E-Train To Masada

A novel by Eli Silberman

The following is a work of fiction. A few characters are real people, however the circumstances and dialogue are products of the author's imagination. The balance of the characters, circumstances, and dialogue are also products of the author's imagination.

ISBN: 0615745652
ISBN-13: 978-0615745657

For Janeice, Jordan and Lindsey

Published by T.S.G. Productions, Inc., 2013

ACKNOWLEDGMENTS

Until you've written a novel the value of a great editor is impossible to comprehend. I was fortunate to have such in Ginny Beards whose advice, tenacity and literary astuteness I am grateful for.

And until you've written a novel in this transitional publishing environment, a knowledgeable guide is essential. Jim Breslin, a writer and publishing advisor, has been helpful to the max.

The Plains, Virginia

The Director of Central Intelligence and the Secretary of State were on the terrace, drinks in hand, out of hearing from the other guests, seemingly enjoying the view of the rolling Virginia hunt country, speaking softly.

"He started out so strong," said the Director.

"Ratings in the eighties," from Madam Secretary.

"Low thirties now."

"The demonstrations. Riots. Draft card burnings."

"Vietnam is killing him."

"He's killing hundreds of our boys a week."

They were drinking gin and tonics, sipping simultaneously as a server in a white apron over a black dress passed by with a tray of skewered shrimp.

"There are people walking the streets of New York that hate him."

"It's not just New York. Most of America has turned against him," added the Secretary of State. "The First Lady is concerned. It's in her eyes."

The farm, an hour and a half west of Washington, was owned by a Senator on the Intelligence Committee, a Harvard classmate of the CIA Director. His wife's addiction to riding to hounds meant the Virginia countryside and a long daily commute for him. In the distant meadow a young girl had just put a halter on a horse and started leading him to the barn.

"Point is it's not impossible he's clinically depressed. Judgment erratic. Good thing he decided not to run, but that's because he knows he won't win. Not because he's losing it."

They focused on the girl and the horse moving in a slow distant rhythm at the other end of the pasture, and changed the subject.

"I heard they flew some lobster down from Maine for dinner," said the Director.

"Perhaps we ought to go in," the Secretary replied.

Others who were mingling in twos and threes had started

moving to the buffet which was on a Regency sideboard in a paneled dining room dominated by an oil painting of the host's wife in canary riding britches standing between two young blonde girls on gray ponies.

They were greeted by their twinkly host who had been a rower in college but now was paddling against the tide of an out of control girth. His navy blue blazer had an excessive number of gold buttons at the sleeve. "So what state secrets were you two whispering about far from the madding crowd?"

"He's usually not this nosey," said the Director, putting an arm around his old friend.

"Let me guess," said the Senator. "Is it what half the people at this party, hell, half the people in Washington, are buzzing about?"

The Secretary of State answered, quietly, "He could be having a breakdown. As a former history professor I can't think of any past president being so, uh, strung out. It's his policies causing the demonstrations. Millions of Americans are also on the verge of a breakdown. Normal people. Good citizens. Just as depressed. All they can do is riot. He can end it."

"But he won't. Too many demons. Too stubborn. Too much pride," added the Senator.

The very bubbly angular wife of the host swirled in, kissed the Director of Central Intelligence on the cheek and said, "Stop talking business you three and get in line or you'll miss out on the lobster salad."

Manhattan

Making his way up Lexington Avenue with the after work crowd filling the streets to the curb, moving both north and south to whatever sanctuaries drew them, Harry Lang had a feeling of being in a civilization that was close to an implosion, to a violent, stupid, self destruction and then the world would be at Genesis again. There was a relentless out of control rhythm that the street rocked and rolled to. It reverberated from Memphis to Detroit to L.A. to the bongo beat of his heart.

The Beatles filled the airwaves from a loud tinny speaker hanging in the narrow doorway of an electronics store with a turbaned Indian salesman smoking a cigarette impassively. It was the last of the truly warm days of September, urban heat coming up from the pavement and joining the fumes of cabs and restaurant exhausts and God's sun burning cancer to enhance the metropolitan haze from Queens before settling down over Great Neck with its temples and textile magnates and Kennedy Airport where foreign airliners with ancient alphabets on their fuselages land as union baggage handlers working with teamster truckers decide what to steal.

The chant from another peace demonstration in back of the 42nd street library tormented his brain, "hell no, we won't go, hell no, we won't go." And the Beatles sang, and he waited for the light to change, bunched up with crowds who couldn't move as cars and trucks and cabs closed the inches between bumpers.

Taxis with off-duty signs made his choices the Fifth Avenue bus or the subway at 53rd and Lex to the 8th Street stop and walk to his apartment in the Village.

The light changed, traffic still deadlocked, then horn blasts. The crowd of walkers bunched up even tighter as office buildings emptied and more people had less space. Lexington Avenue traffic going downtown was blocked by cross-town traffic, and cabbies were making profane gestures as two black hookers in faded pink hot pants and cowboy boots giggled and smoked Salems. An overweight lady carrying a Bloomingdale's shopping bag pressed into him. It was a period when certain men started carrying shoulder bags and he wondered why these guys, these art directors on fashion accounts and space salesman from *Vogue* and the *New Yorker* had daringly stopped wearing J. Press and Brooks Brothers and appeared to be tuned into something he was grappling with. He would get home, turn on the air conditioner and TV for the six o'clock news. This was the year civilization was experiencing a hiccup, a searing cosmic heart burn, an international in scope dysentery, intestine tearing convulsions whereby the bile couldn't decide which orifice to splat from. The traffic opened just enough for single lines to pick trails between bumpers confronting bag carrying humanity surging from the other side, jousting in a specialized step known only to New Yorkers. There were pot bellied men in bell bottoms; "bells," one of the agency secretaries called them, and afros, big aggressive cushions of African heritage bobbing in the crowd, medallions of jewelry on open necked hairy chests, the occasional marijuana whiff as he moved along with members of his civilization selected for the same planetary time frame as his own.

Early in the afternoon at a meeting with others from the big Black and White Advertising agency where he had just completed his third year as a copywriter they had discussed the campaign he created for Kiddie Keds. Holding the diminutive canvas and rubber shoes in his hands he pictured the kids across America who would wear them, in their one story houses with above ground swimming pools and hard working young fathers that were linemen for the county and belonged to the local Fish and Game club, and slender June Alyson mothers committed to good housekeeping and packing lunches. He compared their both researched and imagined small town social discourse to his own childhood in a Brooklyn neighborhood with a collective memory of being helpless in Europe, escaping peasants on the rampage, and mothers who were not June Alyson but rather plump, hysterical products a generation or two removed from the Ellis Island experience. They stuffed their children with latkes and love and took them into the city for the museums and the circus and ultimately raised accountants and neurologists, passing on a tradition of compassion, irony, fatalism. Holding those tiny red and yellow sneakers in his hands, those symbols of an America he read about in *Boys Life* with the Remington .22 ads featuring a comic strip of two teenage boys walking in the fields on the edge of town with a Remington .22 rifle while up ahead their slender June Alyson of a teacher is picking wildflowers and about to be bitten by a coiled snake. One shot from the Christmas gift rifle quickly dispatches the snake and gains the admiration of the young, perky teacher for all eternity.

He was almost at the 53rd Street subway with its descent to the under life of Manhattan, where twice a day riders flowed up and down escalators that frequently didn't escalate, and then waited in the tile and fluorescent aura of the Transit System, the two sheet subway advertisements advising, "You don't have to be Jewish to love Levy's" and "Shop at Ohrbachs." He walked down the steps to the first landing and played his game of picking out those people who would get the E train going to Queens and who would continue to the lowest level for the E train going in his direction to Greenwich Village.

The present was now with him...the President's sad, resolute Texas intonation informed the world, "I shall not seek and I will not accept the nomination of my party as your president," followed a week later by Martin Luther King being bagged with a pump action thirty caliber deer rifle, motivating black populations of Chicago, Baltimore, Washington, Cincinnati and others to stampede the streets in rage, creating anarchy that required tens of thousands of National Guard troops who were avoiding Vietnam to see civil mayhem in their own country, while the Ivy League students at Columbia University occupied five buildings, surprising the college administration and board with their resoluteness regarding the way society treated those blacks who were rioting and, of course, the escalation of Vietnam. Almost simultaneously France stopped operating as millions of workers went on strike and the Sorbonne closed for the first time in 700 years. Thousands were arrested and injured as Gallic riot police banged heads to achieve order. Then a week after France blew, a cheap pistol went bang once, and bang again, as the last hope of bootlegger Joe Kennedy and tens of millions of Americans fell to the floor of the Embassy Room at the Ambassador Hotel in Los Angeles with one bullet in his forehead and the second bullet close to his right ear; goodbye Bobby. As the E train with its electric alto screech stopped at the platform and the crowd surged, he replayed the Democratic Convention in Chicago a couple weeks past when Hubert Humphrey was nominated for president and Mayor Daley's finest used nightsticks with gusto on protesting college students while others were getting their legs vaporized by anti-personnel mines, and their bodies made lifeless by the effectiveness of AK 47s and jungle rot and heartbreak. The Chicago police even entered the convention hall and attacked Mike Wallace.

He stood all the way to the 14th Street station where he got a seat for one stop, getting out at 8th Street, still absorbed with rioting and the war and the red and yellow sneakers in four and five-year-old sizes that made him feel as sad as anything on the front page of the *New York Times.*

"1010 WINS New York, you give us ten minutes, we'll give you the world," was blaring in the little deli where he stopped for half a pound of American cheese, a container of orange juice and a sour pickle. There was a fender bender on the Brooklyn-Queens Expressway, 400 Viet Cong had been killed in a 24-hour battle, and 300 black students had been arrested at a University of Illinois demonstration. As he was getting his change George Wallace was nominated for president by the Texas-American party.

Once he got away from 6th Avenue and 8th Street, the Village was quiet and familiar, with residentially urban streets, three and four story attached buildings, many with shutters, trees coming through cracked sidewalks, homosexual set designers walking their Shih Tzus.

He relaxed in the Village liking the fact that Dylan Thomas had died passing out at the White Horse Bar and that the Lions Head was a gathering place for writers and columnists like Jimmy Breslin and that Jean Shepherd broadcast from the Limelight Café on Friday nights. People who lived in the Village worked in publishing or made films or imported handmade textiles from Tibet. There were few venture capitalists or CFOs down there in 1968, and as he walked these comforting streets loosening his striped tie and unbuttoning his Brooks Brothers collar, Peter, Paul and Mary came softly through the open window of a basement apartment asking, "Where have all the young men gone, when will they ever return?" He pictured scenes from last night's Vietnam war on TV as well as those tow-headed kids wearing Kiddie Keds who fifteen years later would become members of Long Range Recon Platoons, LURPS, and come in from patrol, lean and listless. They would volunteer to be LURPS to get even closer to the randomness, the lethality of it all. These were the kids that knew how to lower and deck a '53 Ford and put Hollywood mufflers on that old Ford, who entered teenage rodeos and actually volunteered for the Marines at seventeen. They were so different from his own gene pool where they went to Hebrew school after public school three days a week so they could get Bar Mitzvahed and a revered education and fight battles only because they had absolutely no choice, as compared to those American former Kiddie Keds wearers to whom killing an enemy, any enemy, was a coming of age rite that made their daddies proud.

His apartment was three stories up, the top floor of a West Village early 1800s building a few blocks from the Hudson River with a working fireplace in the bedroom and one in the living room. The walls were plaster and brick and the floors were antique random width walnut and he furnished it in post college macho with a leather sofa and one of those Abercrombie and Fitch leather rhino stools you could straddle. Books and record albums all over. The TV was in the bedroom where he had a single bed. An Irish girl who spent the night mentioned that he really ought to keep some food in the under-the-counter refrigerator. She had gotten hungry at two in the morning and he was somewhat taken by the shrillness of her admonishment, so he got dressed and went to the all night deli three blocks away and came back with half a pound of rare roast beef which they ate with their fingers.

Although he was glad to be back in his apartment he ached for some relief from the isolation. Feelings about what was happening in the world filled him with frustration, unhappiness that never quite became tears. He ached for somebody who understood his foreboding, but if that somebody appeared he knew the words wouldn't come. Relief was to get out of his suit and into old Levis and sit on the floor hugging his knees watching the boys on TV who didn't go to college carry their dead and wounded and morphined-up war brothers on stretchers to noisy helicopters, eager to soar up and out.

Lately at times he observed the sense of connection amongst the war protestors, the camaraderie of the soldiers, and the solidarity of the freedom marchers with their arms linked on some Alabama street. A murky wisp of a memory was oh so gently gliding around the outer rim of his consciousness from a time when perhaps he too was joined in a spiritual fusion with soul mates in common cause. The memory fragment was from a long ago protoplasmic seed of creation that refused to dry up, to forget the flames of destruction as the temple was defiled, as the final struggle before the dispersion unfolded on the gritty, dry mountain plateau.

Turning on the TV he saw a safari jacketed Walter Cronkite standing outside a hospital tent talking into a microphone. A helicopter landed and stretchers were carried by camo-wearing kids running in the heat to get their fellow Americans to the recent med school grads who were acquiring firsthand experience no teaching hospital on the face of the Earth could provide. A generation of orthopods and neurosurgeons and anesthesiologists and every other American Medical Association specialty was being prepared for careers as caregivers back in the USA, if they didn't have emotional collapses before their year was up. He didn't have the sound on, just the images in sharply defined video. Light outside his bedroom was almost gone; the only illumination in the apartment came from the TV.

While sitting in semi awareness of the present as people's lives were changed forever on the TV screen, he thought he heard a voice. It wasn't coming from the TV, nor was it from the street or the hall. He was alone in the apartment. He almost laughed out loud at how alone. But a voice had clearly enunciated a command. At times lately he felt he was entering the cuckoo fringe zone of New Yorkers who mutter to themselves on crowded buses. He tried to subtract from himself and shear it all down to whatever was his primal beginning.

He sat on the floor wondering how simplistic an organism can I become and not be comatose? How far back to pre-memory can one go before quacking like a duck? He knew that was where the voice spoke from, and his neurological engineering got jammed in reverse and backed into air raids and block wardens with whistles making sure no light showed through the windows in the middle of World War II on his street in Brooklyn, preparing the populace for a possible bombing attack from across the ocean.

The voice he intuitively knew came from a hot, dry, gritty climate that predated, well it just predated. He heard the words as clear as if they had come through his KLH hi fi system endorsed by Jean Shepherd. Every night at 10:00pm if he wasn't in a bar or restaurant he listened to the Gene Shepherd show on WOR AM. He believed in Jean Shepherd.

The voice wasn't loud but it had authority. It enunciated words clearly and there was a stillness behind the words, as if all natural and mechanical sounds held their breath for the moments the voice commanded. Then the vibrations picked up as street sounds and refrigerators and air conditioners ceased supplicating to the voice and felt the courage to resume being whatever they were. It was as if the voice was heard by his heart more than his ears. As the individual words became clear he continued the game of distilling down to some pure form not affected by experience.

As a child he would walk to the ocean after school in the

winter, past the apartment buildings that went practically to the boardwalk, then down the wooden steps to the sand, deserted and cold, seagulls suspended against the wind, hot dog stands and souvenir shops shuttered in back of him, all of wondrous nature in front as he trudged through the soft sand to the harder packed stuff near the water and onto the jetty. He was good at jumping from rock to rock, daring the slippery moss, getting a rhythm, loving the white foam after a wave broke over the jetty. He would clamber to the last rock and look out across the ocean, all the way to Far Rockaway and sky into water. A freighter would appear in the far blue and stay forever. He reveled in being cold and smelling the winter sea, sometimes staying until almost dark, with his back to Brooklyn and his dreams focused on the darkening winter ocean and charcoal sky, wondering if he could see Europe out there between Manhattan Beach on the left and Coney Island on the right. Europe meant combat, bombed cathedrals and concentration camps, long lines of Jews waiting to board trains with Nazi guards in black boots herding them. Men in business suits and fedoras, women in fashionable winter coats and children in knee socks, all in black and white and shadings of gray, like old etchings of San Marco Square during the Renaissance, of men in tights and bloomers with swords dangling from their waists and plumes in their hats, frozen in the 1500s. Then back a thousand years before that to the fading Roman Empire, even a few hundred years earlier to the power of Rome at its glorious peak, seen from the last rock on the jetty, dreaming across the expanse of water wondering what was happening on top of the white cliffs of Dover, and what was going on in those villages in Normandy where the D-Day invasion took place, and what were those girls doing, the ones in the newsreels who kissed American soldiers in Paris when they marched in triumphantly; and he wondered if the knights who went to Jerusalem during the Crusades rode their horses through the same French towns on their way to Palestine that our tanks and jeeps drove through?

Thus zigzagging for hours on end from his own memories to old daydreams of long ago quests, keeping it all in some chronology that had a pattern he didn't yet understand. He knew he heard a voice. He was sure the year was 1968. He was sure what the words were. The voice said, "You must go out from Jerusalem."

He was awakened as usual by the sound of garbage trucks mashing and compacting the leavings of an urban population, the tin cans and kitty litter, orange peels and tampon tubes, neatly tied piles of last month's *New Yorker* magazines and *Village Voice*, plastic bottles of hair conditioner and roach killer, gooey remains of TV dinners and split panty hose, all pulverized and driven to Secaucus, New Jersey in New York City Sanitation Department trucks for final composting into oblivion. As the familiar metallic thrashing brought him out of sleep he lay in that place partway between consciousness and wherever sleep had taken him, feeling his heart back two thousand years.

Living alone as he did the mornings started without the presence of other humanity. Nobody gave off warmth in bed; nobody caused the sound of toilet paper unrolling and then a flush, or the faucet to run. Nobody opened drawers or ran hair dryers or slammed refrigerator doors or hummed "Moon River." No smell of hair spray or coffee or other morning rituals that people who lived with people took so for granted. Not having somebody there at the start of a new day in the big city in the early fall of the year 1968 meant he didn't have to respond or compromise or listen or be alert to nuances of human interaction. He was able to reenter gradually, without intrusion and sometimes didn't turn on the radio or TV, as a discipline for he knew not what. This morning he didn't want to hear the news, or watch *The Today Show*, or turn on the classical sounds of WQXR, or listen to the country and western station that had recently started broadcasting in New York.

He came awake thinking James Joyce must have felt like this when on the verge of melancholy and detachment, and as he listened to garbage cans being slammed on pavement and the truck grinding gears and moving fifty feet to the next set of anthropological leavings he resolved to give *Ulysses* another go. He'd find a copy at one of those used book stalls on Fourth Avenue. His heart was now firmly in place and he stretched long and hard, feeling it in his spine and all the way down to his toes and concentrated on the day ahead. A 10:00 a.m. meeting with the focus group moderator, the research director and the creative and account team on the Kiddie Keds account, a 1:30 p.m. plane to Cleveland, and focus groups with mothers of young children at 5:00 and 7:00 p.m. The next morning they would fly to L.A. for three more groups, and the day after that to Houston for two more, then back to New York. The fate of his campaign would be determined by how the mothers of America responded to the story boards and concept statements that would engender discussion regarding their deepest motives and subconscious responses in the selection of sneakers for their children.

As he showered the hot water helped dissipate the grogginess, a residual effect of journeys in sleep. A slight headache went from the back of his head down to where neck met shoulders and he massaged that spot as the heat soothed ever so perceptibly. Goose bumps formed from the chill as he pulled the shower curtain back and stepped out of the big old-fashioned bathtub drying off quickly, using the towel in the same motion of a shoe shine boy doing the final buffs, enjoying the friction and watching the sudsy scummy water slowly seep down the ancient drain into the leaded pipes that went into bigger pipes that merged into the municipal discharge system where his own DNA was joined with the body fluids of hundreds and thousands and millions of other Manhattanites ritually and therapeutically cleansing themselves to face the hundreds of thousands of millions of challenges that particular day. The drain gave off a low final gurgle, like the death throes of some medium sized jungle beast stoically bidding the world farewell. He decided to clean out the foamy mixture on the bottom of the bathtub when he returned from Houston after the focus groups. He'd remember to get some Drano at the bodega.

It was another sunny unseasonably warm day and the morning smelled fresh for the city. One of those elephant-like machines with rotary sweepers had just passed leaving the gutters wet and refuse free. He got a cab almost immediately, beating out a woman in a suit carrying a briefcase who was a half block up the Edward Hopper-like street but on the other side, so it was easier for the cab to keep going to him. It was a big Checker. The driver was also the owner. A little sign on the dashboard said, "Please don't smoke, driver allergic." It was almost nine o'clock and the traffic from the Village was flowing up town. Crossing 14th Street they left the charm of the West Village behind, passed a restaurant called Asia de Cuba, and got into the more utilitarian and lower rent area toward 23rd Street. He always looked to the Chelsea Hotel to see if anybody arty, eccentric and famous was hailing a cab. Above 23rd Street non-descript stores, very few apartments one would choose to live in, and then they entered the wholesale flower district where girls in jeans were unloading trucks delivering boxes from Mexico and Chile stuffed with colorful assortments of every conceivable species chemically treated to stay fresh for days. The flower district merged into the garment district where traffic was getting mid-town intense, trucks of every size maneuvering into unimaginable spaces, Hispanic rack pushers navigating the streets with samples that would clothe America, buyers and salesmen and designers and models and receptionists in various stages of morning alertness, some carrying little bags with cardboard coffee cups and the freshest, softest New York Danish, all at the start of another day of deals and coterie and showroom intrigue and instant fame through *Women's Wear Daily* and inspiration transformed from a sketch pad to must-have chic, from Main Street to Worth Avenue.

He always looked for real life characters that could play the roles in "The Pajama Game" and "How to Succeed in Business without Really Trying." The sociology of the garment district absorbed him every day as he cabbed through, from the people who owned the coffee shops that operated at a frantic orchestrated pace to the fashion czars in their tailored suits and twelve month tans, oozing opulence in Gucci loafers and British cut pin stripes. His owner operated Checker cut across town, turned left on 6th Avenue, the tourists called it Avenue of the Americas, then went past the back of the library where yesterday's peace march had reminded the lunch crowds and everybody who read the newspapers and watched TV that the visionaries of America had made a bloody mistake and were too stubborn to admit it as boys with white, black and yellow skin mixed it up in a deadly mélange in Vietnam.

The fashion district segued into midtown with office buildings representing architectural and social statements from the '20s to the '60s, from Bauhaus to deco to minimalist, some with names like the Look Building, the Collier Building, the Chrysler Building, the Seagram Building, the Brill Building, all containing companies with minds that fermented, fomented and percolated trends that emanated out to the American masses, eager to embrace what was new and improved, worn or eaten or driven or sprayed on or orificed in by the role models of the moment. They crossed Park Avenue in front of the Pan Am Building, defiantly making its statement about world domination of the skies, a self-satisfied sphinx placed smack dab in the middle of the caravan route; Park Avenue coiling like a concrete intestine through either end of the skyscraper. The cab let him out a block away and as he was paying, 1010 WINS was reporting student riots in Mexico City, eighteen dead and hundreds arrested. The owner operator of the Checker looked at him with a world weary shrug of resignation which could have been in acknowledgment of the dead college kids in Mexico City or perhaps it was a general statement regarding who knows what might happen next and I wish I were back at the bungalow colony in the Catskills for another two weeks.

He stopped at Schraffts in the building for his own cardboard container of coffee and watched as the elderly counter lady with pink skin, fading yellow hair and wire glasses who could have been a nun but worked at Schraffts instead, poured her trillionth cup of coffee since her career began during the Depression. She spoke to her clone-like co-worker about her nephew who had come home from Vietnam and was starting a job bartending in a bowling alley in Edison, New Jersey. He asked for a bran muffin and wished he could go out to Edison and watch her nephew on his first few days in the bowling alley, he bought a *New York Times* and the Otis Company came through once again as he got off at the twenty-eight floor, one of the two creative floors of the six floors that Black and White advertising occupied. He stopped in his office long enough to sip some coffee and read the story in the *Times* about the hundreds who were arrested in the Mexico City riots. The little red and yellow Kiddie Keds were still on his desk. One pair had a likeness of Clarabelle the Clown emblazoned on the front and he tried hard not to feel a lump in his throat.

"Sandra, where's the focus group meeting?" The secretary for his group sat just outside his office. Slightly overweight, always fashionably dressed, she had a new diamond engagement ring and still lived at home in Brooklyn with her parents. Her father was the manager of a big and tall men's clothing store on 37th Street and her mother was in the catering business. He liked Sandra, she had an easy laugh and could see through the agency crap, as he called it. She was taking a night course at the School of Visual Arts. Sandra knew how the world worked, and he thought she'd make a good copywriter.

"In the small conference room on 27." They looked at each other to catch the mood of the day within. Her eyes were large, brown, wise sparkles and her lipstick was Day-Glo red on a broad pale face that projected Brooklyn street smart wisdom.

"You're a nurturer," he said and took the circular staircase down to twenty-seven.

The conference room table seated twelve with a cramped projection room on one end and a screen on the other. The walls were cork and had colorful pushpins in a patternless abstraction where they had recently held various foam presentation boards. The chairs were gray wool and swiveled, carpeting beige. The room had been location for thousands of internal meetings and advertising campaigns that changed the buying habits of America, had billions of dollars in media spent, made millions for Mr. Black, now deceased, and Mr. White, now in his late eighties, always ruddy faced in a tweed sport coat with a paisley handkerchief sticking out of his breast pocket, and spending half the year at the Morgan horse farm in Woodstock, Vermont and half the year in Bermuda with occasional stays in the New York apartment on East 68th Street. Lighting in the room appeared a bit dim and Harry wondered if it was deliberate. Probably wasn't, as he greeted the others drifting in either singly or in talkative pairs. There was the head of the account group, Steve Lester, whose auburn hair was thinning out at a disturbing pace. Steve was raised in Toledo and now lived in Greenwich with his wife and two young daughters at Greenwich Country Day. He had a self-assured manner but would frequently clip his nails in meetings, feet up on the conference table holding everybody transfixed as they anticipated the next click. He would use phrases like, "I suspicion." The head art director never let a meeting end without referring to the account director with "two first names."

"Hi Harry, I love your concept."

"Thanks Steve, let's hope it makes it through the focus groups."

He wondered if Steve would defend it if the client resisted. Steve once told Harry and a couple of others about his grandfather, a traveling salesman for a company that manufactured submersible pumps, and mentioned that he always used to stay in the Physter Hotel when he came through Milwaukee. Harry pictured somebody out of *The Music Man*, and thought it was very American. His own grandfather deserted the Russian Army and emigrated to the U.S. in 1898, about the same time Steve's grandfather was checking into the Physter. Harry found Steve to be genuine, even likable, with a thin membrane of craftiness he accepted as part of the package.

Paula Markham, the head of research, was looking at the discussion guide, smoking a cigarette and stirring her coffee. Wearing her typical tailored suit with jacket removed, an off-white silk blouse and one of her stockings larger than her leg, which she appeared oblivious to. It looked almost sensual in its nyloness, leaving space between the fabric and her skin. Harry thought the same legs needed a face that wasn't as plain. The features begged just a bit more definition, a cosmetic surgeon wouldn't have to do much and Paula would be in the next category of desirousness, but she was destined to spinsterhood, at best a late marriage to somebody fourteen years older. She was a disciplined thinker and had majored in psychology at Vassar. Harry believed she had the same assessment of herself as he did and he valued her insights. There was an edge of benign flirtatiousness to their discussions. She dangled one shoe on the toe of her foot. The leg with the loose nylon stocking was barefoot, the other shoe lying on its side under the table like a miniature beached canoe. "I really like your concept, Harry," she said. Harry wondered if she might occasionally get yeast infections as he waved appreciative thanks and took a seat across from her.

Marv Munchik, the art director, came in with Sandy Stahl, the account executive whose family owned the famous deli on 7th Avenue of the same name. They were talking about Arthur Ashe having won the U.S. Open at Forrest Hills a couple of weeks earlier, and how he couldn't take the $14,000 in prize money because he was an amateur.

"Let's get this meeting started," said Steve. "We've only got about an hour before we leave for LaGuardia. Let's make sure we're all on the same page, and if we're not, let's get it on the table now so we don't confuse the client, who is meeting us in Cleveland. Harry, why don't you run us through the campaign premise again, and then lay out the creative." He put his feet up on the conference room table, took out his nail clipper, and slid down in the chair, relaxed, attentive in charge. All eyes looked to Harry except for Paula who was scribbling some notes and although her head was down she was aware of every nuance. Harry learned that these meetings could become unpredictable, out of control, living organisms whereby somebody's offhand observation could alter the outcome of the campaign, affect careers, cause office cabals to break up and new ones to form. They could even change the pattern of lives if one decided it wasn't worth taking a firm stand on an issue, followed by a sense of shame for not having the courage to publicly go on record, then rationalizing that it was just a product you didn't really care about and more sales would only make the stockholders in the client company richer. Then in a later moment of lucidity, the cowardice of that reasoning would hit hard, causing even more shame, plummeting esteem, overdrinking, rampant sexual conquest, and emptiness in life.

Harry looked over to Munchik who had the concept boards and began explaining his idea.

"Our premise is the mothers of young children are concerned the sneakers fit properly, look attractive, and that they get value for their money. Value translates as durability. If this campaign can convince the young mothers of America that these Kiddie Keds last longer, they will buy."

"You're right," said Steve as he studied his index finger nail deciding there was nothing left to clip. "Convince 'em they'll last longer and I guarantee we'll sell a shit load. That's the nugget right there."

Harry nodded to Munchik, whose grandfather also left Russia in 1898 to avoid serving as Jewish cannon fodder in the Czar's army. Munchik held up a foam presentation board with an illustration of a robot. The robot had a happy face and was walking through the Main Street of Anytown, USA. On the bottom of the board it said in bold type "Anytown, USA." A throng of kids singing, skipping and holding hands were happily following him. Local shopkeepers were peeking out their shop doors and windows smiling and waving. The robot was as tall as a typical five year old and on his robot feet was a pair of Kiddie Keds.

"What we do," continued Harry "is have an ergonomically designed robot built and have him walk across America wearing a pair of Kiddie Keds. A film crew follows in a van. We alert the media in the major metropolitan areas. We show up at local events, Little League games, with the robot. We get *Life Magazine* to cover the human interest side. *Time* can do a story on how we designed the robot. The moms will follow the Kiddie Ked's Walk Across America on the news every day. They'll get the message that Kiddie Keds are sneakers made to last. Across America. It's the durability story of a lifetime. The PR potential is enormous."

"It's big," said Steve. "God damn. It's big. Paula, let's have a final look-see at the discussion guide."

Paula plumed in a demure professionalism and looking at her notes began. "The important thing to probe for is believability. It's a charming concept. It's verging on great. It may even be one of the really great ones. Conceptually. But we've got to feel confident the moms will believe it."

Munchik blurted out "Believe what? That the robot's walking across America? That the Keds are the same type they can buy in the store? What?"

"Well, that's a big part of it Marvin," placating and soothing, realizing Marvin had the volatility of a sensitive high strung child. Every time the creatives put an idea before the group, fragile egos were on the chopping block, exposing their beloved art to criticism of the vulgar over-analytical account group and anybody else who happened to be in the meeting. Being the person responsible for testing ideas, Paula knew as the bearer of consumer reaction to the agency's output, it was at times inevitable the creatives would be shattered by the results and she worked hard to not become their enemy. She worked hard now.

"I know these commercials will produce brilliantly, they'll be captivating as anything we've ever done, but we owe it to the client to ask the right questions. If they just look charming but aren't internalized, don't truly have meaning that turns into motivation to buy, then we haven't done our job. Now Marvin, and you too Harry, what are the questions to ask? How do we set up the research so that the right buttons are hit with moms?"

Steve prepared to answer in a snorting pig-like inhale, but before the words came out Paula said, "let's hear from the creative team first, Steve. It's your baby, guys. What are the pitfalls to look for?"

Marvin began. "The sheer execution of this concept will be captivating as hell. Start with the robot. Three, four feet high. Non-shiny metal. Pewter. Wearing maybe bib overalls. Something red checkered. Kerchief. Hat. Arms move in rhythm as he walks. Dances down the street. It's a kid's wet dream of robot land. When the moms are in the store the kids see a model of a robot and go hysterical with desire. Moms have positive memories of the spot. Kids try on the shoes. Refuse to take them off. Love the brand."

Harry whispered softly to himself, "We're entering da da land."

"The purchase of these little sneakers will give mom primal satisfaction. Think Indian squaws chewing on deer hide to make soft moccasins for the whole family. Sadly our machine age society has deprived modern woman of her natural urge to soften deer hide with their teeth."

Marvin played out his reasoning with deliberate, confusing tangents and insane analogies that Steve thought were brilliant. Paula sensed but wasn't quite sure it was a put on. Harry stared into the wood grain of the conference table and wondered what he was doing with his life.

The sixties had begun with the solidity of the post war American rebirth and President Eisenhower as father figure, out of which emerged John Fitzgerald Kennedy commanding, "Ask not what your country can do for you, ask what you can do for your country," and the first stirrings of *Leave it to Beaver* America getting sensitized to how awful it was to be a Negro in America; then came the Peace Corps with thousands joining up to share our wisdom and technology with indigenous people who lived in mud huts and had National Geographic as their society column, where only brown skinned women were allowed to bare their breasts, followed by women of the enlightened classes burning their bras in public so they too could legitimately let their boobs hang out, and, simultaneously, our elected leaders in Washington in their elected wisdom agreeing that no dominoes would fall in Vietnam. The best and the brightest made the worst and the dumbest decisions, and what began as a CIA intrigue blew out of control as the whole country fragmented itself like a grenade. Middle aged clerics stood up to the overwhelming force of fire hoses because they believed in their cause. Young men tore up their draft cards in front of the FBI building because they had the courage to defy immoral use of the law. Soldiers gave news cameras the peace sign and smoked dope in defiance of the chain of command, court martial or even firing squad material in World War II.

As Harry stared at the wood grained veneer top of the conference room table with Marvin's voice in the background exemplifying what TV commercial directors referred to as room tone, he experienced a sense of not being part of this time and place. The voice from last night echoed in his head, "You must go out from Jerusalem" and he believed there was another place where he would have conviction and defy the authority of the moment. He would defend his *idée fixe* to the end, like a bull in a bull fight who would die in dumb nobility. Disappearing into this space, he wondered if he was destined for a quiet institution in a tony exurb to recuperate from his breakdown in the safety of muted tones and group therapy, under the care of psychiatric social workers supervised by pipe smoking psychiatrists who projected calm on the outside but also suffered from the same twisted forces that made the inmates crack. Part of him was alert to the progress of the meeting, on guard for a question he might have to answer, a statement from somebody that would require response, but his soul had taken a journey to recesses that teased with the promise of familiarity in a hazy terrain once traversed in conflict.

Sandra gave him his airline tickets and cash advance for the three day, three city focus group trip. He stood in his office for a moment looking at the disarray, desk covered with memos, yellow copy paper with ads he wrote weeks ago that had been through the photo session, production, media insertion, and become advertising history; original typewritten copy still on his desk covered by old *New York Times* Arts Sections, used cardboard coffee cups, research reports, unfinished time sheets, pink telephone message slips, some from months ago, and on his window sill several boxes of Kiddie Keds while his coffee table had crumpled up papers from creative sessions with Marv and some of the others. A couple of big layout pads leaned against the small sofa and one was on the floor with part of a shoe print on it. The ceramic ashtray had cigarette butts that were stiff and stank.

"Wish I weren't such a pig, Sandra," and he slowly walked down the hall wondering who would occupy that space when he got a different office, or left Black and White Advertising, or died. Marv was waiting in the reception area, which was covered in the exact wallpaper with parrots and green jungle foliage that hung in the Polo Lounge of the Beverly Hills Hotel. The parrots looked you right in the eye. Those who got it thought it was really creative, but most were unaware. Marv was standing in the reception area chatting with Sam Abruzi, a printing salesman who wore a gold medallion around his open chest that was big as a third world country war medal. Also sitting in the reception area was Freddie Magreb, the film animator, barely five feet tall with greasy shoulder length hair and in great vogue with certain TV art directors because of his frenetic, zany bug-like characters that appeared to have been created through narcotic inspiration. Freddie lived above the "O" of the massive lighted Crisco sign that dominated the night time view across the Hudson from the West Side highway. He'd once mentioned to Harry that when he was in the army during World War II, he had been "shanghaied" into the 82nd Airborne against his will and parachuted into Normandy on D-day.

"Freddie," said Harry, "when I get back from this trip I'll call you. We'll go out for Lebanese food."

Freddie got up and through a giggle said, "I eat Lebanese food all the time at home."

"Have you gotten a response from your billboard?" asked

Sam.

"Nah, not yet." In a moment of entrepreneurial lucidity, Freddie had leased a billboard on 6th Avenue that simply said, "Why doesn't somebody give Freddie Magreb $9 million to make a feature?" Harry embraced Freddie, then pinched his cheek, and he and Marv walked to the elevators. One arrived immediately.

The doors closed Marv said, "Steve went down a minute ago. Said he'd hold a cab for us, and we'll meet the others at the gate. Steve feels useful when he's hailing cabs." The only other person in the elevator was one of those messengers that the photostat houses used who were all marginally demented but not physically threatening. This one sported a soiled t-shirt that said "New York, the Empire State" in small letters above the pocket. He also wore a wool stocking cap, even though the temperature was in the eighties.

"How's it going?" asked Harry.

His reply was a flawless imitation of a pig. "Oink, oink," as he grabbed his crotch in a masturbatory gesture and got off on the eighteenth floor.

They exited the building through the revolving door into late summer hazy brightness on Third Avenue where Steve was leaning against a Checker cab, patiently waiting for the overly sensitive children who had created this winner of a national ad campaign.

The Beatles were singing "Hey Jude" on the cab radio as they left the curb and got into the traffic flow crossing over to Lexington Avenue. Marv sat on one side, Harry on the other, and Steve sat on the fold-up seat facing them with his legs stretched out at an angle. He reclined like a potentate at rest. Even though they all knew the route, Steve said to the driver, "Queens Midtown Tunnel, then the L.I.E. out to LaGuardia. We're on United," as if to prove to the cabbie that he was a bona fide genuine real article New Yorker. Harry recalled hearing that Bennett Cerf was from Wisconsin and had worked on perfecting his New York accent. They passed Grand Central Station on the right then it took almost ten minutes to travel the three blocks that got them across 42nd Street where traffic was faster. They turned left onto 38th Street going in spurts at a walker's pace, fumes mixing with the warm Murray Hill haze, and eventually funneled into the Midtown tunnel. Marv asked Steve his perspective on the Soviet invasion of Prague the previous month and as Steve pontificated on a subject he knew little about, Harry suppressed a laugh knowing Marv was not at all interested in Steve's opinion on middle European affairs. Marv wasn't interested in Steve's opinion on anything.

As Steve's voice blended with trucks and the cab radio and the expressway din, Harry drifted projecting into the next few days. Whenever he left New York on trips such as this he felt like a visitor from another country, even another world, studying the real America. New York was a happening, a boiling cauldron of ethnicity and emotion and edginess, but people lived for real in places like Cincinnati and Houston. He felt the New Yorkers were just as nice as people from Dubuque, but they expressed their niceness aggressively with a spontaneity most of America found offensive or confusing. He also felt as the Vietnam War careened out of control that the riots and peace marches and the mass rage had become so overwhelming that those "real Americans" with biases against New York were forced to confront their own aggressions and perhaps, more importantly, those of their children. He would sample the mood of America sitting in the darkened Focus Group facility, behind a one-way mirror, eating gourmet meals provided by the research company, each outdoing the competition with culinary enticements in their quest for ad agency business, surrounded by both cynics and optimists, the agency people usually occupying the cynic side. Lefrak City passed by on the right side of the Expressway, putting them about halfway to LaGuardia, and Harry mused that those secretaries who were older and not using secretarydom as stepping stones to dramatic and fulfilling careers lived in Lefrak City as did postal workers and teachers and those minions not on the glory trail to riches and sophistication. Each summer when the new crop of college graduates showed up in New York to make their statement, none thought to find an apartment in Lefrak City. And looking past the expressway into the neighborhoods of Queens as the cab sped to the airport, with the Lefrak City's and the attached brick single family homes going on for miles in every direction, the denseness of it all pulsated into him with a not unpleasant beat. It wasn't that long ago that there were farms in Queens; he had heard old relatives say, "We used to drive out to Canarsie to see the cows and get vegetables." And the Editor in Chief of *Town and Country* magazine had told him of an old lady who lived on Beekman Place whose combined life span with that of her uncle stretched back to the Revolutionary War. When Harry looked at him quizzically he explained the old lady was a little girl when her uncle was still alive, and her uncle had been a little boy during the Revolutionary War.

The Checker cab sped on to LaGuardia. Where brick and pavement and roofing tar and Formica kitchens now exist was once swamp and forest and reeds growing in the clear water and quiet starry nights with owls hooting and fish jumping. Now it was Queens Boulevard with Greek bakeries selling baklava next to pizzerias down the street from parochial schools indoctrinating kids in knee socks who would someday rebel against the doctrine in spasms of guilt-filled early sex.

Harry felt a part of him that was not organic emerge within his stomach, spread up to his chest cavity and liltingly float out to all those people struggling and loving and living in Queens. Whatever it was that came forth went back in time to when Queens was rural and then back before that when teepees with smoke from cooking fires stood where dry cleaners and luncheonettes now reign, and fish curing on racks made of branches took up space now occupied by parking meters and fire hydrants. Next he sensed that the thing within that he couldn't touch was drifting further back, going out across Long Island Sound across the ocean to the first millennium; it then turned right, crossed the channel and floated into France as the centuries clicked back like a taxi meter in reverse and it finally entered Italy through the whimpering, smoldering last curtain of the Roman empire. On it floated over the Mediterranean, east to the land of Canaan at the zenith of the Roman period in the year 68. Wherever it was from, a pre-memory genetic visage transporting him, it then came to a stop and hovered over a high mountain plateau. Harry suddenly felt an excitement, a sense of resignation, a willingness to accept his destiny with a valor and determination that made him not afraid to die.

The cab pulled up to the curb at United. Marv and Steve had switched from the uprising in Czechoslovakia to the focus group discussion guide, and as Steve was paying the fare Harry said goodbye for now to his spirit hovering above a massive rock outcropping 2000 years ago. He reentered the modern world of airports and outlandish headlines. Each day seemed a backdrop in a play that featured characters making a fatal stand on convictions regarding the Vietnam inferno, the hate filled terror that had come to characterize race relations, the new overtness of sexual behavior, and the bra burning women's liberation movement. For the middle of the day LaGuardia seemed to have a high degree of bustle. The skycaps professionally assessed that all they had was carry-on luggage and in their black coolness shifted attention to the next cab. The three of them made their way through crowded airport corridors towards the gate, and as Steve stopped at a newsstand to get a couple of magazines Harry noticed that a tall and very paunchy black man wearing a long, brightly patterned robe and a fez was talking to another black man in a tailored navy blue suit. His accent was not deep throated African or Oxford educated British, but rather New Yorkese. They were discussing a lecture one of them had given or was going to give at Morehouse College. Two policemen seemed to be observing the crowd's movement with interest, and as they ambled toward the gate Harry wasn't sure if he was imagining it but there appeared to be a mood of cautious alert. Ever since the Palestinians and Algerians and Baader-Meinhof something or other gang had started hijacking airplanes to get instant worldwide attention for their causes, plane travel had taken on a new dimension.

The rest of the group from Black and White Advertising was already at the gate waiting area and various forms of greeting were exchanged from subtle eye contact and a nod to "hey buddy, we thought we might have to leave without you," offered in loud, locker room camaraderie that annoyed those engrossed in reading or reverie. Paula Markham sat cross-legged, one stocking drooping, hunched over her research papers, hair falling over her face and smoking a cigarette. There were two empty seats next to her and Harry and Marv took them after they checked in. Harry looked around for suspicious passengers, pretending he was a member of Mossad.

They all boarded and Marv and Harry sat on the left side where the rows had two seats. Across the aisle the rows had three seats which meant if you didn't get a window or aisle, you sat in the middle book-ended. If you were having a bad run of luck one of the two strangers overflowed his or her corpulence into your allotted middle space resulting in squirming civility for the entire friendly skies flying experience. Paula Markham had the middle seat a couple of rows up, and although the angular gentleman to her right had been a sprinter in high school and would be put in his coffin weighing what he weighed at eighteen, the lady on her left was the "before" picture in a weight loss ad. Paula bent over her reports and willed herself invisible. Harry nudged Marv and motioned towards Paula. Marv acknowledged Paula's plight with a shrug typifying his fatalistic view of the world. When Harry traveled on business he considered it a bonus to eavesdrop. If he had an extra long wait between planes he could sit in an airport and study the crowd passing by, thoroughly engrossed. The duo in front of them appeared to be on the upper end of the urban sophistication scale. You could see it in their mannerisms, their self- absorption, their impeccable turnout, one in a miniature glen plaid, natural shoulder, three button suit, the other in a charcoal gray, blue striped shirt and maroon bow tie, both close to fifty. The talking one had auburn-red hair that was short and kinky curly.

"I've come to look upon my affairs like medicine. If I don't take my medicine my condition deteriorates, and eventually I'll die. I've got a wife and kids to support. I can't die. So I just keep having affairs. It's like insulin for a diabetic."

The bow tie said, "Thank God for modern medicine."

Harry appreciated the spirit of their exchange, two business associates who traveled together countless times, were comfortable as confidants, and shared this form of urban cynicism that occurs years after complex emotional entanglements, twice a week therapy, and some level of financial success. Harry nudged Marvin and gesturing at the two quietly said, "Hear what they're discussing?"

"Yeah. Seems like a practical enough solution. The wife's point of view would not occur?"

"Nah" Harry said. "If we edited together sixty seconds of their conversation we'd have a wonderful commercial to reduce matrimony in America."

"Why not Europe?"

"Jerk. The Mediterranean countries enjoy the mistress system. And the Northern countries don't stigmatize occasional variety."

"Stupid of me."

The plane increased its speed down the runway. Harry looked out the window and saw heat waves as the jet engines eliminated any possibility of eavesdropping. He leaned back and wondered what the girl that kinky hair was having an affair with looked like. He wanted to know where they went, hotels or her apartment, and exactly what they did, and if the guy's wife suspected anything. As his mind wandered aimlessly the stewardess announced something he couldn't totally hear, and the rhythms of "hell no, we won't go" replayed in his head. He pictured the TV news clips of the shirtless, long-haired, jeans and camo clad, bead wearing, sunglassed, chanting, anger filled crowd protesting the asinine decisions coming out of Washington. They were right of course. Nobody could satisfactorily explain what we would get in return for the lost limbs and emotional carnage and lies. There was no dignity in any of that, but there was courage all over the 1968 landscape. A vision of a short, dark-bearded man with a Roman nose, no more than twenty-two or three, throwing his military medals into a bonfire with raging protest written on his face, so courageous when he earned the medals and again when his gesture told the politicians and generals they were pitifully wrong. But dignity is important, and the times were lacking it.

Harry thought of Hemingway characters and how they suffered their personal tragedies without rage or self-pity, but with Buddhist-like acceptance of life's random selection. Hemingway's people were familiar with war, suffered the pain of combat and the loss of romantic attachments, but there was a sparseness to their expression. Was it writing style, or were his characters simply more dignified than the Vesuvian emoting spewing out with fission-like force now in 1968? The players in the protests, sit-ins and riots weren't at all concerned with standing their ground with grace as the Cape buffalo charged or with killing him well. That would be the behavior of imbeciles. Hemingway's generation survived a war in which millions were nerve gassed, bayoneted, shrapneled and bombed, but they did not deliberately grow beards and dirty long hair or sport cheesy beads and flaunt their objections with aberrant actions. To not behave well, with dignity, despite the awfulness of life, would just not occur to Hemingway's lost ones. Even though an entire generation of French, British and German husbands and fathers were killed with violence equal to that of Vietnam, no vast movement emerged that mandated burning draft cards and wearing clothes of protest.

Harry's seat was back and the monotonous drone of jet engines lullabyed him into half sleep as these thoughts emerged and then submerged. The stewardess' announcements would wake him for a moment, he would wonder if they were important then he'd pull his periscope down.

As the plane began its descent into Cleveland he grieved that he wasn't part of the protests, and grieved he wasn't part of the military. The wheels hit the runway with a sharp screech and puff of smoke, awakening him with a cramp in his neck, feeling needy and alone. He took some comfort when he realized Marv was next to him and Paula Markham of the tiny studio apartment on Irving Place just off Gramercy Park was a couple rows up. The plane slowed and turned and navigated across runways and around gas tankers and food service trucks that moved with purpose on the byways between passenger terminals and runways. He could overhear conversations once again. Kinky hair and bow tie were still earnestly engaged in the same subject they left the New York ground with. Kinky hair, still riding his metaphor, was saying "and for two or three days after each dose of medication I seem to treat my wife better. And she is less argumentative, almost livable with. If I miss my prescription for a couple of weeks it really gets unbearable at home. There's a dynamic going on here no doubt self-destructive, but so far I'm not complaining."

Cleveland

The plane jerk-stopped at the gate and with the chime everyone was instantly up and in the aisle. Harry and Marv sat in their seats as overhead bins were emptied. Then joltingly Harry heard the voice again. It was the same commanding one from last night. "You must go out from Jerusalem." A clear, direct order. Harry looked at Marv to see if he heard it, but Marv was just waiting for people in the aisle to start moving. He looked to see if anyone else heard it, but they were patiently waiting for the line to move. He felt his body experience low voltage currents of fear and attempted to collect himself. This was a critically decisive business trip, the outcome of which could be a huge boost to his career. They were meeting an important client in the airport who had departed from Hartford instead of LaGuardia, then they would get the ultimatum on this campaign straight from the consumer over the next three pressure filled days. Nevertheless, he was distinctly hearing a voice with utter clarity ordering "go out from Jerusalem." Sometimes he would see a picture in *Time* of those metal military coffins loaded into the belly of a huge Air Force transport and fantasize about the bodies in the boxes, the never to be school teachers and auto mechanics and CPAs, and picture them arriving in their hometowns for final insertion into the soil where on Memorial Day little American flags would sprout. He wanted to embrace the dead soldiers and their parents and relatives who would cluster around the gravesite. He'd been feeling this way since his gradual realization that the leadership of the world was making monumentally stupid errors. He wondered, yet again, if he was sliding into unreality and ultimate emotional breakdown and if the directive voice was the catalyst.

Moving down the aisle of the plane with his associates from Black and White Advertising he felt something embedded deep, sending a signal, as if his heart was another being from another time, reaching out with a message he'd better consider with a degree of gravity. The sights and decibels of the airport at full tilt were as some muted abstract painting and he recalled reading in a college psychology course that Freud was convinced our past with its cacophony of emotion and terror and unfulfilled aspirations inhabits our present forever. A revelation that perhaps "our past" reaches further back than our own wet emergence from mother's birth canal. As he was exiting from this dreamy progression he tuned in to Steve Lester's friendliest mid-western vocal chords greeting Burton Hayes, vice president of marketing for Kiddie Keds, and his manager of promotional services, Gertrude Mengele. Harry and Paula had ambled behind the group and were in the cab line talking. Nudging her shoulder he said, "So Paula. What thinks thee?"

"Question is too open ended. Specificity Harry."

"Oh anything. The flight. The Maxfield Parrish mural at the King Cole bar. Life behind the Iron Curtain."

"Methinks the campaign is golden. Unless there's a hidden surprise our consumer research will hopefully echo that. Enjoy the ride Harry."

"I am. I am. Maybe Gertrude Mengele will teach us how to laugh again."

"The campaign is brilliant Harry. Get in the cab."

They required three cabs to get to the focus group facility which was on the edge of Shaker Heights in a suburban office complex. Harry and Marv got into the last cab with Gertrude Mengele. There was no conscious pattern to who shared which cabs, except for Steve and Burton Hays. The cabs sped away like jets roaring off an aircraft carrier, and as they entered the traffic flow Harry caught glimpses of others in animated conversations as they swayed with the vehicles. Gertrude had entered first as Marv held the door in a gesture of overstated gallantry, then Harry motioned Marv in, who sat between them. Gertrude had a hefty figure, muscle rather than rolls of flab, she usually wore dark suits and white blouses with a little frill. Her hair was dark, shiny and cut short, glasses larger than they should have been magnifying her eyes to surreal size. She had metal in her teeth.

Marv once observed that she looked like a navy blue box with legs wrapped in some miracle fabric from DuPont. Gertrude took her job very, very seriously. She thought Burton Hays talked tough but was wishy-washy and too quickly persuaded by Steve and the rest of the agency silver tongues and took pride in the practical perspective she brought to matters involving creativity. Her role was to discipline Burton Hays' fits of fancy when he was under the influence of the agency double talk. She also controlled the budget.

Gertrude harbored a secret. It lay passively in some inner layer of the pulsating red protoplasmic mass that determined her responses to people and things in the world. Her secret was that through her father's line she was related to Dr. Josef Mengele of the medical experiments on Nazi concentration camp inmates. It wasn't a subject her family talked about. But when they did it was in an abbreviated code she first recognized when in grade school, just after the war ended. They lived in Cincinnati surrounded by friends and relatives who also partook of German culture, but were Americans. Her father, as a teenager, emigrated from Bavaria with his family in 1923, and spoke English with an accent that got more pronounced on the beer drinking nights at the local Teutonic Club where men went weekly to target shoot ancient rifles designed for *zimmer scheutzen*, or room shooting. The targets were of various Bavarian game animals, hare, a small deer, just a couple of inches high, and the range was ten meters. After the target shooting they would drink and bond. At the monthly family night out dinner when she was not quite a teenager, she first began to realize her father's cousin was famous for acts spoken of in a whisper. The women would cook schnitzel and cabbage reveling in a sense of *gemultlicheit* in the clubhouse basement as the children chased each other and the adults drank and felt a kinship in their Germanness. Some of the slightly older boys told her she had a famous relative who injected Jews. The information was pronounced like a punch line to a joke, and they snickered in a way that made Gertrude afraid to question her parents.

As their cab arrived at the focus group facility the other two taxis were discharging the group and Steve was already on the curb, stretching his limbs, arms high, spine bent, purging himself of all extraneous content in preparation for the concentration required to comprehend the upcoming consumer input. They entered the facility carrying luggage, briefcases, and over-sized art portfolios, each body indicating a range of tenseness from rigid and jerky to the almost languid movements of the more junior members of the group. In the reception area sat eight women ages twenty-five to thirty-nine, married with at least one child between three and seven, middle income, full-time mothers with working husbands. The receptionist instantly recognized the ad agency and showed them to the observation room where they would observe the group, passing a kitchen with two refrigerators and countertops loaded with trays piled with cookies, chips, and other snacks. Coffee percolated and ice buckets brimmed. Focus group operators knew the observers constantly snacked and when research occurred during lunch or dinner it was to their advantage to bring in a wide variety of gourmet meals, resulting in enthusiastic recommendations for future business. The anxiety of seeing a favored concept ridiculed or, worse, engendering no response at all, seemed to stimulate a variety of chemical reactions in those whose fortunes were determined by the consumer attitudes. Frequently there was a frenzied need to fill the nervous emptiness in their stomachs. The room was semi-dark with a one way mirror facing into the observation space where the discussion would take place. When the process began the light would go dark, even though the moderator would tell the participants that they were being observed. Harry and Marv had been in dozens of research sessions such as this and the one way mirror never seemed to inhibit anybody. There were comfortable theatre seats as well as a wide ledge with additional chairs next to the one way mirror. Very frequently drama the equal of Eugene O'Neil was played out without any rehearsal or script or direction.

Everybody took seats and Steve and Burton sat closest to the one way mirror munching from the dish loaded with a combination of M&M's and mixed nuts. Paula was having a last minute conference with the moderator, a Ph.D. in psychology and a woman of great compassion who had decided the world of qualitative research was more fulfilling than doing therapy or living in academia. Paula and the moderator, whose name was Rhoda, had been on the phone these last few days developing the discussion guide and there was a sisterly professionalism in their interaction that Marv and Harry disciplined themselves to not display cynicism over.

The group would start at 5 p.m. and last for two hours. It would proceed in sections, with the moderator explaining the rules and stressing there were no right or wrong answers, then having the women introduce themselves and give some pertinent data regarding their lives. The plan was to get them to talk about their children and direct the conversation to their children's sneakers, to brands they bought and why. This would be followed by the main event, showing the concept statements including the robot's walk across America, then Rhoda would probe for reactions. The session would conclude with the moderator getting the women to grade each concept from one to five, one being puke and five being pay dirt. These sessions could be painful in the extreme or joyful beyond life itself, depending on how close the respondents favored what the agency wanted to recommend. The discussion could sometimes take a tangent impossible to rein in. One dominant figure might affect the spontaneity of others, resulting in an inaccurate consensus. The moderator had to orchestrate the dynamics of the group's personalities to assure balance. Once in a while groups got so far from the true feelings of the participants as a result of one aggressive individual that if you just read the report without having been there, even if it was indicated, millions of dollars could be spent in advertising the wrong concept. On the other hand, there were examples of focus groups unanimously rejecting a concept the agency had unwavering belief in, and the agency after gut wrenching introspection deciding to recommend producing it regardless of the research, with the client skeptically acquiescing, waiting for the campaign and the agency to self-destruct in an embarrassing suicidal crash. When such a campaign sold hundreds of millions of dollars of product because a few wildly self-destructive agency heroes rejected the research and went with their instincts, the client quietly said thanks. Sometimes the opposite happened. A concept would score higher than the Himalayas in the focus group, but the agency couldn't execute the idea into a compelling TV commercial. Couldn't cast it right, direct it right, light it right, or pin down the essence that sets the great commercials apart from the promotional slop that TV watchers are ray gunned with in thirty second blasts eighteen times an hour. Harry and Marv had concluded there was an inverse ratio among the clients between the size of the corporate testicles and the amount of agency research conducted before a campaign was committed to. It was the instinct guys battling the quantify it guys.

"It's three minutes to six. They'll be filing in in a minute," said Steve. "Somebody kill the lights."

Paula who sat closest to the wall turned down the rheostat. The room was moonless, darkness an enveloping security blanket; the sound of Harry's bathtub drain gurgling down the foamy morning shower just eleven hours ago in Greenwich Village regurgitated in his head. Rhoda walked into the lighted conference room and as the women, referred to as "respondents" by the research professionals, filed in Steve whispered, "Turn up the speakers." Somebody did and their chatter filled the darkened observation room. These eight women were the absolute finest representation that the middle range of American aspirations could offer up. They were the target audience, the mother lode of potential sales that Proctor and Gamble and Kellogg's and Coca Cola brand managers had restless, lustful dreams over. Motivate them to switch brands by titillating the right urge to buy, and bonuses materialized, promotions occurred, careers were solidified, life became good. What these eight women casually commented upon during the next two hours could richly grease the wheels of American capitalism with fat, or slow it down to a rust flaking squeak. For the women, this was not only a night out, a furlough from the mindless mothering drudge that their lives had atrophied into, but they were actually being paid an "honorarium" for their opinions. Each of them had received a call from the focus group company recruiter and had answered a series of questions regarding income, marital status, and age. If they fit the demographics the client wanted to attract they were invited to participate. Harry hugged himself in the dark and thought that if Franz Kafka could observe a couple of these sessions, actually sit next to him in the observation room, and then have a beer, the ensuing conversation would be worth jotting some notes over. "Franz Kafka at the Focus Group," a title for a *New Yorker* poem.

The women offered a few tidbits about their lives. First names were written with magic markers on paper tents in front of each of them. Maxine with fleshy arms and a sweet inflated face was saying in a lilting sing-song voice, "kvetchy" Marv would say, that she had three children, two girls and a boy, aged two, three and five, that her hubby, upon using the word hubby Marv poked Harry, was a driver-salesman for Tip Top Bread. They had just bought a starter house and her mother-in-law was watching the kids because tonight was her hubby's bowling league and his team was two games away from league champions. "That's exciting" said the moderator, and Maxine said it does him good to get out with his friends once a week, and some of the others laughed, sharing their own personal moments of husband liberation. The next respondent, Tammy, said that her husband was a CPA. They had one six year old and were trying for another. She and her husband met at college and got married the week they graduated; they just celebrated their eighth wedding anniversary. Sighs of congratulations and hormonal communion occurred around the table during the warm-up, skillfully piloted by Ph.D. moderator Rhoda.

The eighth respondent to share some personal data with the

group appeared detached and bemused. She was subtle, more observant of the orchestration, curious, suspicious, interested in the process, with a guarded smile bordering on condescending. Harry noted her intelligence and trim figure and immediately had sexual fantasies. In the darkened space he could stare without fear of being observed. He could work on absorbing her aura. He was like the museum goer and she was a 17th century Dutch portrait. She was saying her husband traveled quite a bit on his job. He was a consulting engineer for the Army Corps of Engineers. He was in Idaho this week and she had a part-time job at a nursery school. She had majored in art history and also archeology in college and her hobby was painting. Harry wondered what it would be like to be married to her, to get up in the morning and watch her shed silky, pale blue pajamas from her nice slim body and get dressed and have breakfast together and go on vacations to the great art museums of Europe and attend family functions on various holidays, and whether they would ever reach that condition of sexual nothingness that some of his married friends joked about. All this as he craved her in the darkness of the observation room. He couldn't quite see her name as her name tent was at an angle, so he got up and walked to the ledge, close to the mirror where Steve and Burton Hayes sat. He seated himself, took a handful of M&M's, and felt a wave of titillation at being just a few feet away, what safe intimacy, through the protective barrier of a one way mirror. Her name was Audrey. Perfect. Audrey Hepburn, Moon River, inner demons wrapped in outer loveliness. No last names. Did it end in a vowel? Mediterranean? Catholic yin and yang? Episcopalian? Wish I could get her maiden name.

Then he drifted back to the conversation coming through the speaker; they had somehow strayed to comparing recipes for Apple Brown Betty, but Rhoda, the moderator, deftly directed them toward their children's favorite food, and then got them to talk about shopping for sneakers. A large woman with a take charge voice complained that the kid's feet grew so quickly she had more experience shopping for sneakers than she knew what to do with, and the others emitted female sounds of agreement accompanied by knowing nods. Maxine said she always worried about fit. Somebody else offered that she usually buys them a larger size, hoping they'll last long enough to grow into. One of the other women said you shouldn't buy them too large, but she was tempted to do the same thing.

Rhoda then queried as to whether any of their children ever influenced what they bought. Several nodded in the affirmative, "oh yes" with looks of exasperation.

"If the sneakers are brightly colored or patterned," said Irma Klein.

"Or if they have a cartoon character, especially a Disney character," said Susan Rothenberg, whose background included eleven years of marriage to a former college baseball player who now worked in her family's wholesale food business. All the women rose up in a swirl of agreement about cartoon characters on sneakers being irresistible to kids. Steve slapped Burton Hayes on the back in a spontaneous gesture. Maxine said that the cartoon character shoes seemed to be more expensive and that wasn't fair, and when Moderator Rhoda asked if they all agreed, they once again rose up in motherly union at the exploitation, the cruelness of those children's sneaker companies. And when Rhoda asked if anyone could guess why they charged more, there was a lull in the room, just a few heartbeats, and then Susan Rothenberg blurted out "royalties" signaling a henhouse cacophony of realization. Rhoda asked if it wasn't worth a little more to make their kids happy, knowing she was entering emotionally turbulent seas, but also sensing they were sailing into fruitful seas. In the observation room Steve leaned over and whispered in Burton's ear, "No royalties for our cartoon character." Even Gertrude in her Teutonic quest for the super rational seemed to know they were witnessing a major marketing sperm penetrating a receptive marketing egg.

"My kids don't need characters from Disney on their sneakers to make them happy," snapped one of the participants who had remained uninvolved until that moment.

"But they do love them," said Maxine.

"Yeah, it sometimes feels like an extravagance to pay more, but that's what they want," said Susan Rothenberg whose grandfather founded Rothenberg Wholesale Foods in 1924, and who grew up in Shaker Heights, never lacking for little extravagances. "I don't want to spoil them, but it's such a little thing and it brings them so much happiness."

The discussion flew on automatic pilot with most of the mothers concluding it was terrible for the manufacturers to rape them like that, but if their kids made a big fuss they'd usually give in. And at exactly the right moment, when their minds were still grappling with the moral implications of characters on sneakers versus the added price compared to their children's love and what this all added up to, Rhoda, the brilliant moderator, asked, "What if there was a loveable character that you and your kids saw on TV and in the newspapers, and he stood for all the good things in life, and a sneaker maker put him on the sneakers and didn't charge a premium. Would you buy?" Nodding heads. Dumbfounded looks. Could it be true? Yes. Yes. A chorus of affirmations. It's too good to be true. Which manufacturer? Who's the character? No premium? Yes. Yes. When?

By now there was a slow boiling energy in the observation room. They nudged each other when something positive was stated, they sighed to themselves, clapped silently, fidgeted in expectation, stood up, walked around the room, sat, suppressed the rising optimism as best they could. Even the more experienced who realized this was just the first group, who had seen positive reactions turn to lethargic indifference in subsequent groups with the exact same demographics, even the most jaded in the room heard the Mormon Tabernacle Choir exalting Hallelujah.

Marv showed no emotion. Although inside he soared, he would be gracious, magnanimous in his triumph. Confident. A touch humble. The wisdom of his people, of two millennia of the taunted outsider, gave him a genetic survival system that he might have to call up should the world go mad and the next focus group go all to hell. Harry was also impassive as he fantasized further about Audrey, this time she was shedding her clothes and getting into her silky, pale blue pajamas as they prepared for bed, getting under fresh sheets in a Queen Size Sealy Posturpedic, snuggling close, lights down, bliss.

Rhoda, moderator extraordinaire, was now saying, "I'd like to show you some rough ideas, we call them concept statements, and we'll then discuss your reactions." She went through three ordinary looking graphic depictions of kids at play, and happy families, all with not very memorable headlines, probing them for emotional hot buttons, but there were none. Then she took out Marv's rendering of the robot wearing Kiddie Keds with a big endearing human smile on his cute robot face. The next board showed him walking through town, kids following gleefully, townspeople happily waving, Kiddie Keds resplendent. Under the picture the headline said *Kiddie Keds last longer. Robbie Robot walks across America to prove it.*

"Oooh, my kids will love that!"

"Is he really going to walk across America?"

"Well, if it's true I'd buy Robbie Robot Kiddie Keds in a heartbeat!"

"But how much are they going to cost?" Everyone talking. Real interest. Enthusiasm. High group expression. We like it. We want it!

Inside the observation room Steve Lester was sprawled out in his chair, legs crossed, a self-satisfied smile of victory, ownership of the campaign seized for the duration. Burton Hayes was saying, "It's incredible. Can we really pull it off? Can we build the robot? How much? We might have to ask for an increased budget."

And Gertrude Mengele witnessing the spontaneity of the mothers decided to keep quiet for now but seemed to be moved by it all. She wondered what kind of minds come up with such stuff.

At that moment there was a knock on the door and one of the staff ladies poked her head in to announce dinner was ready.

Paula and Gertrude went out to the lounge area where the caterer had set up the food and returned with plates of Caesar salad and beef stroganoff. Then a couple of others went out to get theirs. Harry looked at Marv and realized they were ravenous. At the serving table Marv said to Harry, "Smells like a winner."

"The food or the campaign?"

"Both." The stroganoff was top quality beef in a rich, creamy sauce giving off expensive aromas. They walked back into the observation room with full plates to enjoy this haute cuisine from Cleveland's caterer of the moment and bask in the sublimity of their creative efforts, having hit the bull's eye. As they seated themselves Harry heard his dream fantasy the lovely Audrey speaking. He noticed that Steve Lester was sitting upright poised to pounce, and nobody else in the room was eating. Gertrude Mengele had a large chunk of stroganoff in her mouth but had stopped in mid-chew. Audrey had started speaking in a low voice, but as she continued her decibel intensity grew.

"We are being violated by these mind-sucking shit heads, they're not in the sneaker business, they're in the exploitation business. Do you see what they're doing? They're obscuring the way you're raising your children by skinning you alive and examining our guts for profit. They're using research that should be used for improving society, and sucking something sacred out of us to sell more crap to kids. These people are despicable. This whole Marx Brothers movie makes me feel like a whore. Don't you know that while we've been in this emotional rat maze of a psychiatric glass house with that fucking one way mirror being observed like some amoeba under a microscope there's a war going on that only a few misguided politicians who are on the payroll of companies like this one want, and people are being blown up to hell while we're in here blithering away like a new species of retard about our deepest sneaker buying secrets. I feel demeaned just by being here, and I feel ashamed for the people putting this freak show on."

She'd been leaning forward and frothing at each of them, but especially to marvelous moderator, Rhoda, and now she sat back in her chair surprised at her outburst, looking as if she might continue into tears, but then another thought lit up her eyes and she leaned forward again. "These kids that will be screaming at you mommies to buy these demented robot sneakers are getting a different world to grow up in. It's all so fucking sick."

Harry silently congratulated her. She was right. For the last three years he had been waiting for someone in a focus group to explode in rage at the tawdriness of the process, at the invasive assault on the soul that these manufacturers and marketers of products inflicted on gullible naïve and so willing consumers of the latest, the most improved, the must have and fashionably necessary via TV commercials, magazine ads, counter cards, shelf talkers, and forty foot high billboards. Audrey hovering away from the warmth of the campfire saw the whole system with a lucidity only those cursed with a destiny of inhabiting the outer fringes could penetrate. And she cracked. She was a focus group moderator's most horrible, sweat soaked nightmare, an intelligent exquisitely clear thinking neurotic battling external demons. What now? The shadowy forms in the observation room were barely breathing. Harry saw that even take-charge Steve Lester was suspended in time, mummified, incapable of command. Harry knew they had just witnessed an event that would become a conversation piece at the agency, at other agencies, at the client, in bars and trade group meetings, on Fire Island and commuter trains and throughout the universe of those most sophisticated shamans of selling whatever to the sucking masses.

The other mommies looked down, avoided eye contact, fidgeted. Ph.D. Rhoda, the masterful, was composing herself. She'd been conducting focus groups for three years and was on guard for an emotional outburst but this plastered her in the solar plexus. She knew she had to placate Audrey and then reassure the rest of the respondents. She sensed her first words would be pivotal in undoing the damage, the potential damage, and she carefully considered what to say, weighing various responses all in the space of a second or two. In the observation room, Marv quietly exhaled the words, "She's great," to which Harry nodded a barely observable affirmation. Steve Lester did one of his hyperventilating pig snorts. Gertrude gradually began again to chew the stroganoff, enjoying the succulence of the highest grade beef the focus group caterer could provide. Paula Markham wondered how Rhoda would handle the outburst, wondered how she would handle it were she conducting the group. She too started eating again, sliding flawlessly prepared Caesar salad with a hint of anchovy bits onto her fork and in a deliberate ladylike gesture into her mouth concentrating all the while on the mechanics of her movements.

Harry was now ready to transcend the illusory clouds of imagination starring the many tiered Audrey and strive for a personal appearance. How to meet her, to sit across a small table with a bottle of wine or maybe just two espressos and pose questions that would cause her to reveal herself, to peel off his own layers with slow, subtle eye contact, like a foreign film that allows the slightest change of expression to speak worlds. She would find him irresistible because he was interested, because his questioning would help her examine her own motives, her being; together they would burrow through the protective barriers, reach the substance, the longed for and consoling no-sophistication center. But without a meeting, nothing. She would disappear into the parking lot, into her car, into the night, forever.

"We can't let her go," he whispered to Marv.

"Yeah, but what would we do with her?"

"Talk to her. Maybe violate her, establish a meaningful, extramarital relationship."

"But you're not married."

"I know that. She is."

"That's unacceptable behavior, you're seriously flawed."

Harry leaned back knowing he was about to seize the moment, but not how. Seconds of silence. He knew somebody, Steve or Rhoda, was frantically covering the options and might do something that would cause Audrey to slip away forever. There's nothing to lose, and the world is mad. I'm on the verge of some sort of emotional breakdown anyway, so here goes. He bolted out of his chair and said to Steve, "I've got an idea," and before Steve could respond he went out the door, down the hall, and entered the room on the other side of the one way mirror. The women were still suffering the aftershock of Audrey's outburst and were startled to have this male figure enter their preserve. Rhoda looked up not knowing if it was the cavalry coming to rescue her or the Indians counter attacking.

"Ladies," he began, "my name is Harry and I'm with the advertising agency that developed these campaigns." He gestured to the layouts spread before them on the table. "Your insights have been very helpful to us. There is nothing more beautiful than a mother's love for her child, and you've all expressed that with great feeling. And for that we're grateful. Once in awhile when we conduct this sort of consumer research we say things we didn't realize we were feeling. Whenever that happens it's especially valuable for us and this has been so helpful we're going to double the honorariums we pay you to fifty dollars. And if I could I'd like to conduct a more in-depth one-on-one interview with Audrey."

Being in the room with the respondents not separated by the one way mirror put these women in another context. He could smell them in the confines and intimacy of that room, their hairsprays, body essences, clothes, their cigarette smoke and even their laundry detergent. Achingly obvious ordinariness previously obscured by the one way mirror, by the drama of the technique, was exposed. Except for Audrey.

Serenity on the surface. Dark observing eyes and lips peacefully Mona Lisa'd with confidence. Intelligence. But something more complex. A searching tilt to the head. A spiritual hunger. Disappointment. Curiosity about what unfair travesty will we be overwhelmed by next. Harry had read somewhere about the ordinary man in war, in combat, fatalistically dealing with the day-in day-out wariness of his predicament, no longer surprised by the unreality of decent strangers trying to kill other decent strangers, and that seemed to be Audrey's demon.

"Would you consent to a one-on-one interview? It will only take a few minutes and perhaps I can explain." He didn't know what he would explain. She observed him impassively, shrugged, the combat veteran, and followed him out. They walked down the hall to the reception area and he asked the perky, mini skirted, part-time receptionist, food server, cul de sac queen, if they could use an office.

"This is Charlene's office, but she's gone for the day. Let me know if I can get you anything." Harry closed the door, sat down in a chair in front of Charlene's desk and Audrey sat in the other chair. There was a picture on the credenza of Charlene's son in a football jersey holding a white Scotch terrier. What now, thought Harry. What about forthrightness and honesty? She's volatile and perceptive and different from the target audience. Risk playing it straight.

"I'm a copywriter with the advertising agency and I've been in dozens of these focus group research sessions. What you just so eloquently blurted out is something I've felt for a long time but haven't had the courage to express. I want to congratulate you on having the balls that I don't." Maybe "balls" is too familiar, he thought. But on the other hand she used profanity during her explosion, but she was exploding. I'm supposed to be the voice of reason. But I am being perfectly straight with her. Where is this going? Where do I want it to go? I want this to be the beginning of a conversation, get past her focus group rage to whatever the human chemical mixture is that results in a desire to know more, go deeper, ignite the thin flammable thread lying dormant in us, testing how hot the flame will get, how far it will spread, from bland neutral eye contact to… this is stage one. I am nothing. To her at this moment I am a zero ad agency guy interested in selling sneakers to kids, the bad guy. What do I say? How do I comport myself, present myself, so she is surprised? More than surprised. Intrigued. The first step from bland zero to…interest. I know things about her. She said things about herself in the warm-up session.

"Did you say you majored in anthropology?" A distant flicker of light. Very distant. Buried. But something. Continue. "Did you ever do anything with it? Study tribes? Live in the ghetto? Go on digs?"

"Digs are archeology," said dismissively. Bored. But response. Blow on it.

"Sorry, anthropology and archeology seem so close. But have you ever been on a dig anyway? You look like someone who might." Shifting in her chair. It's like fishing in clear shallow water where you can see the fish. The lure hit's the surface with a plop but the fish is wary. Indifferent. Then a feeble strike.

"Yeah, I've been on a dig. But where the fuck are you going with this?" Going on instinct, no forethought, spontaneous.

"I wanted to understand you. Your rage is justified. I didn't want to let you walk out. When did you go on the dig?"

"About five years ago, '63."

"Where was it?"

"Israel."

"Where?"

"Masada."

Several of his organs heard the word Masada and responded. His lungs trembled. And his heart sobbed. He was aware of internal backfiring but it was the voice again that caused his unease. It was quiet, as close as you could get to no voice, but clear as menacing thunder. "You must go out from Jerusalem." He felt there were two of him, the physical being with loosened tie and business stress in this focus group facility in Shaker Heights and some other form of life that was also him but whose personal history and memory of experience was dim, as if from a stranger passing through the neighborhood and causing a stir, leaving a spell. He tried clinging to his previous state of being in charge, of directing the conversation to a level of intimacy with this woman he wanted to touch, but the voice which only he heard took away his sense of control and replaced it with a sucking quicksand descent into a fearsome vulnerability. Like holding onto driftwood in a shipwrecked sea he grasped at whatever rationality was in his proximity. Three times the voice has spoken. Is there a pattern? What the hell triggers it? Is it a message, or madness? The early stages that one doesn't take too seriously but others notice at first as quirkiness, then eccentricity, distraction, and your behavior enters a spiraling ascent to the other side of the star studded universe and you're simply bats living your own reality having nothing at all to do with anything at all.

"Something happened at Masada. What was it?" As he asked the question he felt he should know.

Audrey who rarely used profanity sat in this windowless cell-like office, a volunteer captive, wondering why she wasn't embarrassed at losing it so thoroughly with that group of bowling league bridge-mix eaters. Although she frequently had thoughts like those expressed she rarely voiced them and never with such spontaneity and anger. Because her husband had been away more than usual lately, because of the military build-up, she'd been alone a lot, especially in the evenings and there was an uncomfortable diminishing of anticipation when he returned. She had the part-time job at the nursery school which was why she'd been included in this focus group debacle in the first place. She painted and read a lot and was living the everyday pain and rage at the Vietnam war millions of others felt, but hadn't yet expressed it by attending a peace rally. She was ready for a personal public statement. During her time alone the phrase "personal public statement" came to her lips and she did a painting with those words appearing in a dark abstract haze. She had seen a picture of a girl who lived in her dorm at Kenyon College on the front page of the *New York Times* in a Gay Rights march, and the husband of one of the mothers at her nursery school, a lieutenant in the Marines, had come back from the war without his arm. She lived each day with a sense of unease. The dreams she had when she got her degree were fading; she had to think hard to recall the life envisioned when fresh and open and eager.

She questioned if it was the endlessness of the war, the images of blacks running and looting through burning American cities, the assassinations and the hippies marching and chanting and smoking pot while sitting cross legged in some park. Had her spirit been so diminished by events she had no ability to control? Sometimes she had a hint that were the world kinder, she still would have been diverted to this off-loading ramp because that's how she was stamped. The freshness and hope that Jack and Jackie Kennedy created in 1960 as the presidential campaign set expectation to a rapturous level mirrored her own anticipation at the vision of a fulfilling and audacious life. Now her hopes plunged downward as the Washington aristocrats and military elite created national turmoil and spiritual sickness through arrogance and blundering. No, it wasn't how she was stamped. It was how the times were stamped. Fucked by the fickle finger of fate for being born in a time not of your choosing. And she found a sad smile in that.

"Masada," repeated Harry, seeing she had drifted. "I feel I should know what happened there." I'm not sure what this guy is after, she thought, but he does seem earnest. I really disrupted their flow when I lost it. So tell him about Masada and then scram.

Harry was struggling with internal currents rising to conflicted consciousness. The more charged of the electrical surges were commanding he engulf her. Yet the more practical current was dictating those civilized controls that separate human species from other animal life. Decorum. Rules of engagement. Gradualism. When he studied her in the small space they occupied he knew her with the intimacy of many lifetimes and was frustrated to madness that he was still outside her own secret emotional life. The mysteriousness of attraction was confounding. He knew if there were eight equally beautiful women on the other side of that one-way mirror this one would cause the yearning. As his old Aunt Sadie from Flatbush would say with a shrug, "Go know."

"Okay," she said. "The dig at Masada lasted two years. Volunteers from all over the world. I was there for three months. People would rotate in and out. When you're on top of that plateau and feel the hot dry wind blow and look out toward the Dead Sea, you feel you've passed into the world of the ancients. You're on top of that place and the people who walked that gritty terrain two thousand years ago didn't feel it any differently than you do."

Hearing the tympani of her voice caused within Harry hopefulness for inner peace, and resignation that it was eternally beyond his reach. She spoke quietly, occasionally looking at him. It was slowly becoming apparent that what she was saying seemed to have a meaning for him that was beyond casual.

"You really don't know the story of Masada?"

"I feel as if I may have known it at one time, but I can't pull it up. Please go on. It would mean a lot."

She distractedly fidgeted with the top button of her shirt. "Masada affects people. It overwhelms you. For many people it consumes, with the intensity of a love affair. In order to understand I have to tell you about Josephus." As she went from a walk to a trot Harry saw a young college instructor delivering a lecture, evoking respect from peers. He was on the verge of understanding this was a woman of complicated layers she was oblivious to, that some element within him was stimulated by that particular scent, and he was making preparation for a dance of fertility.

"Josephus was a chronicler of the times. At first he was an officer fighting the Romans, but then he switched over to the enemy and became a favorite of theirs. He served as a historian of sorts, writing about the battles and events with an emphasis on the years 66 to 72 C.E. Although Jewish, he wrote in Greek which some upper class Jews of the time spoke. The less than upper classes thought that an affectation and were disgusted by it. Josephus wrote several volumes called *The Jewish Wars*, they've survived to this day. What is so haunting and magical about Masada is that just about everything Josephus wrote two thousand years ago was eerily accurate. You see ghosts up there. They talk to you." As she recreated her own evocation of Masada he wanted to hear the ghosts talking, to touch them as he touched himself, to experience her through them.

"According to Josephus, there were 960 fighters including women and children. There's some controversy as to how long they were on Masada. One theory says several years; sieges at the time rarely went longer than a few months. They had lots of water and supplies, so it could have been a year. One point everybody agrees on is that the group, called Zealots, were pretty hard-boiled. They really hated the Romans and were ready to kill other Jews if they considered surrender or co-existence. They were almost eager to die. Masada is about thirty miles southeast of Jerusalem. The revolt against Roman occupation gathered real momentum in 66 A.D. and by the year 73 the Romans had quelled all resistance. Although some Jews stayed on, most left the country. Dispersed. The beginning of the Diaspora."

And Harry said, "Dispersed, Diaspora. But what exactly happened?"

"I guess I strayed. I haven't thought about this in a long time." There was a knock on the door and Steve Lester's head appeared.

"How're ya doin' Har?"

They didn't realize how private their conversation was until Steve's gawking presence intruded. Harry recovered and shifting to the Steve vernacular said, "Hey Stevo, Audrey and I are getting into some deep issues that are proving valuable. We need a little more time."

Steve looked at them with great relief, eager for additional insight into the consumer mind, winked at Harry, said "gotcha Har" and receded behind the closed door.

"So what happened at Masada?" he said, obliterating Steve's being like a quick swat at a pesky fly. The room purified, Audry picked right up.

"The Zealots were in an untenable situation, holding out against the most powerful nation on Earth, and there were under a thousand of them, including women and children. They knew the Roman Tenth Legion was on its way, sixteen thousand hardened warriors, most of whom were Romans rather than conscripted locals. Whether the Zealots were under siege for months or a year or longer, they knew they didn't have much of a future. As they analyzed their options, being the believers they were, a miracle from God was no doubt high on their list."

"It sounds like what we're going through with Vietnam," said Harry.

"A miracle from God. For those who believe," switching subjects as naturally as he did.

"Are you a believer?" he asked.

"Moments when I feel frightened. Empty. The way the Zealots probably felt on top of Masada, but I don't turn to God for relief." She was perplexed by her answer. It came out without any forethought. The question had taken her by surprise. A personal question from a person she did not know, yet she was eager to answer. A long time since having a conversation in which someone was interested in what she was saying. She looked at him searching for a clue as to who he was. When on the Masada dig she had been told the ancient Hebrew word for face and the word for inside are exactly the same, recalling that as she tried to remember the word and peer inside. As she herself was in the midst of a turmoil that would not pass, her receptivity to the anguish of others was especially keen. She looked at his eyes without appearing to gaze deeply and saw he was sad and intelligent and wrapped in solitude. And his neediness extended to her like a protrusion with an energy all its own. "Punim." The Hebrew word for face and inside was "punim." Harry perceived that a shift occurred and he thought, he hoped, he had progressed from a faceless non-entity to a gradation of humanity perhaps worthy of exploratory probes. Could he possibly get her out of this focus group office to a friendly neighborhood bar where the locals went for the sense of familiarity he sought even though he knew it would only be experienced from the fringes? He searched for the right words realizing it was a gamble as the possibility of her rejecting his invitation meant he would probably never see her again.

The best he could come up with was, "Uh, look, please don't

consider me presumptuous, but this conversation has a relevancy I don't quite understand and I was wondering if there was some local spot we could go to and continue our talk?" His benign and casual exterior masked an increased heartbeat as he prepared for a negative response and her exit. But she had caught a glimpse of his interior and had the ability see his fragility. Most women he had selected were incapable of recognizing messages of emotion from a man, so he was stunned to a gloriousness too exquisite to savor when after a contemplative few seconds that seemed like being submerged in the sea, she said,

"I know a place."

"Good. I'll tell old Stevo we're leaving."

It was dark now and cars seemed to be moving with a purpose. People who worked late rushing for the sanctuary of their homes, a late dinner and television, then under the covers for seven or eight hours, only to repeat the battle of office politics and assembly line tedium in the morning. Others rushing to their night shift jobs in factories, all-night diners, fire stations, parents returning from PTA meetings and Little League. Harry followed close to Audrey, not quite tailgating; he dreaded getting separated, not knowing their destination. Audrey got off the highway and they were in a quiet suburban neighborhood of middle management families. The houses were not large, neat yards, some with boats or campers, well-cut lawns, dim lights inside with the dull shadowy glow of TV's flickering. This America was as far from Manhattan as Bora Bora. Harry thought that many young people who migrated to Manhattan were formed in places like this. Why did some leave to fulfill dreams of ascension in the world of creativity and expression, while others remained in places like this? You pop out, fall in love with your mother, and the die is cast. New York for some, Cedar Rapids for others.

Audrey was now easier to follow as there was practically no traffic. They came to a quiet main drag with frilly, fancy shops and a tavern with a small green neon sign, "Pat's Place." They found parking right in front of Pat's. Entering phase two. She was languid. Moved like royalty, Audrey Hepburn playing a modern day princess, taking the attention and servitude for granted. But not raised with ladies-in-waiting, with needs attended to before she realized she had them. Royalty and outrage in the same body. They entered Pat's Place. Perfect. Darkly lit. Wood booths. Billiard table. A few neighborhood couples quietly having drinks. Three male buddies at the billiard table, laughing, enjoying the comfort of having known each other since middle school. On the jukebox, the Beatles. A waitress who worked there decades and wise in the knowledge of this suburban Cleveland community took their orders and because she had developed an instinct of figuring out what the relationship was between couples decided theirs was new and sweet and had a possibility for volatility and deep hurt. They seemed like social and intellectual equals. It would be very good with them, and also conflicted. The clairvoyant waitress returned with a chardonnay and beer, then focused on how many hours before she'd be through her shift and in the arms of her new boyfriend.

"I like this place," said Harry.

"Yeah, I come here once in a while with my husband and sometimes with my girlfriends."

At the mention of her husband Harry was jolted into a danger zone. He was in a bar, at his suggestion, with another man's wife. There could be consequences.

"What does he do?"

"He's an engineer, a civilian engineer with the Army Corps of Engineers. Travels a lot."

"Good marriage?" My God, how can I ask that?

"Used to be. Right now he's in Idaho. Been there about a week. Not sure if it's still good. Wish it was. Just not sure." Once again confusion by how easily she could be candid with this man she knew nothing about.

"What about you?" she ventured.

He knew he would give her the depth of it, as much as he understood. "I'm in a depression of sorts. See a shrink twice a week. Cannot stand what's going on out there. The war. Young soldiers trying to survive a nightmare. Being spat upon when they return. Peace marchers being arrested. Suffering as deeply as the teenage Marines. The assassinations. I die a little every day. Spending my working day generating creative ideas about products and companies I don't care about and convincing those poor, sweet, nitwits in the focus group they'll burn in purgatory for having deprived their kids a certain brand of sneakers. Bad in relationships. Certain women go for my piercing blue eyes and magic personality. I always make them unhappy. Rudderless on the inside, faking determination on the outside. Lately I've started hearing a voice. It happens in the oddest places. Airports. My apartment. Taxis. The voice says, 'you must go out from Jerusalem.' It's as if I've heard the voice in another life. Some string-like vestige of another time. First time I've said any of this to somebody that doesn't have M.D. after his or her name. Thank you."

In very few words he had synthesized his travail in an even and flat voice, eyes ever so slightly moist. A boiling kettle spurting steam on the inside, and Asian passivity outside. Except for the eyes, the telescope to the primal guts, punim. Her eyes dilated with subtlety that perhaps only a psychiatrist or a lover would register. "I think we've got the same thing." Buried in their sadness was the exquisiteness of connection between female moistness and male matter. The comfortable sounds of the billiards game quietly filling Pat's Place as background ambience mixed with The Beatles as they took long, slow drinks.

"Tell me about that voice. Do you think you're cracking?"

A quick laugh. "I may be cracking, but it's authoritative. It's real. If that crazy voice is a sign I'm going kookooboo, then I've already gone off the edge."

"Sounds like something God would say. As if it's a line in the Old Testament. 'Go out from Jerusalem.' My father is Jewish."

"Don't know the Bible well, but why in hell would God be talking to me? You know this conversation is certifying both of us as being candidates for an upscale mental institution at the end of a long tree-lined drive surrounded by shrubbery."

"Yes, yes, I know the perfect place. It's in an expensive suburb in Westchester County, New York." They both nodded, smiling.

And as an afterthought Harry added, "and tweed coated, pipe smoking psychiatrists directing Masters of Social Work in how to conduct group therapy."

"Yeah, that's the place."

"Tell me more about the dig at Masada. How did you get interested in it? What made you decide to go?"

"I will, but I want to hear more about the voice."

"Deal."

"For you to understand, I have to start with my father's family. They were from Berlin. They owned textile mills. A big house in the city. Twelve inside servants. The opera every Saturday afternoon. Another house in Zermatt. Big skiers. Athletic. Cultured. They got out sometime in 1938. They bought their way. Bribed the right Nazis. My grandfather had been shifting money to U.S. bank accounts for years. He was smart and because the mills had worldwide business he used his contacts in New York to help get the money out. Unlike many who fled the Holocaust they arrived with sizable resources, but nothing approaching what they had in Germany. My father was born in 1908. He was about thirty when they left. Traveled first class on the Queen Mary. There are old photos. Men in expensive overcoats, cashmere with fur collars, homburgs, the women in high fashion of the time. Looking at those freeze frames from the past you would never know they were on a journey that altered their way of life to its very core. There had to be endemic fear and sense of loss and shame at leaving their homeland of over 300 years. My father was deeply, deeply humiliated. He left behind a love affair that could have been a marriage, a young countess from Luxembourg he met at Zermatt. Back in the twenties the intermarriage rate was almost fifty percent. Our family was so wealthy and powerful and Teutonic that their Jewish heritage didn't bother many of their own contemporary pure Germans. My father speaks French and Italian without a trace of an accent, in addition to his native German. His English has a slight foreign tinge, but you have to listen carefully to pick it up.

"So after war breaks out in 1941 he wants to join the army and go back and do his share. The army discovers Daddy's background and language abilities and he goes into the OSS. He had the European equivalent of an Ivy League education and was totally comfortable in the world of international aristocrats as well as the lumpenproletariat. The latter because he spent so much time learning the textile business from the ground floor. After boot camp and the OSS school he's back in Germany posing as a mid-level Reichstag diplomat in well-tailored civilian clothes and with all the necessary documents. He's on a train from Munich to Berlin and has a small compartment all to himself. Somewhere halfway, an SS captain struts in, mutters excuse me, and shares the compartment. Something about the SS captain looks familiar. What causes every beat in his body to quicken to a sweat producing four minute mile pace is that the captain registers that same look. He knows my father, but can't place him. The SS officer opens his briefcase, takes out a bottle of brandy and offers some. A friendly sharing of alcohol. They gesture a toast and attempt conversation. Both try to identify in what context they know each other. The Nazi is collegial rather than suspicious, and my father is very frightened.

"After his third drink, the SS captain is getting talkative and they "Heil Hitler" each other. My father asks where he's from and he says Berlin. Then he asks what was his job before the war. The Nazi says he was in charge of trucking and transportation at a Jew owned textile mill. The big one, Sonnenshein & Sons. The recognition occurs simultaneously. They are no longer Aryan equals. The SS man's face is a reflection of what's going on inside. Punim. It's an expression of resentment my father has been the target of many times. It's what the lower middle classes feel towards the privileged when in daily contact. The unfairness of life. Why should those lucky ones be born into wealth and prestige, while I struggle to put bread on the table? It's an inbred seething. They come home exhausted and can never afford all the Christmas gifts they'd like to give their children, while those stupid fucking lucky ones are being driven home in Dusenbergs. A constant rage with a low, medium and high setting.

"The SS man slips down in his velvet covered compartment seat and squints, rattler like. 'You are Sonnenshein.' And my father remembers his name. Karl Klages. Obsequious Karl. Now with the authority to vent his lifetime of humiliation.

" 'We heard most of the Sonnenshein's left for America. Why are you here?' And my father makes a decision to not deny who he is. He tells Klages that he has been asked to work for the Reichstag because of his worldwide influence. Klages doesn't totally buy it.

"'But you are a Jew. That is not possible.' Father builds his case as Klages drinks more brandy, no longer offering any, only partially convinced, and says, 'I must check your documents.'

"Father's OSS training tells him to stand firm, confident, and arrogant. Klages backs off. Drinks another. Then says, 'You are a Jew. I don't believe you. I must turn you in. At the next stop.' Then Klages says, 'On your knees Jew Sonnenshein. Suck my schveinvessel. In your mouth, now.' Father's first thought was that he'd heard in training that several of the ranking Nazi leadership were homosexual and would have all-male parties at the big houses and castles they requisitioned. Then a survival plan. He knew what he must do. He got to his knees and the former employee of Germany's largest textile mill, revenge, sweet revenge, unbuttoned his fly and his pink toned, semi-erect, urine fouled penis popped out like a Jack-in-the-box. He grabbed the hair of a scion and major stockholder of Sonnenshein and Sons and pushed his penis into my father's mouth. He thrust and gyrated as father tried not to vomit. When father knew his former employee was about to ejaculate he got his six inch switchblade from the inside of his suit pocket and in one motion snapped it open and with all his strength stabbed through Karl Klages' uniform and into his chest. As Karl Klages' sperm was spurting my father withdrew the knife from his heart and pushed the man's chin up with his open palm and sliced through the artery of his throat. Blood spurted like a water pistol. As Klages was more dead than alive, my father found an imbecile-like laugh emerging from the violence. The French, he recalled, referred to an orgasm as the little death.

"He sat down. Gathered himself. When he thought of that Nazi dick in his mouth his impulse was to slit Klages' throat a second time. He had to get off the train quickly. The attendant had just passed and announced the next stop in ten minutes was Furth. As the train started slowing down he laid the SS captain Karl Klages on the double seat in the fetal position and covered him with a blanket. He then looked his clothes over. Miraculous. Just one spot of blood the size of a pfenning on his Dunhill tailored jacket. Could be a food stain. Goulash soup. He wiped the switchblade on the inside of Klages' blanket and put it back in his pocket. He felt the Walther pistol he carried under his shirt, in its concealable holster, picked up his small Louis Vuitton bag and assumed the officious pose of a rising Reichstag diplomat. In the aisle he found the car attendant and informed her that the good SS captain was sleeping and requested that no one enter the compartment. She agreed immediately, being totally committed to the Fuhrer. The train proceeded at a maddening snake-like crawl for what seemed a doomed lifetime. At Furth my father got off with the dignity someone of his rank would project and ultimately hitched a ride with a major driving to Berlin in an Opel. When my father finished he broke into convulsive sobbing and held me as he sobbed."

Harry now knew why she moved with such grace, and that she had insides constructed of steel. As he was about to ask where Masada came into the picture Audrey said, "When I was at Miss Porter's School, in the 11th grade, I was writing a paper on World War II and while home for Christmas asked my father exactly what he did in the war. It wasn't a subject he talked about. He told me this story and with tears said that ever since that terrifying incident he has lived in the spirit of Masada. I didn't know what Masada represented and he simply said we are ready to die with nobility and courage as we face those who will destroy us. It was a metaphor for how he lived his life. That's why I went on the dig six years ago."

"Now you. The voice."

Harry had one more question. "I'll tell you what I know, which ain't much, but I'm curious about one more thing. Who is your mother? Who did your father marry?"

After a pause, an oversight, she said, "It must have been early in 1940. The Sonnensheins working hard at building a retail fabric business and father was in Cleveland negotiating something, I think real estate, and his business hosts here in Cleveland recognized his international courtliness, and when they heard that he rode invited him out to see Chagrin Valley. It's the foxhunting area. While there they introduced him to my mother who had just come into the clubhouse from schooling a horse. She comes from an old Cleveland family. She was almost healed after breaking off her engagement to another product of the Cleveland Social Register and she thought my father resembled Errol Flynn. They married eight months later and I came along ten months after the wedding. Now the voice."

The waitress appeared asking if they'd like another round. Neither had noticed the empty glasses. Appraising each other for mutual consent, nodded, and the local doyenne of who's doing what to whom in her domain reaffirmed her first impression that this couple was going to make hanky-panky.

Harry began. "I don't know what research has been conducted by the high priests of mental health professionals in our time, but I'm sure some studies exist on people who hear voices. And what odds would you give that the voices truly do come from some other physical presence rather than deeply out of whack fucking, emotional disintegration?"

Audrey said, "I like the intensity with which you say 'fucking.'"

"So if all our western European sensibilities dictate it's hallucinatory, where does that leave me? On the other hand, people have bought into the hearing of voices for millennia. I'm not Christ. Not Moses. Not Jacob. I'm Harry Lang living in

Greenwich Village and working at an advertising agency. When people like me admit they're hearing voices it's lockdown time for the inmates. All the nutsies get sedated and have highly substantive conversations with the voices. Although when I hear that voice say 'you must go out from Jerusalem,' it's not some misty distant hallucinatory smoke. I'm sure if I had a tape recorder on I could broadcast it for all the world to hear."

"Seriously now, do you think you're actually hearing something real, or are you truly that fucked up?"

Harry took a long time to answer. He cupped his face in his hands with elbows on the table and closed his eyes. He'd asked it of himself. Finally...,"The coward's answer would be, I don't know. But I don't believe I'm a coward. I frequently bring up memories from the past. A mother not capable of emotional connection. A distant and depressed father. Not realizing that combination would handicap anybody for a lifetime. I do not feel sorry for myself. That's what I was dealt. I'm tenacious. I will fight my way out of this demon fog. I also think too much about past girlfriends. As soon as they would express seriousness, love, I would hightail it at a Masai warrior's pace chanting across the Serengeti. I am cursed with that defect."

His face was still cupped looking down at the table, as if free-associating in el shrinko's haunted office. He now looked straight at Audrey. "Were you to point a cocked pistol at my head and say 'choose or your brains will be splattered onto that wall,' I would say the voice is real. And that answer puts me either in a mystic's robe or a straight jacket."

They searched each other's inside spirits. Consolation? Affirmation? For a first encounter they had both revealed much.

"After you explained the story of Masada I felt the voice trying to speak. But it decided not to. Do you feel it's possible to have lived other lives? Centuries ago? Reincarnation? It felt so familiar. Every detail on Masada I knew. Like I was there. Could I have been a Zealot? On Masada?"

Audrey said, "I believe anything in this world is possible. Anything from other worlds is possible."

Harry jolted upright. "This is such madness. How we came to be sitting here." Then retreated. Audrey waited. Their silence was such that any sounds from the bar had clicked off. It was easy silence and it lasted.

Eventually Harry said, "I've got to go. I mean Masada. I'm going to go to Masada. Tomorrow. Come with me."

And with impulsiveness Audrey had been suppressing since her wedding day she simply said, "Let's do it."

Harry and Audrey left Pat's Place and stood on the street. They both had things to do. Harry would check into his hotel and order their airline tickets. Then he would call Steve with some excuse as to why he had to leave the focus group junket. Audrey had to get a message to her husband with a story she had not yet thought out clearly. They exchanged phone numbers, then a quick squeeze and separation, wondering if they would ever see each other again.

Audrey drove home to the empty house with a head throbbing in conflict. She had decided to attend the focus group session because the prospect of another evening with a box of pizza in front of the TV was unbearable. Then she lost control and in a surprising eruption of invective and profanity simply blew. Followed by the most heartfelt exchange of private inner life. Harry had a magnetic field she found disarming. She saw he was sad and vulnerable, and there was something else. The word came out of her mouth in the isolation of her car. Risky. As compared to her husband whose patterns were predictable. He was a mistake. She exhaled as the realization impacted her. Her husband was a mistake. And as she took the next breath in, a deep one, the madness of what she had just committed to with this man she'd only known for a few hours expressed itself in a panic attack. Her breathing switched to a fast gagging response. The familiar streets she drove through registered as unknown territory. Flashbacks of her father, stylish in the toniest houses and clubs, thrusting a knife into the SS officer's heart, a photograph in the house she grew up in, of her mother as a debutante smoking a cigarette with a mocking expression, her husband in a plaid flannel shirt and baggy jeans watching a football game. The idea of calling this Harry and pulling out caused her excitement thermometer to go down. She turned in to her driveway and sat there depleted.

Harry made two wrong turns before he found an all night gas station and got directions to the Holiday Inn. Driving along the Interstate back to the vicinity of the focus group facility near the Holiday Inn, Harry's logical dimension was in combat with his gone amuck emotions. Just hours ago this woman Audrey did not exist. This married woman Audrey. And in the morning they'd be flying to Israel to experience something, he didn't know what, or why, on the top of Masada. That she had so quickly agreed to go indicated they had each touched something submerged in a murky byway. But even so, had he fallen for a raving mad enigma? She'd erupted so uncontrollably in the focus group. Was she irretrievably gone out there in the stratosphere? But she was insightful, and intelligent, and confident. She was interested in what he had to say, and also revealed intimate nuggets from her past. Not first meeting guarded trivia. Why would she say yes if she hadn't also been slammed with their quick acting chemistry, their fusion across the little table at the tavern? Perhaps their subtle olfactory essence was compatible. Could it just be primal smell and biology? Parallel psychosis? Harry too believed anything was possible on the fucking planet. At the words "fucking planet" he wondered how many couples around the planet from Cleveland to New York to London to Tel Aviv, around the whole fucking planet were coupled together in sexual fusion. Hundreds of millions? And how many hundreds of millions at that particular moment were orgasming? From slickly decorated bedrooms in Beverly Hills to hovels in Sao Paulo to Levittown boxes to Manhattan studio apartments. Would it be possible to harness all that ejaculatory energy and run refrigerators?

He saw the Holiday Inn sign projecting its artfully devised welcoming assurance of safe harbor and felt the way a returning Arapaho hunting party must have felt at seeing their teepees in the open prairie distance. Minutes later he was going through the arduousness of airline reservations, which when finally completed caused a tedium breakdown. He was sprawled on the bed still in his suit unable even to loosen his tie. And he too felt panic beginning to flame, the early stages of a volcano slow boiling its fiery outrage. As a result of the hundreds of hours on Dr. Weinstein's couch Harry analyzed why the panic. Would Audrey have second thoughts and not show? Or perhaps worse, she would show. Would her husband discover any of it? Did she want him to? He then remembered their seamless thrilling fusion at Pat's Place. And as his body traveled into blessed sleep he was doubtful he and Audrey would last, given what he was, and then was scared to panic that it would.

A couple of hours headachy sleep passed when he heard something in his room. He was wide awake when he realized it was the voice. "You must go out from Jerusalem."

He whispered, "Oh fuck off," trying to get back to sleep, his last conscious thought coming from the years with Doctor Weinstein again, and having to do with Audrey saying "let's do it" rather than "let's go." And then he was shamed and uneasy for having blasphemed the voice.

Audrey also had a bad sleep and in the morning was still conflicted. She had been raised to conduct herself with honor out of conviction. The phone rang. "Good morning. It's me," said Harry. "How'd you sleep?"

"Not great."

"Me too." They both knew each was struggling with what they had agreed to. Harry said, "I've got our plane tickets all set. 11:20 out of Cleveland to New York. 9:00PM El Al New York to Tel Aviv. We'll have plenty of time to stop by my apartment so I can throw some stuff in a bag." The clock radio clicked on and caused her to recoil.

News blasted out that the People's Army of Vietnam was amassing a force that could be as devastating as the battle of Ia Drang in 1965. The Secretary of Defense was calling for an increase in the draft, and a demonstration in Washington of Peace

Marchers and Vietnam Veterans Against the War had battled the Capital police with several vets, some in wheelchairs, being handcuffed and taken to jail. Then came a commercial preparing America for the introduction of the breathtaking 1969 Camaro.

Audrey said, “I’ll meet you at the airport." She then called her husband. It was two hours earlier in Boise, Idaho, but he wasn’t in his room. She knew he was frequently inspecting dams or flood plains at the earliest times and left a message that since he was away anyway she was going to New York for a few days to catch up with a friend from Kenyon. It was the first time she ever lied to him, had a quick sob, shivered, and tried to concentrate on what to pack. It hadn’t been the way she hoped for a long time. She thought back to when the disconnect may have begun but there was no starting gate and until yesterday she hadn’t imagined a finish line. They didn’t have raging disagreements; they hardly ever raised their voices, either in anger or ecstasy. It was a slow beginner’s slope skiing to a place without content. His trips got longer, she realized she missed him less, her painting was a way to pass the time but caused no growth, and she still hadn’t committed to graduate school in archeology. She was close to thirty and Peggy Lee sang *Is That All There Is*? She didn’t hate him. It’s just there was nothing. She craved something. Didn’t everybody crave something? Returning to Masada with a man she’d logged three hours with was risky. Crazy risky. Now that was something.

Steve Lester was puzzling over Harry’s call. He said there was an emergency of a personal nature and had to return to New York. The kid was creative as all get out. With a little discipline from the account group he usually came through with cracker jack campaigns, the kind that would hit you in the face. Sometimes took a bit of selling from the account group, but the kid was good. Knew he was seeing a shrink. But what the fuck, half the creative department was seeing some sort of therapist, hell half of New York was. Wasn’t like the Midwest where people had solid values. Didn’t get themselves all wrapped up in this emotional baggage bullshit. But Christ, that’s what made it New York. It was the big time and he loved it. If old Harry had some sort of personal bullshit going on, what the hell. We'd show some sympathy. Great copy writers ain't that easy to come by. And you gotta face it, an advertising agency makes its name and profits from the creative product. Doubt if the client would ever notice Harry's missing in action. We'll just hope today's research in L.A. starts out as great as Cleveland. If it wasn't for that psych case bitch that blew her guts out we'd be uncorking champagne. Sure as hell was an alluring screamer though.

After Harry spoke to Steve he called Marv Munchik. "Where the hell are you Har? The next group of imbeciles loved it even more than the first. If your girl-friend hadn't lost it, Steve told us we'd be drinking campaign. I mean champagne. Paula said she'd never observed two focus groups in a row respond so favorably to a campaign. Where the hell are you?" With a calm he didn't have to fake Harry described his evening with Audrey, and told him they were actually leaving for Israel in a couple of hours.

"So my son, you are making aliya. It's a mitzvah. Don't wear out her snatch. And send post cards. Don't forget your Valium."

Harry said, "Marv, there's something really, well it sounds too dramatic but there's something about this that goes beyond our stewardesses in Third Avenue bars. Something intractable is pushing us to see where this goes."

And Marvin Munchik said, "You've got my number if you need me. What fools we mortals be. William Shakespeare. Got to meet my traveling companions in the lobby. When are you coming back?"

"Don't know."

Marv said, "Enjoy the promised land."

The Cleveland airport registered a hum drum predictability that contrasted with Harry's brain and heart screaming for guidance. He managed to get their tickets and when he turned from the counter saw Audrey walking down the corridor in sandals and jeans carrying a small knapsack. If this were a movie what type of music would they mix, he wondered. Montivani

French horns, or something whimsical, The Syncopated Clock, turning the moment into a comedy. They sat down and there was an awkwardness.

Then Audrey said, “Let’s do it.”

Ein Gedi

El Al flight 1210 landed smoothly at Ben Gurion Airport. They had slept for most of the nine hours, emotionally finished, her head resting on his shoulder. The plan was to rent a car and find a hotel at the Dead Sea near Masada. The airport was crowded, soldiers patrolling in twos, sub machine guns slung low. Both had a sense of being watched but neither felt uncomfortable. Outside it was hot and glaringly bright, diesel fumes and confusion everywhere. Harry had rented a small Mercedes thinking what the hell. They sat in the car and looked at each other. "We are unquestionably out of our fucking minds. There's nothing rational about any of this. We hardly know each other."

And she said, "I feel guilt. Scared. Like I'm defusing a bomb."

"Bomb defusing is one of my specialties."

It was mostly a primitive road going south and the only suitable accommodations in the Masada area were at a kibbutz Audrey remembered from when she was on the dig. Kibbutz Ein Gedi, founded in 1956 by a group of young people called Nahal, was an agricultural-military unit. Very utilitarian. The sleeping situation had been a worrisome issue for Harry and he was relieved their room had twin beds. Something about whatever it was that was happening between them on this journey would be cheapened had they shared the same bed. Although Audrey was prepared to adapt there was a harmony in not sleeping together. Without any discussion they had come to agreement.

Each showered, put on fresh clothes, got in their separate beds and fell into one of those jet lagged on again off again naps. Harry thought that whenever he'd been with a woman for the first time the little acts of brushing her hair or himself putting on his underwear had a somewhat uncomfortable rush to intimacy even though they had just been naked and in bed. Having heard Audrey in the shower and then seeing her in a change of clothes and with wet hair was that sort of moment.

It was late afternoon when Audrey felt herself coming awake and was confused. Where am I? On top of a scratchy wool blanket. Soft mattress. Just laundered smell from pillow case. Harry. Masada. Doing it. Hungry. Harry's eyes opened. She was sitting on her bed. "You okay?"

"I'm okay." She massaged the back of her neck. "Just coming out of it. Let's see if we can get something to eat." Her voice was soft, and an octave lower, a late night bedroomy voice Harry had heard before in a foggy warm memory he couldn't touch. Wherever it came from, a desire to caress her very lightly pulsed in him as a lover's ache. Instead he went to the bathroom and splashed his face with cold water. They found the dining room after wandering around in the heat and asking someone where it was.

A group of teenagers in shorts and blue shirts were at one table and several soldiers with their Uzi's and M16's were relaxing over coffee and soft drinks. The soldiers acknowledged them with friendly gestures, some appreciatively lingering on Audrey in a respectful way. It was cafeteria style and an older man who moved with a slight limp gestured they should sit anywhere and then help themselves. At the food counter Audrey said, "When I was here in '63 we ate lots of tomatoes and cucumbers and feta cheese. And hard boiled eggs."

"You mean no rare prime ribs and cottage fries?"

"Have some vegetable soup." Back at the table they seemed to exhale the previous twenty-four hours, their impulsiveness, Cleveland, New York, airports, the flight, the drive, the questions. Tiredness and anxiety lifted and they looked around with a traveler's eye for the first time. Others, lean and tan from outside work, were coming into the dining room. Harry picked up something else. Purposefulness? Their pride. They'd been there. Wherever *there* was, it toughened them. Audrey was feeling it as well. She was so pensive it seemed her mind had taken over her reality. Eventually she said, as if broadcasting from some distant tower, "The Israelis are different." Harry wondered if she would say more, but that was it. At the same moment they both noticed a man standing at the table with a plate.

"Americans? May I sit?" As he sat and put his plate on the

table he said with a gesture, “It was getting crowded." He spoke with an accent. German? Audrey noticed it was a cultured speech pattern. A faint beam signaled familiarity. “What brings you to Kibbutz Ein Gedi?”

“We’re going to Masada tomorrow.”

“Are you touring through Israel? Where else have you been?”

“No. Not really. We’re just here for Masada.”

“Just Masada? Nothing else?”

Audrey said, “I was on the dig in ‘63. We were talking about it yesterday. In Cleveland. Harry didn’t know much about the history. So we came." The man didn’t appear to think it was odd.

“Do you live on the kibbutz?” asked Harry.

“No. No. I just came out from Jerusalem. I live in Jerusalem. I’m also going to Masada tomorrow. It’s only a short drive from here but it will be dark soon." When he said he came out from Jerusalem Harry felt a mild electrical shock. The man looked to be in his late 60’s, lean, angular face with lines, thinning steel colored hair and horn rim glasses. His blue grey eyes were slightly magnified and Harry felt the tear reservoir had gone dry. He knew nothing could surprise this man. Psychoanalysts who had heard every human maladjustment and entanglement on the planet had the same reserve. Harry half rose from the table and offered his hand. “Harry Lang, and my friend Audrey Sonnenshein” as she extended her hand formally, Eastern boarding school and once again Harry thought Audrey Hepburn.

“Doctor Rheinhardt. Stefan Rheinhardt," with the emphasis on Stefan, interpreted to mean call me Stefan.

“Psychiatrist?” asked Harry, and not appearing surprised Dr. Stefan Rheinhardt nodded.

Audrey looked at Harry. “How did you know?”

“I didn’t even know I was going to say it."

Doctor Rheinhardt looked at Audrey. “It sometimes happens.”

Audrey said, “Have you been to Masada before?”

“Once. When my son was commissioned in the army. After

training the army does the ceremony on top of Masada. It's very symbolic."

"Where is he now?" asked Audrey.

"He was killed last year in the Six Day War. He's gone. So I came out from Jerusalem to be on Masada again," said without emotion.

"I'm so so sorry," said Audrey. Harry looked down, it being understood Audrey spoke for both of them.

"Everybody in Israel has lost someone. The fighting is always with us."

That's what Audrey meant when she said the Israelis are different, thought Harry. They ate, dining room chatter all around filling the space. Audrey's mind was doing laps. Where's his wife? Other kids? What's his office look like? Where did he go to medical school? Harry was on the same track.

"May I ask where you're from. Originally?"

"We were all from Vienna."

"So Viennese psychiatrists actually do exist. And you knew Freud I assume." Stefan Rheinhardt, M.D. acknowledged Harry's attempt with the smallest of smiles and said, "Dr. Freud and I were colleagues. His daughter Anna and my wife were good friends."

Harry quietly said, "Oh," thinking why am I such a flaming asshole?

Now Audrey. "You've been to the U.S?"

"I have delivered a paper at Harvard."

Audrey said, "Harry was trying to be funny."

Dr. Rheinhardt, with more of a smile, "I do understand." Audrey was feeling maybe this Doctor Reinhardt has a role in wherever this journey is taking them. She wasn't controlling any part of it. Just going wherever the wind blew.

Then Harry said, "This is a pretty barren landscape. Why a kibbutz out here?"

Doctor Reinhardt explained, "This area hasn't been inhabited in over 500 years. The kibbutz was started in the early fifties. The weather patterns are such that out of season vegetables can be grown here. Out of season they get a premium. But just like anywhere in Israel, there is ancient history. In the bible it says David hid from Saul in the caves around Ein Gedi. In the book of Samuel it states David dwelt in the strongholds of Ein Gedi. And in more recent times, say 2000 years ago, the Zealots from Masada would come down and raid the town for food and supplies. The Dead Sea Scrolls were found in caves just a little to the north."

Although Audrey was familiar with some of it this was all new to Harry. He pictured David in the caves and the Zealots on the rampage, ruthless, taking what they needed from their own blood, leaving destruction as they returned to Masada, carrying what they had stolen. And here was Doctor Reinhardt going to the place where he last was with his son, the same place the Zealots returned to 2000 years ago, fleeing from violence, creating violence. What was this Viennese psychiatrist hoping to find, what was it that he himself was searching for, and then there were those Kiddie Keds haunting him with the Vietnam war for background ambience. From his drifting around in other places he heard Audrey saying, “My father left Berlin when he realized it was all lost. His family went back centuries in Germany. Unlike many others my family had assets in the U.S.”

And he heard Doctor Reinhardt saying, “Sonnenshein? Berlin? The industrialists?” Fusion. Comforting familial fusion in Ein Gedi. Audrey saw that Stefan Reinhardt was E.S.P-ing her thoughts and without her having to ask he said, “It had gotten impossible to go on in Vienna. The Nazis had us on our hands and knees cleaning the streets with toothbrushes. We escaped with Sigmund and Anna in 1939. We may have been the last Jews to leave Vienna before it was impossible. They got to London. The best we could do was Paris. A cousin was a professor at the Sorbonne and he took us in. It was a very tense time. The Parisians knew the Germans were going to take over; my wife was pregnant. The day they marched in, June 14, our son was born. The Germans took down French flags and replaced them with swastikas. As the German armored cars drove down the Champs Elysees men and women wept in the streets. Dr. Freud had tried to get us to England but he had died the previous September. In June the French signed an armistice with Hitler. All German political refugees were to be turned over to the Reich. They put a sign on the Eiffel Tower *'Deutchland siegt auf allen Fronten.'"*

Audrey translated, "Germany conquers on all fronts."

He went on. "Frightened Parisians fled. In cars, trucks, bicycles, foot. Everywhere was panic. We knew there would be round ups and deportations, the camps. Sigmund said our pasts are always with us. He was right. Enough though. I saw some baklava by the desserts. Shall we?"

As they got up Audrey said, "Since we're all going to Masada in the morning why don't we go together?" They lingered at the dessert section, made selections, each poured a cup of coffee, and returning to their table Audrey wasn't sure Doctor Reinhardt heard her. He put two cubes of sugar in his coffee, stirred, sipped, and said, "Why not?"

Back in their room, in their separate beds in the dark they talked. "I know this man," said Audrey. "He's one of those people you meet through serendipity and it's as if you've shared your most private thoughts. It's instant trust. It's not as if you want to trust. You just do. Remember when you mentioned other lives? If there is such a thing that would explain it. The absolute lunacy of you and I on a kibbutz in Ein Gedi. Hitting the pause button on my marriage. Could all of this be part of the script? Chiseled out by some spirit in antiquity? I noticed your reaction when he said he came out from Jerusalem. I feel it wasn't coincidence. We are all supposed to be here. It's so strange. Once in an anthropology class on Australian aborigines the professor, a Margaret Mead type, said the abos live in reality, but they also live in what they call dreamtime. But dreamtime to them is as real as their reality. Can we even imagine what it was like to leave Vienna? As he spoke I saw my father leaving Berlin. And dreamtime put me with him, as an infant wrapped in a pale blue blanket and he wore a homburg and Chesterfield topcoat. I was in his arms and those red and black swastika flags were everywhere. It was as if I was born before I was born in Cleveland. I was looking through a telescope from the wrong end. Do you know that in 1838 two Americans were the first to rediscover Masada. They observed it through a telescope from Ein Gedi. From this very place. Of course you don't. I think one of them was named Robinson. They never made it to the sight. Then some time in the 1840s an Englishman named Tipping, a painter, did get there and his sketches and descriptions were as accurate as anything we had on the dig. I regret not going to grad school in archaeology. Once as I was digging and sifting, a shred of cloth appeared. That evening at our nightly meeting it was identified as being from the Zealot period. Two thousand years ago it was part of somebody's cape, tunic, socks, something they wore, and as I felt it in my hands the thought of it being worn by a Zealot, touching his skin, was overwhelming. I started sobbing. I'm almost sobbing again just thinking about it, being here, Doctor Reinhardt, his infant son in Paris, killed in Israel almost thirty years later, the terrain, the spirits."

A Chopin piano sonata was on the radio in the next room. They would have liked it to be just a bit louder. As Harry entered the first stage of sleep he saw his sixth grade classroom. Mr. Schloss, the first male teacher he had, was in front of the room. He had just written the words "BUT SHE'S MARRIED" on the blackboard. In a very short time they were both sound asleep.

Roswell, New Mexico

On a morning early in July, 1947, the foreman of a ranch 33 miles south of Corona, New Mexico, got in his old pickup truck to drive around the ranch looking for damage from the most violent thunderstorm he'd ever been through. He was searching for injured or dead cattle and sheep as well as downed fence lines. Some miles from the main ranch house Duane Harkum came upon a sight he didn't know what to make of. Getting out of the pickup he felt wary, as if a mountain lion might be stalking from behind. Debris he couldn't figure out was covering a section at least as big as two high school football fields, maybe even four. Roswell Army Air Force Base was less than sixty miles away, and other military installations were in the region so occasionally pieces of an experimental weather balloon would land on the ranchlands in the vicinity. But he never felt threatened when coming across remnants from one of those. He would gather the rubber and dispose of it, since livestock could choke or suffocate if they got into it. Various pieces of some unknown pewter colored material were everywhere. He picked one up and when he squeezed the fabric-like substance it sprung right back to its previous shape. It was impossible to tear. He took out his pocket knife and it wouldn't cut. He walked over a rise not feeling at all comfortable in this familiar landscape when he automatically constricted to not pee in his underpants. About a hundred feet down the gentle slope was what appeared to be a large saucer shaped contraption with a big jagged opening where part of it had been ripped off. Duane Harkum determined it must have hit the ground mighty hard. He wished real bad that he wasn't standing there. He'd left the ranch house thinking he might find a steer standing on three legs or a sheep hit by lighting. He'd handled injured livestock hundreds of times and would know what to do. He was confident about any situation that might come up on the ranch, but this was a totally different deal. Having known nothing but the open range his whole life, he was a man of primal instincts. In those few seconds he could tell this was big time trouble. Every beat in him was going at a fast gallop, and he sensed the familiar routine of life fading into a foggy night. Then his eyes squinted in a man of the plains sort of way. There were four small unmoving bodies not of the human species all tangled up inside the thing, and one sprawled out on the ground. They must have been less than four feet tall. When he heard what sounded like some kind of animal in distress he wished that 30-30 Winchester back in the truck was in his hands. He slowly backed away, unconscious of his movement, then turned and ran, not knowing he was running until he found himself sitting in the truck breathless. He waited until his heaving body was calmed and decided to head on back as fast as the old Ford could handle the terrain. As an afterthought he cautiously got out of the truck and had a very long pee, figured he might have pissed a quart, and as he stepped back up on the running board hesitated, looked around, hopped off and quickly gathered up some of the debris.

For the last couple of weeks folks all over Chavez County had been buzzing about weird flying saucers in the sky. Come to think of it last night in the middle of all the thunder and lightning one big boom louder than any thunderclap did get his attention. He thought maybe the Roswell Army Base was running some tests. People knew they were in charge of the atomic bombs dropped on the Japs. It gets damn hot in the high desert country this time of year and though he wasn't much of a sweating man, the stick shift and steering wheel were slippery from dampness on his hands. His heart was still pumping faster than it ought to as he braked to a jerky stop in the house yard. The young neighbor kid that helped around the ranch was leading a horse out of the corral. After telling the boy what he'd just experienced, and feeling foolish talking about it, the kid rode home and told his parents what Mr. Harkum had just seen. Then they came by and heard it straight from Duane. He showed them some of the stuff in the truck. Besides the pieces of indestructible tin foil there was something with pictograph writing. By mid-afternoon everybody within thirty miles was talking about it and several either drove trucks or rode horses out to the area and witnessed it all. Some of them were talking about giving those dead creatures from God knows where a Christian burial. Almost everybody left with souvenirs.

Duane Harkum tossed most of that night and the next day drove into Corona and showed the fellas at Wades Bar and the Corona General Store the practically weightless material that wouldn't tear, stay crumpled, or burn. Duane was hoping someone would know what to do and finally he drove the seventy miles to Roswell to see Owen Swett, the Sheriff of Chavez County.

Sheriff Swett, knowing that Duane Harkum was a solid member of the ranching community and had rarely ever had a drink, saw that he was uncharacteristically wound up pretty tight as he described what was out there. Swett dispatched two deputies to investigate. While they were gone Harkum was calming down when the local radio station phoned Sheriff Swett for any news he might have. It had been quiet in Roswell over the 4th of July weekend and just when he was about to say nothing much going on, he looked at Duane Harkum. "Wait a minute. Might be something here for you." At first Duane was reticent, but when Swett put the phone in front of him he repeated the story and it was no longer a slow news day in Roswell. After listening to Harkum, Tyler Dunn, the radio announcer, suggested Harkum contact the Army base and then come over to the station. Swett called the base commander's office and spoke to the N.C.O. who answered the phone. Once again Swett handed the phone to Harkum who was getting agitated at all this explaining. When finished going over it again he still wasn't sure what to do and just knew this was going to get worse. God damn thunder storm. Sheriff Swett reminded him the radio station was waiting, and feeling trapped he left forgetting to say goodbye. Driving to the station he wondered if they might pay him for all his trouble and then remembered the frightening little bodies and what sure as hell sounded like moaning. What if they did come from Mars or Jupiter or the other side of the moon? What if there's more on the way? What the hell they want with some honest ranching folks? Americans. Shit, we just fought one war. Hope the people at the Army Base don't think I'm a deranged lunatic. Maybe we ought to go to church next Sunday. After talking to this radio announcer I'm heading back to the ranch, doing chores, and then just gonna forget.

Tyler Dunn guided the rancher to a back studio, offered coffee, which he was glad to get, turned on a tape recorder and asked Harkum if he would mind talking about what he'd said on the phone and if he could remember even the smallest details. Harkum wasn't happy being asked to repeat the same damn thing so many times and Joyce saw reluctance turning to hostility and thought the cowboy might get up and leave. Tyler Dunn was a small town radio personality with aspirations of getting hired by one of the bigger stations in Albuquerque and then maybe on to L.A. or New York. He was not going to allow what could be a national news story walk out. Raised on a farm himself he knew rural attitudes could mean unflappable independence and stubbornness. "It would scare the bejesus out of me if I ever came across what you did. Not sure I'd know what to do." Harkum took two quick swallows of coffee as if downing shots of whiskey and said, "I don't know what to do either. Been a couple of days and nobody's taking charge. My sheep ain't crossing the area where all those pieces of whatever the hell they are got scattered. They're skirting around about a mile to get to water."

"Anything else strange like that?" Tyler Dunn poured some more coffee and for the next half hour guided Duane Harkum when necessary to repeat for the tape recorder what he'd seen. Dunn didn't doubt one word and realized this could be the interview of the century. He wanted more but Harkum was getting fidgety and he risked asking if they could talk some more tomorrow. A shrug of annoyance was the answer. As they walked to the reception area an army major and a captain were entering.

"Mr. Harkum?" For the second time that day he felt like he was in a nightmare, confined in an upright coffin, terrified, unable to get out. "I'm Major Gladden and this is Captain Fleischer. We were hoping you could come with us to the area where you found the debris."

By this time Harkum was exhausted, depleted, and angry.

"Can't do it. I'm going home."

Major Gladden said,"We know the area is on the ranch. Be okay if we just followed you?"

Harkum's voice was dry and gravelly, the sound of a man without hope and capable of acts he would later regret. "I just knew it was gonna be like this when I spied those space beings."

Major Jack A. Gladden was the senior intelligence officer at Roswell Army Air Force Base commanding a squadron with responsibility for the atomic bomb. He had been in charge of security and intelligence briefings at the base on Kwajelein in the Pacific theatre. Kwajelein was home to Operation Crossroads which tested two atomic bombs. He and Captain Fleischer were now following Harkum's ancient truck in an Army vehicle at a tediously slow speed. Back at the radio station Gladden had said in an unthreatening way that they couldn't force Harkum to take them to the sight, and he really didn't want to get the FBI involved, who could force the issue, and he sure hoped it wouldn't be too much of an inconvenience. When he mentioned that they had their orders and were obligated to inspect the alleged crash site, Duane Harkum just gave up. Both officers saw that Harkum didn't have the temperament or curiosity to deal with whatever it was his bad luck to come upon. They felt sorry for the cowboy. Eventually they got off the hardtop and traveled on a dirt road, then a track that looked like it was made by covered wagons. When Harkum stopped the truck he didn't get out and the two Army officers saw his arm pointing straight ahead. "I'm staying in the truck" and he pulled his ten gallon hat down over his eyes and put his head back. There were a couple of neighbor's trucks parked close by, and in the distance someone waved. They started walking, stopping frequently to examine the scattered debris, taking their time, gradually coming to realize they were at the very beginning. Like the Pilgrims landing at Plymouth Rock. Like Pearl Harbor.

Then both slowed their pace as if delaying another shot soon to be heard round the world and went over the rise and down the slight incline on the other side, practically in Duane Harkum's footsteps. Major Gladden felt the very same way when he was in the first group to view the film of Hiroshima taken from the Enola Gay as the bomb exploded and ended the war. The two career Army Officers got closer to the crashed space craft, saw the motionless Aliens, thought they heard a weak moan and not knowing if it was radioactive stayed where they were. They knew when they reported in this was going up the chain of command up to the highest level of the Pentagon, up to the White House. Both officers appreciated the quiet desolate high desert terrain because in just a few hours the United States Army would be all over the place with trucks and jeeps and soldiers guarding a big perimeter and other soldiers retrieving the debris, following orders, hearing rumors within the ranks, very few realizing what, where, why, or who.

Taking a couple of steps backwards before they turned, just as Harkum had done, Major Gladden said to Captain Fleischer, "Let's follow Harkum back to the house and hope there's a phone so we can advise Colonel Shortridge. Something tells me I should stay out here while you drive back and make a full report. I'm sure you'll be returning in force. By then it will be close to sunrise in the sagebrush."

Captain Fleischer said "Yes sir," in a relaxed tone.

Duane Harkum thought of calf roping at the rodeo because he now knew exactly what that calf felt like when it was laying on the ground hog tied and helpless. It was almost dark as he drove back to the house with the jeep not too far behind. Didn't think it was possible to feel so downright low and once again it whacked his brain that all this shit was something way the hell beyond his capabilities. Guess those two in that Army jeep ain't got much of a choice either. Now that the government's in it I'm getting back to what I know something about, which is running this ranch, and to hell with answering any more questions.

As the sun appeared through the morning haze a jeep, an Army green Chevy and a black Ford drove into the ranch yard. Two M.P.'s and two FBI men in dark suits entered the house and a few minutes later the M.P.s escorted Duane Harkum to the Army sedan and drove back to Roswell Army Air Force Base, followed by the FBI in the Ford. He would be detained for six days. Major Gladden, feeling achy from having dozed most of the night in a too soft and faded easy chair and wishing he could shave got in the front passenger side of the jeep, Captain Fleischer got in back, and a sergeant drove to the crash site. At least a hundred and fifty soldiers could be seen. There were others out of sight. Perhaps fifty were clearing the area of debris, some on their hands and knees. Others had been issued live ammunition and were spread out on the edges with orders to shoot any civilians who came too close. There were several half-ton Army trucks, two Army ambulances, two State Police Patrol cars, the Sheriff's car, and the local Emergency Services vehicle. Colonel Shortridge, Commanding Officer of RAAF Base, was standing next to one of the ambulances with a Lieutenant Colonel and a Master Sergeant. Gladden walked over to Shortridge, saluted, and asked if anything was radioactive. He shook his head no and said, "The Pentagon wants us to keep this quiet. No press. No interviews for now. We've got to keep the lid on."

Gladden hesitated, and then stated the obvious. "With all the local civilians that have been here taking souvenirs and telling everybody they know about the UFO crash we've got a big problem."

Shortridge said, "Washington has the FBI on that one. Think they can keep them quiet. The troops have been ordered not to speak to anyone about what they're doing or it's a court martial and life in the brig."

"What about the bodies sir?"

"We've got four in the ambulances. They're getting the last one now."

Gladden looked in the direction of the crash site and saw four soldiers carrying a stretcher. "Mind if I check out the area sir?"

Shortridge said, "Of course not." Gladden headed to the stretcher. The body was no more than four feet long, oval shaped head and eyes, two tiny holes for a nose, very small slit like mouth, hands had four fingers, no thumbs. As the Major walked alongside the stretcher the Alien's eyes fixated on him and without words seemed to be in touch with Gladden. It was a clear message: I know I'm going to die. You must stop dirtying the Universe. It is not good for your people. Or for the others. You have little time. One hundred of your Earth years at best. Then Masada.

Masada

They left Ein Gedi in a grey quiet early morning before the sun appeared, so they could watch it rise at Masada. Doctor Reinhardt sat in front with Harry, pensive and far away, visiting his son. Audrey in back with her knapsack, sandwiches, and sodas the lady in the kitchen had given them. As Harry navigated into the parking lot at the base of Masada the absence of conversation between these three active minds during the short drive seemed right. Harry had once told Doctor Weinstein that when he was growing up a lack of conversation was interpreted as something being wrong. Quite the opposite with us three he thought.

A few soldiers were relaxing around some army vehicles, there were also some civilian cars and groups of teenagers eager to get to the top and witness the sun rising on the mountain plateau. Harry shouldered Audrey's knapsack and they stood a moment, heads bent back, gazing at the top of the mountain, gazing inward to the bottom of their existence, each knowing something past had guided them to this monument. The only route to the top meant going single file on what for over two thousand years was called the snake path. It was on the Eastern side of the mountain, could be tricky in parts, the sun would rise as you climbed, and it ended at the ancient main gateway. As they walked across the parking lot to the beginning of the trail Audrey quietly spoke to Harry. "Every young person in Israel makes this trek. It's looked upon as a sacred gesture. Israel is surrounded by nations that would happily blow the whole country to oblivion. They all tried last year and were shamed by their defeat. Every Israeli knows they will try again. And again. The population has a siege mentality. Guns everywhere. When they fight if they lose, it's the end. Of everything. When I was here five years ago we relished climbing the snake path every day. One day some of us got a ride on an army helicopter and it was like cheating. We wanted to walk in the footsteps of the Zealots, the

Romans, King Herod, and thousands of Israelis whose collective memory brings them to this place."

"We will talk about that," said Doctor Reinhardt as they started the trek with him in the lead. "Yigael Yadin's book, *Masada: Herod's Fortress and The Zealot's Last Stand* was published two years ago. Although it's the story of the excavations, it's more about Israel being a warrior state, assuring it stays a warrior state. Never Again and Masada. Yigal is thinking bigger than archaeology."

Audrey said to Harry, "Yigael was in charge of the dig. Organized it. Got the financing. Volunteers from all over the world. He'd been a general in the army and is an archeology professor at Hebrew University. Walking this trail again is stirring up memories. Every day was filled with meaning. We were bringing the dead back to life." Her words floated along as the walking and the heat required a more conscious effort, and the thought came to both of them that Doctor Reinhardt was on a very personal dig all his own. We are as well thought Harry. He mouthed Audrey's words, "Every day was filled with meaning." He mouthed them again. With each step he cadenced a word. Every. Day. Filled. With. Meaning. To the beat. Every. Day. Filled. With. Meaning. And then a march. One. Two. Three. Four. Meaning is what we're looking for. Could it be her being here has nothing at all to do with you ol' Har? She's looking for her meaning and thinks she left it up there on top five years ago. Playing hide and seek with meaning on top of old Masada. Old Smoky Masada. She's pretty god damn smart. I wonder if she gets it. Maybe not yet. Maybe I ought to tell her. Maybe I'm wrong. So many god damn maybe's. Maybe I shouldn't be thinking god damn after how God shafted the Zealots. They worshipped him and he fucked them anyway. So I guess it really doesn't matter. God damn. She really looks good from behind in those shorts and sandals and sweat splotches on her shirt. Did I lose my meaning as well? Can't lose anything you maybe never had. Another god damn maybe. Maybe meaning can't coexist with all those maybes. Banish maybe and enter meaning. When the Israelis whacked Egypt, Jordan, and Syria last year in six days all of New York partied. It was better than the Yankees winning the World Series. It was louder than Times Square on New Year's Eve. Same in 1948, 1956. Took two thousand years to get their act together. Thank you Hitler. Thank you Queen Isabelle. Thank you Roman Empire. Thank you all. We ain't leaving. We got meaning. For an old guy Doctor Reinhardt's a walking machine. And look at Audrey's body language. A woman with a mission. She's loving this.

About halfway to the summit, they rested and drank from the same canteen. The vista was steep promontories and hills, rough and beige and brown and blue and very dry. Doctor Reinhardt looked at his American companions as if deciding something, took another swallow, and continued his steady pace. Some parts of the ancient trail were washed out and they had to pick their way, on hands and knees at times. A group of teenagers came up from behind but the trail was too narrow for them to pass, so the two groups became one and there was a sense of unity. Collective memory marching together to celebrate nine hundred and sixty men, women, and children killing themselves two thousand years ago.

One final clamoring and they were off the path and on the plateau. Doctor Reinhardt again studied them with interest, as if he expected them to speak. "I'm going to find a spot to sit. We'll find each other later," and strode off. The two of them stood close, not eager to move, slowly adjusting to where they were and what had been. Harry felt Audrey leaning into him and realized he had his arm around her. Eventually Audrey said, "I think our journey has just begun." Harry thought about that and decided the journey was not just about them. He saw himself as a child at a Saturday matinee and on the screen it said "The End." No movie. Just "The End." Then he said, "Two thousand years ago these people thought they were cutting edge of all that is modern. And two thousand years from now some archaeologists digging in the remains of, say, LaGuardia Airport will find some scrap of a Boeing 707 from 1968 and figure out it's how they traveled in ancient times." As they started walking he removed his arm. Audrey said, "Let's start at the Northern palace."

An Israeli tour guide with a group from Hempstead, Long Island, was talking about King Herod's reasons for building a luxurious palace in such an inaccessible spot and they listened for a minute. They could tell he'd delivered the speech dozens of times but was still making it interesting. Audrey motioned to move on and they walked through the ruins to the edge of the cliff. Looking down they could see the outline of where one of the Roman Legion's encampments had been. Ein Gedi, the Dead Sea, and the Judean Desert were in the far distance, appearing as in the time of Herod, the Zealots, the Romans and all the others whose bones were now dust buried in the sand.

"It's as if we're gazing at the past, out there, all around us, but we're on our own dig looking for fragments from the future. We're archaeologists, but looking forward. Reverse archaeology. Counter intuitive. Many mental health professionals would probably put me on medication, blithering like someone on the fringe. Maybe we should ask Doctor Reinhardt for a diagnosis. He also hears voices, Doctor." They leaned against the railing, arms close. Once again Harry found their silence to be neutral. It was a non-anxiety producing silence and lasted. Then Audrey started talking about the Northern Palace as if she had already been on the subject, taken a breath and now continued.

"So the Northern Palace was the royal residence. The architecture is Hellenistic, but with Roman influence on the upper terrace. That's where the bedrooms were, and sitting rooms, and this spectacular semi circle veranda looking out on what we're looking at. The royal family occupied those rooms, and the next level down, at that outcropping, was a large reception hall. The main banqueting room was on the lower terrace. This was a big square space decorated with painted half columns on pedestals, stucco walls and a colorful podium. There were large windows and hard plastered floors. The palaces of Pompeii had similar layouts. We actually found remains of the wall paintings. When our work was finished for the day I would sometimes come here by myself and imagine what the place looked like in the Herodian period, with people eating and flirting, and excusing themselves to go to the bathroom, doing all the things we do today. But they owned thousands of slaves, and entertainment for them was watching captured enemies be torn to shreds by tigers and bears in coliseums back in Rome. And I wondered how could they, when they could design something beautiful like these palaces and build bridges that are still standing today. And then a moment of truth and it made me very sad. If today in our huge sports arenas the sport was watching people get torn up and devoured by wild beasts we would have sellout crowds every Sunday afternoon. People would pay to watch fellow human beings mauled and eaten alive. They'd sell beer and hot dogs and cotton candy and it would be a fun outing for the whole family. And before the main event we could have gladiators going at each other, so in addition to animals killing humans they'd have humans killing humans. If you didn't buy season tickets you couldn't get in. Demolition derby with blood and intestines. So we're not that different from the Roman citizens. Our symbols are different. Today a cross says religion. In the first century it was like the electric chair. In the first century the concept of ascension meant you were going up above the clouds way way up into heaven.

"The idea of rising up up and away was actually a belief even before Christ. Twentieth century science tells us there are star systems and universes and gases and freezing temperatures and it's unlikely you'll get to heaven no matter how high you ascend. But a mother's love for her child can't be any different than it was then. A father's need to protect his family is the same. Today's great thinkers have nothing on Socrates, Plato or Aristotle. With gunpowder and atomic bombs we can kill more people faster. With jet engines we get wherever we're going in hours instead of weeks or months. But their hearts looked like our hearts. We haven't learned anything new about our souls. Archaeology can tell us how they made sandals, or how they stored figs, but not what if anything happens after we die, or if the man made theories concerning what it all means mean anything at all, or why millions marry the wrong people. And can't you just hear someone who has a complete set of Reader's Digest Book Condensation's saying, 'Audrey, enough with the sophomoric questions'?"

Harry's arm was still on the railing, he rested his forehead on it and even though it was already close to ninety didn't mind the sun. He could smell her sweat and thought it was very pleasant. Sweet smelling sweat. Because of her diet? Soap? Inner life? What if the whole world smelled like lilacs when they sweated? Might be less violence. How can you kill someone when you like the way they smell? Unless you're killing your own wife and children to save them from man-made travesties. Probably be able to live with it if you also killed yourself. "Since you're my tour guide what's next?"

As if anticipating the question Audrey said, "The casemate wall is a must see."

"You mean like the Statue of Liberty, or Versailles?"

"Something like that." Harry was pleased it was he Audrey was talking to as they walked the circumference of the wall. Although her tone was matter of fact she loved showcasing her knowledge and Harry felt an intimacy that made obvious the loneliness within. He was giving her the opportunity to feel proud and it made him feel good.

"King Herod's architects designed the casemate wall where the Zealot's families lived with thirty-seven towers for defense. During the dig we found evidence of numerous ovens, bathtubs, cooking stoves and storage areas in the wall complex. We even found ashes from their cooking fires and utensils and perfectly preserved wicker baskets, even remains of wooden door jambs. The top of the casemate had rich soil in which they grew crops. When the Zealots took over Masada they actually found stores of wheat and wine and dried fruit that Herod had brought in almost a century before, all perfectly preserved and edible. They also found enough armament to equip an army of ten thousand.

Herod was living in fear that the Jews, and he was Jewish himself, might revolt against him to restore the former regime. He was also terrified that Cleopatra in contiguous Egypt would convince Antony to wage war so that Judea would come under her rule. Herod knew Antony was consumed by passion for Cleopatra and might just do it." After a pause she added, "I never felt more alive than during the weeks I spent here. Thank you Harry, for bringing me back."

Another long easy silence and then Harry, "It's weirder than hell but it's as if you brought me back. Have you ever remembered a place you spent lots of time in, had relationships, experienced events you equate with that time and place, like a dorm room and college friends, or an office you occupied at some job with co-workers, the house you grew up in, and in your mind it's remained the same as when it was a part of you years before? As if the same people, the same conflicts and laughs and daily dramas were still there. But then you return and it's all gone, it's somebody else's space, events, life, and even though you know this is how it is, you feel let down. Why are my memories not still here as I left them? Who are these strangers superseding what was? They're nice people but they've altered my precious past reality. You feel loss. Older. When you leave there's sadness. The people you're talking about, Herod, Eleazer, the wives and children, something of them hasn't left here. They're watching. They want to tell us something."

They moved on together, strolling around the casemate wall as Audrey described some of the finds and how they were interpreted. More than once others touring Masada overheard her descriptions and stopped to listen, some even asked questions. When reaching the southern tip of the plateau they sat down on the ground, backs leaning against the ancient wall and looked to the north where the main palace had been, imagining in unison Zealot families living out an ordinary day. Harry transposed a seventeenth century Dutch painting depicting in great detail a moment in the life of a tavern yard with peasants at a table looking tipsy and children playing on the ground next to a sleeping dog, and a nobleman's horse tied to a post as he flirts with a barmaid, but the year was seventy something and the locale was the Judean desert. The children of the Zealots were chasing each other, two Zealot women were out for a walk, a group of men were having an animated conversation. Harry's painting morphed in to wide screen live action as his characters went about what he imagined would be their usual activity during the siege. Then his camera panned down the mountain to the Roman encampments, soldiers drilling, platoons doing calisthenics, slaves and mules working in the sun constructing the siege ramp, military procedure taking place. He envisioned coliseums in Rome where different forms of human and animal life were tearing each other to bloody pieces, before shifting his thoughts to Paris and the German occupation. He heard Audrey as if in a tunnel saying, "Doctor Reinhardt." They both started to stand but Doctor Reinhardt waved them back, and he sat with them, all three with backs against the wall. Addressing Harry and gesturing at the ruins, he said, "So, what do you think?"

The sun was at its highest position. Tour groups were bunched at various spots, engrossed in their guides' narratives. Occasionally a warm wind gusted through, then dissipated, leaving stillness. Harry was pensive for long moments. Nobody seemed impatient. It appeared Doctor Reinhardt wasn't asking just to make conversation. Harry began speaking without any pre-formed thoughts. Having made numerous presentations to clients in which there was an end game, to sell them on an advertising concept, there was always a progression as he developed a rationale, knowing where he was going. But this was free form, Weinstein's couch.

"I think we're on this ancient mystical rock formation sitting here with you having this conversation because we've allowed instinct to take over. Three days ago I was in New York play acting at life and she was in Cleveland edgy, seeking, and a few hours after we met decided to come to Masada. Nobody's driving our train. We're just passengers. No map. No desire to steer. You asked what I think. I was thinking Eleazer Ben Yair would have made a great ad guy. If he could persuade his target audience to kill their families and then themselves he could sell any product in the world that has an advertising budget. He'd win gold medals at the New York Ad Club show. I was wondering if I could have made that decision. And what is it we're looking for as we dig two thousand years into the past? Besides technology and medicine we've made hardly any improvements. We haven't made any progress at all with the real questions. Why Vietnam? Nazis? Why we love? Stop loving? What really is out there beyond our universe? Maybe we're the Martians to Aliens in some other universe. Why are some people born with deformities? Some whacko? Why do some starve and others inherit fortunes? We have theories. We don't have answers. Freud was asked what makes for a happy life and he answered work and love. So you have work and love and find yourself in Buchenwald and no more happy. I'm probably getting into your area Doctor Rheinhardt, but as I think about it, that's what I was thinking. Shall I go on?"

The three of them were shaded from the sun by the wall, but it was hot and they shared the same heat, the way in which they drank from the same canteen. Ghosts of Masada blew around with the breeze. Doctor Rheinhardt said, "Another colleague from Vienna, Viktor, Viktor Frankel, would ask his psychoanalytic patients why they didn't commit suicide." The ghosts in the breeze thought that was funny and smiled.

Then Harry asked, "What happened after the Germans entered Paris?"

Doctor Rheinhardt hesitated, and both Audrey and Harry thought the question might have been impudent, but he made eye contact with both of them. "It was miraculous we got out of Vienna when we did. It would take another miracle to escape Paris. Two miracles in the same year may be too much. My cousin knew a White Russian émigré musician who for a price could get us forged travel documents. Risky. But where would we go? The U.S. wasn't letting us in. Shanghai was a possibility. The British had closed Israel, but some were being smuggled past the blockade. A provision in the armistice signed by the French stated that all Jews were to be surrendered to the Germans. People were being imprisoned, tortured, deported, executed. In my profession, almost immediately after the occupation the French Analytical Society had only two members left. Ironically, *L'Illustration* portrayed the German soldiers as handsome, decent and correct. People we knew were taken to Gestapo headquarters and just disappeared. Gone. Roundups. The French weren't Nazis, but some were complicit. The concierge in your building could be counted on, or could be dangerous. We had an infant, which would make travel more complicated. So we made the decision to stay. We paid a lot of money and got I.D. documents that gave us a chance if we were stopped on the street. We were now good Austrians living in Paris. I volunteered to work for the French Red Cross, which gave us another layer of cover. At that time we didn't know how the war would end. Four years we lived day to day. It could have been so much worse. Then the American Army entered Paris, and in 1948 we came here. Twenty years ago. My wife was killed in a bus bombing in 1955. She was a pediatrician. So you now have the contours of one life. But almost everybody you meet in this country lives with loss, with wounds. The Masada syndrome is in the streets of Jerusalem. Shall we try some of those sandwiches?"

Audrey reached in to her back pack. "Looks like egg salad," not revealing how diminished she felt for allowing discontent to have taken over when she never had to consider being stopped in the street and detained, tortured, sent to die in a concentration camp. She'd been adrift too long. Perhaps this mad trip is not without purpose. Be alert. Look for signs.

There were three bottles of warm orange soda with the sandwiches and Harry said, "Perfect vintage for egg salad." Doctor Reinhardt held up his bottle in a toast and the three of them clinked, not having realized they were hungry. The weak zing of the warm carbonation went down just right, each traveling their separate paths. Distractedly observing the tourists, Harry said, "Do you mind if I ask you something? You fled Vienna, you survived the German occupation of Paris, you get here to start a new chapter, lose your wife and then your son violently. How do you do it?"

Doctor Reinhardt finished the first half of his sandwich, took another swallow of the orange vintage. "My friend Viktor Frankel wrote a book about why he survived four concentration camps. The Nazi death machine would dehumanize through starvation, overwork, replacing your name with a number. You know all this. You could be beaten, shot, gassed, on a whim. They confiscated your belongings. Luck would decide if you lived another day. Viktor came to the realization that he possessed one thing they could not take. And that was his attitude. Those who maintained a sense of personal dignity, despite it all, increased their chances of surviving. Those who found a way to create meaning in their lives, not withstanding their situation, had an edge. Out of his concentration camp horror he developed what is now known as the third school of Viennese psychiatry. Logotherapy. Logo is the Greek word for meaning. The hurt never stops. But attitude, meaning, is the dressing on the wound. What is it that drives some people to the long, painful at times, expensive journey of psychoanalysis? It is the need to know what the truth is in one's self, one's own existence. You are trying to get at it in your own analysis Harry."

"But I didn't mention I was seeing a psychiatrist," said Harry.

"And I didn't tell you I was a psychiatrist. As I said, it sometimes happens. Residue from early stage evolution perhaps. Instinct in the animal world is what keeps it alive. As an environment changes the animal's instinct remains the same. If the animal cannot adapt it becomes extinct. Perhaps there was a stage in our evolution when external changes were more than our instincts could deal with. Whereas some animals became extinct we humans saw our brains get bigger, resulting in a greater ability to learn, to realize there is such a thing as a past, a future, the concept of awareness of ourselves as entities unto themselves. As instinct diminishes, it is replaced with the need we have for meaning. Success in business, desire for more and more pleasure consumes most of us. Then some unbearable loss, and we ponder what it all means, where is our own personal truth. An anthropologist studying western man would conclude that honesty is elusive. An analyst and a patient strive to identify the irrational and find reason. Truth. As we breathe the air on Masada, the same air of the Zealots, I wonder if the suicides were irrational, or a final act of truth."

Audrey asked, "What if Eleazer Ben Yair was your patient? Psychoanalyze Eleazer. Would he still have decided that death for all was the better choice than life under the Romans?"

Doctor Rheinhardt offered an embryonic smile. "A question to ponder. In the 1930's Doctor Frankel was head of what we called the Suicide Pavilion at the General Hospital in Vienna. He treated over thirty thousand women vulnerable to suicide. They had little to look forward to. An existential vacuum. An empty hole within. Meaninglessness. A conversion must take place to a life with purpose. Eleazer on the couch? Who knows?"

The three of them finished their egg salad sandwiches and relaxed over the last of the warm orange soda in the sun on top of Masada enjoying what there was between them. "You won't even try to predict where it would go if Eleazer Ben Yair was a patient?" asked Harry. "When you see someone two, three times a week over a couple of years or more, they tell you everything, things they wouldn't dare speak of with anyone else, you analyze their dreams, discover their mother caused all their unhappiness, over time they forgive, you live their marriages, break ups, breakdowns, give them Kleenex as they sob uncontrollably, get them through bad bosses, unlucky business failures, determine at what point they're fixed, if ever. You won't even predict what someone who's either a psycho murderer or a courageous leader would have done two thousand years ago? This is so disillusioning Doctor Rheinhardt."

"That's very good. Well said Harry. But what we do is a balance between science and art. Neither can be predicted with any certainty."

And Audrey commented, "I read about an exercise in meditation. Try to make your mind go absolutely blank. No deliberate thoughts. Thinking not allowed. And then see where it takes you. You can never predict."

"I can predict that lunch period is over and there's more yet to see. You two go on and we'll find each other later." He watched them continue their walk around the casemate wall and thought they appeared natural together, as if they'd known each other three years and not just three days.

He'd come out from Jerusalem to the top of Masada with a specific purpose and didn't anticipate joining up with two engaging young Americans. On the snake path, a thought softly emerged that the girl was hitting chords in the same key as his wife, and the boy was causing the sound of cymbals with the thumping of his son's heart. Randomness in life is perhaps a synonym for "we just don't yet understand." They are pleasant to be with, but focus on what brought me here, which may or may not be coincidence.

Dr. Rheinhardt's colleague from Hebrew University, Ehud Ben Dov, Chairman of the Archeology Department, had mentioned over coffee as they sat in a sidewalk café that he'd come across a puzzling ostraca from the dig at Masada. It had taken on huge significance when combined with a piece of papyrus from a letter of a Roman officer which never made it back to Rome. The letter, written in Greek, indicated an educated officer, and the design on the parchment was not Zealot. Back at his friend's office, cluttered with articles from past millennia, Dr. Rheinhardt realized that the two thousand year old shard possibly depicted three flying saucers. The scrap of papyrus, in a fine handwriting, mentioned three mysterious discs hovering over Masada as a possible sign from one of the gods. Of and by themselves the finds would be of interest, but together they provided corroborating evidence of a possible anomaly. In addition, a student of the professor had read that on one of his voyages Columbus made a journal entry about flying discs following the Nina for several frightening moments and then dissolving into the sky.

He thought about how only a month before while at a psychoanalytic conference in Austin, Texas, one of the psychiatrists talked about a retired army officer in treatment who had become non communicative, depressed, and taken to sleeping with a light on. The officer was a decorated veteran with no history of depression or other emotional issues. He had a successful career and a solid marriage. In therapy he kept returning to an incident that occurred in 1947 while stationed at a base in Roswell, New Mexico. He spoke of an encounter with a space Alien who telepathically communicated with him. The message from the Alien was that we, Earthlings that is, are polluting the universe and if we don't stop we will know Masada again. The psychiatrist then asked the Israeli psychiatrist to explain what happened at Masada. Not until Rheinhardt was on the plane back to Israel did he connect the officer's case history with shards and the papyrus fragment in Ben Dov's office.

Nine hours in the air from New York to Tel Aviv and he knew he would go to Masada by himself to think, and then meet with Ehud Ben Dov. So here I sit, he thought, with tangled memories of Vienna and Paris and my wife and my son and Eleazer Ben Yair in therapy and UFO's and that young man's question, how do you do it? Attitude? Meaning? They are only techniques. Strategies. With some they are helpful. Others don't possess the discipline. They go on. They cry without tears. They will never laugh. In time perhaps a smile for a moment, and then deadness, darkness, death. So what do I know? Forty years a psychiatrist and asking what do I know. Acquisition. Socialization. Human contact. Without that question, insanity. So is this insanity? UFO's over Masada two thousand years ago? Space Aliens on Earth communicating a warning without words? As I recall, that Texas psychiatrist appeared to believe his patient, or allowed for the possibility. So what am I doing here on Masada? Do I expect to see a flying saucer? The Messiah? Superman? And what would peer review determine? "Doctor Reinhardt believes Aliens from other worlds are sending messages." Not good. Unless Aliens from other worlds are sending messages. If so the foundations of western civilization would crack. So Pope, did Jesus die for Alien's sins also? So Billy Graham, can you also save Alien's souls? So Talmudic scholars, in seven days God created the heavens and the Earth. But these guys, these Aliens, probably come from beyond the heavens. And what if they don't like us? The Nazis didn't like six million and murdered them. All together over a hundred million were killed. So the Aliens decide we're not their kind of people then all six billion of us have a choice. Allow the Aliens to slaughter us? Or choose suicide instead? Masada.

Harry and Audrey followed the casemate wall imagining the anguished sounds from two millennia ago, the children who if they lived today would be wearing Kiddie Keds, the mothers serving macaroni and cheese, the fathers on assembly lines or dentists, not having to choose slavery or family suicide. Audrey said, "Was it any different twenty-five years ago in Poland, in Germany, than two thousand years ago where we stand? It never stops. There is good and evil. Some skull dug up in Africa twenty-five thousand years old was once a human who lived among good natives and evil natives. The evil that men do lives after them. The good is often interred in their bones. Shakespeare? John Donne? Archie and Veronica? Did Iago love his evilness the way the good love their goodness?"

Exploring on at a languid pace and feeling the heat of the Judean desert Harry said, "Hitler is synonymous with the evil side. But to most of the German people he was their beloved leader. Same with whoever headed up the Ku Klux Klan. Attila the Hun. To the millions who believed in them they weren't bad."

Moving on slowly, not noticing they were walking in step, Audrey said, "Mother Theresa. Good. Even the worst of the evil see her as good."

"Abraham Lincoln. Everybody thinks he was a courageous kind hearted icon. Except for a majority of Southerners. But this sounds like a philosophy class that leaves you without answers, just more confusion. I wonder if Israelis laugh less than other nationalities because of all the tattooed numbers, the ceaseless fucking battles for survival. Let's think of something we can laugh about. Marx Brothers, Abbot and Costello, Amos and Andy belly laughs. Does Doctor Rheinhardt have any of those side splitting tears-running-down-your-cheeks laughs in him? What do you suppose he's doing up here? He seems to want to be alone as if he's doing some really deep thinking, but he also appears almost relieved when we meet up."

They had stopped to examine the remains of a room with patches of surviving lime plaster and two stone benches. Audrey's face said far away thoughts and Harry was sorry he had intruded. Perhaps a couple of minutes passed and she finally spoke. "I think it was in this room that I found several pieces of pottery and an intact vessel. It was so beautiful. We also dug up thirteen coins. It was early in the dig and although I was beside myself I wanted to behave professionally so I didn't allow my excitement to burst out. We figured out this room and that adjoining room could have been used for storage because they're in a relatively remote spot. It's been so long since I had such a feeling of completeness. Maybe these last three days, this journey we're on, was prescribed by whatever forces determine the destiny of our planet. Because who really knows anything about anything? Did you say that or was it me? And yes, Doctor Rheinhardt looks like he's trying to solve some sort of mystical ancient puzzle and we are a welcome intermission. When we meet up his curtain comes down. When we wander on his curtain goes up. I think we're all working on the same problem. It's all so out there I can't define it. Let's bring it up with him."

And Harry said, "Whatever the 'it' is."

Masada, 68-73 C.E.

In the year 68 CE Jerusalem was a city in tears. Caesar had dispatched his most effective statesman, Flavius Silva, with all the men and resources he would need to subjugate the people of Judea to the will of Rome once and for all. Those defiant ones had rebelled against taxation and refused to kneel before the Roman gods. The worst amongst them were the Sicarri, consumed with piety and rage. So violent and determined were these outlaws that they took as much pride in murdering their brethren who acquiesced to Caesar as they did a Roman. Although Silva was a gentleman and preferred negotiation, the rebels had become increasingly formidable and unwilling to compromise. An example had to be made of these fools or other colonies might get ideas and also foment insurrection. His last option had involved devastating brutality. The temple of the Jews was burned and the people slaughtered. As the city smoldered and bodies littered the alleyways and bazaars, those that could fled. The Diaspora had begun. It would last two thousand years.

Eleazer Ben Yair, leader of the Sicarri, had slipped out of Jerusalem avoiding the sentries of the Tenth Legion, eventually arriving at the mountain fortress Masada, constructed by King Herod during his building frenzy in the previous century. The formerly grand palaces and support buildings were crumbling but would serve as sanctuary for the nine hundred sixty men, women and children who had survived the carnage. As Eleazer climbed the snake path he knew this was their final stand. They would continue the revolt as best they could. When supplies became scarce they would raid nearby settlements like Ein Gedi, or Qumram to the east. Herod's engineers had designed a technologically brilliant fortress. There were views of Lake Asphaltitus, breezes to ward off the intensity of the summer sun, areas for growing vegetables and, through ingenious architecture, a water system that channeled occasional torrential gushes so that the reservoirs and ritual baths were usually full. There were even steam rooms and hot and cold pools for the pampering of the King and his retinue. Strategically the fortress was practically unreachable.

Feeling old as he arrived at the top he entered through the main tower and the guards were relieved their leader had made it out from Jerusalem. In his quarters he acknowledged fatigue and slowly drank a cool goblet of water. His efforts to suppress flashbacks of the fighting were unsuccessful and a memory repeated of a young boy, perhaps seven or eight, and a smaller girl, his sister or cousin, both wearing white tunics with purple colored bands and sandals with thongs going up their little calves in the same style as adults, wandering the streets clinging to each other bewildered and hopeless, slipping in the red goo on the cobblestones. He wondered if his own Sicarri women— in colorful dress with hair braided smelling of perfume and femininity, yet conditioned to be lethal, to quickly draw their curved daggers from under stylishly draped mantles and stab anyone thought to be traitor or Roman—were responsible for making these children of Judea orphans.

He couldn't control his mind's roaming back to Jerusalem and the fighting, the shouting from the city walls to the Legionnaires encamped on the sloping plain, the burning of the temple and the torture he had imposed on the priests when they chose to negotiate with Rome in order to salvage what they could of their prestige and opulence. He drifted back to childhood and the struggles, feeling his parents' vitriol toward Rome was more important to them than he was. The aloneness creeping up reached a level of abandonment for which he found relief solely in battle. But now fatigue was causing fuzziness and he questioned his past actions as visions of barbarities flashed and he wondered when in his calling as a soldier and commander he had shed humanity and why his hatred for Rome spilled over to his own blood, to his tribe that accepted the Covenant but was also willing to swear allegiance to Caesar.

This questioning was not good and he shuddered recalling the viciousness of his own hand against those aristocrats who as a sign of their status chose to speak Greek rather than Hebrew. He would become enraged at their airs, the supercilious slights that allowed those wealthy and entitled to wear finely woven cotton and write on papyrus in a sophisticated cursive arrogance that made him feel so belittled. Why these doubts now, when it was fortitude and conviction his people required? The Tenth Legion would eventually encamp below and find a way to end the siege. Eleazer Ben Yair and his refugees had little choice but to resist. If captured they would be sent to Rome or its territories as slaves or human entertainment to be ravaged by wild animals in coliseums. Tens of thousands had already been decreed slaves and were property of Roman masters throughout the Mediterranean.

Months passed. Hope diminished. The Sicarri on top of Masada observed the Legionnaires below encircling their fortress with a series of camps and constructing a ramp that would serve as their highway of attack. The holdouts lived with increasing desperation. Eleazer had eliminated all options but one.

The group gathered around a long wooden table that had absorbed years of spilled wine and slothful eating during Herod's reign. The dim light muted the faces of the men whose expressions were dark and weary.

Eleazer spoke. "We are at the end my brave men. There is but one tactic for the dawn. Our decision to neither serve the Romans nor any other God, for He alone is man's true and righteous Lord. Now is the time to verify that resolution by our actions. We refused to submit to a slavery involving little peril. Let us not, along with slavery, deliberately accept the irreparable penalties awaiting us if we are to fall alive into Roman hands. It is in our power to die nobly and in freedom, a privilege denied others who have met with defeat. Our fate at break of day is certain capture, but there is still the free choice of a noble death with those we hold most dear. Our enemies fervently pray to take us alive, but they can no more prevent what we must do than we can now hope to defeat them in battle. Not even the impregnable nature of this fortress can save us, not even our ample provisions, our piles of arms and abundance of every other requisite will save us, for we have been deprived manifestly by God Himself of all hope and deliverance. The penalty for the many wrongs which we madly dared to inflict upon our countrymen let us not pay to our bitterest foes the Romans, but to God through the act of our own hands. Let our wives die not dishonored, our children unacquainted with slavery. When they are gone let us render a generous service to each other, preserving our liberty through honor with death.

Even though we have been taught that man's highest blessing is life and that death is a calamity, still the crisis we face must be borne with a stout heart, since it is by God's will and of necessity that we are to die. Un-enslaved by the foe, let us die as free men with our children and wives, let us quit this life together. This our laws enjoin. This our wives and children implore us. The need for this is God's sending. The reverse of this is the Roman's desire, and their fear is that a single one of us should die before capture. Let us deprive them of their hoped for enjoyment at securing us. Let us then enjoy their amazement at our death and their admiration of our fortitude."

The room was quiet, a long silence of resignation, and then his commanders left for their final hours with loved ones. The dry wind on the plateau gathered force. Fast moving clouds playing tag with the moon.

Eleazer slowly walked around the casemate wall of the entire plateau they occupied during these final years, hearing sobbing and moaning from the apartments within the enclosure. He had issued an order to burn food and supplies so as to deprive their foes, but ordered some be put aside as a sign to the Romans that this was by choice. Soon he would join those given the task of going from room to room administering what had to be done for those not yet gone from this life.

Eleazer Ben Yair reached the Northern Palace, descended to the lowest level and for the last time surveyed the Judean desert, the Dead Sea reflecting moonlight, and far off the town of Ein Gedi where they had plundered wheat and olive oil and left a bloody mess. His arms were on top of the railing and he rested his forehead with eyes closed. We never succumbed. We eliminated many who did. We are fighters. Killers. The first to revolt. And now the last. Am I proud we made death preferable to the alternative? If I allow these thoughts of doubt then courage will leave my soul. Without courage I am not alive. But with courage I will soon be dead. There is nothing but endless darkness into worlds of more endlessness.

He rested at this roadblock having no desire to journey on and with eyes still closed was alerted to a signal, pinpoints of illumination guided directly to his innards. Lifting his head and looking to the sky were three large brightly lit discs circling, disappearing, reappearing, hovering, and like lightening shooting over the Dead Sea, reflecting red and blue beams, returning in a blink, noiselessly suspended, and then nothing but stars in the heavens.

He returned to the tower over the entrance where the Tenth Legion would ram through at dawn, intent on what they predicted would be a violent but quick finale to the rebellion. The men were waiting, the ones who had drawn lots and been selected for the final task of entering each apartment where the scene would be repeated. Puddles of blood, children embraced by parents, eyes with nothing in them, necks sliced open, some still dripping. Our message to you, Roman Empire, is that you can never own our dignity, our honor, or boast that you won the last battle. Listen to the echo of our laughter.

He told his waiting men that two older women and five children had gone into hiding, and it was to be respected. Then he showed the three flying discs he had drawn on a piece of broken pottery and described what he had just witnessed. He said they were from other worlds and not good for humanity. He said it was a reaffirmation of the path they had chosen. The last holdouts then embraced and in communion sat on the floor, each ready to offer his neck. Eleazer's mind was stuck on the flashing red and blue objects that had hovered over him. Simultaneously he envisioned his commanders and himself lifeless on the mosaic floor. They were wishing he would get at it, but the puzzle of the three flying discs gave them extra minutes of life. It troubled him that he was to die not knowing what they implied. The flames and smoke from the fires they had set combined with the sound of ballista balls from the Roman artillery on the siege ramp, created a violent backdrop for their final moments. Through his disc in the sky trance Eleazer saw they were to die as they lived. The men waiting for his sword saw their Commander smile. With his smile Eleazer knew the discs had been sent to teach the people how to exist without killing each other. What irony. He knew they would return.

Jerusalem

The drive back to the Kibbutz passed quickly compared to the drive out. The talk came easy and Harry saw that Audrey could be chatty. Her words overflowed, filling the car with gushes of new energy as if a double dose of a fast acting super powered vitamin had been mainlined on the top of Masada. Her knowledge of first century life in Palestine was another layer off the onion. Harry realized that although their souls had merged almost immediately back at the focus group they were still strangers. Spiritually wedded but on distant planets. Audrey asked Doctor Rheinhardt what his plans were and he said he was driving back to Jerusalem. She then said they were going to Jerusalem as well, which was a surprise to Harry. At an almost imperceptible vibration from Doctor Rheinhardt, Harry sensed the psychiatrist in the back seat knew they hadn't planned to go to Jerusalem until that moment. It was in the dawn's disappearing darkness they'd left Kibbutz Ein Gedi and in the evening dimness that they returned. The three of them got out of the car and Doctor Rheinhardt said to both of them, "I am having dinner with the head of the Archaeology Department and I believe you both would enjoy meeting him so please join me for dinner if you have no other plans. I'll give you the address of the restaurant, but you can follow me. It should be easy until we get close to Jerusalem. If we get separated the restaurant is across the street from the King David Hotel. I'll just get my bag and settle up and I suppose you'll do the same. Shall we meet in fifteen minutes?"

Harry's head was a mélange of thoughts as they followed Doctor Rheinhardt's Citroen. A single flailing spermatozoa was circling an egg in metamorphosis. The female linkage in this chain of events had begun to shed flakes of vulnerability on the snake path. Something lying dormant was preparing for the sun. Harry thought it would be a strong growth. Although he was happy to be going to Jerusalem for dinner with two intellectuals, he couldn't decide if he felt diminished when Audrey announced that decision without any discussion. On the one hand, it was obviously a spontaneous moment and he just knew enthusiasm had been a dead issue with her for a long time. On the other hand could he last with a woman who was happy? And out of the dimness he heard her voice for what was probably the second time. "It would be nice if we could check into the King David Hotel. I don't think you heard me the first time. You look so cute when you're thinking deep thoughts." Ah sweet acceptance. All doubts gone. But what if she was reading my mind and thought she ought to say something nice. I really am a neurotic fuck.

"The King David Hotel would be great. And thank you for acknowledging you've fallen in with a real cute looking fella." She squeezed his knee and then rested her hand on his leg and it was a wonderful drive in to Jerusalem.

They checked into the King David and left their bags at the desk not wanting to be rude and keep Doctor Rheinhardt and his friend waiting. The crowded restaurant had an urban sound of people expressing opinions on subjects great and small. Aproned waiters from middle Europe were coming and going with a staccato rhythm, professional and contented as the diners. Audrey saw Doctor Rheinhardt and waved as they navigated to the table. Both men stood with an old fashioned courtliness and Doctor Rheinhardt said, "My two American friends, Audrey Sonnenshine and Harry Lang, Professor Ehud Ben Dov." Harry noticed the elegant way Audrey extended her hand, with a slight bend at the wrist, as if she expected it to be kissed. Ehud Ben Dov was in his early fifties with a well fed waistline, just under average height and although he was in slacks and an open necked shirt probably wore a size forty-two short sport jacket. He had a close cropped grey beard, a powerful handshake and laugh lines around his eyes. Harry decided he was one of those people you like immediately, are never disappointed in. He could tell Audrey would certainly agree. As soon as they were seated Professor Ben Dov looked to Audrey. "Stefan tells me you could teach a university level course on our first century C.E. And he is impossible to impress. We will have a lot to talk about." A quick blush and Harry saw she was very happy. "And you were on the

Masada dig in '63. An international event. It will take years to compile the final report. And you Harry, do you have an interest in archaeology?" Harry realized he was feeling proud for Audrey, in the way a parent revels in a child starring in the school play. As he thought about how to answer the question, a question of his own having to do with how pleased he was that this girl sitting there was beaming and if that meant he might be swimming into another dimension. She can be chatty and she can beam. How come I like that? So here's how I'll answer the professor's question.

"Vietnam. Assassinations. Students rioting and getting shot, jailed. Cities in flames. All of it. So maybe studying what was happening two thousand years ago when the world was just as crazed allows us to not focus on today's madness. It's a constructive way to escape. Of course there's the possibility we learn something about our place in the universe. Can archaeology do that?" And on that beat one of the animated waiters appeared with menus and announced that the pot roast was excellent tonight and that a whole roasted fish was the special and disappeared. Everybody took their time concentrating on what to select. The waiter reappeared for their orders.

"Our place in the universe Ehud," said Doctor Rheinhardt. "A good place to start."

Putting a pita with hummus in his mouth Ehud said, looking at Harry, "Wherever you stand in this ancient land you can dig up the past. Walk out on the street, take a jack hammer through the pavement and you will find our history. In this country archaeology is the same as praying. Since the destruction of the Second Temple by the Romans, since Masada, 'next year in Jerusalem' was our people's obsession. So Doctor Rheinhardt, the topic at hand."

Audrey was complete. It had been so long. The three men surrounding her seemed like blood relations. She was high and heard an angel chorus. Everyone in this restaurant was her family. She wanted to embrace the three at the table, hold them in a hug. Stefan and Ehud were having dinner to discuss something. And Doctor Rheinhardt was now Stefan. Professor Ben Dov was Ehud from the start. Something about Ehud said he was not of the refugee class. She meandered on... he is a Sabra. Born in Israel. What was it? No sense of gratefulness to be here. No spiritual stoop. He is a warrior. Like all Israelis born a warrior. He's not programmed to adjust his behavior to fit in. He was born fitting in. Unlike my father, coming from German Jewish aristocracy, impeccable manners, money, war hero, but forever indebted because America allowed him in. France, Israel, allowed Stefan in. Did he invite us to dinner because I was manipulative? Rule that out. Psychiatrists don't get manipulated. What did he mean by the topic at hand? Return to Earth. Tune back in. Stefan is speaking.

"At the conference a psychiatrist said that a patient of his, a retired army officer, no history of anything, good marriage, successful military career, had recently presented with extreme anxiety, started sleeping with the light on, remote, wife concerned, insisted he get professional help. After a few sessions he brings up an incident that occurred over twenty years ago outside of Roswell, New Mexico, near his base. A local farmer had called the base commander to report a "flying saucer," his words, had crashed on the ranch and there were Alien bodies. The officer, a major at the time, was sent to the ranch to verify it was probably a weather balloon or some army experiment. The officer told the psychiatrist there indeed was a crashed spacecraft and several Alien bodies not from this world. One was still alive and while being carried on a stretcher to an army ambulance he communicated telepathically with the patient that we are destroying the planet and unless we stop dirtying Earth there would be another Masada. My colleague at the conference had heard of Masada and knowing I was from Israel asked what exactly happened there. Although he didn't come right out and say he believed that the incident with the Alien actually occurred—this would be professionally damaging—my sense is that he did. So at twenty five thousand feet above the ocean on the flight home, your shard with the flying discs, the papyrus letter, jolted me awake. Could it be? Flying objects over Masada during the siege, the suicides? Space beings in our time delivering a message of Masada? So I spent the day there to reflect, to decide if it's possible, if anything should be done, can be done. Ehud, the letter, the ostraca shard, have you given them any thought since our meeting?"

The Chairman of one of the world's most acclaimed university archaeology departments said, "I asked some doctoral students to research it, see what they find." Turning to Audrey, "You have read Josephus's description of the siege, the last commanders of the Zealots drawing lots?" She offered a small affirmative movement of her head. "Twelve ostraca were found next to the Water Gate near the storehouses. Eleven of them had names inscribed, all in the same handwriting. The twelfth was indecipherable. One of the names was Ben Yair. The others were nicknames 'the Hunter,' 'Son of the Valley,' 'Son of the Baker,' 'Grida.' It is thought these were the lots they drew to accomplish the final killings, the last one killing himself. The epigraphic material with the flying discs was found in the vicinity of the twelve shards. Which could indicate it was created in the last hours before the suicides and by someone not a scribe or artist, possibly by one of the twelve. The Roman officer's letter that was never sent could have gotten lost during the confusion of the final night and the shred of papyrus that was discovered somehow survived."

He paused as their first course was put on the table. The American couple stared at their plates not seeing food. Ehud Ben Dov continued. "1504 BCE. Egypt. Thutmose the Third. A papyrus from that era states there were circles of fire in the sky. They must have crashed because the writing on the twenty-four hundred year old papyrus describes a body one rod high and an unbearable stench." He picked up his fork. The American couple mimicked him, not tasting the food. "The prophet Ezekiel in 592 BCE speaks of a flying craft in the sky and four living creatures telling him the Israelites have transgressed. Unless they obey the commandments they will suffer punishment. More recently a book from 1493 in a museum in Verdun describes with drawings from 1034 a cigar shaped craft in the sky and a globe with orbs. These finds have been authenticated as being from those eras. Did they actually see what they drew or recorded? There is a similarity. I believe they all witnessed something. Did your army officer get a telepathic message from a space being? Some would think we are delusional just having this conversation. But delusional is your expertise Stefan."

"If we put delusional aside for now," Doctor Rheinhardt said, "it appears sightings, maybe even contact, have been recorded for thousands of years. I accept that something was observed over Masada on the last day of the siege. Descartes wouldn't approve of my science, what science, but intuitively this Army officer is not hallucinating. So looking at this as an experiment in human behavior, our own behavior that is, do we attempt to save the population of the world or simply have a pleasant dinner? What is the saying Ehud, save one life and you've saved all of humanity. Save all of humanity and..."

Both Harry and Audrey were coming back from their speechlessness. The puzzle these two men were examining actually seemed to match the otherworldliness of the last few days. Audrey understood this more quickly than Harry and asked, "What if it's all true? What if all humanity on Earth is in danger of annihilation by beings from out there somewhere because we're destroying our planet. Who do you tell? What can they do? They may think you're mad."

"Aha" said Professor Ben Dov, gesturing in the air. Then seeing embarrassment on Audrey's face immediately said, "Forgive me," and turning to Doctor Rheinhardt, "So Stefan?"

"Of course those are the questions." He smiled at Audrey without condescension. "Perhaps our only course of action without risk for now is inaction. But we can take a small risk and go to someone in our government and see what they know. Intelligence. Files. Someone must be in charge of, in charge of what? UFO's? Aliens? Anomalies from other dimensions? You're well known in military circles Ehud. Mossad. The most critical decisions in world history were made by intuition."

Ehud's eyes dimmed to seriousness. In the 1948 War for Independence he did things that earned great respect in the Hagganah. In the 1956 war as a Company Commander the military establishment chose him for a secret operation with minimal odds for survival. He and the men under him were among the most decorated fighters in the IDF. His ancestor's remains from the time of the Second Temple to the present were absorbed in the holy Earth. Anyone in government would be happy to receive him. Investigating further though, was this something he wanted to do? He and Stefan had been friends from the moment they met at a university faculty function twenty years before. An ancient Israeli family and the most recent of arrivals. Together they were what the country was. With their wives intellectual life in Jerusalem was joyful. Cafes. The symphony. Dinners at each other's apartments. Then the bus bombing and in addition to a life extinguished so was the magic of four civilized minds at play. Then last year Stefan's son. So Stefan now carries within what it means to be Israeli. Of course I will make some phone calls.

Harry and Audrey saw Ehud Ben Dov's eyes go from high voltage to black out and back again in seconds. "I'll call Ariel tonight," he said to Stefan, and then to all of them, "shall we order dessert? Baklava, cherry pie with ice cream, bread pudding, three flavors of sorbet. Let's order one of each and share."

Conversation through dessert and coffee was not dominated by anyone, Ehud discussing some of the digs the university was currently involved with, Audrey remembering some of the finds from five years ago and also speaking of her father's background which the two Israelis listened to carefully, asking for details. Harry was amusing on life in Greenwich Village and what it was like inside a New York advertising agency. Doctor Rheinhardt appreciated Harry's entertaining style and also saw the festering. It was one of those evenings where people new to each other share intimacies the way old friends confide in each other. Leaving the restaurant Ehud said, "Come to my office in the morning. You'll enjoy seeing some artifacts we dug from the Earth of this land," looking at Harry, "and I'll have one of the graduate students give you a tour."

Almost before he finished the sentence Audrey said, "Thank you. We'd love to. Thank you." Harry felt her respiration accelerate from zero to sixty in five seconds. Saying their goodbyes she gave each a hug, not an air kiss type hug. Her thermometer was just under boiling as the couple crossed the street back to the King David Hotel, bodies close.

The two men turned and strolled into nighttime Jerusalem. "It was good of you to invite them Ehud. From what I gather the girl has not been productive. And the boy bright but not yet fully formed, if anyone ever is. Both seekers. They could be our children. So I chose the empty seat at their table last night in Ein Gedi. In need of blood relations."

"You're talking like a psychiatrist. And Ariel will tell you to go find a good one for yourself. I'll call him when I get home."

Their room at the King David had two large double beds. Harry was reminded of a line from a Country and Western singer at a recording session in Nashville. A definition of ambivalence, when your sixteen year old daughter returns home at four in the morning, with a Gideon Bible. He sat down on a small sofa with his legs propped up on a chair and hands clasped behind his head. Audrey stretched out on one of the beds. She wanted the three men she had dinner with to know at that very moment she loved them very much each having touched her heart, and that's where it was coming from, her heart, in ways that had been dormant, mummified, that hadn't ever announced, surprise, we're in here holding hands and dancing, a kazatska, a hora, a two step, do-si-do, feel us Audrey, send out the vibes, shake, rattle, and roll, allow yourself the joyfulness, because we come, and we go, we've whipped you up, like turning egg whites to meringue. Oops, your husband. You are married Audrey. But don't think of him yet or we're outta here. Just close your eyes baby 'cause right now there's nothing you can do about it.

Harry appreciated the sight of her form on the bed, her femininity, and then looked at the other bed and that's where he would sleep. He felt his lips form a sad smile. But it was okay.

At 7:00AM Stefan and Ehud entered General Ariel Sharon's office. Stefan saw between them the brotherhood of shared combat. Sharon gestured to a coffee pot on an electric burner and they helped themselves. The general had a distracted smile and seemed to be focusing on the next subject or some other issue before his smile disappeared. The two warriors spent a minute on family updates while men and women in uniform passed by the office, many looking like high school seniors. Ariel Sharon closed the door and got right at it. "I'm sorry but I have less than five minutes. A helicopter is waiting. What I'm going to tell you is considered top secret by most governments but we have other issues that occupy us. This conversation is unofficial, but exercise discretion. I told Ehud on the phone last night there was a UFO crash in New Mexico in 1947. It's true. There were Alien bodies and they were autopsied at Bethesda Naval Hospital near Washington D.C. Any military or civilians who saw anything, the craft, the debris, the bodies, were informed they would disappear forever if they ever spoke of what they saw. They were told their families would be in grave danger. This information is from Mossad," looking at Ehud. "We know there have been other crash sites, most recently in Siberia. The Russians are more careless than the Americans. We know that Barry Goldwater was very curious about the New Mexico incident. Even though he was a Reserve General Officer he was shut out. According to Mossad, Curtis LeMay was so annoyed at Goldwater's nagging to see the bodies that he lost his temper, which he has a lot of, and ordered Goldwater never to mention the subject again. Our Air Force Intelligence has a report indicating that in 1954 President Eisenhower was at the Muroc Experimental Base in California and met with representatives from an Alien world and was told that we are much too aggressive on Earth and should not use weaponry that pollutes the atmosphere to solve our global problems. They said we should be kinder to each other. Tell that to the Arabs. Our source tells us, believe it or not, I happen to, that the President signed a treaty of some kind with the Aliens. When a new President is sworn in the military immediately makes a detailed presentation. What makes the Eisenhower intelligence plausible is that he was on vacation in Georgia quail hunting the week before, and when he left for California the word was he went to play golf. Unlikely a President would take unplanned vacation days following a vacation. A UFO also landed on a base leased by the American Air Force in England. The base is known to store atomic capabilities."

The look on Ariel Sharon's face said there was more, but what does it matter. He got up and put his arm around Ehud and then shook Stefan's hand. End of meeting. As they were leaving he said, "So if I need a psychiatrist I know where to go?"

The two friends left the building, their civilian clothes contrasting with the military khaki all around. A colonel and a general entering the building noticed Ehud and made a slight detour to greet him, every movement conveying respect. The brotherhood of combat arms. When the two officers left, Stefan Rheinhardt said to Ehud Ben Dov, "Thank you for doing that. It was an imposition on you and on Ariel. You know I'm grateful."

The tending to overweight, unprepossessing war hero, shrugged him off saying, "It was only five minutes. He knows he didn't have to. It's a subject I haven't ever given much thought. It can probably make you meshugah. If you're free come by for dinner tonight. I'll check with Naomi." Ehud made eye contact for a moment longer than usual, which Stefan acknowledged, signaled he would, and they walked in different directions to their cars.

Doctor Rheinhardt had a scheduled meeting with interns he was supervising, and as he drove to the hospital he searched for the Greek word for melancholy. Don Quixote jousting with Aliens. To save humanity or not to save humanity. No longer an issue. I will allow myself to experience a sense of foolishness, hope it doesn't last, focus on what I do, what I know something about, and not analyze why I had a need to save humanity. My son gone. My wife gone. They are my humanity. Doctor Frankel. Attitude can last for so long.

Harry woke before Audrey and must have been dreaming about Kiddie Keds and the robot because he decided he must call Marvin. Audrey was still asleep in the other bed, on her side, arms embracing the pillow, long dark hair in an intimate tangle hiding secrets. Between the covers and the hair camouflage she was deep in happy slumber. He got out of bed and into Levis, brushed his teeth, then sprawled out on the sofa waiting for this very contented woman to reenter. The blanket molded around her fetal position curves, undulating terrain yet to be traversed. This is day three he thought. They're back in New York with the research results, I'm in this room in the King David Hotel in Jerusalem with a woman I've spent three monk-like nights with, but it's okay, haven't heard the damn voice since we got here, spent a day on a mountain top plateau where two thousand years ago husbands and fathers slit their family's throats and then killed themselves, had dinner with two brilliant Hebrew University professors who discussed whether Aliens from other worlds are planning to annihilate humanity, and the desk clerk said there's a buffet breakfast. My traveling companion seems to be moving her hands, stretching her left leg out from under the blanket, turning head, rolling onto her back, stretching both legs outside the blanket, eyes opening, sitting up, feet now on floor, a good morning smile, a surprise caress of my unshaven face on way to bathroom, door close, toilet seat down, flush, shower on, on for long time, off. Reappear in hotel terrycloth bathrobe. No speakee. Modestly into jeans and tee shirt. "Good Morning Harry," as she sits down close on the sofa and gives a hug. They quietly hold hands each knowing the other is happy. Reluctant to speak because it is all so perfect Harry finally says, "This is going to be a good day. Don't know where it will take us but this odyssey does have a destination. How 'bout I get shaved and showered, we'll get some breakfast and then figure out how to get to the university."

As Harry drove to Mount Scopus where the Department of Archaeology was, he focused on finding a phone to place a call to Marvin in privacy and also hoped for a few minutes alone with Doctor Rheinhardt. He would ask Professor Ben Dov how to reach him. They parked the car and entered academia. People were there to learn, or to teach. Faces didn't have that profit motive look. There was no effort to move product off the shelves. Nobody cared about package design. Or competitive pricing. Or market share. Not a world where clients left agencies and people were chucked. There was a softness, like a love song. Jerusalem unfurled below. They had entered a preserve. No hunting allowed. Harry said, "This sure ain't Madison Avenue."

Audrey followed up with, "Sure ain't Cleveland either." They asked a young girl in an army uniform with a book bag where Professor Ben Dov's office was and she said that was where she was going. As they walked along together Audrey asked, "Are you studying archaeology?"

"Master's program. Working on my thesis. Professor Ben Dov asked if I would show some Americans around, and you must be them. Where in America?"

Audrey and Harry answered in unison. "Cleveland. New York"

"I have relatives in New York. They own a luncheonette on West 37th Street. In the garment district." Her voice was a low octave and gravelly. She spoke English with the guttural pronunciation of 'ch' that Hebrew requires. "Professor Ben Dov's office is on the second floor, but as we're walking I can give you some history. The department was founded in 1934 as the Department of Archaeology of the Hebrew University of Jerusalem. Until 1948 and the War of Independence we were located right here on Mount Scopus, but in 1948 the department was moved to the new campus at Giv' at Ram. Last year we became the Institute of Archaeology and moved back here to Mount Scopus to the original building. A very generous group, the Belgian Friends of the Hebrew University, helped with funding.

Our museum has over 30,000 objects, inscribed cuneiforms, jewelry, weapons, glassware, the largest ancient coin collection in Israel."

Audrey said, "I found several coins when I was on the dig at Masada five years ago. Maybe some of them are here in the museum. We never introduced ourselves. This is my friend Harry Lang, and I'm Audrey Sonnenshine." Harry looked for some meaning in the word friend.

"I'm Rivka." As an afterthought. "Shatsky." They stopped at a display case with bits of cloth and remnants of sandals. Rivka continued, "The Masada dig was in the news constantly. I went out there one day with a friend. Just to watch. We hitchhiked. I was sixteen. I'd like to hear what it was like. How long were you there?" As Audrey answered Harry watched the conversation between the two women progress to where each was curious about the other. Harry was invisible. It was okay though. He liked seeing the two of them oblivious to everything but what each was saying. Guys didn't do it that way. They entered Professor Ben Dov's area still talking, unaware they were at their destination.

The short, slightly stocky warrior scholar appeared saying, "I see I don't have to introduce you. Rivka will show you around. The museum. The library. Have some lunch. Come back when you're finished."

"Is there a phone I could use?" asked Harry. "I'd like to place a collect call to New York. Is that possible?"

Professor Ben Dov thought a moment. "The back office. There's a phone on the shelf."

"Why don't the two of you go on" said Harry. "I'll find you."

They left immediately and the professor took Harry to the phone and closed the door gesturing he'd see him later. Harry found a straight back chair, brought it to the phone and sat down welcoming the quiet. It occurred this was the first time he'd been alone in four days. Falling asleep with someone breathing and shifting just a few feet away, using the bathroom in the morning, the scents that humans leave behind, the toiletries, the wet towels–this was not the routine he knew. Whenever a girl stayed the night she'd usually zip into the bathroom then get a cab home to her own morning routine, and off to her office. What would life be like with Audrey in the morning and Audrey in the evening? For years. For life. And I sit on this hard back chair wondering if my me is still here. Must be the middle of the night in New York. Marv's snoring away on East eighty-second Street in his third floor brownstone apartment back from the focus group junket. Hope I can place this call without having to look for help. The operator spoke perfect English and two minutes later the phone was ringing in Marvin Munchik's apartment. Harry heard his friend say he'd accept the call, his first words after having been awakened at four A.M. were, "Did you nail her Har?" Ignoring that, Harry's first words were, "How'd the rest of the groups go?"

"Is that a genuinely sincere question Harry?" asked Marvin.

"C'mon Marv" Harry begged.

"Okay" said Marvin. "Because you have a perfect attendance record and stopped masturbating in class I'm going to tell you. But can you keep a secret?"

"Marvin, please."

"You and I" said Marvin, "are now looked upon at the Black and White Agency as advertising geniuses. Every cunt in every group in every city loved the campaign. Paula made a public statement that in all her many years of doing focus groups she'd never experienced a grand slam. The client is coming in his pants. Even the Nazi bitch is quivering, like she's just been to her first book burning. And Steve Lester is strutting like one of those testosterone filled male birds showing all their splendid plumage as they do a mating dance. Except for your paramour losing it at that first group in Cleveland we're sitting on a big time winner. Careers will be made Harry. Bonuses. Profits. Riches. Calls from Jerry Fields with job offers. You'd better get your ass out of the promised land and back to reality. On the plane back from Dallas Steve said he hoped you solved your personal problem and are back at the office. Oh, your name didn't even come up once while you were on your neurotic escapade. Seriously Harry, we creative geniuses have work to do. Sandra is worried she hasn't heard from you in four days. Remember Sandra? Your secretary? We have a meeting tomorrow afternoon, which would be this afternoon, to decide on production companies. They want to get this on air really quick. There's legalities. All the bullshit."

Marvin, respecting his friend's long silence, could tell a lot of processing was occurring in Jerusalem. At last Harry said, "Would you mind telling Sandra I'll be in the office tomorrow. And to please ask her to let Steve's secretary know. I'll call you when I'm back in New York. And thanks Marv. Go back to sleep."

Harry was grateful to be in the quiet back office of Professor Ben Dov's domain. He knew the time had come to untangle this jam-up of complications. The King David Hotel could take care of booking a flight. He had to talk to Doctor Rheinhardt before he left. Then there was Masada. From when Audrey told him the details back at that bar in Cleveland to yesterday when he was there and seemed to inhale all of Masada deep into his diaphragm like a yoga exercise where you see your breath, it was all hauntingly familiar. Even when he wasn't consciously thinking about it there it was, with an edginess. And when he envisioned the rocky dusty plateau he realized an implacable resolve. And what about the voice that convinced him he was probably going round the bend? Thank God it finally shut the hell up. God? And now just a few minutes ago his professional triumph. He was an advertising hero. Gold medals at the ADDY show. Stories in the *New York Times* and *Advertising Age*. Love it. Enjoy it. It's fragile. If he left the agency in one week his name would never come up. And then last night's conversation between two respected intellectuals taking very seriously the possibility of Aliens from other worlds creating a space age Masada. Then there was Audrey. And oh dear. She does have a husband.

He attempted to make his mind go blank. Erase the equations to nowhere on the blackboard in his brain. Start clean. But start what? I'm in an existential hole. Never read Sartre but existential hole it is. If I were a glass is half full kind of guy I'm inhabiting a wild and wonderful life. Career shooting to the stars in a glamorous business. Involved with a woman of depth and beauty. Intelligent friends, most seeing psychiatrists, possibly lived another life two thousand years ago. That's pretty neat. Impulsive at times. Open to life's frequent weirdness, like Aliens among us! So I chugalug the half full glass and there's nothing inside. Just an empty glass not accomplishing its purpose in its glassiness. Do electrical engineers meander like this? They're constructed linear. Never without a slide rule. Bet James Joyce couldn't learn the language of slide rule if Bloom's life depended on it. Think I'll just stay here 'till the girls get back.

He had gone into a headachy semi-doze having mini flashes of the conference room back at the office, the E-train screeching in to the 14th Street station, leaving a faceless lover's apartment into nighttime Second Avenue, when he heard a voice he thought was from his dreaming but was Audrey's as she came through the doorway with currents of happiness electrifying her eyes. "When we realized you couldn't find us we thought you'd be back here. Come on. We're meeting Rivka for lunch. Did you make your call to New York? The museum they have here could take days to go through. It's fantastic. This whole place is so energizing. We sat in on a class for a few minutes. We met some people from the University of Southern California here for a dig at a place called Khirbet Mazra'a. Oh, and we ran into Ehud and he invited us to dinner at his apartment tonight. Doctor Rheinhardt, Stefan, will be there too. I'm sorry I know I'm speeding. There's just so much. What are you smiling at?"

"I was thinking you're not the same woman that blew a gasket in the focus group. When was it? Four distant days ago? Bi polar women have always had a certain allure."

She crossed her eyes and made a clown-like face. "Think you're man enough to handle that?" and she brushed against him. "I'm not the same woman. Or maybe it's the woman that once was but she drove off the turnpike at the wrong exit and just kept going 'till there was no gas. Anyway, I'm feeling too good to try to figure it out right now. We're supposed to meet Rivka in fifteen minutes at a place a couple of blocks from here. She said it has some outdoor tables."

They found the restaurant just as a group was leaving one of the outdoor tables. Rivka hadn't yet arrived. The waiter saw them looking at the table and with one gesture signaled they should sit down and he'd clear it off in a minute. The ash tray was filled with butts and there were empty Pepsi and Orange soda bottles and plates with ketchup smears and leftover food. There were university students, a few soldiers in uniform, professors, beards, ponytails, smokers, and the waiter looked Arabic but wore a mezuzah around his neck. Audrey said, "I like it here." Harry saw Rivka coming down the street and thought that Israeli women in Army dress gave off a sexiness, visions of thighs and calves and panties under the skirts, much more fantasy than civilian skirts. She wasn't especially attractive, or unattractive, but the low hoarse voice indicated I am a woman not easily convinced of anything and very much worth getting to know. She lit up a Lucky Strike with a military type lighter and slowly blew out the smoke, watching it ride the breeze and disappear. "My cousin, the daughter of my aunt and uncle who own the luncheonette in Manhattan, she also works at an advertising agency. A big one. Thomas? Walter Thomas?"

Harry said, "J. Walter Thompson. I have friends there." Rivka said, "She is in the media. She buys magazine space. She graduated from NYU two years ago. My aunt and uncle live in New Jersey. Teaneck. My cousin has an apartment with two roommates on West 72nd street."

Audrey said, "We only talked archaeology. I didn't realize that. Have you been to the States?"

Maybe in two years. I finish my army enlistment next year and then a year full time to get my degree."

Harry asked, "What do you do in the army?"

"I teach recruits how to take apart their guns. We still have Uzi's. And M14's. M16's also. Courtesy of your government." Rivka started to smile. "I don't pass them 'till they can do it blindfolded. Like in your John Wayne movies."

Harry also smiled, "I'd better not get on your bad side."

Rivka said, “Better not.” The waiter appeared and Rivka and Harry ordered coffee and burgers and Audrey a Pepsi and a burger. Then Audrey said, “Tell Harry about the dig we talked about. I hope we can see it.”

“It’s at Hazor” she said. It’s the largest biblical era sight in Israel. About two hundred acres. Twenty-two strata of occupational debris, twenty-one superimposed cities. Temples. Fortifications. Water systems. In 1928 a British archaeologist, Garstang was his name, did some limited excavations. The Rothschild Foundation came up with funding and Yigal is heading up a team. They’re there right now. It’s very exciting. I have a few more days off from the army and was planning to have a look. Come if you like.” A sharp anxiety jolt sped through Harry top to bottom, side to side, since he had yet to tell Audrey the latest news regarding his ascending career and his presence in New York being a requirement.

“What do you do after your Master’s?” Audrey asked.

Rivka had a last inhale of the Lucky Strike. Harry noticed the way she smoked projected sensuality. He saw her in bed lighting up and deeply inhaling after making love. The man in bed with her was faceless. “Teach. Write. Digs. Study for a Ph.D. Try to understand.” Audrey nodded that she got it. Rivka said, “I never asked what you do.” It was just a casual question but Harry was so curious in Audrey’s response he controlled an impulse to stare.

“That’s a hard question. I studied art history and archaeology. It’s a transition right now. You answered it though. Just trying to understand.” Rivka nodded. An honest, vague answer, thought Harry. Honesty out of vagueness. And Rivka knows all of it without hearing any of it. In a plain physical sense nothing outstanding, but I know men fall in love with her. Figure it out ol’ Har. Because her smoking style is alluring? Nah. There is a completeness there. No narcissism. She catches your emotions and sends back that she has. And she knows how to take guns apart. Not bad. Then Audrey said, “Maybe graduate school. In archaeology.”

And Rivka said, “Here?” Before Audrey could answer the

waiter interrupted and nobody ordered anything else and the check was left. Rivka looked at her watch and as she got up put some money on the table. Harry said it was on him but she left the money and said she'd see them that night at Professor Ben Dov's.

Each within themselves on the drive back to the hotel, silence again not uncomfortable. Entering the lobby and as if it had been discussed they walked to the coffee shop. "All of this has been so good," said Audrey with her elbows on the table and her face between her hands like a butterfly, "But I'm so guilty being here with you." The tears appeared slowly without sobbing. They traveled halfway down her cheeks and were stopped where her fingers formed a dam. "I just don't know what to tell him. My husband. It's been so blah for so long. I've got to contact him and I can't lie. Life has been a red light that's not changing. It's really not his fault. The marriage. It's hopeless. Maybe the red light will go to yellow. There's such a gap between what I've become and what I want to be. Rivka has so much serenity. She has the meaning Stefan talked about on Masada. Meaning, Harry. It means back to school. Just saying those words out loud is a relief. Did I just make a decision? Fuck. I think I did. Now I've got to tell him. Oh God, I'm so scared."

And Harry wished he could hold her because there were no words. Say it by feeling the warmth. Wait a bit he thought, before his news. About to walk the road to forever. Holding hands? Separate roads?

Back in the room she undid her sandals and kicked them off by the bed then lay down on her back. Harry went to the window and gazed at the ancient city, not registering. The empty temporary vacuum of hotel rooms.

"Harry, come here. Come next to me." He turned from the city and sat down on the bed. He touched her hand. Held it. With her hand in his he felt her face. She gently pulled him down, tucked her head into his arm and went fetal, her knees into his side. "I need to be held," she said.

Their breathing harmonized and in a while Audrey said, "Let's just stay like this. Okay?" Soon she was asleep and Harry loved holding her and didn't question why he wasn't imagining what it would be like for both of them to be naked. Late afternoon light entered the room.

He felt her coming awake, say thank you, and kiss him on the lips, like two lovers absent the lust. Her kiss was not without hints of what might be, just wasn't to be now. They got off the bed and went to the window. In almost a whisper Harry said, "I spoke to New York today, to my office. Tomorrow I've got to go back."

She turned to face him and clasped her hands behind his neck in a kneading motion pulling him closer. "I want you to stay but I'm relieved it's working out like this. Now I can honestly tell my husband this trip took place with a friend. You understand? All this happened, I mean you and I, being here, because we're in parallel traps. We're trying to struggle free without tearing off an emotional limb. We're both fighting to stay intact Harry. You know that, don't you? The way this script is written I stay here a few more days, by myself, and un-fog the lens, get clarity." Harry clasped his hands around the back of her neck and they were links in a chain.

Mrs. Ben Dov was a slender, angular faced woman with pulled back dark hair and brown eyes that said it's okay, be yourself, I understand. She wore bracelets and gold strands of necklace and Harry saw she was one of those women that had it, and whatever the it was the camera would love it. He also thought this is Audrey in thirty years. "Come in Audrey and Harry. I'm Naomi." It was the greeting of relatives, not strangers, and when Naomi gave Audrey a hug they were simply reconnecting from the many past lives they had together. It was a top floor apartment in a near elegant building. When Stefan Rheinhardt and Ehud Ben Dov came in from the balcony Audrey gave them each a hug and it caused Harry to go lumpy and suppress tears that came upon him suddenly, surprisingly. There was a big platter of fruit and nuts and a pitcher of orange juice on the cocktail-less cocktail table. As they started to sit down the doorbell rang and Naomi said "that's Rivka." In tailored black slacks with a stylish belt, white silk top and hair down, Harry thought this woman does not look like she takes guns apart in the army. As they greeted each other in Hebrew Rivka gave Ehud and Naomi a kiss and said in English, "My aunt and uncle." A very mild whiff of lamb and cinnamon came from the kitchen and the conversation got to high gear without hesitation. Harry waited for an appropriate lull, which didn't seem to be an immediate possibility, to ask Doctor Rheinhardt if he could speak with him privately. The conversation went from the El Al flight that was hijacked by Algerians in July to Eisenhower's seventh heart attack, to a recent bus bombing in Jerusalem, to the King David Hotel having new ownership, to Bobby Kennedy having been assassinated by a young Arab, and they all expressed opinions on everything and the Israelis were interested in what Audrey and Harry thought about all of it. As Rivka was asking Audrey how long they planned to stay Doctor Rheinhardt got up for the bathroom and Harry waited a couple of minutes to intercept. The bathroom was down the hall next to a bedroom and Harry had his chance.

"Doctor Rheinhardt, could I steal you for a minute? There's something I'd like to ask in private."

"Of course," and he directed Harry through the bedroom to another balcony. A sliver of a moon, occasional traffic sounds from below, and a mass memory from thousands of years of ceaseless defend and attack in every direction.

"I'll get right to it, and I hope this isn't rude, asking for free professional advice. About a week ago I started hearing a voice, which convinced me this could be creeping insanity rather than ordinary Manhattan neurotic. It was real and close and repeated the same sentence every time. It would happen in my apartment, at airports, subways, in the office. The voice said, 'You must go out from Jerusalem.' Tomorrow I am going out from Jerusalem, back to New York, and I was hoping you could tell me something about crackpots that hear voices."

Doctor Rheinhardt stroked his face, studied the Jerusalem

night, seemed to be thinking about something in some far distant world and said, "No Harry. I don't mind. You're with a very distinguished group. Joan of Arc heard the saints speaking, urging her to battle the English and make her country free. A German poet, Ranier Rilke, heard the voice of an angel, a bad angel, and it inspired him to write the *Duino Elegies*. Let's not leave out Moses. Auditory hallucinations can be caused by a deluded mind, severe psychological issues, schizophrenia, bipolar conditions, and certain defects of the brain resulting in losing one's sense of reality.

Harry said, "All of them apply."

"Some people with no psychological issues can also hear voices caused by drugs, transitional states, for instance between sleeping and waking, or states of religious experience. High levels of negative emotionality and distress as well as intense creative inspiration can result in auditory hallucinations. This latter group shouldn't be tagged as being sick. Some are even encouraged to embrace the voices as a positive force in their lives. Cognitive therapy can be effective to take control. From the time we've spent together I would say you're not sick, but have been experiencing emotional distress and also perhaps a state of very productive creativity. You're not sick Harry. When the stress is addressed, I predict it will pass. Where shall I send the bill?"

"It's a relief to know I'm not a deranged homicidal maniac." Doctor Reinhardt had his almost a smile expression and put a hand on Harry's back as they returned to the group. The change from being outside on the balcony discussing a worrisome subject contrasted with the emotional coziness in the room. "So you're returning tomorrow. A business emergency?" asked Ehud.

"It's a little complicated," said Harry. "You might say this trip didn't have a lot of planning. I was in Cleveland with some others from my office doing consumer research and Audrey explained the story of Masada and that she had been on the dig and I said let's go. The next evening we were on an El Al flight."

"You left your colleagues just like that." Rivka's husky voice was making a statement, not asking a question.

"It is rather bizarre," said Audrey, and Harry thought she sounded like a socialite in a restricted country club. As Naomi left the group for the kitchen she said, "Let's hear more of this bizarre story in the dining room" and Rivka and Audrey got up to help.

The contemporary and sparse dining room had a large oriental rug and a Scandinavian dining table and chairs. The three women were each carrying a platter and Naomi motioned "Sit anywhere. We're very informal in Israel." Audrey and Rivka sat on one side, Stefan and Harry on the other, and Ehud and Naomi at either end.

"We've been making wine in this country for thousands of years," said Ehud as he opened a bottle. Looking at Audrey, "so please continue."

"I was one of the consumers being researched and behaved very rudely and upset things and Harry came out from behind the one way mirror to help and we started talking and Masada came up and here we are. The lamb is delicious." Harry looked at Naomi as she started to speak and he crossed the moat into her mind knowing she got it immediately, all of it, as if her quantum waves had shadowed them from the focus group to this moment.

"But you've left out the best parts. The atmospherics. The magic." She was a guest on a late night talk show, Jack Paar, and was teasing the host.

"It's not something I could ever see myself doing," said Audrey. "I mean getting on a plane to Israel with someone I'd known only a few hours. I'm so glad I, we, did or we never would have met." In one blink Audrey's eyes included everyone. "I would have kept putting off decisions, like graduate school."

Harry wondered if she would mention her husband. Naomi looked to Harry. "People in advertising are imaginative. Creative. Out with it. The drama."

Harry had some cous cous on his fork as he took a moment and then said, "It's a movie. The female lead is Audrey Hepburn. The male is, well I'm not sure, but it opens in New York, scenes of Greenwich Village, midtown, taxis, street sounds, bright color, cut to conference room, male lead speaking, airport, plane lands in

Cleveland, focus group research room, female lead has emotional outburst, advertising exploitive, Vietnam, profanity, violence all over, embarrassed silence, male lead enters, chemistry, cut to neighborhood tavern, life stories, more chemistry, female lead relates experience on Masada dig, male lead hears commanding voice say it is written the two of you will travel to Masada tomorrow, cut to top of Masada, mystical and moving, meet welcoming Israelis, convergence, ancient connection needing no explanation as family of Jews, dinner in beautiful Jerusalem apartment, UFO's, building a nation, lead characters each on own quest for purpose, relief from emptiness, fade to long hazy dissolve, cut, next action not yet on screen."

They stopped eating. Rivka said something in Hebrew. Naomi started applauding. The others joined her. It lasted just a moment then Rivka spoke. "I just said you are both so fortunate. To be able to act on impulse just like that."

"I've never been impulsive to this degree," said Audrey.

And Harry said, "Events gradually unwrapped. I just went along."

They all looked to Doctor Rheinhardt, as if he knew something they didn't. With a shrug and almost a smile he said, "It happens."

When coffee was served Professor Ben Dov returned to the rocky plateau. "There's a lesser known history regarding Masada. The early settlers of Eretz Yisrael came mainly from middle Europa. The leaders of the Zionist movement had a vision for this nation. Farmers. Fighters. Self sufficient. But in Poland, Germany, the Pale, they weren't allowed to own land. Some countries banned Jews from the military. Pogroms happened. They were overwhelmed, murdered. No legal recourse. Fearful. Subservient. Helpless. Israel's founders knew that centuries of humiliation must be transformed to a new spirit necessary to develop and defend the country. The reason Moses wandered in the desert for forty years when in just weeks they could have reached Canaan was because a population of slaves didn't have the attitude or ability to settle the land. A generation had to be skipped. So we needed a symbol. Just like in advertising Harry, we had to create an image of the new Israeli. Strength. Resolve. Independence. Count on no one but ourselves. Glorify ultimate personal sacrifice in protecting the land. Masada was perfect. General Yadin was brilliant in organizing the dig to reinforce the philosophy of, we fight to the end. The approach is necessary given that every country in the region would rejoice to see us massacred. What is not publicized though is that with close to a thousand suicides at Masada no remains have been discovered. About twenty skeletons were found but there is no evidence they were from the Zealot period, or even Jewish. It's true a siege took place, and as Josephus writes, the Romans built the ramp and fighting did occur. But where are at least some of the nine hundred and sixty skeletons? And there are some who feel that because suicide is forbidden in Jewish law, perhaps this should not be instilled as part of our national character. I disagree."

Audrey asked, "Does this mean it's possible they weren't the heroes Josephus describes? That maybe they surrendered and were brought to Rome as slaves?"

Rivka said, "It's known that suicides took place at other sieges of the time. Almost everything Josephus wrote regarding Masada has proven to be accurate. But he did defect to the Romans. He might have exaggerated events. Or felt conflicted. We just don't know." And Harry said, more to himself than the group, "We just don't know more than we do know."

The White House

The President of the United States stepped out of the shower not feeling any better. When they moved in he had the White House plumber turn up the pressure as high as it would go and install a showerhead that worked like an afterburner. In the evening the jet stream on his head, neck, and back would make most men lose consciousness but for him it washed away the tensions of the day. His life in politics had brought him to the top job because he could cajole with finesse, force comprises that usually tilted in his favor, and he married well. But this war in Vietnam was such a damn mess and getting worse that he just knew it was going to end his presidency. His Director of Central Intelligence had called a half hour ago and requested a meeting even though it was close to 11:00PM. The massive Turkish towel was somewhat of a comfort as it wrapped around his waist and touched his ankles like the grass skirt of a Hawaiian hula dancer. With drops of water clinging to his body hair, he tried to get comfortable in an easy chair in the sitting room off the bedroom. Charles Calhoun, whom the British Ambassador referred to as the President's manservant, said the Director was waiting outside and could he get them anything. "Decaf for me and ask the Director what he'd like." Even though the head of the CIA was a Harvard holdover from the previous administration, the President over time, surprisingly came to enjoy his company. In the beginning it was better than even money on Capitol Hill their backgrounds would bring out an unkind small town Southern brand of sarcasm from the leader of the free world. A hardscrabble country boy who started out as a teacher interacting with a model American aristocrat whose early years included Choate, Harvard, correct clubs, and a Social Register marriage. But he seemed to laugh honestly at the President's crude barnyard humor, didn't speak upper crust lockjaw, and he had served as an enlisted man in the Marines during the war. Additionally, the Commander in Chief decided he was god damn smart.

"Come in Reggie. If this is more bad news about Vietnam I'll have Charles put some bourbon in my decaf."

The Director didn't flinch that his boss was practically nude and still dripping from a shower. "No sir. This doesn't concern Southeast Asia."

"Sit yourself down Reggie. Did you tell Charles what you'd like?"

"Just a Coke sir."

"You look as worn out as I feel Reggie. This war is a disaster for the country. Those coffins rolling off the planes at Dover every day are bringing grief to too many families, too many towns. Walter Cronkite on TV broadcasting in front of helicopters delivering our boys to field hospitals all bloody and shot full of morphine is one damn sorry state of affairs. The Joint Chiefs don't have any good options. Just more troops. Every time that's announced there're more demonstrations in the streets. Kids burning draft cards. More troops. Bomb the shit out of the NVA. Napalm thatch hut villages. Get deeper into the rat hole." The White House steward knocked and came in with a tray he set down on a coffee table. "Thank you Charles. We'll help ourselves. We won't be needing anything else." The President leaned back in the chair crossing his legs and exposing his pubic area as if he was in a locker room at a men's club. "This job just ain't fun anymore Reggie. How's your daughter? She's starting her second year, isn't she? Is it Smith? Or Vassar? Sorry but I get them all confused." The Director of Central Intelligence really liked this man.

"It's Vassar Mr. President. And she's decided to major in Political Science."

"Tell her not to get into politics." After pouring cream in his coffee the President said, "Well I know you didn't come here at 11:00PM to listen to non-stop bitching about the god damn war. What's goin' on Reggie?"

"General Majeski has been sitting on some intel I thought you ought to know about."

The President put his cup down and said, "Majeski? That sumbitch is so dumb he couldn't figure how to pour piss out of a boot if the directions were written on the heel. What's on the Air Force's mind now?"

"It has to do with the Edwards Air Force Base meeting President Eisenhower had. The one that never took place Sir. General Majeski informs me they've asked for a second meeting. Naturally with you Sir. This is uncharted waters. For all of us."

The President stood up holding onto the towel around his waist and in a whisper said, "Shit" then went to his bedroom to put some clothes on.

Jerusalem

During the thank you's and goodbyes Rivka said she was driving close to the King David and could drop them. As Harry shook hands and got a hug from Naomi it was a true goodbye. With Audrey it felt as if she lived in the neighborhood and they'd talk in a couple of days or bump in to each other at the grocery. Doctor Rheinhardt looked sad, having known more than enough goodbyes in this life. He gave Harry a small wave and the door closed.

As Harry got in the back seat the Buick smelled new. Rivka said, "It's my father's. He may be financing a car importing business." Money too, thought Harry. The girls talked about the dig they'd be going to in the morning and he pictured himself in the air tensing up over the usual ambushes patiently waiting for him. Pre production meetings were the beginnings of making a campaign come to life. Looking at director's reels, getting bids, casting, deciding on locations, picking voice-overs, music, were all things he enjoyed. Getting a commercial to look like what was in your head required dominating decisions on every detail. Everybody had strong opinions and frequently the copywriters and art directors who thought the whole thing up would lose control. There were fatal duels over what appeared to be minor elements in the commercial, but losing the little ones could mean mediocrity. When somebody on the creative side consistently endured in these skirmishes and was right, they became known as stubborn and difficult but with that came respect. From the first pre production meeting to the final edit and sound mix, unsolicited opinions were like twelve gauge blasts of buckshot to the creators of the commercial. During filming there was a rule that only one agency person could speak to the director, and all suggestions had to be relayed through that one person. The rule applied to everyone on the set, including clients. While companies from Elkhardt to Detroit to Parsippany to Turin to Pittsburgh manufactured, extruded, stamped, cooked, processed, built, pumped, brewed, sewed, welded, mined, pickled, and painted products, the end product of advertising agencies is persuasion. Harry's awareness that the drive back to the hotel was the start of his return trip had ignited neurotransmitters that pulsed out these spasms of insight, causing his throat to constrict and neck to tighten. Layered on this x-ray was the undiagnosed Audrey condition. Will it linger, like a good movie or pass quickly like a hangover from one extra glass of Champagne? Not to forget it could be forever, like someone born with a wonderful smile. They're still talking, here's the hotel, and Rivka, this is ciao and shalom and see ya. Harry leaned over to the front seat and said, "Do you think you could teach me how to dismantle an Uzi?"

Rivka said, "I could, but you'll have to join the Israeli Defense Force."

He squeezed her shoulder and got out. Audrey said, "I'll be down here at 8:AM." He watched her drive away thinking of her thighs under an army issue skirt.

They were quiet in the lobby and the elevator and the walk down the hallway to the room. Both beds were turned down, the only light from a low lamp. They sat close on the small sofa, then he put his arm around her and they slouched back, hibernating in the dreamy shadowy space not afraid of wherever it was to go. Audrey played the first theme, a French horn solo. "I'm staying a few more days. Find out about the Masters program at Hebrew University. I feel comfortable here, the way I haven't in so long, maybe never. The people, the Masada attitude, it's so like my father. I'm going to call him tomorrow. Tell him where I am. The marriage. So much more. I want to walk around the university. The streets of Jerusalem. You and I. Do we let go? It's been only four days. There's so much in my heart reaching out to you. We were so irrational doing this. What was it Rivka said? She envies our impulsiveness. For so long I've been unable to face it. My marriage. My emptiness. Thank you God in heaven for impulsiveness. Going to graduate school here in Jerusalem, burying myself in history, our history, my father's side of the family history in this land, maybe touching things our ancestors held, it's already filling that sinkhole of hopelessness. God damn you Harry. Why us now?" There was a repressed spasm, a single sob as she burrowed in deeper, feeling to Harry like the recoil of a small caliber pistol, and an emotion that was new to him whispered that if they ever did make love he would want her to know he was joyfully giving her his love. Wow. Sex as an expression of love. What a concept. No post orgasm depression. So is it practical or neurotic that I wonder if that would last. He very gently massaged her head with his fingertips.

"We were impulsive, but we're also cautious. We aren't trying to control anything. Without really saying it we agreed to sail wherever the wind wanted us to go. Let's not jinx it. Of course there are words I'd like to say. Take you back with me tomorrow. Sculpt our clay. Your decisions concern your life before we happened. Our trip hasn't ended. We're traveling together. Wherever it is we're going. There's a poem, written at the turn of the century, can't remember who wrote it but it takes place on the ferry that used to go from lower Manhattan to Hoboken. It's about this guy who sees a girl on the ferry wearing a yellow dress and carrying a yellow parasol. He can't stop looking at her. He wants to embrace her. Their eyes meet only briefly, and it means nothing to her. The ferry docks in Hoboken. She goes her way and he goes his way. But for the rest of his life a day doesn't go by when he doesn't think of the girl in the yellow dress with the yellow parasol on the Hoboken ferry. You don't own a yellow dress, do you?"

"So sad, so beautiful. Yearning for a dream that will never be. Let's just have this moment in the dark and only time will tell if our dreams fuse."

In the morning they were in their separate beds. Harry woke in the middle of the night and controlled the need to slip in next to her, to feel her breathing and smell her body. This is like a two pack a day Camel's smoker trying to quit, is what he thought, and it was even worse than that because he knew she wouldn't ask him to leave. They hardly spoke as she got ready to meet Rivka and he packed to go to the airport. When there was nothing else for him to pack and it was almost eight o'clock they had a long kiss and neither of them wanted it to end.

I'll call when I decide what day I'm coming back, probably over the weekend." She left the room with a smile that was a Chinese menu of emotions. Harry was in solitary confinement for a couple of hours and then it was time to go.

Manhattan

The buildings of Manhattan stood solid and in sharp focus with an artist's fluffy sky as the El Al flight did a tourist's Circle Line loop waiting for traffic control's final instructions. The calming familiarity of home thought Harry, feeling an intimacy with all that was happening down there in the congestion and noise and unhealthy air. If the Long Island Expressway was being kind he could be in his apartment by 4:00PM, change into a suit and tie and be at the office by five. Customs checked his passport, commented "quick trip?" and minutes later he was in a cab with a back seat that had very little spring left. It was slow funneling into the Queens Midtown Tunnel and then the usual cabbie careening.

New York was baking in a late September heat wave and his apartment was humid with a stale coolness from five days of non-use. Call Marvin, he thought. Then shave, change, prepare for re-entry, cab uptown, decide how to handle questions about absence, brace for the expected unexpected. Call Marvin now.

Marvin Munchik was in Steve Lester's office when Marvin's secretary called Steve's secretary to say Harry was back and on the phone. "I'm on the way in Marv. Can you talk?"

Marvin said, "It's Harry, Steve. He'll be here in half an hour."

Harry said, "Guess you can't. Can we meet in my office before Steve?"

Marvin said, "Sounds great." And then to Steve so Harry could hear, "I'll give him a brief rundown on where we are and then let's all get together."

"Good plan Marvin. I'll have my girl assemble the troops. And tell Harry we all hope he fixed his personal problem."

"That's high empathy for Steve. See you in a few minutes." Harry shaved fast, changed clothes and knotted his tie on the way down to the street. As the taxi passed Union Square and then cut over to Park Avenue South, the entire cast of the past few days was in a slow dissolve, players waiting in the wings coming into clear focus. Because of one-way streets the cab let him out a block from the office and he pushed through the going home crowds and bus exhaust. As those who worked in the skyscrapers and shops of Manhattan ended their day, Harry was about to start his after ten hours in the air between worlds. The newsstand in the building had a stack of the *New York Post* and left over *New York Times*. A few familiar nods as the crowded elevator emptied and a solo ride up. The receptionist on his floor was blotting her lipstick preparing to leave and with a sincere smile said, "Welcome back Harry."

"You look even more beautiful at the end of the day Marsha." She blew him a kiss. His office door was open and it felt so familiar, as if he'd just come back from the men's room. Melancholy constricted his throat at the sight of a box of Kiddie Keds on the window vent combined with the view of the United Nations building and the East River a few blocks away.

"So you don't call, you don't write, what's an office wife to think," and Sandra's voice chased away the flash of sadness.

"At least I'm consistently insensitive Sandy," and a quick hug was more comforting than either had expected. "What's the mood around here?"

"Everybody's wondering where you've been mystery man, and you and Marvin are the creative geniuses of the month."

"Being AWOL is a court martial offence dickhead," as Marvin entered and slouched down on the sofa. "You can buy me a drink after the meeting and tell your lies. Steve is assembling the troops and we can keep them waiting in suspense for five more minutes. You look lousy. We've been looking at reels. Talking to a mechanical engineering company about building the robot, might be a glitch or two to work out. All of New York was spiritually crippled without you."

Sandra said, "Do you want me to stay?" and Harry said, "See you in the morning." As she left her look said, "I'm glad you're okay."

Like many art director-copywriter teams Harry and Marvin knew each other in ways that only co-workers who spend more time together than husbands and wives do, and they communicated in ways many spouses do not. "Burton Hays and Stevo showed the campaign to the CEO of the conglomerate that owns Keds and he announced that if we pull this sucker off there could be business from other divisions. Which turns the pressure cooker up to high steam. We've got Jennifer Corn assigned as the producer, so we can sleep easy on that end. This is going to be the most expensive commercial this client and the agency have ever produced."

"Well it beats writing statement stuffers for a bank account."

"We'd better get our asses to the assembled troops," said Marvin.

Paula sat in the conference room with one high heel shoe dangling off as usual, studying a research report, Steve and his assistant account exec, Val Massimo, were talking to Jennifer Corn and her nameless assistant, and when Harry and Marv walked in, Steve, with what appeared to be some level of sincerity said to Harry, "Hope you got things straightened out buddy."

"Thanks Steve. Appreciate your words." Steve acknowledged that man to man.

"Seems the legal department has some issue in the copy area and in the claims area. They won't allow us to say our robot walked across America unless we walk the little guy across America. That'll take forever and this sucker has to be on air real quick. It's a copy problem and nobody's better at solving something like this than you." Harry nodded thinking that was a complement-trap. "The lawyers just got to us on that one last night, so we're real glad you're back. The other problem is more technical. Lawyers tell us the networks and the competition could challenge our claim that the robot character is proving that Kiddie Keds last longer unless the action of his feet works exactly the way a human kid's feet work. We're talking ergonomically here and it's complicated. We're getting an orthopedic surgeon to consult with the company making our robot. This one could be a challenge, but there's no way in hell we ain't solving it. Hell of a lot at stake for everyone." Harry and Marvin both registered that the prospect of new business, especially from an existing client, created lust and madness in the neural workings of Madison Avenue. “Val wrote up all the details in an inter-office memo. Should be on your desk. Client’s visiting the agency one day next week for an update. The doctor and the mechanical guys will be here. Jennifer’s got all the director’s reels and we’ll give our recommendation for a production company. We all have thoughts on that so get up to speed Harry.”

Marvin controlled the impulse to say something sarcastic since that was infringing on creative department decision-making authority and its motto of don’t tread on me. Paula went over the executive summary of the final focus group report and as the meeting continued Harry’s jet lagged brain drifted back to the top of Masada, UFO’s landing on Earth, thinking the advertising business was a perfect occupation for those from other worlds. I’m back, he thought. Back.

It was just past 7:00PM when the meeting had run its course. Between hazy remissions Harry had solved the copy problem but would save it until end of day tomorrow. Steve was now thinking about the next train to Greenwich but he did give Harry a gentle male bonding punch in the shoulder and said, “If you want to talk about anything drop by any time tomorrow,” and with a wink meaning your personal problem started to leave the conference room feeling very much the man in charge.

Before he was out Marvin said, “Steve, to recognize that the soul of man is unknowable is the ultimate achievement of wisdom. It’s a concept with legs Steve, but I’m saving it.” Paula’s pen abruptly stopped as she looked up at Marvin admiringly and then swiveled her chair as she tried not to laugh, and Steve’s face went to blankness causing Harry to think of a frontal lobotomy.

With Grand Central back on his mind Steve said, “Bat it around Marv, see where it goes.” The conference room door closed and Paula allowed her laugh full expression as she found a Kleenex and said, “The Delphic Oracle.”

Marvin said, “Naw. I saw it on a menu in a Greek restaurant.”

The cocktail lounge at the Barclay Hotel was close to the office and the piano player usually went back and forth from classical to Cole Porter. They each ordered a Heineken and picked at a small bowl of high end mixed nuts with little chunks of an orange colored sugar dusted dried fruit not easily identified. Harry said, "I know what's on your pornographic and unprincipled mind Marvin so I'll start out by saying there was no penetration or frontal nudity."

Marvin feigned a heart attack and said, "All that distance, crossing oceans, airplane food, possibly being hijacked, for what?"

Harry's expression changed to thoughtful. "So much happened, it's a puzzle with the most important pieces missing. Something in a dream that disappears just when you're about to identify it. Nothing was planned, it was life in free form. We fail at controlling so much of what we think we need, and without trying to affect anything, something I didn't realize I was dying for is almost visible in the distance."

"Hasn't appeared? Going to appear?" asked Marvin.

"I'm probably whacked out," said Harry." "I wasn't getting the Mister Stability of the Year award when we left for Cleveland. Then going to Israel with this girl that popped her cork in the focus group, climbing to the top of Masada into a time machine going back two thousand years, meeting Israelis living lives that trivialize our own aspirations, experiencing tribal bonds, envying their sorrow." The piano segued from a Chopin sonata to a song whose lyrics repeated in Harry's head, "Let me know what June is like on Jupiter or Mars."

"Then having dinner in a restaurant with the head of the Department of Archaeology at Hebrew University and a psychiatrist who actually knew Freud and hearing them discuss flying saucers and Aliens from other worlds attacking Earth."

Marvin said, "I think you need a good night's sleep and a session with your shrink, but I just remembered something on the news the other day when we were in Texas about UFO's being reported in Nevada and Utah and Colorado all on the same day.

They even interviewed a couple who said something hovered over their car while driving through the desert at night and then it just disappeared. They didn't sound like weirdo's. Then some Air Force officer said it was experimental weather balloons. The couple sounded more convincing than the Air Force guy. But on much more important subjects, what about your lady friend?"

"She could be a fleeting enigma in time, or we could spend the rest of our lives in blissful union, that's the range. We've been intimate in all ways but physical. She's married, soon to be unmarried. Likely be going to graduate school in Israel. Layer upon layer of complexity. On the verge of maybe finding herself, lucky thing. Feels comfortable. Once this jet lag goes I'll wish she were here. Probably back over the weekend. That's the executive summary."

Marvin said, "Sounds perfect. Just about the right level of shakiness. You look more haunted by the minute. It's very becoming. This campaign we've got is one of the biggies. Everybody's talking about it, going to want a piece of it, put some of themselves into it. Claim some of it. We're into detail time. Until it's in the can we can't let our guard down. Tomorrow will test all our skill sets. Skill sets is such a putrid phrase. I want to hear more about your adventure, and your girl, but unless you want another beer I'm pretty wiped out myself. I'll get the check. I'm really glad you're back Harry. Don't fall asleep in the cab."

Jerusalem

Audrey was in front of the hotel a few minutes before eight. A few minutes after eight Rivka drove the Buick up to the entrance and a Moroccan doorman held the car door open. The girls started talking immediately and the three hour drive to Hazor would not seem long.

"Last night was a special evening for us. Thank you so much. Is Ehud your uncle on your mother's side or your father's?"

"Uncle Ehud is my mother's older brother. She had another brother, also older. He was in the paratroops but was killed in '56 in Suez. He was only married one month when he died. His wife was beautiful. She's in the States now, teaching biology at Hunter College. She comes back every summer. She hasn't remarried but she's had offers. She'll always be part of our family."

"Everybody we've met has someone close to them who was killed," said Audrey.

"It's part of who we are. I doubt it will ever stop completely. Neither spoke and then Audrey brightened. "I wish I had time to research Hazor."

As Rivka dealt with Jerusalem traffic and the near misses of Israeli driving she lit a cigarette steering through tight spots with one hand and the lighter in the other. "In Solomon's time, Hazor was ten times bigger than Jerusalem. It's in the upper Galilee and looks out over Lake Merom. The buildings and fortifications are similar to other tenth century B.C.E. cities, like Meggido and Gezer. There's a unique six chambered gate to the city and the administrative buildings were probably built under the same rulers as Meggido. The underground water collection system could sustain high urban populations. There was extensive agriculture, important trade routes, the usual stuff that cities grew from. There've been several excavations since 1955. Yigal, Professor Yadin, recently started the current one."

Audrey said, "I met him a few times during the Masada dig. He gave a couple of lectures to the volunteers. He'd never remember me but I had one conversation with him. I'd mentioned that our history in the U.S. goes back only four hundred years, and he said what would your Indians have to say about that? His expression seemed to say how sweet and naïve you American kids are. I don't think he was being condescending."

Rivka said, "There's no place for naiveté here. We wouldn't survive. We're cynical. Fatalistic. Maybe a little like your boyfriend?" Rivka was concentrating on driving so she didn't catch the blink of confusion on Audrey's face. In that flash she thought, boyfriend? I'm married. Then, but it's over. Then, Harry assumed to be her boyfriend. Then, can't remember when I've been linked to somebody called a boyfriend. Takes longer than five days to become a boyfriend. What is he? Will I wish he were here tonight? Tomorrow? Next week? Nothing but empty space for so long. Then a burst of possibilities. A piñata all my own. I will not get overwhelmed. It's all good. And I don't live every day with the possibility of someone I love getting killed. Who do I love anyway?

"What makes you think Harry is cynical and fatalistic Rivka?"

Rivka inhaled, the smoke came out her nostrils in two streams. "I don't know. Maybe I saw some Israeli in him. Doctor Rheinhardt would shrug and say 'it happens.' It happens. The way you met, came here, it could be a movie. When I got home last night I lay in bed and couldn't stop wondering if I could have done what you did. I finally fell asleep. Not knowing. What if he turned out to be dangerous, an escaped rapist but a good actor."

"I never thought he could be a rapist." Of course I wondered if I was bungling into a big mistake. But my life seemed like 360 degrees of mistakes. Both of us wore signs that said 'breakable.' I trusted him. When we act on impulse perhaps we've been preparing for years, but oblivious, so we call it impulse. And because I came to Israel with a breakable man I'd just met, I've decided to end my marriage, go to graduate school and possibly even move here. Forgive me if you hear a hysterical laugh." Both of them smiled.

"You seem so even Rivka. I know you want to finish your Master's when your active duty is over. Then maybe teach or do research. Anything else?"

Rivka shrugged. "Maybe write. Possibly museum work. I'm open. One thing at a time."

"Is there a man?"

Rivka got another cigarette. "Shlomo. He was thinking about staying in the Army. Engineers. He made captain. But his family real estate development business was also a possibility. Office buildings and shopping centers."

"What would you like him to do?"

Rivka concentrated on the highway and impassively said, "Shlomo was killed last year in the war." Slowly Audrey started heaving. Then sobbing and gasping. Her body shook and the tears made her face look like she'd been under a sprinkler. She put her head in her hands and moaned. Rivka watched the road as she put her arm around her.

Audrey thought compose yourself you soft little girl from Cleveland. I will never ever again feel sorry for myself. God give me just a few drops of their courage. Masada. I now get it. Her sounds of anguish powered down and coasted to a stop, but she kept her head in her hands, partly because of embarrassment. Eventually she looked up and accepted the brightness of day. "I'm sorry. I'm so sorry Rivka. It's just everyone we've met. So many tears. Dreams gone. Doctor Rheinhardt. His wife. His son. Your mother's brother. And you. Shlomo. Compulsory army service for teen-age girls. My mother's tweedy Wasp relatives are…" and half a sob, "why do they even come to mind, and my father, he's one of you, you'll see. Yigael is right. Sweet and naïve."

Rivka put her hand back on the steering wheel. "I think you may be one of us also."

Audrey wiped her eyes with a tissue, blew her nose, then said, "Thank you, but I don't think I qualify. I've never been threatened or persecuted or had to escape to a different country. I always felt safe and sure of my place. And I wasn't raised the way you were, knowing as a little girl I'd serve in the army, accepting that people I love might be killed by enemies all around us. As a child I went to dancing class, riding lessons, tennis. I never wondered if a bomb would be exploded in the Chagrin Valley Country Club by Palestinian terrorists. I've not been conditioned for fatalism. For Masada."

Rivka looked at Audrey. "It's not too late."

At about halfway they stopped for coffee and a sandwich and Audrey brought up Hazor again. "How long will the dig last?"

Rivka said, "It will continue for months. As long as there is funding. The search for the stuff that dead people left behind so we can figure out how they lived has a price tag. Doctor Yadin has a talent for procuring funding. He thinks they may find cuneiform tablets from a royal archive that could help us understand what life was like in Canaan up to the time of the Israelites. He believes the Jews destroyed Canaanite Hazor toward the end of the Bronze Age. He's found ashes that were three feet deep."

"When we found ashes at Masada we could see the flames and feel the fright and hear the Roman Legionnaires," said Audrey. "It was entering another life. The entire experience was another life. Awakened at 4:00AM, light breakfast and to the site, work as the sun came up, use a small brush to examine a whole room, entire buildings, eat another breakfast around nine, dig in the heat, the anticipation of coming upon something, a valuable find, valuable for understanding their existence, not being aware of the tiredness till early evening when someone would give a talk on the day's finds, then dinner, conversation with people from all over the world, and falling asleep on a cot in a tent, aching from the tiredness and dreaming of some great discovery the next day. The leaders of the dig, those who weren't going to leave in two or three weeks, from the University, the Israel Exploration Society, the museums, they knew geography, anthropology, history, sociology, architecture, ancient languages. I was on intellectual overload the entire time. I wonder if it would have been the same on a Mayan or Celtic dig instead of one in Israel. Probably not. Religion was never anything my parents thought about. Either the Episcopalian side or the Jewish side. From time to time my father would talk about his past in Germany, but until I was in college I knew very little, except that they were a very established well known industrialist family. I've seen framed photographs of a big house in Berlin and family members on a patio or riding in the park, but I know very few details. When he brought up what he did in the war and the meaning of Masada, I felt cheated that I didn't know more about relatives that were only images in a picture frame. The words anti-Semitism stood for aunts and uncles and cousins I never knew, never would know. Then I heard about the Masada excavation and nothing could stop me being part of it. It was transformative. Like these last few days."

As they left the restaurant two jeeps parked next to the Buick and Audrey noticed the friendly matter of fact acknowledgement from the young soldiers. She thought that whenever she passed soldiers in airports back home they were invisible. In the car Audrey said, "In the States you never see soldiers carrying their guns, but here it's all so casual. The way they're slung low over their shoulders so natural, so symbolic of Israel, so necessary." Rivka shrugged.

A couple of hours later they were at Hazor walking through the rubble of ancient buildings. The sunlight felt like a heat lamp too close, but didn't appear to affect any of the people working delicately with small digging implements and brushes. Rivka pointed to a group in the distance just sitting down at a table under a large umbrella and said, "There's Professor Yadin." As they approached there were waves and everybody seemed to know each other. Rivka made introductions. "Audrey was on the Masada dig."

"I'm sure you wouldn't remember me Professor, but I sat in on every one of your talks at the end of the day."

Yadin studied her face as if he was looking at an artifact. "The American that forgot the Indians inhabited her country for fifty thousand years before Columbus entered the picture." At that moment Audrey made her decision to move to Israel.

With mention of Masada the conversation switched to the ethics of using archaeology to further a particular ideology, such as suicide being the solution to maintaining one's honor. One of the people at the table was a Lutheran minister and bible scholar from Munich who was introduced as Reverend Kleinmetz. "The question requires specificity," he said.

"How exquisitely Teutonic," said the woman to Professor Yadin's right. Audrey noted her red hair and that she said it with a smile. Her khaki shorts and shirt covered a toned tan figure and Audrey wondered if she and Professor Yadin were sleeping together.

Reverend Kleinmetz smiled and said, "Ours is a rather specific language, but of course it's necessary for the new Israeli to be a patriot, a soldier, and that requires preparedness for the ultimate sacrifice. It's a nihilistic view, death as a way to preserve honor, but considering recent history it's a philosophy for self-preservation. General Yadin and I know each other well enough so I can be frank."

Yadin added, "As some of you may know, Reverend Kleinmetz was there for us during our War of Independence." Audrey heard her mother's quiet voice advising that relationships around this table were layered in complexity beyond her ability to even attempt understanding. Then her mother's voice faded into her own and she heard herself, as if broadcasting from a small speaker on top of the umbrella pole.

"Half of me, I mean my father's side of the family has a heritage in Germany dating back at least two centuries. They were a well known Jewish industrialist family, he left with some resources and married my mother who is from a prominent Episcopalian Cleveland family. I tell you that because I have a question which is late in coming and makes me feel embarrassed and naïve, but can anyone explain why there is anti-Semitism?" The words came out as if programmed in some part of her that just had a grand opening. Then it seemed as if her clothes had dissolved and she was the only one at the table totally nude. Audrey could hear the dry heat. So that's how heat sounds, she thought.

The red head was the first to say something. "Reverend

Kleinmetz? Specificity please."

The Lutheran clergyman bible scholar looked to Audrey seeing that she was flustered. "It's a centuries old question and will be studied centuries to come. I witnessed the disease unite Germany in madness. Friends, parishioners, family, were complicit. What I can tell you is that most of them felt righteous in their campaign to eradicate the Jews because in their souls they were on a crusade to eliminate evil in the world. The Jews were evil. The despisers of the Jews were criminals who in a righteous effort believed that banishing all that was evil in the world would automatically result in a better world. Anti-Semites possess a positive attitude and are committed to the propagation of Aryan humanity through removing evil. It's passed on through mother's milk."

The conversation was akin to asking why do I have brown hair. Again Audrey spoke. "But what did we do?" Saying the word "we" was an official stamp, reaffirming the decision she just made to live in Israel.

Professor Yadin moved the rudder to a different course. "Are you here on a study program?"

"I plan to be. I'm going to apply to the Graduate Program." Yadin said, "If you're a friend of Rivka's we wouldn't be allowed to turn you down." Audrey knew he was simply being charming but couldn't contain her blush. Then the talk shifted back to whatever they'd been discussing and she and Rivka excused themselves to explore Hazor.

It was well into dark when they left and on the drive back to Jerusalem they were friends with no secrets. Audrey decided to stay another day, then fly back, spend one night in New York with Harry, prepare for meeting with her husband, see parents, a lawyer, apply to Hebrew University. She was already making lists of things to do in preparation for her sky dive to a new Earth.

The White House

The Director of Central Intelligence stood when the President reappeared wearing an old pair of khakis and today's dress shirt not tucked in. "Sit down Reggie, it's just the two of us. What should I know?"

The Director opened his briefcase. "I had a hell of a time getting this file. The level of security is so high it doesn't even exist. I read some of it while being driven over here Sir. A meeting apparently took place with two of them, the Aliens, through the night of February 20th, 1954 at the Muroc Test Center in California. In addition to Ike were some others, Doctor Edwin Nourse, an advisor to Truman and the first Chairman of the Council of Economic Advisors from 1944 to 1953. And a Cardinal James Francis MacIntyre, Bishop of the Catholic Church in L.A. Also some Generals and there may have been a retired reporter from Hearst. The two Aliens were quite tall, had white hair, pale blue eyes and colorless lips. They could pass for being from one of the Nordic countries and easily disappear in a crowd. It states they communicated telepathically. The report emphasizes that our nuclear capability was of concern to them because it does something to time and space and negatively impacts extra-terrestrials on other planets. They communicated that we are overly aggressive with each other, use destructive violence and kill our own species to solve global issues. A treaty was offered stipulating that we were to eliminate our nuclear weapons in exchange for the Aliens teaching us to live in harmony. President Eisenhower rejected it.

"The press was curious as to Ike's disappearance for twenty-four hours and the cover story was he chipped a dental cap while eating fried chicken and had to have repair work done. His press secretary, Jim Haggerty, called an impromptu press conference to explain why the President was missing and a dentist that supposedly did the work was produced at some point. After the dentist died his wife was interviewed. She had no recollection of her husband having the honor of working on the President. White

House records show no dental work on Eisenhower in February of 1954."

The President paced, hands in his pockets, gazing at the design on the carpet. When he sat down the Director of Central Intelligence said, "There's more Sir. Another meeting was held at Hollman Air Force Base with terrestrials from another planetary system. They're referred to as The Greys because their skin looks like the belly of a lizard. They too wanted us to give up our nuclear capability in exchange for advanced technology. Additionally, we were to allow them to do experiments on cattle and some humans so they could test implanting procedures. They wouldn't harm the people, who would have no memory of the experiments. Negotiations ensued. We didn't agree to eliminate our nuclear weapons but a treaty was signed, specifying a very small quota of people to be abducted. In exchange we got some very advanced technology. It's referred to as the 1954 Greada Treaty but Congress knew nothing and it was never ratified, so it's unconstitutional. Besides, the Greys haven't adhered to their end of the Treaty as there is evidence many more people than agreed to have been experimented with."

The President started pacing again. "What do you think Reggie?"

"General Majeski and the Chairman of the Joint Chiefs are the only ones in the loop at this point. They feel the meeting should take place."

The President stopped pacing and firmly said, "I asked what you think."

"I agree with them. We've got to have the meeting. If I may Sir." The President stopped his pacing, "It doesn't get more bizarre than this."

The highest elected politician in the world walked to the window of his sitting room in the living quarters of the White House and stared at the black sky and dots of stars, "You're god damn right about that Reggie." He eventually turned from the window. The Director rose. With his arm around him walking him to the door, the President sighed, "How do we get in touch with them?"

"We don't Sir. They said they'd be back to us."

"As one public servant to another Reggie, I'm going to ask an off the record confidential question."

"Sir?"

"You scared?"

"You're god damn right about that Mr. President."

"Me too," and as the door closed he added, "Tell that pretty wife of yours hello."

After accepting the job as head of the Central Intelligence Agency Reginald C. Elkins insisted a certain retired Master Gunnery Sergeant from The United States Marine Corps be his main driver. They'd been in the Pacific together and any casual observer sensed the relationship went beyond senior government official and obscure government employee. He got in the front seat and said, "The President would have been a good man to have in our platoon."

A light was still on in the bedroom as the Director's car turned into the driveway. "Thanks Gunny. 0530. I know it's way over your shift time. I can have someone else," but before he finished the sentence his combat arms fellow Marine said, "Aye aye sir. 0530."

He turned the light on in the kitchen and for one moment felt safe hearing the sound of the refrigerator and seeing the toaster and Mix Master on the counter. Just an ordinary American kitchen, he thought, and tonight it has the same effect as a martini. The old Golden Retriever waddled in wagging its rear end in joyousness. He scratched her ears and remembered a Christmas puppy for his five year old daughter now away at college. His mind drifted. Could have been a history professor at a hard to get in university writing books about dead politicians and the wars they started. Wouldn't know about our government's lies for years. He opened the cupboard and found some Oreo cookies. Of course the Aliens are right. We on Earth shouldn't be accumulating thousands of nuclear weapons to solve our global differences.

"Would you like some milk with your cookies little boy?" His wife in light blue pajamas and barefoot looked even better than she did twenty years ago when they married.

"The Pres says to say hello to my pretty wife."

"Finish your cookie and come up to bed so your pretty wife can give you a back rub."

"But we hardly know each other," he said.

She started on his neck and before reaching his shoulders he was asleep, dreaming of little green Aliens doing acrobatics on the dome of a flying saucer parked in front of the White House. And then the alarm rang him in to a grey dawn.

Greenwich Village

Greenwich Village was Audrey's favorite part of New York. She couldn't sleep on the plane with her brain running like a semi-trailer truck with worn out brake pads speeding down a steep incline. The cab driver spoke with a Yiddish accent and as she paid she noticed a faded number tattooed on his arm. "Thank you lady," and she left a too large tip. Her clothes were near grungy from five days, and after a shower she hoped they could stroll through the Village and find a dress shop. She pushed a buzzer with his name on it and still hadn't decided anything. When she phoned from the airport their electrical currents were strong, but seemed to travel through different wiring, like using an adapter plug for foreign power systems. His apartment was on the second floor of a four-story townhouse and on the stairs she heard his door open and they met on the landing with a welcoming bear hug embrace.

"Give me your knapsack. Flight okay? Been thinking about you. You're finally here. Come in. I even dusted."

"Oh Harry," she said. "Let's take a minute and just look at each other. Before our crazy trip life was a closed spiritual box. I finally broke out and breathed some clean air. Uncorked the bottleneck. It's like a graduation. Decisions I was to frozen to make, frozen for years, felt the sun. Everything at last feels right."

"Come in. Let's sit down and look at each other sitting." After airports and recycled air on the plane, Audrey liked the way the apartment smelled and seemed to melt into its coziness sinking into the sofa. She breathed in and had a long exhale. "I'm sorry to be jabbering but I can't help it. There's just one glitch left and it's you. Us." Then enunciating each word separately she said, "What are we going to do?"

"You've got to learn to stop beating around the bush Audrey,"

"Would you make me some tea?"

"Lipton or green?"

"You decide."

As Audrey listened to sounds of making tea she examined the room searching for clues. Nice hi fi system, lots of records, books, TV on a shelf, dark wood shelves, Navaho design rug, two potted plants appear happy, magazines and newspapers seem current, pair of loafers sticking out from under the sofa. Passes, but just barely, the cleanliness test. Lacking a woman's magic wand.

"How about a chocolate covered graham cracker with the tea?" he said handing her a cup.

"My favorite. Bring the box. After we talk and I get showered let's take a walk and find a shop where I can buy a dress."

He sat down cross-legged on the rug facing her with his back against the old brick fireplace. "You go first," he said.

"Mmm. Good grahams. So the topic is, and I repeat, what are we going to do?"

And Harry said, "The topic is, what do we want to do?"

Audrey said, "We travel well together."

"Very well."

"What do we want to do?"

"Didn't I just say that?"

Their eyes were having fun. "Seriously, ever since you walked into the focus group room after I went into that raging breakdown we both knew our neuroses were a perfect match. Returning to Masada, the wonderful people we met, and you, all of it together, I'm ready to love life again. I've even stopped being scared about asking my husband for a divorce. I think he'll be relieved. Instead of 'what do we want to do,' what do you want to do Harry?"

"We're both cautious. We may have thought it but neither of us has yet said the most complicated word in the dictionary. I'll spell it out, coward that I am. L.o.v.e. I'd like to continue our journey. We allow the combination of you and I to grow roots. Nurture it under normal growing conditions. A little fertilizer. Some weeding. Plenty of sun. Natural growth. None of our choices are Hollywood endings. You move to Israel. I stay in New York. Have a long distance relationship. Hate that phrase. Sounds like we're in a pop psychology advice column. You'd get more involved in your life four thousand miles away. Same with me. Meet others. Pain. Gradually disengage. Or, you put the kebash on Israel. Move to New York. Big sacrifice. Resentment. Or, I go to Israel with you. Table career. Resentment."

"There's something else," said Audrey. "The first affair after a divorce isn't supposed to work out."

"There is that," said Harry. "And it's only been a week. We could simply let go and move on with whatever was to be before our trip. Of course there is the possibility we'd spend the rest of our lives wondering what might have been."

"Yes, the girl in the yellow dress on the Hoboken ferry."

"I wonder," said Harry, "how this very rational conversation would end if one of us said those three little words."

Audrey looked at Harry, looked out the window, looked at him again and said, "I think we care too much for each other to inscribe anything on jewelry after just a week."

"Maybe," said Harry, "it's not yet decision time. So far this rudderless ship has taken us to some magical ports. If we try to steer we could jinx it."

"That's what people do. Try to steer their lives. Goals. Could be we only know what they are once we attain them. Could it be the randomness of the last few days wasn't random at all?"

Harry said, "So if we put off making any decisions about you and me whatever happens will happen and that would be the goal we didn't know we had? I think that's what I meant, but it does sound like a cop out."

She got up from the sofa, walked over to him, kissed his head and said, "And now my shower."

They walked on Bleeker Street her arm comfortably in his, anonymous with the Sunday crowd in the Village. "What sort of shop are we looking for?" he asked.

"Remember, we're just drifting Harry. I'll know when I see it."

"You mean like pornography?"

"Exactly." They got to Sixth Avenue and drifted towards 14th Street, window shopping and people watching, joined in shared serenity. She gently pulled him to a shop window with light summery dresses on mannequins without heads. He sensed serious assessment, but whatever hormonal systems were activated soon diffused and she pushed on. A pizza shop tantalized with aromas of oregano and olive oil on warm baked dough. They aimlessly turned onto 12th Street going toward Fifth Avenue. Passing the New School for Social Research she tugged his arm toward the entrance. "My father once mentioned that a distant relative of his, a professor at Heidelberg, foresaw what was coming and he and some other academics decided to get out of Germany. Sometime in the 1920's they immigrated to New York and he was one of the founders of this school, originally called The University in Exile. They then turned on Fifth Avenue and just north of 13th Street was a more expensive dress shop and in one fluid movement the window display was approved and Harry found them inside. He sat down on a velvet covered stool knowing something out of the feminine mystique had just occurred. Audrey scanned the goods, made two selections, was shown the dressing room, and in what seemed like seconds reappeared wearing something casual and sophisticated. She assessed herself in the mirror, looked at him for reaction; he nodded yes feeling slightly intimidated by her stunning appearance. A repeat with the second dress, which she told the saleslady she'd wear, but buy both. As Harry observed her telling the saleslady to put her jeans and tee shirt in the bag with the other dress he saw his spread eagled body free falling as in a dream, an eternity of free fall into the thin air of intimacy. He figured if he could fight through the nausea it might really be good.

Then they were out on the street with her arm back in his as she handed him the shopping bag. "This is the first time I've seen you in a dress," he said.

"That sounds suggestive," she said.

"You do look rather tasty."

"Does that mean you'd like to eat me?"

"I suddenly do have hunger pangs."

"Now that you mention it," she said, "some dinner would be lovely."

"There's a little Italian restaurant a couple of blocks the other side of Washington Square."

Shirtless muscular shiny blacks were sitting around the fountain broadcasting loud waves of primal sexuality on the bongos, a girl in a colorful peasant skirt was strumming "This Land is Your Land" on the guitar to a group that hummed and softly sang, a kid in an N.Y.U. tee shirt was juggling, and a mime was making people laugh and feel sad. They exited the park onto MacDougal Street where marathon chess games drew a silent assortment of Village characters. Motorcycles roared and sirens screamed an urban symphony as tourists and locals bunched together passing darkened coffee houses advertising poetry readings. Everybody was there for the eccentricity. The restaurant was a few steps down, not yet crowded, pleasant and subdued. Harry said, "Chianti bottles with unlit candles and both waiters from Naples, what more could a kid from Cleveland ask for?"

As they were seated Audrey said, "I'm not going to have a meltdown if you tell me you take all your lady friends here," and Harry felt her sandal rub his calf.

"Only the seriously neurotic ones who look irresistible in clingy summer dresses and bare legs with sandals."

"Compliments will always give you wiggle room. Do you think we could start out with an iced double espresso?" The Neapolitan waiter overheard her as he handed them menus and smiled yes. "I think we ought to continue the conversation I avoided earlier by escaping to the shower."

"You're right. It only has the potential to affect the rest of our lives."

"Well, it truly does," with a getting down to business expression.

"Look," he said. "You get on a plane back to Cleveland tomorrow, deal with ending your marriage, wrap up that part of the Audrey story, say your goodbyes, might take a couple of months, and off you go. And tomorrow I show up at my office and give everything I've got to make this ad concept I haven't told you about come alive. Could be the award winning campaign of the year, big bucks, promotions, job offers. Everything people in my business covet. Could take a couple of months. We have memories of this wondrous week, bypass all the complications, and just fade out. We end it now. Very adult. That we've shared the same bedroom, even the same bed, and been abstinent, it's an overwhelming statement. All of America is getting liberated, most well adjusted narcissists would have fucked their brains out, and that we didn't seems okay. There was an almost moment, but the tenderness would have been violated. Never been there before Audrey. Some internal approval mechanism was activated. It seemed the noble thing. We were affirming that we care, honoring our potentiality. Does one of us have to trade personal growth in this life to fulfill what we could be together? Will it be a left brain or right brain decision?"

The iced espresso's arrived and the waiter saw they were a long way from ordering. Audrey concentrated on stirring two sugars into the espresso. The stirring continued, like a thirty-three and a third long playing record. She said, "The Vietnam war. Madness. Destruction. Ripping the soul of our country to shreds. But there will be a time when it becomes a non-issue. The next generation will not care. Nobody beyond historians is agonizing over World War One. When tomorrow you go to your office and I get on that plane it's very likely someday we will be a non-issue. Shouldn't we resolve this by tomorrow?" They tasted the iced espresso.

"Of course," said Harry, "we could talk out a resolution like the two intelligent beings we are, and then change our minds. Makes one confront the big unanswerable. Define our lives. How to feel good about ourselves. All the clichés. Purpose. Goals. Love. When I look at you I feel good. Why? Will it endure? Will we tire of each other? We haven't yet had a disagreement. We will. Conditions change. We have less than a week's knowledge of each other. Is that enough for one of us to give up other parts of our lives? When people think they're in love they sometimes do. In time there's respectable odds they may no longer be in love. Then what? Could be we're an exaggerated moment in time and our emotional states found temporary relief."

"Let's test how temporary," said Audrey, "and do nothing. Suspended animation. Tomorrow comes and *que sera*. If life becomes unbearable apart, that's our answer."

"And we'll always have Paris," said Harry.

"Who said that?" asked Audrey.

"Humphrey Bogart in *Casablanca*."

"It is the right decision, isn't it?"

They both laughed. Then Audrey said, "I'm suddenly ravenous. Shall we order?"

"Just one more question," said Harry. "Are you still interested in whether I'd like to eat you?"

"Why Harry, I'm a married woman."

The Ranch

The President and immediate family were taking a few days at the ranch over the Thanksgiving holiday. His announcement that he'd not be running for reelection had been a ten thousand-voltage jolt to the country, his party, even the inner circle. Vietnam had defeated him. The polls verified what his stomach told him. Ever since that speech his sense of humor had gone into remission. The First Lady worried he was spending more time alone. They discussed how the historians would treat him and both knew the war would overwhelm everything. Uncharacteristically he'd taken to long walks and was reading more. He was still CEO of the nation but secretly wished January 20th would come and the new President be sworn in. The Secret Service missed his country boy humor and remembered a couple of months back, at the ranch, when he allowed a few favorite reporters to follow as he drove a pickup across the range. Getting out to relieve himself one of the bolder reporters asked if the President wasn't concerned a rattlesnake might bite it off, and the President replied, "It is part rattlesnake."

After coffee and pecan pie on Thanksgiving Day the First Family, like millions of other Americans, was watching one of the many football games on TV. The President would have preferred the rivalry of high school teams in any small town to the major spectacles, and the *Washington Post* had his attention more than the screen. When a commercial came on he suddenly put the paper down and leaned forward. The scene was the Main Street of the type of town in which traditional high school football rivalries are the major news. A smiling mechanical robot about four feet high wearing a pair of red sneakers was waving to shopkeepers and cheering families like it was a Fourth of July parade. A long line of happy dancing five and six year olds with laughing applauding mothers and a couple of adorable cocker spaniels and labrador retrievers was merrily following him. The announcer enthusiastically explained that Kiddie Keds last longer than any other sneaker you can buy and to prove it Robbie the

Robot was skipping, hopping, and walking through cities and towns across our great land in the same pair and challenging any other shoe company to attempt this test. He went on to say Robbie's escapades would be in the news with additional announcements, so you can follow his progress, and to check your local paper to see if Robbie is coming to your town. The accompanying music got the President's feet tapping. The commercial ended in a crescendo of trumpets and cymbals and quick cuts of ecstatic faces and Robbie the Robot doing the two-step. The President sat back in his big cowhide easy chair and said, "Whoever the hell thought that one up is a god damn genius." The First Lady and the Secret Service were relieved to see a happier President for the rest of their time at the ranch.

The White House

On the Monday after Thanksgiving the Director of the CIA, the Secretary of State, and the Chairman of the Joint Chiefs with their number twos were in the Situation Room quietly awaiting the President. Decisions from years past that affected the destiny of the world hung in the air, and even these veteran defenders of the American way experienced spurts of fear and doubt simply by being present. They all stood as the President entered and sat down once he was seated. He started the meeting by saying, "I hope everyone enjoyed the holiday with your families. These jobs we have hardly allow enough family time. I imagine what's left of the turkey population is glad this weekend has passed." They all laughed in the way subordinates respond to the boss's jokes. Many in the room were relieved the President seemed less stressed. "I spoke with some of you from Air Force One yesterday on this situation. I needn't remind you this is above Top Secret. Where exactly are we?"

The Chairman of the Joint Chiefs began. "They asked if it would be convenient to have the meeting on Thursday. Their approach is very diplomatic. They appear to have an understanding of our protocols. They even provided a list of topics for discussion. We determined the best location for the meeting..."

The President cut him off. "Will you share the topics please?"

"Yes Sir. They've observed that the Twentieth Century thus far has been the most violent and destructive since life began on Earth and predict it will get worse. They plan to discuss that. They are concerned that our way of life is causing the world to be dirtied by pollution that is rapidly increasing and almost unstoppable under current conditions. They say it will not only eventually diminish life as we know it on Earth, but will affect other planetary systems. Next. They want to understand human and animal reproduction from conception to birth. Finally sir, they want the bodies back."

The President quietly said, "What bodies?"

"The 1947 UFO crash at Roswell, New Mexico. We retrieved four Alien bodies. They've been asked by beings on some other planet to request their return."

The President said, "You mean as long as they're in the neighborhood why not ask?"

"Yes Sir. They referred to the bodies as the Dimuins. Might translate as diminutive."

The President addressed the Director of Central Intelligence. "Where might these Dimuins be Reggie?"

"We located them at Area 51. They're refrigerated."

"They've been on ice since 1947?" asked the President.

"We don't know how long they've been at Area 51. We haven't been able to locate much documentation."

The President looked at the Secretary of State. "I imagine our experience with intergalactic diplomacy is somewhat limited, Madam Secretary."

"We are developing a plan working with the Joint Chiefs and Central Intelligence. As Reggie indicated, we can't find much of a paper trail on the 1947 occurrence."

The Chairman of the Joint Chiefs spoke. "Their technology is far advanced from anything we have Sir, so we start at a disadvantage. We're collaborating as to what might be our negotiating strengths. We're going into this at a disadvantage."

The President addressed the General. "Didn't mean to cut you off before Stan. Where is this going to take place?" General Stanislas Mijeski knew the President blamed him in part for the Vietnam disaster and was pleased he called him Stan. "We've determined the best location is Area 51. It's secure. Nobody can get within miles. The press shouldn't be an issue, and the bodies are there."

"You should be aware the Aliens suggested Area 51," added the Director of Intelligence. "They indicated they possessed some familiarity with the location. Although that concerns us, nothing can be done. And we do agree it is a good location." They waited for a response. The silence was uncomfortable. Nobody fidgeted. Their gaze was locked on him.

Finally the President spoke. "Could this be a trap? Is there danger of an attack? Can our defensive systems handle this? I recall a speech General MacArthur delivered after Truman fired him in which he said all the nations on Earth will have to join forces for the next world war and it will be fought intergalactically, or some such words."

The Secretary of State said, "We've each been in contact with our counterparts in the Soviet Union. If missiles are fired they mustn't think they're under attack. They've been surprisingly cooperative. They appear to be amenable to sharing their own experiences in this, uh, new category of concern, for possible collaboration."

"Nobody can really speculate intelligently what this end game could be," said the President.

"This is obviously new to us," said Reggie. We know there are nine planets in our solar system, including Pluto. Beyond that there's endless vastness with probably millions of planets. The feeling amongst people who study this is that it's not unlikely some have conditions that can sustain life. At the risk of being labeled a whacko, nobody at an MIT or Harvard is willing to go on record beyond that."

The Chairman of the Joint Chiefs said, "We'll have specific details for Thursday completed late tomorrow, or whenever you can see us Sir."

Looking calm and in-charge, the President said, "I'll be available late tomorrow. I know you've got people standing by for what would have been my 7:00AM briefing on the war. Have them come in."

Area 51

On Thursday the most secure room four levels underground at Area 51 contained a meeting that had been going on for forty-five minutes. The military commander and top civilian in charge were the only permanent base personnel in the chain of command with knowledge that this meeting had been scheduled, and they were not privy to anything else. The President and his party had arrived on a military plane with fighter jet escort rather than Air Force One. The Secret Service informed the base security detail in individual interviews that if they recognized any in the party it would be a federal offence with permanent consequences should they reveal what or who they observed. As the oddest top-secret experimental aircraft were taking off and landing at all hours it wasn't particularly noteworthy when a cylindrical shaped vehicle executed a vertical descent before any radar picked it up. A windowless panel truck transported its occupants to a remote building. It was agreed the meeting would not be tape recorded, but note taking was permitted. The President, the Secretary of State, the Chairman of the Joint Chiefs of Staff and the Director of Central Intelligence had arrived as well prepared as was possible, given so little precedent or past history. All of them had climbed to the top of their professional lives by assessing risks, and nurturing their vanity and extreme sense of confidence, being addicted to situations involving a vulnerability that most people can't tolerate, for the sheer thrill of triumphing. Their emotional conditioning was comparable to the fitness of thoroughbred race horses.

They began the meeting wired as Olympians at the start, so it was astonishing they not only didn't feel threatened by their guests, but rather experienced an odd sort of familial kinship in their presence. With a genuine collegiality they listened as it was explained that the twentieth century is the bloodiest since humanity appeared on Earth, that it took only a few years during World War II to murder hundreds of millions. They were made to understand that with Earth's nuclear arsenal the same mass slaughter would be practically instantaneous. The Aliens were emphatic in pointing out that industrial development, much of which grew to facilitate international aggressiveness as well as provide treasure for the most ruthless few, is poisoning all things natural on Earth. Man's exponential procreation and tendencies for settling international disagreements by killing will result in quantum levels of unchecked pollutants, eventually affecting other worlds. One of those worlds closest to Earth will be diseased first. They implied that because man is a danger to himself and the Dimuins, they hoped to infuse us with a love response and defuse our knee jerk response of inflicting pain and killing one another. They emphasized governments on our planet have caused billions of young children and old women, conscripted men, humans at every stage of life to be bombed, burned, gassed, shot, starved, stabbed and strangled for reasons now irrelevant, now forgotten.

The Secretary of State saw they were not being lectured. The Chairman of the Joint Chiefs perceived no hostility. The Director of Central Intelligence didn't detect a covert message. The President knew that he, more than anyone, was the star example and their message had validity. It was he who ordered the bombing of the Ho Chi Minh trail network of supply routes. He even participated in selecting areas to be bombed, making it a more personal act. Of course it was a strategic military decision in a time of war, but was private vengeance also in play? When it was clear that an army of rice eating peasants in black pajamas from a third world country was whipping the ass of the United States of America, waves of futility practically paralyzed him. The realization that he wasn't courageous enough to end it was crippling. These seemingly nice folks from some science fiction world were stirring up his own pot of turmoil.

Stanislas Mijeski pulled up from his fighter ace past a day over France when he delivered close air support to soldiers on the ground in Normandy and one of his bombs was off the mark blowing up a farmhouse instead of a German tank. On his second pass he destroyed the tank, but saw the bodies and parts of bodies of the family that had been in the house. From that memory he skipped to a period after the war when he decided to make the army his career and discovered he was gifted in the complicated and sometimes odious art of internal military politics, which rewarded him with a star on his second tour at the Pentagon.

The Secretary of State was thinking ahead to what the United States' position should be on whatever it was they were yet to negotiate, which was not at all clear. At the same time her brain switched on a channel to thirty years ago when as an embassy employee in Austria she'd met Adolph Hitler at a reception for the Olympics and thought he was charming. She swallowed a gulp of self-loathing, and a millisecond of a question as to why now?

The head of the CIA was on guard for any subtle message that might imply a threat but so far nothing. He did experience an undisciplined flash to the future, envisioning his college age daughter in ten years with a solid marriage and an infant child, wondering if what was occurring at the moment would harm the imaginary grandchild. His mind ran on as he considered how the very congenial emissaries from a distant aura as yet not admissible by our standards of science were now speculating that human biology while not identical to their own might be similar. He considered that should we ever consent to a limited experimentation in procreation, the outcomes could be useful. The poisoning of both our atmospheres is of graver consequence than war as a solution to failed diplomacy. As the nation on Earth with the most advanced destructive arsenals, could not the will to soften the nature of humankind be also within our capabilities? Should we request it, he thought, they will guide us. Although we are of different worlds, there are life forms an incalculable distance beyond their own planet that deem us to be of a similar genus.

His mind rambled as he thought of those among us with evil tendencies who quest for power, control, unlimited wealth, who circumvent the moral imperatives, the rules, who make the rules and commit legal murder through war. Moral authority or personal will power does not suppress the impulse for destruction...they would deny they are responsible for evil...to avert ultimate suicide we must understand what happiness is...we must achieve joy...as we teach our children to read we must teach them to breathe...we are alive because we breathe. The universe breathes through us. Cosmic oneness will come through our breath. Their mission on Earth is to let us know they are there, not to be feared, and will return when they must.

Two windowless vans approached the cylindrical space vehicle at the most isolated section of Area 51. Four body bags were placed near the entrance to the craft and as the vans drove off two figures appeared and together with the figures that exited the second van, the body bags were placed in the cylindrical object. In moments and without any sound it hovered off the ground and then ascended at a speed that caused it to vanish in seconds. Nothing at all registered on the technologically superior Area 51 radar system.

The President said it would be nice if they had some coffee and General Mijeski pushed a button to relay the request. In less than a minute a steward entered escorted by a security guard, with a coffee service for four, and quickly left not looking at anyone. They helped themselves, the President gesturing for the only lady in the room to go first. The ordinary sounds of spoons being stirred in cups and the familiar aroma of coffee relaxed them back to a reality that validated the last couple of hours had actually occurred. Their silence was a show of respect for the processing taking place in each of them. The President had big hands, but held the cup delicately, obviously liking the coffee and aware no one would speak until he said something. "I don't want anyone to hear about this meeting, even those who know it took place. Tell them that is a Presidential directive. No leaks. Nothing in our experience prepared us for what we just heard. The public isn't prepared. I've never given it much thought. Some day something like this was going to happen, but not on my watch. After the new President is sworn in he must be informed.

Helen, as Secretary of State you take the lead in preparing a document for him. A short one. Work with Reggie and Stan. I find it difficult to disagree with anything we just heard. The twentieth century is the bloodiest since recorded time. I want to hear what you think but I do tend to trust them. At this time I can't imagine any reason they'd be less than sincere. I believe we've just received a neighborly warning with long-term implications. Unless you believe in miracles what they conveyed must happen. Will it though? Learning to love thy neighbor, not kill him when we can't agree could be impossible. On the other hand, the last couple of hours would also have seemed impossible. Our first priority though is to protect and defend. We've got to look at all options Stan. Collaboration with the other world powers Helen? Vietnam complicates everything. I'm thinking there is an action we can take immediately though, for the American people. Let's continue this on the flight back to Washington."

The military plane they flew in had a private bedroom and office for the President, including a communications system equal to Air Force One. It was used mainly when the President's agenda was not for the press to know. Even those at the highest levels of government and the military were ignorant of its existence. A small group of those who usually accompany the President was in the plane wondering what was going on, having been briefed with few facts. Knowing this was above top secret they asked no questions. The President acknowledged them, removed his jacket and loosened his tie, signaling it was okay for the others to get comfortable for the four hour flight. When they reached thirty thousand feet a Navy steward brought sandwiches and soft drinks.

General Mijeski poured a Coke, hesitated, and then said, "Their mention of breathing has me stumped."

The head of the CIA said, "A couple of years ago I was at a dinner party with my counterpart in India. It was very informal at his house and afterwards it was just the two of us in his library and the subject of Tibet came up. Then we got on mysticism and he mentioned Prana. As I now recall, he explained Prana is a cosmic force that flows through the universe, through our bodies, and provides us with intelligence, radiance, and joy. We inhale Prana through our breath. He said that when we are aware of our breathing, deeply inhale and exhale, our bodies get rejuvenated and our minds feel pleasure and rejoice. Prana can lead to good health and a state of bliss. It's more complicated than just learning how to breath, but I do recall saying wouldn't it be wonderful if all the bad guys in the world were required to practice Prana. He said, and I believe he was serious, Prana is for the good guys as well."

The President said, "Teach everybody on the planet how to breathe and we get world peace and clean air. I wouldn't put that in the briefing document for the new Commander in Chief." He cleared his throat. "I do have a concern however, that we can do something about. Someday this encounter could become public knowledge. I hope it doesn't, but it could. And they did indicate they were going to return. Could be six months. Could be twenty-five years. Can you imagine the hysteria, the mass panic? The immediate impulse would be for a military response. The population would feel helpless. Doomsday. It is our duty to prepare the American people for that inevitability. It must be subtle. Gradual. There's nothing more I can do about the war in Vietnam. This has the potential to be a bigger disaster. Unless we take action now."

In recent months as the President exhausted all options for the war, his reclusiveness and uneven behavior had caused some, including those on the plane, to wonder about his stability. Although he now appeared himself again they were conscious of his moods, and the Secretary of State was on alert. She spoke for all of them. "Where are you going with this?"

"Advertising. It gets politicians elected. It persuades people to buy billions of dollars worth of any kind of product you wish to name." The President clasped his hands together. "We need a brilliant advertising campaign that will prepare the American public for the possibility of extraterrestrial beings conceivably being a reality. They need to be educated that Aliens are not that much different than we are. They are not our enemies. We welcome them as friends. We've got to get ahead of this. Control it. If it ever gets out that their President and advisors met with Aliens from unidentified planets, half the country will think the world is coming to an end and the other half will think we've gone mental."

The plane was in some mild turbulence that meshed with the human turbulence caused by the President's words. The CIA chief was wishing he'd wake up soon in bed next to his wife. The Chairman of the Joint Chiefs was thinking all of this was above his pay grade. The Secretary of State reasoned the President's idea might not be that off the mark. She was the first to respond. "Several questions to analyze. Can we do this without including others in the administration? Can we find a budget without going through Congress? What if the Aliens don't return for decades? Will the effort be for naught?"

General Majeski said, "They could turn hostile. These past couple of hours could be a set-up. We should be prepared for all eventualities. That means bringing in more people."

The Director of Central Intelligence looked at the President. "This will be very tricky advertising to develop. We'll have to find the right people. But what if Stan is right and they do have another agenda?"

As the President rose to go to his office he said, "All good questions. Work it out.

And Reggie, there's a commercial on the television right now. It's for some kid's sneakers. It has a robot in it wearing a pair of little red sneakers. Whoever thought that one up is a genius at understanding the soul of America. Have somebody talk to them." As the President was entering his private quarters he turned his head, "Washington's fingerprints are nowhere near this." The door closed.

The State Department

During World War II it was not uncommon for Washington to suggest movie scripts to Hollywood that would dramatize America's fighting spirit and portray sacrifice for the war effort as noble and patriotic. *Sands of Iwo Jima* starring John Wayne and *Battle Cry* with Van Heflin did just that. With this in mind Meyer Kaminsky, Executive Vice President of MGM Studios was asked to meet with—summoned some might say— Billy Jessup, Chief of Staff to the Secretary of State, and Louis Mortimer, Ph.D., from Central Intelligence. Billy Jessup had been a Congressman from a rural district in Texas on the Foreign Relations Committee. Louis Mortimer had a doctorate from Yale in 19th century German history. After Hitler invaded Poland, the new Ph.D. was recruited as an analyst with a small group that in time became the OSS. After the war he decided to have a career in government. Meyer Kaminsky, from Brooklyn, had been in the second wave on D-Day, earned two bronze stars and a purple heart, and in 1946 got a job in Hollywood at a talent agency. Jessup started the meeting. "Thank you for coming so quickly Mr. Kaminsky. We hope it wasn't too inconvenient."

"When the government calls, besides, I was in New York when my secretary got to me with your message." Meyer thought it could be his imagination but the way Jessup pronounced Kaminsky had the tone of a football jock all in good fun teasing the class book worm. Jessup continued. "Everything we discuss in this meeting is understood to be classified."

Louis Mortimer said, "Before we begin let me say that my wife and I loved your last movie. It should win an Academy Award."

"Thank you. Looks like it could be in the running."

Jessup resumed. "As I'm sure you know, occasionally, in the national interest we come to Hollywood with suggestions for a movie theme. What we're going to discuss is not a script but a classified assignment with Central Intelligence. Typical CIA," he chuckled, "so it's deliberately complicated as hell, and this is just a piece of the whole. Very few, including the Secretary's Chief of Staff have the complete picture. Perhaps you ought to take it from here Louis."

"This program has multiple parts," began Mortimer. "This is just one piece having to do with the missile race we're in with the Soviet Union. We want them to deduce that we have missile technology so far ahead of where they are that they become intimidated and softened up for any upcoming negotiations. We know there have been, and brace yourself, UFO crashes in Siberia, and intelligence tells us they are convinced Aliens from other worlds are observing life on Earth and may even be among us. A fringe but influential group in the KGB suspects these Aliens have been in contact with us and that we've made a treaty with them stipulating they will provide us with weapons technology ahead of anything that exists on Earth. We'd like to reinforce that suspicion."

There was a pause and Meyer Kaminsky said, "Sounds like a movie script."

"That's just part of it. We want to have an advertising agency create a campaign that will appear to the Soviets as if we, the government that is, are preparing America for eventual contact with life from other worlds. But it must appear to the KGB that Washington is attempting to mask any involvement. That should reinforce their suspicion." Mortimer paused making sure Kaminsky was following. "Additionally, the ad agency should in no way suspect we're orchestrating any of this."

"I'm waiting," said Kaminsky.

"We'd like you to go to the ad firm and tell them you're looking at a script in which the President of the United States is losing his mind and is convinced Aliens will be landing on Earth, and so has commercials produced that lay the groundwork for such a possibility in order to avoid panic in the streets. And MGM would like to give them the assignment of creating those commercials. Tell them your scriptwriters are not advertising professionals and that's why you're coming to them."

Meyer Kaminsky's reputation in the movie business was that of someone able to analyze complex problems quickly, and create calmness when the big egos got hysterical. They were waiting for his response but he'd let them wait. Something about their proposition wasn't totally kosher but it eluded him. It was imaginative, audacious, sneaky. He was a patriot but not a "my country right or wrong" person. It actually would make for an intriguing movie. He would do it but just now was going to be a bit circumspect. Think time was over. "A couple of questions. You're asking me to deceive the ad firm. I don't like doing that. Can I be assured this will never go public?"

A moment of impatience and Jessup simply answered "Yes."

"How do we handle the advertising agency's compensation?"

Jessup spoke again. "We've thought of that. Billing is through MGM and we'll reimburse you through a C.I.A. company."

"Timing?"

"We'd like to see their ideas in a couple of weeks. If we like what we see we'll get an okay from the next level up and give the go ahead."

"Who will my contact be?"

"The Secretary of State asked me to stay on top of this, but Mr. Mortimer, if I'm unavailable."

"One more question. Do either of you truly believe beings from other worlds might be among us?" He said it quietly and not as a challenge, but with a demeanor they saw could be formidable.

Jessup spoke first. "Research tells us at least fifty percent of Americans would say we're not alone in the universe."

"And what would you say?"

With theatrical reserve Jessup said, "I would say I just don't know."

"Mr. Mortimer?"

Mortimer was enjoying this. "They are amongst us, and most are at the highest levels of government."

Kaminsky laughed. Jessup didn't.

"Seriously." Mortimer closed his eyes. "I would say anything in this world is possible, including that."

Jessup started to stand and said, "There's an ad firm in New York called Black and White Advertising."

"I've heard of them," said Kaminsky.

"There's a Harry Lang and a Marvin Munchik that work there. We'd like for them to get this assignment." Kaminsky and Mortimer also got up. Jessup extended his hand. "It's been a great pleasure meeting you Mister Kaminsky." Meyer Kaminsky shook hands with a hard grip. He did fifty pushups and fifty sit-ups first thing every morning.

"My pleasure Mister Jessup."

Louis Mortimer winked at Meyer Kaminsky. "Call me if I can be of help."

Manhattan

The CEO of the Black and White agency had joined the firm when those of a certain background who didn't go into law or banking or investments could find acceptable employment in advertising. His grandfather had been at Princeton with Mister White's father, and the agency back then was as white shoe as any old-line law firm. He'd been with Black and White for close to forty years and with some detachment watched as the influence in the industry shifted from account service and country club relationships to the creative effectiveness of the ads. It started at a competitor called Doyle Dane Bernbach and an ad for Volkswagen with a simple shot of the little car and a headline that said "Think Small." Detroit was selling tanks with tail fins that gave America what was termed a boulevard ride. The transformation came to be known as The Creative Revolution. Clients now expected campaigns to not merely increase sales but to dramatically increase sales. It didn't hurt if they also won awards and became topics of popular culture. Those with the talent and discipline to generate the great concepts became international stars. It was a cliché that an Italian art director and a Jewish copywriter working as a team generated a high percentage of the award winners. Madison Avenue's Renaissance artists and tortured novelists collaborating to create masterpieces that enrich America's corporate ego and profit margins.

The Chairman of Black and White was in his office waiting for the famous movie producer Meyer Kaminsky to arrive, and simultaneously thinking it might be time to pass the torch on to the next generation at Black and White. Although he'd met with new business prospects hundreds of times and the old enthusiasm was no longer pumping hard, he was curious as to what MGM had in mind. Mister Kaminsky had said he was impressed with their Kiddie Keds commercial and asked if Harry Lang and Marvin Munchik could be available for the meeting. Their campaign had resulted in an unimaginable volume of publicity for the agency and the creative team. The star system certainly had its advantages, but some of the older generation were uncomfortable adapting to it. Although Lang and Munchik received enviable jumps in compensation and were even offered contracts by Black and White, there was always the possibility some competing agency would steal them. They were to be kept happy. When two days ago Lucy Doyle, the Chairman's secretary, called asking them to attend a meeting in the Chairman's office with somebody from MGM Studios, Marvin said to Harry, "Oh goodie. We'll get to see his framed photos of the 1939 Newport to Bermuda race." They tried to get more information and even called Lucy back. Miss Doyle, the second employee to be hired during the flapper era when the agency was founded said all she knew was that Meyer Kaminsky was coming. That was enough. This was big time Hollywood, not some provincial martini drinking narrowly focused executive from Cincinnati or Detroit. Marvin said, "My only original thought is that it's a mystery wrapped in an enigma." Steve Lester even strolled into Harry's office probing for information. He put his feet up on the coffee table, clipped a couple of nails and casually rambled away, eventually casting his Kaminsky bait. When he surmised Harry was as curious as everybody else the clipping stopped and the visit ended.

"A Constantine Stanislavski performance in nonchalance," Harry commented as Steve disappeared down the hall.

The elevator from the twenty-eighth to the thirty-fourth floor was a supersonic flight to a different country. No rubber cement fumes. No pushpins. No voices or music or posters in offices. Instead a designer ambience of beige carpeting, wheat colored walls, oil paintings, polished antique reproductions, quietude. It was leaving a Kandinsky painting and entering an Andrew Wyeth. Agency gossip had it that forty years ago Mister Black and Lucy Doyle had an affair that ended the week of the 1929 stock market crash. Lucy never married and continued to be in love with him to the present day. Some thought Lucy's apartment on Beekman Place was part of the affair settlement. At the annual company Christmas party she never disappointed by consuming too many whiskey sours and somebody from the creative department usually got her home in a cab. Lucy and the creatives enjoyed what she referred to as a very special relationship.

The elevator door closed behind them. Harry straightened his tie saying, "Try not to be the cynical wise ass that you are Marv." Lucy saw two of her favorites come through the reception area and got up with a smile to show them into the Chairman's office.

"Mister Kaminsky arrived a few minutes ago," and she knocked on the door opening it at the same time, closing it when the Chairman got up.

"Meet one of the hottest creative teams in New York Mr. Kaminsky." He rose from the sofa taking their measure and shaking hands in one motion. The Chairman put his arms around both of them conveying the sort of affection typical in corporate life with employees that produce significant profit. As they got comfortable around the oversized butler tray coffee table the Chairman said, "Mr. Kaminsky was just saying he flew in from L.A. last night."

"Please call me Meyer. I've often thought that making TV commercials and making movies require similar talents. The best of both are art forms that touch emotions. It's a lot harder to do in thirty seconds compared to two hours. You have my admiration."

Marvin leaned forward in the easy chair, "I plan to quote you on that, but depending on how many scenes a movie has would mean each scene is like shooting a commercial. Might take us three years to produce that many."

Harry said, "Of course if you're here to ask us to come to Hollywood and make a movie we'll have to get a leave of absence."

The Chairman chuckled and snorted at the same time saying, "They're loved and needed right here. Besides, these two New Yorkers would never get used to L.A."

Kaminsky said, "You may be right. I'm a New Yorker, Brooklyn, and it took a long time."

Harry raised his hand as if in class. "Brooklyn also."

Marvin said, “Bronx.”

The Chairman felt like he was crashing the party and decided not to say Old Westbury. Marvin was getting comfortable. “Two generations back, before the Bronx, it was Kiev.”

Kaminsky said, “Bialystok.”

Harry said, “Some little mud-hole village deep in the Pale.”

Once again the Chairman held back knowing 1693, Salem, Massachusetts, would make him the interloper in his own office.

Kaminsky sat back saying, “Let me tell you why I’m here gentlemen, and please respect that this is confidential. Should we decide to proceed you’ll all be asked to sign a confidentiality agreement. We’re about to begin filming a movie in which the President of the United States is behaving erratically and his cabinet and those closest to him fear he’s on the verge of a breakdown. What is particularly worrisome is that he is convinced Aliens from another planet are going to be landing on Earth. But he thinks they mean us no harm. The President is positive they are biologically close to what we are, and are friendly. He has discussed this with his closest advisors and they all agree, possibly humoring him. Should it happen they say, there will be mass panic. The President feels it’s his responsibility as Commander in Chief to inform the citizens they are not under attack. The way in which he wants to do this is by having TV commercials produced that convince citizens that should ever beings from a distant world arrive they are not to be feared.” Kaminsky stopped. “Questions?”

“We’re with you so far,” said Harry.

“Our screen writers are not ad men and can’t seem to come up with subtle and believable commercials. A suggestion was made we go to the professionals, an advertising agency. So the assignment is to create an ad campaign convincing America that we are not alone in the universe, and if Aliens ever visit us, we will accept them as friendly Aliens, almost as distant cousins. And because of your robot campaign we’d like to give you the assignment.”

The Chairman cleared his throat as if about to deliver a

speech. “We’re certainly flattered that MGM Studios would select Black and White Advertising for this very exciting project.”

Without appearing rude Kaminsky ignored him and looked to Harry and Marv. “Reaction?”

Harry said, “It’s not impossible something like that could actually happen.” Kaminsky sat up straight. Harry continued. “Not long ago I was with some intelligent accomplished people who believe there really could have been a UFO crash in 1947 in Roswell, New Mexico. The government says no way, but who knows?”

Kaminsky said, “I seem to remember something about that. I suppose anything is possible.”

Marvin spoke to Harry. “What if, as we’re coming up with ideas we fool ourselves into thinking it is for real? Could sharpen our thinking.”

Kaminsky noticed Harry gazing to something within. He said, “I’d like to see something in ten days. Possible?” Marvin said, “If the Lord made heaven and Earth in seven we ought to come up with something just as innovative in ten.”

“I know we selected the right team for this. Any questions call me direct.” And then to the Chairman, “Send me whatever your usual agreement is.”

As they got up to leave Marvin said, “Meyer, come over here and see these wonderful photos of the 1939 Newport to Bermuda race.”

Back in Marvin’s office Harry reclined on a giant size leather cushion that was a whimsical substitute for a chair. Marvin was at his drawing board doodling as they talked. “Is it odd that somebody as high up as Meyer Kaminsky would be the one to come by the agency?” Marvin was intent on his doodling as Harry went on. “He did say his screen writers were stumped and was emphatic this must be kept confidential. Why confidential? It does sound like a great story line for a movie. Our real president is so fucked up he’d be perfect for the part. Ten days to convince America that if Aliens drop in we should bring out the good china.

This is undoubtedly one weird fucking assignment."

Marvin said, "Thank you for sharing your stream of consciousness thoughts." He stopped doodling. "If I were an Alien I'd get out of my space ship, look around at what's happening on Earth, get back in and go home."

Harry said, "That could be a commercial. It would show everyone they're smarter than we are. But it has to be subtle. That's a good thing because I sure as hell don't know what they look like."

And so the creative process begins, conversation seemingly leading nowhere, verbalizing, drawing free form, catalytic energies eventually sculpted into persuasiveness that moves Americans to wherever it is the client wants them to go. At five o'clock Harry looked at his watch. "Gotta wrap it up pretty soon. Appointment with the incredible shrinking man at six."

"I'm going to hang in for a while," said Marvin without looking up. "See you in the morning."

Doctor Weinstein's office was on Central Park West and for three years twice a week Harry used the cab ride across town as a slow dissolve to whatever subconscious surprises might emerge to clear the haze. The doorman and he usually had a blink of eye contact, the elevator opened directly into Doctor Weinstein's apartment and a small waiting room. A few minutes with *Travel and Leisure* magazine, previous patient exits, again no eye contact. Harry enters low lit office, Doctor Weinstein asks how are you, Harry removes jacket, loosens tie, and lies down on sofa which looks like a copy of one in pictures of Sigmund Freud's office. Sometimes there is a blankness of words in the analyst's cave. Other times, like this session, a geyser of unpredictability. "Met with Meyer Kaminsky today. He's originally from Brooklyn. Does the same trust happen when people say they're from Des Moines? Brooklyn is just different. It's not Ebbets Field or Coney Island or, I don't know, Prospect Park. It's deeper than familiar landmarks. I think it comes from Cossacks on horseback chasing our grandparents. Or it's the Yiddish accents and working in the garment district? Just stating 'I'm from Brooklyn' to someone else who's from Brooklyn, I don't know what I mean, it's like sharing a life raft." Harry stopped talking. The psychiatrist said nothing. Harry listened to the hum of the room. It wasn't too bad just lying there, but then he thought, I'm paying for this. These are expensive pauses. But the pauses are also part of whatever the hell I'm doing here. "Why am I here?"

Another silence, then Doctor Weinstein spoke. "Why are you here?"

Eventually Harry said, "Because I'm fucking miserable. I shouldn't be. I've got a career. I'm making money." Another jammed up psychoanalytical blackout and Doctor Weinstein said, "What else?"

"Audrey is gone. The week we were together could have been the beginning. Our talk was spontaneous. We wanted to know more. Have more. She could come just so close. I respected her. She was married and her morality made me ache. I've brought it up before. It's all so evasive. Was it really her studies and my career that stopped us? Or were we both scared shitless to give happiness a chance and needed an out? Maybe that's why I'm here. We didn't make love. Haven't had sex with anyone since she left."

Another long psychoanalytic drift, then Harry said, "Doctor Weinstein, why is it with Audrey I just said 'we didn't make love' and with other women it's 'I haven't had sex?' "

Doctor Weinstein said, "That's very good Harry. Any thoughts?"

"Wish something funny would come out of all this. I can't seem to focus on one single issue today. Let's see. There's Brooklyn heritage. Kaminsky bonding. Audrey. Too frozen to pursue each other. Hardly any angst at throwing her a kiss goodbye. And I haven't even gotten to the Aliens."

Doctor Weinstein said, "Let's back up to Audrey."

"I'd rather talk of Aliens, but here's one perfect for the shrink's couch. One night in Israel as I listened to her breathing in bed I fantasized about all the positions we could try and then the thought occurred that sex could actually be an expression of love. Eureka! We never did it but I thought it's okay. Then I felt melancholy."

"How do you feel now?"

"Melancholy, which is why I want to talk about Aliens. I think it's important. First in Israel. And now here." Harry ignored Doctor Weinstein's silence. "MGM is doing a movie in which the President is losing his marbles and convinced that Aliens are coming to Earth, but they're friendly Aliens and he wants to avert mass panic by having commercials produced that subtly communicate if Aliens pop in not to worry. They are friendly Aliens. So Kaminsky asked us to come up with the commercials to be in the movie. And by coincidence when I was in Israel I met a psychiatrist who believed that a UFO actually did crash in Roswell, New Mexico in 1947. A lot of people think it's not impossible." After a long stretch of quiet Harry said, "What do you think?"

Doctor Weinstein said, "I suppose it's not impossible. I'd like to hear more about Audrey."

Harry went in to a long Freudian paraglide. As he was thinking there wasn't much to say the words began. "She was amenable. Nothing strained. No demands from her, or me. Neither of us needed to control the moment. She was unsettled. A woman between life's phases. Sometimes strong with opinions. But also fragile. A beautiful strong vulnerable woman. Her vulnerability was appealing." A sudden halt. Then turning to look at Doctor Weinstein, "Could it be her vulnerability made me feel needed? I've turned her off, but talking about her, envisioning her, I think I want to see her. Mustn't block out that her archaeology and my work were more important than a shot at happily ever after. Neither of us demanded...anything."

Doctor Weinstein said, "Can you go deeper? Is there something here that's not apparent?"

"If anybody can suck it out of me it's what I'm paying you for." More silence ticked away then Harry said, "When I was about six years old I was in the bathroom taking a six year's old crap when my mother barged in with the plumber to look at some pipes. Never knocked, never apologized or even acknowledged I was there. I didn't exist. When they left I felt pissed and embarrassed and demeaned. I should have told her to go take a flying fuck. Next time I'm in West Palm I'm going to do it. I'm going to crash her condo meeting and say, 'Mom, go take a flying fuck.' So what would be the extreme opposite kind of childhood? If I were raised by English nannies I'd probably be a British faggot with crooked teeth and a picture perfect family, living a secret life as a cross dresser. Audrey where are you?" Harry was aware his breathing changed to a livelier tempo. "I saw Audrey as she is. There was respect. For what she is. When my mother walked in on her six year old on the pot respect died. So do I spend forever grasping at respect? I see Audrey as she is. She looked inside of me as I am. Understood. And respected. Effortless two way respect. That's a god damn good deal. Wouldn't you say?"

"I would say."

"So if we just figured out why I'm lying here wrapped in misery there are still the Aliens. The movie seems plausible. I wonder if there were hard evidence that other worlds are observing us and planning to make themselves known, what would change? Would all the nations on planet Earth join hands in peace? Would our differences matter? Would we still be ready to kill for oil, for territory, religion, or profit? Their technology would make ours appear to be at the cave drawing level. Would we maintain our dignity? What if everybody on Earth suddenly felt like an invisible six year old taking a crap? There's something about this assignment I can't put my finger on. Kaminsky didn't say anything specific to arouse suspicion."

Nothingness in the room as Harry's memory sifted through every moment of the meeting searching for a missed nuance. Then very slowly, as if talking in his sleep he said, "Mothers often can tell what their children are feeling. Siblings and twins and husbands and wives do get on the same frequency, even at a distance. Could it be Meyer Kaminsky was involuntarily broadcasting a signal I picked up, and although I can't interpret it the waves are saying you ought to know there's something else going on here? It sometimes happens. Like when Audrey went berserk in the focus group and everybody froze. Even though she couldn't see through the one-way mirror was she sending a message that said, 'Harry, get your ass in here because we are entwined and the spiritual script indicates we're taking a trip'? This sort of thing is blown off by labeling it intuition, or gut feel. Don't you experience it with patients, hearing their words before they're spoken? Have you ever had a new patient walk in and before they sit down you've got them diagnosed, know how long they'll stay in treatment, and predict outcome?"

Doctor Weinstien replied, "There are theories that telepathy in humans is a vestige of archaic communication between people before readily intelligible forms evolved, at which time telepathy was left deep in the human subconscious. Under certain conditions, different in different people, the archaic can get activated, or so the theory goes. There have been experiments with latent precognition, but nothing has been proven. It's an interesting area of study. Some say that because it can't be proven scientifically doesn't mean it's not possible."

Doctor Weinstein started to get up. "We've gone over. We'll continue on Thursday. Next time bring me a dream."

Harry decided to walk awhile before getting a cab. He was on the park side of Central Park West heading into the gusty chill coming from the south. Thanksgiving was past and Christmas rolling in. He left Doctor Weinstein's office feeling sad and incomplete, thinking the gloom of the season was just another layer to push through. It was beyond dusk and the gothic like apartment towers on the other side of the street broadcast a warm yellow glow from windows in a checkerboard pattern up to the most expensive penthouses on top. Many of those apartments had large living rooms with working fireplaces and he pictured families sprawled out on rugs reading and discussing their upcoming Christmas skiing vacations, sending him into a spasm of aloneness and an impulse to call Audrey in Jerusalem. But he wasn't sure what to say. They'd both agreed the best decision for now was no decision. He noticed that his instant replays of their week together resulted in a smile. Smile on my face, sadness in my stomach.

At Columbus Circle where he planned to get a cab he decided to keep walking. Left on Central Park South and over to Fifth Avenue where the department store Christmas displays were dazzling. He knew the window dressers sketched out their designs in July when they viewed the new winter fashions while the city sizzled and steamed. He turned his collar up and moved in sync with the crowds, shoppers in from the suburbs, out of towners enjoying the city action, Manhattanites focused on their destinations, dinner dates, lovers. Below 42nd street the intensity was less so and he could quicken his pace. At 34th street he hailed a taxi and when they got below Fourteenth Street some of his loneliness skipped out. In his apartment he poured a glass of orange juice, changed in to Levis and a turtle neck, slouched on the sofa with a pad and started thinking of commercials that would prepare the good citizens of the U.S. of A. to greet Aliens with flowers and marching bands. Later he would get a burger at the White Horse bar. The thought of phoning Audrey in Jerusalem was somewhere back on Central Park West.

Hollywood

Hank Wood had been Barry Goldwater's Chief of Staff for seven years. In 1964 when Goldwater lost the Presidential election Wood decided to leave the battlefield of national politics and start making some money. It took two years before he found his new career as head of public relations for MGM Studios. His knowledge of how the media operates and his Washington contacts were substantial qualifications and he happily adapted to life in Hollywood. Besides, his relatives from Arizona much preferred tours of the back lots at MGM to those of Congress.

The valet parker at Trader Vic's greeted him by name and the maître d' told him Mister Kaminsky was at the usual table. His childhood on a small cattle ranch followed by Arizona State contrasted to Meyer's in Flatbush and attendance at N.Y.U., but both enjoyed stories of their different Americas. When they'd first met at a political fundraiser there was easiness between them. Kaminsky had answered his questions concerning the movie business and the conversation was not strained or empty. As they were leaving Hank Wood asked if he could stop by next time he was in L.A., which he did two months later. Not long after he was renting a house in the Hollywood Hills.

Neither of them ordered anything alcoholic and after conversation regarding publicity for MGM's potential Academy Award contender, Meyer shifted the conversation to Senator Goldwater. "I've heard rumors the Senator has a more than casual interest in UFO's and was wondering what you might be able to tell me."

Surprised at the question Hank asked, "Something to do with a script?"

"It's a project I'm involved with and I'm curious what the inside scuttlebutt might be. You've probably heard things during your years in Senator Goldwater's office." Hank was thinking there's a reason for his vagueness, which I will respect. And I can't recall anyone ever saying you're not to talk about this. I do wonder what this is about, and he can tell I'm wondering.

Meyer said, "If you're accused of treason count on me for a letter of reference."

"If you'll also pay my bail I'll tell you everything I know." They both smiled, the usual warmth not having cooled.

"So tell already."

"Barry knew something happened in July of 1947 near Roswell Army Air Force Base. Even though he's a two star general in the Air Force Reserve and a United States Senator, he couldn't get anybody in high places to confirm anything. Butch Blanchard, General Blanchard that is, was a friend of Barry's and commander of the base during whatever happened. That morning he went public with a statement that a flying disc, UFO, crashed on a ranch near Corona, New Mexico. That afternoon he retracted. The Senator knew they muzzled Blanchard. Later he heard they had recovered four Alien bodies that were in a special room at Wright-Patterson and he wanted to see them. He called his good buddy General Curtis LeMay, four star and Chairman of the Joint Chiefs. LeMay was mute. Barry was persistent. LeMay lost his temper and advised Barry he was never to bring it up again. Rumor was LeMay chewed his ass good. When the Senator reminded him he was on the Select Committee of Intelligence, the Four Star told the Two Star to go to hell. I think it affected their relationship permanently. Barry once confided that during the war he wanted to be a fighter pilot and fly P-47 Thunderbolts but instead they had him delivering aircraft to different combat areas. Never quite got over that. He did get checked out in a SR-71 Blackbird, which is an impressive accomplishment and he was proud of that. The two of us were once on the train from D.C. to Philadelphia and I forget how it came up, but he mentioned his friend Senator Russell from Georgia was on a train somewhere in Russia and saw what he swore was a flying saucer a few hundred yards away flying level with the train. A Lieutenant Colonel from our embassy was with him and also saw it. I asked if he believed it and his answer was that some at the highest levels of the Pentagon don't refute that Alien races have made contact. Nobody ever speaks on record. The Senator said an underground government exists and is calling the shots. As you said Meyer, there are always rumors. I believe the Air Force deliberately sends out misinformation. There's interagency secrecy. The C.I.A. and F.B.I. don't talk. The military branches are competitive. Nobody knows what the N.S.A. has. Congress is so far out of the loop they could be convening in Siberia."

Meyer said, "You and the Senator do talk from time to time. Anything mentioned lately?"

"It's been a couple of months. If you like I can snoop around with some friends in Washington."

"Could you do it soon?"

"I'll start this afternoon."

Meyer knew Hank was thinking this might not have anything to do with the movies. "Thanks Hank." The thanks meant for not asking questions.

Driving back to MGM Hank was thinking that Washington taught him there are moments when it's prudent to keep questions to yourself. Some questions are never asked. Meyer didn't talk around issues, like most of the pols he knew. The ability to avoid a question by switching subjects midway through the answer was Politics 101. Goldwater flunked. Maybe that's why he did so poorly in the election. And why Hank stayed with him for seven years despite unease with some of his positions. Hollywood tilted more to the left. Hank was a couple of clicks right of center. Meyer a couple left. If both were in Congress there would be easy compromise. Washington and L.A. shared a never-ending bumper crop of big egos. Duplicity was a draw. Hank had decided that Hollywood style mendacity was like a pure stream, and Washington's a polluted river. In Washington the double crossing was camouflaged by concern for the public good. Hollywood has no moral high ground. It's accepted for what it is. Ego. Money. Sex. When Senators and Congressmen have big houses with swimming pools and staff they keep it quiet. With movie stars and Hollywood producers it's a stop for tourist buses. The shame is in living simply. He'd been to parties at the castles of the monarchs of Washington, and the palaces of the sultans of

Hollywood. The message on their faces was the same. All this is mine because I am dominant. I outsmart those I compete against. When necessary I have destroyed them. I am shrewd. I am powerful. All this is mine because I earned it. I deserve it. You have been chosen to be here to admire these riches. Do admire me. Don't fuck with me. That's what Hank Wood saw on their faces beneath the mask of a gracious engaged host. The exceptions were those whose grandfathers or great grandfathers made it and passed it down and were raised with it and had no need to make anything of it. Those usually were the thoughtful politicians. Hadn't yet come across a Hollywood version of that species.

Two days later Hank called Meyer to get together. Meyer said he was meeting someone at the Polo Lounge at seven and could he be there at six? The Polo Lounge in the Beverly Hills Hotel vibrated Hollywood. Mercedes, Cadillacs and Porsches lined up to get parked, engines running but the cars empty because everyone was too important to wait. On some days the staff that parked these cars could make in tips what a dentist to the stars earns. The room itself was usually crowded with an A list of screenwriters, producers, agents, publicists, actors, the royalty responsible for Saturday night at the movies.

As he entered Hank noticed Lee Marvin at the bar with two exotically stunning Oriental women, and saw Meyer being seated at a table for two against the wall. He'd been around long enough to attract a wave or two as he joined Meyer.

With a parody of a Brooklyn shrug Meyer said, "So already?"

"So already you never know what you'll get 'till you ask. I may have learned more than we'd both want to know. My sources let on that Senator Goldwater has recently gotten back to fishing for U.F.O intelligence. Seems there's whispering in Congress that the President has been uncharacteristically reclusive. Some have concerns about his emotional condition. Gossip says a psychiatrist has been coming to the White House. His utter failure to resolve Vietnam may have finally caused him to go a little soft. Considering there are so many different agendas and players you never know who or what to believe. Hang on though Meyer. It gets better. Or worse. Barry's heard the President is concerned that Aliens are coming to Planet Earth. Yup Aliens. If it's true, meaning if the President is having a breakdown and is worried about civilizations from other galaxies making contact, some in Congress might like to see him relieved. Even with just a couple of months left. That's beyond calamitous."

It was unusual for Meyer's inner circuitry to signal his brain anger and fear before a reasoned assessment, but there it was. Reflexive memory and a flash of the ramp on the landing craft splashing down and being helplessly seasick and petrified as his platoon faced the waves and mud and dead Americans and German armament at Normandy twenty-four years before.

He sipped his ice water. "There's more," said Hank. "My source says it could all be true. The President flipping out. Aliens. She says Barry hopes none of this leaks. Even if it's all rumors can you imagine the upheaval? Not only with us but around the world. It's insane just talking about it."

Meyer emptied the glass of water. "You haven't spoken to the Senator?"

"Not lately." Meyer admired Hank for holding his questions. He hoped some day he could tell all. His unease back at the State Department now clarified. The deception wasn't on the Russians. It was on him. And the ad agency. He'd put his anger aside and concentrate on the bigger issue. Someone in government, maybe the President, has intelligence that beings from another planet are going to appear on Earth. And legitimately wants to prepare America for that inevitability. It's understandable they're fearful of revealing anything to the populace, including me, until the possibility has been tested, accepted. So what do I do, if anything? Take notes Meyer. Really could be a movie.

"Can I assume that since people are speculating about this in Washington there'd be no harm done if I mentioned some of it to others?"

Hank watched Meyer thinking. He almost asked, but held it.

"Correct assumption. Nothing's confirmed, and rumors are consumed like chocolate soufflé in Washington."

"I'm on the red-eye to New York tomorrow. Couple of days of meetings. Back after the weekend. And once again Hank, thank you."

Jerusalem

Audrey loved Israel. She loved Hebrew University. She loved that her divorce was proceeding without rancor. She loved living with Rivka and her parents until deciding on an apartment. She loved the prospect of studying archaeology when the new semester began. She loved now. Her plans didn't go beyond getting her Master's degree. Rivka's father was away on business more than he was home, frequently to London and New York. She and Audrey had confided much to each other and late one night over hot chocolate in the kitchen it came out she thought her father might have an occasional affair. It was said not as an accusation, and when Audrey raised her eyebrows Rivka shrugged, "Successful men seem to generate excess testosterone. The nicer ones may fight the urge, succumb, feel remorse, but they're helpless."

Audrey said, "If you loved the man would you still be so philosophical?"

"Of course not." They clinked their hot chocolate mugs.

"My divorce is almost final and I hardly think of him. If he had an affair I might be jealous for a minute, and then hope he's enjoying himself."

Rivka said, "What about Harry?"

"For now he's a dangling participle and we agreed to leave it that way."

In her throaty voice Rivka said, "I don't know dangling participle."

Audrey laughed. "It means we were both too chicken shit to commit."

"That I know."

"We had one week. We were like a lawn mower that needed one more pull to start. Neither of us pulled. I do think about that week though. He's so sweet."

Rivka said, "Puppies are sweet. Halava is sweet."

"Is there something wrong with sweet?"

"Not if you want a puppy."

"I don't want a husband. I'm getting rid of one. Right now digging up ancient lives, learning a new language, just being here, I feel so good about all of it. Who needs a husband?"

Rivka said, "Since Shlomo was killed I feel the same way. Doctor Rheinhardt said mourning would last a long time. He knows. I almost forgot. I'm meeting him for coffee tomorrow. There's a café near the hospital. He asked if you were free to join us. Something on his mind."

It was just past the lunchtime noise, a couple of young doctors in scrubs looked at Audrey and Rivka with interest, then resumed their conversation. Doctor Rheinhardt arrived at the same time, both girls gave him a hug, Rivka lit a cigarette, and Audrey saw his face was skeletal. Conversation about nothing much and then Doctor Rheinhardt said, "A young woman, a first year medical student, is the only relative of a rich aunt in New York who died and left her a considerable amount of money. The law firm in New York thought it would be wise for her to show up in person for all the legalities and decide what to do with the contents of the aunt's apartment which include antiques and artwork, all part of the inheritance. She knows no one in New York and asked if I knew somebody trustworthy she could call upon. She's very capable, having spent six years in Army Intelligence, but wants someone not with the law firm to help her through it all. Just be there. Dinner. That sort of thing. I thought of Harry."

Audrey took a moment. "He'd be perfect. Would you like me to call, or I can give you his number." She would have gladly spoken to Harry but was surprised at her gratitude when Doctor Rheinhardt said he would.

"I may have his number with me," and as she got her address book out said, "When is she leaving?"

"They'd like her in New York Saturday. She's leaving Friday."

"That's tomorrow," said Rivka. "Who is she?"

"Shoshana Blime. Old French family. They owned a chain of pharmacies. Her parents emigrated in 1932. Her uncles bought her father out when they left. The Nazis deported the whole family in 1943. Auschwitz. Shoshana thought she'd make the army a career, but then decided on medicine. Worked for Ariel her last couple of years and he called your uncle, who called me about medical school. She's going to be an excellent physician."

Rivka glanced at Audrey. "Harry is so sweet. He won't mind at all."

"Doctor Rheinhardt, Stefan," Audrey said, "have you not been feeling well? You're looking tired."

He took off his glasses and rubbed his eyes. "A touch of the flu. Long hours. You're thoughtful to ask Audrey." Looking at his watch and getting up said, "I'll see if I can reach Harry right now. Then I have a patient. Shoshana will be relieved. Give your aunt and uncle my regards," and he moved like a man struggling with a mathematical equation.

"Something's working on him, and it's not the flu," said Audrey. "Should we be worried?"

"I'll call Uncle Ehud."

Manhattan

When Harry answered the phone and heard the Israeli accent he thought it must be Audrey, but the operator said it was Doctor Rheinhardt calling. Of course he'd be happy to meet Shoshana Blime and help her through the next few days. The law firm had booked her into the Gramercy Park Hotel and she'd be expecting his call. Doctor Rheinhardt's voice stirred up a blended soup of elation, reassurance, affirmation, and a yearning for courage. When they clicked off the week in Israel was an unreality, something he'd read in a book. He was hoping it would come up next session with Doctor Weinstein when the phone rang again. It was Meyer Kaminsky saying he'd be in New York Friday and would like to get together with him and Marvin. Harry said that would be great and immediately called Marvin because they hadn't yet come up with anything to present. Marvin said, "Oh fuck."

Harry replied, "Can't dispute that" and wrapped the cord from the receiver around his neck. He hung up, got unwrapped, and said, "Oh fuck."

Meyer suggested The Player's Club off Gramercy Park at 6:00PM, and in the cab Harry told Marvin he'd been asked to baby-sit someone from Israel for a few days and she was staying down the street at the Gramercy Park Hotel. Her plane supposedly landed late afternoon and he'd left a message to expect a call around 8:00PM. Marvin's response was, "We still haven't figured out what to tell Meyer."

"I suppose we could start with the truth."

"You mean admit these two hot shots been coming up dry?"

The cab stopped in front of the townhouse that had been converted to a club for the theatre arts set. "It's not that bleak Marv. We probably have about a dozen concepts. It's just we hate every one of them." As they paid the driver Meyer's cab pulled up behind and the greetings could have been between cousins. Entering the building Meyer said, "It's away from midtown and usually pretty peaceful." There were just a few in the bar and as they sat down somebody trying to be discrete gestured toward Meyer and mouthed his name to the woman with him.

"If you've been wondering about our progress, we have too" said Marvin.

"Yes. I am. Not being an ad guy, if it were me I'd be staring at that blank page in the typewriter with a brain just as blank."

Harry said, "You're not far off. You might say it's a professional challenge."

Marvin interrupted, "It's one challenging freakin' professional challenge. We do have some concepts, and we can talk them. Some may be good, but we hate them all."

Meyer laughed. "I could tell immediately you were perfect for the job."

Harry said, "Up till now I was sure we could create advertising that would sell anything that was for sale. Anything. And as Marv said, we do have some campaign ideas, but if this were not a movie, if it were reality and I was the President's media advisor, I'd tell him to forget advertising, come up with the speech of the century, go on TV and come clean. I'd consider changing the script Meyer. Have the ad agency or somebody he listens to request a meeting and convince him advertising ain't gonna do it and the President needs the balls for straight talk to the people. Could be a scene with devastating dramatic tension. A catharsis for the President. Just as your script writers aren't ad people, I'm not a script writer, but if it were the real deal that's the way to go."

Marvin said, "That sounded good Har. Did you know you were going to say that?"

"The thought didn't occur until the words spewed out."

As Meyer was deciding what to do with this very intelligent advice Marvin said, "Who is the sponsor?"

Meyer got it immediately as Marvin explained. "Every campaign has a logo. This movie President wants to keep the government out of it. So as far as the consumer goes, who's paying to advise America Aliens are on their way and they're really very nice? Is there anything about that in the script? We thought about coming up with a fake NGO. Americans for Intergalactic Love, or The National Association for the Advancement of Cooperation with Pluto."

I don't want to lie, thought Meyer, especially to these two, but here goes. "The basic premise for the film is sound, but there are still some glitches we're working on. It's like *Casablanca*. One of the greatest movies of all time was being written as they were shooting. They didn't know how to end it until they were at the end. You'd be surprised how that sometimes happens." Simultaneously his conscience was saying you're lying for the government, but your shame refuses to recognize that. A lie is a lie is a lie. And here's an extra blast of shame for lying to two very sincere guys. This is not you Meyer. With what you learned from Hank and now this you're getting sucked into a murky pit. Louis Mortimer. Call him.

"I did read that about *Casablanca*," said Harry. "Anyway, one concept we developed opens on a vote being taken at the United Nations. Camera pans from one representative to another, each country voting yes. Different nationalities. Suspense builds. Some in turbans, robes. The vote is unanimous. Admit them. Song,'It's a new world comin' ' fades up. Voice over says something about if other worlds came to Earth they'd also want to work for peace."

Marvin said, "That one sounds better here than it did at the office."

They both looked to Meyer. With a big smile and a thumbs up he said, "That's very, very good."

Marvin was now more confident. "Next one is animation, like Walt Disney, bright colors, crowds and crowds of people, thousands of them, welcoming band, in the distance very large friendly looking spacecraft gets closer and closer, lands, band playing, people applauding, Aliens, looking pretty much like us, start filing out, carrying suitcases, holding kids, older space Alien couples, and the voice over says something like, 'For years America has welcomed peoples from other lands with open arms.

It's what makes America the great country it is. Some day we may be greeting immigrants from neighboring planets. Sound impossible? The land of opportunity offers a future for all who want to better themselves.' Copy not exactly right yet, but that's the broad strokes."

"I love it," said Meyer. "Great use of whimsy." His predicament was forgotten as other TV commercial concepts were discussed, and a few minutes after eight Harry said, "Yikes. This person from Israel is expecting my call. Obligation."

Meyer said, "There's a pay phone by the rest room."

When Harry returned Marvin asked, "How was your obligation's flight?"

"Arrived early. She checked in and took a nap. Said no jet lag yet. I told her I was a block away with some friends and invited her to come by for a drink. She wanted assurance she wouldn't be intruding, but was planning to take a walk anyway. Said she'd be a few minutes."

Marvin said, "How'd you get trapped into this?"

"A very kind gentleman I met in Israel called yesterday to ask if I could be available, maybe show her around. Said she'd be here just a few days, has to meet with some lawyers. It's just paying back someone who was very nice when I was over there." Meyer said, "I've never been. When were you there?"

"Last September. It was an unplanned trip. Impulsive you might say." Meyer was interested.

Marvin looked to Harry. "May I?"

"Can I stop you?"

"Here's the short version Meyer. Harry meets this girl in Cleveland under very dramatic circumstances, they have a drink, she'd been on an archaeological dig at Masada. Harry, entranced by the girl and by Masada, says let's go, and the next evening they're on an El Al flight. What I just described could all unfold on the screen as the titles come on and a full orchestra plays that old Mitch Miller hit Tzena Tzena..."

Harry interrupted. "It's a long complicated story Meyer. Right now I'm wondering what you think our next steps are with the commercials. Deadline's sometime next week. Should we storyboard what we've got, or keep at it?"

As Meyer was searching for an honest answer and vowing he would never lie to them again, a woman about thirty with auburn hair to her shoulders, Lauren Bacall eyes, a clinging cashmere sweater and stylish jeans entered the bar, did a quick confident inspection, and as she aimed herself toward their table with a natural athletic stride, was observed by the few left in the room with some interest. "Are one of you gentlemen Harry Lang?"

The three of them stood up. "I am."

She extended her hand. "I'm Shoshana."

As Harry held her chair three sexual fantasies simultaneously erupted, Marvin's commencing at the two symmetrical attractions under her pale pink cashmere, Meyer's at the intersection of where her long legs formed a "V" under the jeans that might have been acquired at a boutique on the Via Veneto, and Harry's at the back of her graceful neck enhanced by the merciless intoxication of a very soft perfume blended with a dab of pure feminine skin. "Shoshana?" said Harry, noticeably reassuring himself.

"Shoshana Blime. You seemed in the middle of a discussion when I interrupted."

Harry settled and said, "We were only talking about Aliens from outer space invading Earth. Nothing important. This is Marvin Munchik, and this is Meyer Kaminsky."

"Shalom," from Marvin.

"Hello, and Shalom," from Meyer.

"Meyer Kaminsky. Would I have heard your name somewhere?"

Marvin gestured with his thumb. "Hollywood."

"That's it. You're the famous movie producer."

Kaminsky gave the same gesture to Marvin. "And he's the famous advertising executive."

Then looking at Harry Shoshana said, "And what are you famous for?"

"Nothing yet. I'm just a kid."

"I don't believe that," said with a playfulness hinting that I can be lots of fun when I choose to. "Were you truly discussing Aliens when I crashed your party?"

Meyer's answer was, "You speak English with hardly an accent."

"Most Israelis speak some level of English. The Army sent me to language school. They do a good job."

Harry said, "When I was in Israel I met a girl who taught recruits how to take apart their guns. What did you do?"

"Intelligence. But I left the Army after the Six Day War to go to medical school," then looking at Harry, "that's where I met Doctor Rheinhardt who coerced you into this," pointing at herself.

"He didn't have to coerce. I'd be happy to do anything he asks. How is he?"

"I don't really know how to answer. He's always seemed reflective. Distant. Or maybe it's sad. Lately perhaps more so. A few weeks ago I sat in on a discussion he had with some other doctors and he mentioned a conversation with another psychiatrist at a conference in the States who described a patient, a retired Army officer, who claimed to have communicated telepathically with an Alien retrieved from a UFO crash twenty years before. The Alien was being carried on a stretcher to an ambulance and this officer said the injured Alien transmitted that he knew he was going to die, and there could be a global repeat of Masada. Meaning the population of Earth would all choose to commit suicide rather than face whatever. Doctor Rheinhardt said the psychiatrist saw nothing clinically wrong with the patient, tended to believe he wasn't hallucinatory. So one of the other physicians, a psychotherapist, said that under hypnosis a patient of his describes being abducted by Aliens regularly since she was a child. She describes being put through many gynecological exams by the Aliens, and in her twenties being impregnated."

"By the Aliens?" asked Marvin.

Shoshana lit a cigarette. "She had a miscarriage and the doctors were perplexed because there wasn't any blood. The psychotherapist checked with one of the doctors who verified it. Said it was an anomaly. Ever since the miscarriage the woman doesn't remember any abductions. Her therapist had her take a series of psychological tests, which confirmed his belief that nothing seemed abnormal. When the meeting ended I walked out to the parking lot with Doctor Rheinhardt and he seemed far away. When I drove off he was still sitting in his car. Haven't seen much of his ironical smile since then."

After hearing this Meyer decided he must call Louis Mortimer in the morning.

Harry noticed Marvin's expression change to how he looked when they were in Third Avenue bars as he was about to overwhelm a target of interest. "To avoid those scary chase dreams tonight, with your permission I'm going to change the subject Shoshana. You're in the spotlight. Tell us everything. Did you have a happy childhood? Were you a good student? What's your favorite movie? Where'd you acquire those jeans? What's your opinion of the Lincoln-Douglas debates? What books have you decided not to read this year? Is there a special man? Have you ever been in love? What do you think of vegetarians? Do you own a dog? A parrot? Why are we here? Do you believe in monotheism?"

She had an uninhibited laugh with her head tilted back. "Write them out and I'll stay up tonight typing an essay."

Harry asked, "Does Israeli intelligence have a file on UFO's?"

"We have other more immediate issues to deal with but there is some data. What I can tell you is that there are those in the military who do take the phenomenon seriously. Including abductions."

Meyer said, "Does your government consider them a threat?"

"There are more immediate threats. But I've heard rumors we've exchanged information with other countries. Our Mossad and your CIA. What I can say is that many sightings in your country and mine have been in the vicinity of military research facilities having to do with atomic weaponry. France and Russia as well. Seeing Doctor Rheinhardt's reaction to the abduction discussion worries me."

Meyer wanted to change the subject when Harry did it for

him. "What're your plans for the next few days?"

"Tomorrow one of the lawyers is meeting me at my aunt's apartment at 10:00AM. There are decisions to be made regarding the contents. Many are quite valuable. That will take up most of Saturday. Sunday is unscheduled. I might do some sightseeing," looking at Harry. "All day Monday is with the lawyers, and back home Tuesday. If you're free tomorrow Harry I'd be grateful if you came to my aunt's apartment."

"Of course. I'll pick you up at 9:30." The conversation was easy and fun for a half hour and then by psychic signal the four of them rose to leave. As they walked out Harry said to Meyer, "We haven't resolved anything about the commercials."

"I'll be in touch on Monday." Marvin and Meyer shared a cab uptown. Harry walked Shoshana back to her hotel.

At 9:00AM Saturday morning the phone rang at Louis Mortimer's house in Fairfax, Virginia. He wasn't surprised it was Meyer Kaminsky.

"I'm in New York and flying back to L.A. tomorrow evening. I know it's the weekend but is there any chance we might meet?"

With no hesitation Mortimer said, "Can you be at the Army and Navy Club at 2:00PM tomorrow?"

"I'll be there."

"Bring some juicy Hollywood gossip."

Meyer switched his return flight to National Airport and made a reservation on the Sunday 9:00AM train to D.C.

Shoshana was waiting in the lobby when Harry entered the hotel at 9:30AM. "Sleep well?"

"The sleep of the jet lagged. In and out. Plus thinking about today. I only met my aunt once when she visited us in Israel a few years ago after her husband died. He made quite a bit of money in the scrap metal business and in real estate. We were the only ones she had left. My mother visited her twice here in New York. But she's gone also. Going to her apartment like this is something I'd rather not do. Especially alone. So thank you Harry. I have the address. It's on Central Park South. Somebody from the law firm will be meeting us there. They've been very accommodating. Because of medical school I couldn't take more than a couple of days so this lawyer is giving up part of his weekend."

"Did the lawyers say what it is exactly you're supposed to do?"

"I inherited everything. Take what I want. Give instructions how to dispose of the rest. I'm really not interested in taking anything, so I suppose most of it will go up for auction."

The law firm sent a young associate with the key and after letting them in and looking around he left, leaving his card and home phone number. There were six rooms of expensive furniture, a decorator's eye being obvious in the mix of contemporary and antique. Abstract paintings and oriental rugs. Although the apartment was filled with nice things the air was depressing, as a place vacated because of death can be. They inspected every room, Shoshana lingering over some framed photographs as if expecting long gone relatives to identify themselves. Many of the pictures were of Paris before the war, some duplicates of ones she knew. The pictures of men in business suits standing in front of pharmacies were of her uncles and the family owned stores. She looked in closets. Opened medicine cabinets in both bathrooms. The living room windows looked north at the park, framed by the buildings on Fifth Avenue to the right and Central Park West to the left. Shoshana sunk into a cushiony sofa with her eyes closed and Harry thought she might fall asleep. But then sat upright and got a pad from her handbag.

"I'd better make a list. It's so overwhelming and sad. First we should go through the apartment, check the drawers and desks for anything personal or of value. Letters, cash, that sort of thing."

"You're sure you want me to do this?" Harry asked.

"Doctor Rheinhardt said you could be family." Harry understood. "Next is an inventory. Just the things that look super expensive. I'll have the law firm find a professional to place a value on everything. Then I'll need advice in selecting the right auction house. And a real estate firm to sell the apartment. Law firm again. Decide what to do with her clothes, her shoes, find a charity. I know there's more, but if we can do number one and two today perhaps I'll start to relax. Depending on when we finish next on the list is you taking me to dinner."

Harry saluted and said, "Yes Ma'am."

In a drawer with night gowns and brassieres they found a small metal box with $5000.00 in twenties and fifties. In one desk were checkbooks from three different banks and several Israel bonds totaling $50,000.00. One folder had stock certificates and un-cashed dividend checks going back three months. In the back of a closet in the den was a carton containing military ribbons, photographs of German soldiers, and a holster with a Luger. Shoshana showed Harry a picture of a smiling corporal in a World War I German uniform. "My uncle. As a German citizen, a Jewish German citizen, he was conscripted and sent to the Western Front. When the war ended and economic conditions got unbearable he managed to immigrate to Argentina. In the 1920s he somehow got to the States. It was never clear if he got in legally, but he eventually became a citizen."

Shoshana had put a pile of documents on the living room floor and as Harry was packing them in a small Louis Vuitton suitcase she was reading a packet of old letters found in a bottom bureau drawer. The letters were written in the 1920s between her aunt and uncle when they were courting and during the early years of their marriage. Shoshana is thinking she only knew her aunt as a woman at the end of her years, yet the writing is of young people in love, of passions and the life they will have. In one of the letters her uncle writes of conversations with somebody he's buying a building from on the upper West Side. The man is a diamond merchant who projects a deep and soulful peacefulness. They talk and he mentions he is a student of the Kabala. The uncle questions him. The man explains that Kabala has to do with the emanation and transmigration of souls. We are vessels for the divine light, for the soul, which has a pre existence in higher spiritual spheres. We live in parallel universes, and should tap into the energies of the universe. Reincarnation is a Kabala belief. The uncle jokingly states so now it's out. Our souls and past lives inhabit other universes, which solves the question of is there life on other planets. Shoshana rereads the letter. She is not a superstitious woman but the conversation with doctor Rheinhardt and then last night with Harry's friends causes her to recall meetings in the army when the subject of UFO's and the Soviets came up. As she adds the letters to Harry's pile she thinks perhaps jet lag combined with coming into all this wealth is making her brain go mushy. For just a moment she considers that IDF Intelligence training taught her to not discard quiet voices from within.

As the lights of Manhattan came on she had four pages of lists and notes. "I can't continue this," she said. "Find the envelope with the $5000 and I'll buy dinner, if you promise to come back with me tomorrow. If you can't promise I'll buy dinner anyway."

"I promise."

They stopped off at the Gramercy Park Hotel where Harry waited in the lobby while she freshened up, and then walked the few blocks to Pete's Tavern. The decibel level was just under annoying as neighborhood Saturday night out couples and foursomes mingled into an organic hive of chatter. The bar was three and four deep as they waited for a table. Shoshanna said, "After spending the day with secrets and accumulations of lives lived and gone it's rejuvenating to be in this noisy present. Those letters were a form of time travel. A dead person's consciousness from forty years ago rises up from the ink. He wrote to my aunt that according to the Kabala our souls get recycled. We're vessels."

"Did he believe that?"

"I don't think so. He made a joke out of it. Said something about that proves there's life on other planets."

Harry said, "This is a topic that's come up a lot lately. Meyer Kaminsky is producing a movie about Aliens coming to Earth and

Marvin and I are doing some commercials that will be in the movie."

"I don't understand."

"The way Meyer explained the film the President is losing his mind and wants to do an ad campaign preparing America for the possibility of Aliens coming to Earth. Meyer wants an ad agency to develop the commercials."

Again Shoshanna heard that whisper. "A coincidence, but recently a friend still in Army Intelligence mentioned that our embassy in Washington heard rumors a psychiatrist has been visiting the White House."

Harry said, "He's no doubt doing group therapy sessions for the entire cabinet and their advisors. All of them should be institutionalized. My imagination just snapped into overdrive Shoshanna. This President is not totally evil. Being from a southern state he showed courage for civil rights. And he's improved health insurance for millions. Could it be he does have a conscience and because of that can't cope with Vietnam anymore? An internal standoff between good and evil causing an emotional collapse?" The headwaiter waved above the crowd that their table was ready. Following him, Harry saw the way Shoshanna moved attracted glances that said she must be somebody. After they were seated he asked, "Did Intelligence have any policies you know about regarding UFO's? The subject's come up so frequently, starting in Israel in September. I'm getting an odd feeling."

"Trust your odd feelings," she said, smiling and looking serious at the same time. "I'm not aware of any official policies, but it is discussed from time to time. I saw something that said there are hundreds of millions of planetary systems where it's not impossible life as we know it could exist. Doctor Rheinhardt didn't reject that patient's claim to have been abducted. He believed that she believed. Being impregnated by an Alien? Who knows? There being no blood when she had a miscarriage is baffling. Why do you suppose you're getting an odd feeling?"

"I think Meyer Kaminsky's been holding something back. It's

not that I don't trust him, quite the contrary. He's going to be in touch on Monday. I'm wondering if I ought to bring this up."

Shoshanna looked around the room. "Listen to that inner voice. Then you'll know."

As they ordered dinner, the waiter was extra attentive. Harry thought of Rivka. Both were Sabras. Both were in the Army. This is what women's libbers admired and John Wayne types couldn't deal with. Harry felt very good being with a woman other women observed with wariness and men's eyes followed with steamy imagination. She felt his gaze. "God gave you beauty and intelligence. And your aunt gave you riches. So what now?"

Just like at the Players Club she tilted her head back and laughed. "Is this leading up to a proposal?"

"I'd be too neurotic for you. I hear voices. I kick in my sleep. I had a hysterical mother."

Another head back open mouth laugh. "You're funny. So what now? I thought I'd make the Army my career. I'd made captain fairly quickly. The work was challenging. Wars are lost and won on Intelligence. During the Six Day War I was in the field. Egypt. My reports were helpful. But seeing charred bodies of soldiers, limbs without bodies, regardless of which side," her voice got softer, "it changes you. So something said go to medical school. As far as the army, like all Israelis I can get called up any time. Unlike your soldiers in Vietnam, influence, money, political connections don't get you out. Nobody wants out. When we have a war Israelis from all over the world rush home to put on their uniforms."

Harry said, "When you get back you'll be one very rich medical student."

"That can't be denied. I hope I'm not being naïve, but it doesn't matter. It's a comfort, of course, but I have everything I need. And at least I won't be marrying for money." She felt his gaze again.

Harry said, "A line up of Israeli tycoons will be very disappointed." She held steady returning his gaze. Their appetizers arrived.

The Army and Navy Club

Sunday morning a few minutes before 9:00AM Meyer boarded the First Class car of the New York to Washington train. It was half empty. He found a window seat, opened the main section of the *New York Times* and reclined back slightly. Traveling by train was pleasant. He enjoyed the coziness, the big windows on the mural of America, white tablecloths in the dining car, the Negro, he corrected himself, African-American waiters, the ability to walk around without seatbelt lights, he even liked the electrical smell on the platform. When he went to L.A. after the war it was by train, and life had been good. A short lived marriage to an actress who became rich, famous, and the star of millions of night ejaculations ended without a scandal. The war was still with him, but less frequently. He was very good at what he did, had a reputation as an honorable human being, desired by beautiful women with little depth, and he accumulated more assets than he could have predicted. As the train left the black tunnels of Penn Station and extruded into the smokestacks and junkyards of a sunny New Jersey day, he was beyond regretting what was agreed to. He'd made a commitment, but it was like buying a car. No matter what the price there was that sense of being screwed. He needed clarity. Good odds Louis Mortimer expected his call. So what to say to this tall Wasp in a gray tweed sport coat and all his hair, once black like Cary Grant's, now white? Might have been raised Episcopalian, but seems Unitarian. Seemed principled, but were there limits? Meyer concluded he's authentic. I will not be subtle. Probably figured out why I'm coming anyway.

He buried into the *Times* with The News of the Week in Review and then went to the main section, and by Trenton had gone through most of it when a small item easy to miss zapped him: "UFO's sighted in Nevada, New Mexico." The story reported that one hovered over a car out in the desert at three in the morning causing the ignition system to malfunction and then come back on. Rancher with wife mystified and frightened.

Several spotted throughout New Mexico. Air Force says light refractions the cause. Meyer decided he had a conversation starter, but couldn't concentrate on the paper until the train reached Philadelphia. At Wilmington he reread the account looking for something he might have missed. Between Baltimore and Washington seeds of resentment started sprouting. This was diverting him from the business of Hollywood, from enjoying the weekend, from being straight with the ad people, from being straight with Hank Wood. He'd given for his country from Normandy to Berlin. Getting involved with the government meant rules. Adhere to protocols. Accept the culture. A strict chain of command. The straight jacket tightened as the train closed in on Washington. If it were possible to bail he would, surprised the thought even occurred.

The Army and Navy Club was just two blocks from the White House and as Meyer entered its refined military ambience he considered that Presidents and generals do make bad decisions and the citizens who actually do the fighting are helpless functionaries. He announced himself and was shown to a small conference room where Louis Mortimer was drinking coffee and reading the *Washington Post*. As they shook hands Mortimer pointed to the paper and said, "Never any good news out of Vietnam."

"Thanks for taking the time. You did say get in touch if you can be of any help and I think you can." Louis Mortimer was lighting his pipe. "Why don't I get right at it?" The pipe smoke was mellow and Meyer thought it perfect for the scene, but stopped thinking movies. "I met with the ad agency on Friday and the concepts they've come up with are outstanding. They've delivered."

Mortimer said, "I've seen the kids' sneaker commercial so I'm not surprised."

"Louis, since our meeting at the State Department I've felt something wasn't a hundred percent. Couldn't shake it. Couple of years ago we hired Barry Goldwater's former Chief of Staff to head up P.R., Hank Wood. I asked Hank to snoop around

Washington, especially since it's known Goldwater has an interest in UFO's. Rumors are the President may be having a breakdown. Convinced that Aliens are on their way and wants to prepare America for Alien arrival through an advertising campaign. Psychiatrist visiting White House. Some in Congress talking about having him relieved." He stopped for eye contact. "Some of this sounds awfully familiar Louis." Mortimer was finding his tobacco rather pleasant. He put the pipe down.

"We considered others before making you the unlucky winner. Liked your war record and reputation for being a straight shooter. We knew Hank Wood worked for you and anticipated you might ask him to sniff around. I wanted to give you the honest facts but was overruled. Sometimes the State Department is sneakier than Intelligence. This is a situation straight from the Oval Office. Everyone would prefer not to be involved. He's masterful at politics but the relentless stress, primarily Vietnam, would have driven lesser men round the bend a lot sooner. He is genuinely concerned about Aliens on Earth, appropriately so, and does want America to be psychologically ready. Apparently he saw the robot commercial and figured whoever thought that one up would understand how to do commercials on the Alien issue. He feels panic and hysteria would occur were it known the government is behind it. That's why no speech. And that's why this ruse. The wild card was that the intermediary might get suspicious. Others concluded it was worth the risk." He found his pipe. Meyer was now positive Louis Mortimer was Unitarian. Embers in the bowl glowed as he drew in the smoke. "Not to worry Meyer. Being the duplicitous scoundrels we are there is a plan B."

Meyer said, "May I ask a personal question?"

"You certainly can ask."

"Are you of the Unitarian faith?"

"Born Episcopalian but attend the Unitarian church."

"Thank you. Plan B?"

"Plan B. The President is out of office in a few weeks. It could easily take that long to complete this advertising campaign.

We proceed as directed, just taking longer than anticipated. The new president is sworn in. The former president is out. No authority. Perhaps he's in some sort of intensive therapy program. There's no paper trail. Deep six the whole deal."

Meyer said, "Duplicitous scoundrels does seem apt. The ad agency proceeds. Then I inform them we're halting production of the film."

"Indeed you can. Though it does sound a bit duplicitous."

Meyer bowed his head. "Learning from the pros. On the subject of government mendaciousness, would it be okay to come clean with the two fellas at the ad firm and with Hank Wood?"

Louis Mortimer was unhurried. He examined his pipe. Meyer's body language said take all the time you need. Mortimer was pensive. "Perhaps after the inauguration and by them signing an oath of confidentiality with a government official as witness it might be okay. I'll check. Is there anything else I can do?"

"Yes. Relieve my curiosity. There was a blurb in the *Times* this morning about UFO sightings out west. What does our government really know?" The emphasis was on "our." "Is there a threat? What can you tell me?"

"I'll tell you what I can Meyer. It's actually quite a lot. They are real, but not all the same. We are being observed from perhaps six different planetary systems. Around 1947 there was an increase in activity. The Roswell crash and recovery did happen. In 1952 we did shoot one down just outside D.C. and recovered some fragments of the craft. Another encounter. France. July 1, 1965. An oval shaped craft landed and a farmer, Maurice Masse, witnessed it. He saw two beings about four feet tall emerge. As he approached one of the beings pointed a tube at him and he fell to the ground paralyzed. He says they came to him and appeared concerned. He heard them converse in a gurgling language. They returned to the craft and silently ascended out of sight in seconds. About twenty minutes later he could move, managed to get home, call the authorities. Local police and other officials came out, examined the spot. Found indentations in the ground and later a high level of radium.

Maurice Masse was treated for mysterious burns. His sleep patterns disrupted for months. He was known as an intelligent and modest man, wanted no publicity. For years after he felt they were in communication. Never the same. There have been incidents like this all over the world. We have photographic evidence, luminosity and radar readings, auto and aircraft interference, ground traces, destruction of vegetation and other cases of inhibition of voluntary movement."

Meyer quietly said, "Holy shit."

"That's a rational reaction."

Meyer then said, "Who, what, when, where, and why?"

"Nothing I'm telling you hasn't been published in one form or another. Their own planets might be deteriorating and they're looking at Earth as a new home. They might want to colonize us, exploit us, like the Brits did with brown skinned people during empire. Perhaps they have experimentation in mind, like we do with rats. The abduction theory is that they are breeding with us and developing a hybrid race. A more upbeat possibility is they see that we are a mad and violent people and their mission is to teach us to love one another. Like missionaries going to Borneo. Or they just might be looking for a new exotic vacation spot. Who knows?"

Meyer was leaning forward and now sat back. "You losing any sleep over this Louis?"

"Not with Vietnam, the Phoenix program, Russian missiles, the Cold War, a President curled up in the fetal position, and Christmas shopping."

"That's a hell of a lot to ponder during idle moments," said Meyer. He breathed in deeply, had a long slow exhale and continued. "What you're saying is they have the technology to travel from light years away, billions and billions of miles. They stay in touch telepathically, their vehicles go poof and they're gone. Spooky. Unbelievable. Not that I don't believe you."

"Look at it like this," said Mortimer. "If five hundred years ago somebody said we can get to England in six hours instead of eight weeks, or it would be possible to talk to friends, or enemies, a thousand miles away, or have chariots that travel faster than the fittest horses, it's not out of the question you'd be burned at the stake. All of these miraculous technologies happened in the last hundred years. Space beings could have a fifty thousand, or even five hundred thousand year head start on us. Some of our big thinkers speculate that if this became public knowledge hundreds of millions might be so paralyzed that suicide would be preferable to submission. However, we didn't become the world's most fearsome nation by sitting on our red, white and blue asses. Defensive weapons systems are in development. We're collaborating with other countries. Including enemies. General MacArthur said intergalactic hostilities would unite the nations of our world."

Meyer Kaminsky watched Louis Mortimer fiddling with his pipe and after a moment said, "What you're not telling me is no doubt where this story begins. I'm not suggesting you reveal anything further, but sounds to me like we occupants of Earth are getting a message and our leaders know what it is and the implications are not good, so they clam up and deny."

Mortimer started to get up and said, "I believe we understand each other on all matters we discussed. Now our agreement was you'd bring the latest Hollywood gossip."

As they left the meeting room Meyer said, "What I'm about to tell you has not yet hit the press but the latest Hollywood gossip is that Liberace has proposed to Debbie Reynolds."

Masada

Stefan Rheinhardt, M.D. had many friends, was well known in medicine, academia, publishing, the media, Israeli society. He kept a basket with the many invitations that came in the mail and was diligent about responding. In forty years of practicing psychiatry he'd seen patients experiencing pain in almost everything fate could bestow on a life. And now as the seventh decade was near the loneliness inside was sucking his vitality as a leach attaches and sucks blood. When violence blasted his wife's limbs and organs through the wreckage of the bus and onto the street it was the love between son and father that sustained him. The 1967 war eliminated the son. Left were well meaning friends and his work. As the melancholy metastasized he questioned whether his treatment of patients going back forty years meant much. He knew the theories, had read the journals, written for them, attended the conferences, given seminars, speeches, interviews. Alone in the apartment absent the sounds of family life he suffered forty years of former patients' turmoil as repentance.

He understood all that is known of psychiatry, totally. But so what? He also understood this condition of isolation was connected to another dimension that was as murky as theories of dream interpretation. Since learning of the UFO crash in New Mexico his dreams were variations of being floated up to a distant luminescence where diminutive beings in skintight layers were attempting to communicate something of gravity, something having implications for friends, acquaintances, strangers, and finally masses of population on into infinity. He would start to wake convinced the beings knew they were failing the mission of getting a message to him and wished they were capable of a broader range of emotions. He'd studied Freud, Jung, Adler, everybody, on the interpretation of dreams, but psychoanalytic grasping trivialized his nocturnal ascension. In his aloneness Masada emerged and the fortress beckoned like the distant glow in his dreams.

It's quite chilly, he thought starting up the Snake Path thinking frigidness and aloneness are complementary. It was late afternoon and he had the trail practically to himself. Setting a strong pace he reached the plateau in good time not really understanding why the rush. But for a small group of soldiers who waved there was emptiness on top. He was grateful for their acknowledgment. The wind pushed from behind turning chill to coldness. At the three-tiered palace he went down the ancient stone steps to the lowest level. Leaning against the wall looking out at the Judean desert and the Dead Sea breathing in another dimension, he knew it was right to be there. From the depths of this dimension appeared the slender silhouette of his wife as she was forty years ago, beckoning, they were dancing slowly, her hair brushing his cheek. The music went softer, grew distant, then she was gone. Now someone was holding his hand, his son, ten years old, walking together watching rowboats on a lake. The son looked up and smiled. Then the little hand in his dissolved and there was nothing, the wind now more aggressive, blowing from where he faced, and the increasing coldness was a song of life as a joke. Darkness came slowly from above, a lighting director preparing the audience for a scene change. This production has had few laughs. He replayed acts one and two looking for joyfulness, lightness, exhilaration. When lovemaking was new all was happiness. There were several new loves before marriage. After marriage he was true, and when the new became familiar, pleasure lasted. The Nazi pollution in Vienna and then Paris suffocated all that was good. Their son, professional insight and recognition, the ordinariness of a night out with friends, serenity between husband and wife, there was all that, he thought. Hardly any residual.

And now return to Masada, a mystic looking for a sign. Something anomalous. Something science cannot explain. By all measures the patient had died, then returns. Thousands of doctors have heard it. The formerly dead patient has floated up and describes in detail everything occurring in the operating room. The patient knows joy and love like never before and frequently would prefer not to have booked a round trip. But does, having discovered a connectedness to humanity that is life changing.

Now the ironical smile. Seventy years and the unfortunate convergence of time and place delivered him to this outcropping where King Herod lived in pleasure and the Zealots died in pain. The weather was becoming angry but that was fine. He was waiting for a bus in the rain. The anomalous bus.

There it was, headlights from infinity, three of them circling wide, then smaller. They hovered, illuminating Doctor Stefan Rheinhardt in this time and place. No fright. No joy. Take me. Or leave me. But tell me. They were now over the plateau and he followed, back up the three levels to witness the landing. Two had vanished. One on the ground. A glow from nowhere, the way military flares change night to day. He observed the group of soldiers trying to operate their radio but it was inert. Stefan Rheinhardt saw them confer and decide to approach the craft as he was doing. One of them shouted, "Don't get too close. It could be radioactive." The lieutenant, the sergeant and the corporal came to him and the four stood together in the frigid light. He noticed their youth and saw them as sons of this place, of Abraham and Moses and the Zealots and yesterday's battles and tomorrow's. He loved them as he did his own dead. Between them was sanctuary. As if they were one, the message through the walls of the craft was delivered:

The blackout of 1965 in the Northeast of the United States was not a result of overload or a human mistake. Atmospheric poisons from Earth are increasing. Earth will gradually become a desert, and the places beyond uninhabitable. When your betrayal ends, the pollution will stop and life can continue. Your leaders must believe we can turn off your power to save our own planet. Thou shall not kill the ecosystem or each other.

The craft lifted. Vanished. Natural darkness replaced light.

No being had appeared. It was telepathy from inside the vehicle. The three young soldiers and psychiatrist were in spiritual oneness. Was it reality? Simultaneous group hallucination? Synchronicity? Doctor Rheinhardt knew he was more prepared for this than they were. "Let's get to a place out of the wind." They found a room a few feet under the casemate wall and sat on the same stone benches the Zealots had.

Doctor Rheinhardt said, "Let's establish that we all saw the same thing."

The lieutenant was hesitant and shaky but did look at the other two and say, "It seemed to be a round disk, perhaps thirty feet around. It appeared from the sky. There were three of them, but two seemed to disintegrate into the air." He was rubbing his eyes and forehead.

The others nodded agreement and the sergeant added, "The part of the plateau where we stood was illuminated, but we couldn't see any source for the light."

The corporal appeared less unsettled. "Did you hear, well not exactly hear, but feel the thoughts coming from the craft?"

"We should record this while it's fresh and we're together," said Doctor Rheinhardt. The sergeant got a small notebook from the map pocket inside his field jacket and started writing. When he stopped Doctor Rheinhardt said, "I'll state what the thoughts were that came from the craft and see if we all absorbed the same message. If you don't mind sergeant, get it down. I'll speak slowly." The corporal held a flashlight on the notebook. "The energy from the vehicle was telepathically reaching us with these thoughts. We on Earth are out of control regarding the pollution we're creating. This will increase and affect other planets. It can ultimately destroy everything on Earth. Should we learn to stop killing each other the pollution will diminish. The Aliens caused the blackout of three years ago in the States, as a message. They can switch off everything on Earth if necessary." His expression was one of incredulousness at the words. He paused until the sergeant stopped writing. "Is that consistent with your recollection?" They agreed.

The lieutenant now had another thought more troubling than what they'd just witnessed. "When we report this they could send us to the division psychiatrist. It's so bizarre. They'll think we were hallucinating. It will get on our fitness reports. Can affect our time in the army. Our careers. Are we sure we should bring this up at all?"

Sefan Rheinhardt looked at each of them with caring. "Gentlemen, I am a psychiatrist. We'll report it together."

The radio was now functioning perfectly and the lieutenant repeated the incident first to another lieutenant, then a major, and finally a colonel. He handed the receiver back to the corporal, looked at the spot where just a few minutes before they stood in the light from nowhere. "They're sending a helicopter."

Thirty minutes passed and the chop chop of two 'copters before they saw them. Dust and sand blew without pattern as the crafts flared and landed on the plateau. Before the rotors stopped soldiers were jumping out, a major approached, casual salutes, and a retelling of the episode. Doctor Rheinhardt was asked if he would mind a helicopter ride to Tel Aviv with the other three. Someone would drive his car to Jerusalem and then get him home. One of the soldiers came over, saying he was in the same company as his son and was honored to meet the father of an officer he served with. A reflexive embrace and Stefan Rheinhardt and three young companions entered the helicopter. The group from the second helicopter got to work inspecting, testing, measuring. As the first one rose up and accelerated two other choppers were coming in.

Stefan Rheinhardt and the three soldiers separately related what they'd witnessed to a colonel from the Air Force and an officer from Mossad. The lieutenant and two non-coms were shown to another office where a major thanked them, suggested not discussing the incident with anyone and to their relief indicated they were to be commended for the way it was handled.

The Mossad representative was a Ph.D. in psychology whose

thesis was on Carl Jung's theories of symbolism and dreams. He knew of Doctor Rheinhardt's reputation and when they were alone it was two professionals conferring.

Doctor Rheinhardt turned down an offer of coffee saying that only recently it kept him awake.

"This has been most unsettling. Everything the young men reported happened. I experienced it exactly as they did. I've asked myself if it could have been a *folie à trois*, a shared paranoid induced delusional disorder. But the lieutenant and non coms are not psychotic. For whatever self-diagnosis is worth, nor am I. You were presumably called in because you have some background in whatever it is we're facing. So what do we really know?"

"Only theories, Stefan. The last few years there's been an increase in activity. Sightings. Claimed abductions. All we really know for sure is there's something out there. In France. Russia. Brazil. The States. We've been in touch more or less informally. Hard evidence? Evasive."

"Roswell?"

"Sources tell us no question about it."

"Abductions?"

"Appears to be a pattern. Mostly women. Mean age about thirty. They typically remember some form of contact with beings. Usually between 2:00A.M. and 5:00A.M., but it could happen any time. Mostly they're home in bed. Sometimes in a car. They remember being floated up to another dimension. Put on an examining table and studied. Probed. Focus on reproductive organs. Instruments inserted. Other beings present. All report assurances they would not be harmed. Sometimes feel a familial attachment. Loss of memory and find themselves back where the abduction began. Several hours unaccounted for. In following weeks some have symptoms of pregnancy. Many report multiple abductions. Male abductees recall being stimulated to ejaculation and feeling helplessness and rage. In the main these are average productive people."

Doctor Rheinhardt said, "Standing next to the craft the three of us received the same thought that the great blackout on the east coast was caused by them. A warning of what they're capable of."

"We know that this year in the middle of the night the lights went out on the Brooklyn Bridge and every car on the bridge stalled. UFO's were seen and when they were out of sight things returned to normal. People in the cars were terrified, but the incident never got credence."

Doctor Rheinhardt said, "So what now?"

"So now we have a car standing by to get you back to Jerusalem."

Manhattan

At 9:30 Monday morning Harry exited the elevator facing after-weekend reentry to a never-ending battering ram of New York ad agency agita. It took till lunch on Saturday for agency employees to shake the previous week's elevated blood pressure, but immersion into home and family, school sports and supermarkets, wives, girlfriends, dinner out, kid connecting and married sex unclogged at least some of the tension induced cholesterol buildup. Then Sunday afternoon the demons arrive. Normal life begins a slow fade, segueing to office memos, client meetings, deadlines, business lunches, airports, company intrigues, bottom lines and moments of doubt as to life's choices. Sandra was at her duty station and smiled with the words, "Coffee boss?"

He nodded yes, said, "Good weekend?" and was in his office mildly tranquilized by Sandy's knowingness, a beautiful colloquialism bred into girls from Brooklyn and Queens. All of it caused Harry to assume a mental crouch. Meyer Kaminsky, Shoshanna Blime, the Alien commercials, Doctor Rheinhardt's voice, all of it. Ed Sullivan's opening line, "We've got a really big show," summed it up. This cast had been joined together for a really big show, but they weren't blind xylophone players or Romanian acrobats. Harry saw himself floating into an intergalactic extravaganza, Meyer orbiting with him looking apologetic, Shoshanna with her uninhibited laugh directed at Meyer, Doctor Rheinhardt's face frozen in his ironical smile, and Audrey and Rivka firing Uzi's at flying saucers.

"Where are you Harry?" It was Sandra with the coffee. "I said coffee lady's here twice and you never heard me. Wherever you are, take me with you."

"Sorry Sandy. What time is it in L.A? 6:30? Too early to call. Let's try to reach Meyer Kaminsky around 12:30. And I can't take you with me. The Mann Act."

Marvin entered the office looking quite happy with himself. Sandra said, "Well if you're too chicken to cross state lines with an eager minor I'm leaving."

Marvin closed the door. "Saturday night Harry. It was Churchillian in magnitude. Art Kane had a cocktail party at his studio and knowing there'd be numerous succulent maladjusted models and eager for conversation not intellectual in nature, I showed up around 10:00PM. It was smoky and boozy and close. I immediately got a drink and saw this obviously bored brunette with firm medium size breasts putting a cigarette in her mouth. I approached and said that if I had a match I'd offer a light. She had laughing eyes powered by cynicism. High cheekbones. I think she might have been in a Chanel ad. No response. So I said, I can't decide whether or not to have a sexual fantasy about you. She lit her cigarette, exhaled smoke at my face and said, 'why fantasize?' Harry. She said why fantasize? I had a verbal blackout. Twenty minutes later we were in my apartment taking our clothes off. I lived the dream Harry. I'm sure we'll never see each other again. It was perfect."

"I'm so very happy for both of you Marvin. A tender moment that will undoubtedly last into your geriatric years. But have you given any further thought to our Alien spots? Not just the commercials. Something else is going on here. I really like Meyer Kaminsky but do you think there's more to this assignment than he's letting on?"

"What makes you say that?"

"It's more than just a feeling. The other night Shoshanna mentioned Israeli Intelligence reported rumors our President may really be cracking. I went queasy. It was an 'aha' moment. You know how once in a while we come up with a concept that feels right? We just know it's the answer and the client will love it and it will be an award winner. That was the feeling. I'd gamble everything on this instinct."

"So what are you saying?"

"What if Meyer's movie isn't a movie? It's 1968. Two assassinations. War that only a few repressed politicians are getting their rocks off over. Race. Equality. Liberation. The people demanding better. If anybody's in charge of humanity they're fucking up. Ozzie and Harriet and Lucy and Desi are archaeological debris. If Aliens are a reality they've picked a vintage year to do whatever it is they have in mind. I guess I'm saying life could be imitating art. You and I may have been given the responsibility of creating a smooth transition for the Alien takeover."

"That's pretty much on the fringe Har. When's the last time you had a little nooky?"

"Concentrate on what I'm saying Marvin. Clamp down the wise ass comments. Do you give it even a ten percent chance? Five percent? One percent?"

"Hmmm. Even at one percent that's a one percent chance intelligent life exists on other planets. I'd give that five percent. Do they want to come here? Another five percent. Now what are you saying about Meyer? You think he's part of some government conspiracy? He's not the type. He's a likeable, sincere successful guy from Brooklyn."

"Exactly."

Marvin stared at Harry. "Hmmm. Let's say the government did put him up to it. But up to what? And why us?"

"Us because of all the Robot campaign publicity. Remember? We're advertising geniuses. That's as far as I get. I'm going to call Meyer on the West Coast."

"What will you say? Ask if he's a government agent?"

"I'm not sure. I suppose we could lead up to it. Just be straight."

"Did you say we?"

"We're in this together Marv. At least be in the room."

"You're the seeker of truth. I'm just a sex maniac."

"12:30."

An hour with *Advertising Age*, another hour walking the halls conversing, flirting, battling tidal waves of doubt, a half hour back in the office alone constructing how the call to Meyer might begin, unfold, end, and looking at the clock a dozen times. Marvin appeared at 12:20.

Figure out what you're going to say?"

"Uh uh."

"Thought so. Let's try and call him right now."

Sandra reached Meyer's secretary and signaled Harry to be on the phone before Meyer got on. Marvin slouched into the sofa with his feet on the coffee table.

"Hi Meyer. Good flight back? Didn't realize you left from Washington. National Airport, usually less hassle than LaGuardia."

"Enjoyed our drink at the Players Club."

"Yeah. Shoshanna is a very alluring woman. A very rich, alluring woman. She's flying back to Israel tonight. Asked if I'd go with her to the airport. I had dinner with her Saturday night. Oddest thing. She mentioned a friend in Army Intelligence said their embassy in Washington reported rumors our President may be having a mental breakdown. Psychiatrist spotted at the White House. Apparently also reported gossip is he's got Aliens from outer space on his mind. Thinks they're on the way. What a coincidence, or does MGM have a mole in the White House? On the other hand, maybe the White House has a mole at MGM?"

"Leak it to the press? That would really be a riot. Sell a lot of newspapers."

"Maybe I am on to something. Sure. We'll have storyboards ready for you next week."

"Sounds great. Let's stay in touch. See you next week."

Marvin remained sprawled on the sofa. "Did we learn anything?"

Harry still had the receiver in his hand and stared at the phone as if expecting it to say something profound.

"Harry. Hang up the phone and talk to me."

"One thing's for sure. Meyer's got the hots for Shoshanna."

"Can't blame the man for that. But that's not why we called. Did you notice I said we?"

"He knows I was fishing, but he wasn't biting. He couldn't have been blander; he's holding back. He's too straight for it not to show. Shoshanna said go by instincts. Right now instinct is saying run and hide."

Marvin sat up. "Do you think we're going to die?"

After the conversation with Harry, Meyer was disgusted with himself. He got down on the floor and did fifty push-ups. It helped alleviate the disappointment in himself as two aspirin just barely calm a bad headache. He'd observed through the years that screen writers, artists, composers, those labeled "creative," were directed more by intuition than most of the world, so he wasn't surprised that advertising copywriters and art directors are also high intuition. He replayed every conversation with Harry and Marvin searching for anything that would make them suspicious. Nothing. Was a moment's facial response, tone of voice or unconscious gesture responsible for the betrayal? Just the use of the word betrayal caused a shudder of self-loathing. He thought any involvement with government results in a diminishment of principle, and down he went for twenty more push-ups. His calendar was filled with meetings the whole day. Government intrusion was unasked for distraction. He would simply not allow resentment to pile up. Lock the whole odious mess up in a box and get back to making movies.

Washington D.C.

1:00PM in Washington and Louis Mortimer was being shown in to the office of the Director of Central Intelligence.

"We've got a problem Louie." He seated himself thinking no preliminary small talk wasn't good. "After our 7:00AM briefing the President asked me to stay a moment. He was curious how far along we are with the advertising project. After the pessimistic intelligence from Vietnam it was not a subject I would have thought on his mind. Told him I'd look into it and get back this afternoon. Louie. He said he'd like to see the TV ideas soon. This weekend if we could. At the ranch."

"Shouldn't be a problem. I'm told they've developed some excellent ideas."

"Said he'd appreciate it if the two fellas that came up with the robot commercial, the ones he hopes are developing the Alien advertising, could come down to the ranch this weekend and show him what they've got."

"Jesus Christ."

"I know."

"We'll have to let them in on it."

"Have the FBI check them out, sign the necessary secrecy documents. National security. Patriotism. Hit them hard with the consequences."

"Our contact man from Hollywood. Meyer Kaminsky. I'd suggest he come along. Already been vetted. Good man."

"Your decision. Just let me know if there's any screw ups. When you write your memoirs Louie, this could be a good chapter for comic relief."

Hollywood

Since meeting Shoshanna at the Players Club Meyer tried not to think of her long auburn hair and fine facial bones and was also not very successful at turning off the echo of her laugh. If she weren't on her way back to medical school in Jerusalem he would have contacted her. He was imagining what they might do together over a weekend when the phone rang.

"Hello Meyer. It's Louis Mortimer."

"Hello Louis. Something tells me I'm going to regret this call."

"There's no question you will. Have any plans for the weekend?"

"Well since the person I'd like to spend the weekend with is 8000 miles away the answer is no."

"Would you take the President as a second choice?"

"A distant second."

"It's not a mandate Meyer. Although I did hear the I.R.S. was interested in examining the last ten years of your tax returns."

"Checkmate."

"This has come up rather unexpectedly. The Pres wants to see what the two gentlemen from the ad agency have. Asked if they could be at the ranch Saturday. I volunteered you join the party. If you could be in New York and bring the two from the ad agency to a law firm on Park Avenue, Walker, Condon, Oppenheimer, I'll meet you there and we'll spill the beans. Tell all. I've arranged a private jet out of Teterboro 7:00A.M. Saturday down to Texas. Couple of hours at the ranch and back to New York in time for dinner on the town Saturday night. No big deal. You'll all have something to tell your grandchildren."

"You do think of everything Louis."

"We're a full service intelligence gathering arm of the government."

"I know this is a dumb ass question Louis, but could this conversation possibly be taped?"

"Dumb ass question."

"Well thanks for this gift of life interuptus."

"Knew you'd express your gratitude Meyer. Perhaps someday you'll make a movie out of all this."

"Perhaps. If you'll be a consultant."

"Anything you want Meyer."

"Bye."

Meyer got out a pad thinking Louis is one of the good guys. He began writing.

1. Tomorrow call Harry and Marvin.
2. Tell them meeting Friday. Clear Saturday.
3. Will make even more suspicious. Say something.
4. Glad truth will be out.
5. After Saturday no need me? Hope.
6. Now back to work. Forget gov.
7. Shoshanna?

He put down the pen, studied the list, and enjoyed a long purging exhale.

Manhattan

Shoshanna had the hotel arrange a limo to the airport. As they settled in she said to Harry, "I hope you approve of the way the princess is flaunting her gold."

"This indulgence is most welcome by the princess's devoted minister."

"I'm really so grateful to you Harry. I hope it wasn't much of an imposition."

"Shoshanna. You're beautiful. Intelligent. Have a wonderfully wicked laugh. And rolling in dough. No imposition."

"Someday I'd like to come back. See New York without the stress. Go across the country. The West Coast. L.A."

"I know a famous Hollywood producer who might volunteer to be your tour guide."

"Meyer seemed very nice. He was married to that beautiful actress, wasn't he? I forget her name. They're divorced. Aren't they?"

Harry calculated at least a fifteen year difference in age. "Divorced a few years. He's known as a gentleman in the entertainment business." Although they were both looking straight ahead Harry knew the expression on her face was molded by hormonal evolution. They entered the Queens Midtown Tunnel.

"The law firm will be talking to auction houses. The sale could take place next summer. Depending on my studies I might come back."

Harry said, "Ask Doctor Rheinhardt to come along. He might enjoy the trip."

"He doesn't seem to be enjoying much lately. He's pained. Within himself. We're all concerned."

Harry recalled their conversation on Masada. "His work is healing psychic pain in others. Forty years of it. Is anyone capable of helping heal Stefan's own pain? Heal the healer? I once asked him about that. He said having meaning in life is the way. But the pain is always there. Wife gone. Violently. Son gone. Violently. Can work and friends ever compensate?"

Shoshanna said, "Totally compensate? Never. Helpful to some more than others? I think so. Doctor Rheinhardt? He's such a gentle person. But also strong. Maybe you reach a point when strength ceases to work."

At times the traffic slowed but the limo kept a steady pace through Queens to the airport. Harry said, "I've taken this route dozens of times on business trips. Did you know a couple of hundred years ago this was all forest and fields? These miles of row houses and apartment buildings are civilization. Look around Shoshanna. Man advancing to the future. Civilization."

The area at El Al was three deep with taxis and confusion. The limo driver said, "I'll try and stay right here. Or I'll be circling." Harry and Shoshanna got out and stood at the curb in the bustle, then went through the constantly revolving door to the packed ticketing area. She held both his hands, looked at him and gave a hug. "Thank you Harry." Another hug.

He said, "Let me know how Doctor Rheinhardt is." Another hug. "And if you're coming back next summer." She went to the line. He walked back to the curb, turned once and waved.

When Harry arrived at the office Tuesday morning there was a message to call Meyer Kaminsky. He found Marvin working at his drawing board. "Message to call Meyer. Let's do this together."

Marvin continued sketching, "The 'we' team rides again."

Back at Harry's office Marvin said, "At least we've got story boards finished."

"It's ringing." Then, "Hi, it's Harry Lang returning Meyer Kaminsky's call." A few moments pass as Marvin sprawls out on the sofa and Harry looks out the window at the silhouette of the Empire State Building ten blocks south.

"Morning Meyer. Things are fine on this end. Storyboards ready."

"Great. How's the movie coming? Issues?"

"Sure. We can make a meeting on Friday."

"Law firm? I'll write down the address."

"Saturday? I'm open. Marv's right here. I'll ask."

"Okay for a possible all day meeting on Saturday?"

Marvin said loud enough for Meyer to hear, "I'll have to break a date with Shoshanna."

"He's just being a wise ass Meyer. She flew back last night. I will tell him. Meyer says she'd never go for a crude lout like you."

Marvin got up and took the phone. "Elegantly stated Meyer. A complement. Will you be free for dinner Friday night? Great."

He gave Harry back the phone. "See you Friday Meyer. Thanks. You too. Take care."

Marvin said, "What's that about a law firm?"

"That's where he wants to have the meeting."

"Why a law firm? Why not here?"

"Guess we'll find out on Friday. Think we ought to call Lucy Boyle and get in to see the Skipper?"

"Let me think about that. I'm thinking. Naw. Fuck him."

"Sure about that?"

"Of course not. But fuck him anyway."

Manhattan

Walker, Condon, Oppenheimer had a relationship with Central Intelligence reaching back to the O.S.S. days of World War II. It had offices in New York, Washington, D.C., Chicago, London and Buenos Aires. Most of the attorneys had Ivy League law degrees and some had been Congressional staffers or with the State Department. Several clients did business internationally, many with foreign governments. When strangers would occasionally utilize a conference room nobody appeared curious as to whom the visitors were. The firm was very busy and very profitable.

On Friday Harry and Marvin walked the few blocks to the meeting discussing what might cause Meyer to hold it at a law firm. Cars and taxis were in ticking heart gridlock on Park Avenue. An older lady in a three-quarter length sable coat, bowed stick-like legs and a proud strutting miniature Schnauzer on a leash crossed to the median choosing to ignore everything. The Schnauzer wore two little red ribbons. The light changed but only pedestrians could move. Marvin said, "Maybe they'll ask us to sign something."

"What?" said Harry.

"I don't know. Something legal."

"I wouldn't sign anything without checking with Mister Newport to Bermuda 1939. Meyer said there's some issues with the movie. Remember the rumors Shoshanna talked about. Maybe the President really did go cuckoo and Washington gave the word to halt production."

"That's really imaginative Har. No wonder you're an advertising star."

"We'll find out soon enough. Here's the building."

The receptionist was a still desirable shoulder length gray haired woman in her sixties wearing a tailored outfit often seen on the very rich or the very kept, very upper crust kept. Marvin saw undulating red lips and a tennis fit figure. A warning voice commanded not to flirt.

"Have a seat. I'll have someone show you to Mister Kaminsky and Mister Mortimer. It's in conference room C." They each sat in chairs that could have come from a drawing room at Blenheim. "I think we're going to be executed" whispered Marvin.

A very tall smiling young woman in a tweed skirt and long dark hair appeared and in a soft accented voice, possibly Portuguese, said "Please follow me gentlemen."

"Love to," said Marvin and she turned her head back with an even bigger smile. They followed, enjoying her collected canter from behind.

"Conference room C," she said and Meyer Kaminsky waved them in.

"Say hello to Louis Mortimer. Louis, Harry Lang and Marvin Munchik."

As they all shook hands it was obvious this patrician, in a tweed sport jacket and shined cordovan loafers, had something to do with why they were meeting in a law firm. Meyer and the patrician appeared comfortable with each other.

"Louis also works in an agency but not advertising. He's with the government and has something to tell you."

Mortimer began. "What we're about to discuss should be considered confidential and we ask that it remain between the four of us. I know this is an unusual situation for you, but there are times your government calls upon private citizens to volunteer their services in the national interest. I did say volunteer. Meyer was asked and agreed to volunteer. In so doing he found himself in an uncomfortable predicament. We gave him no alternative but to be less than forthright with both of you." Marvin was about to say, "Can we un-volunteer in advance?" but decided that was not a good idea. Harry was thinking since he hadn't marched in any peace demonstrations or volunteered to fight in Vietnam, wherever this Mortimer was going might be a chance to partake of something bigger than winning awards or introspection on a shrink's couch. "Meyer couldn't be straight with you because the highest level of your government told him not to. The President has decided the country ought to know there may be a time when we're faced with the reality of life from other galaxies coming to Earth. He's decided to prepare America for that possibility. Through T.V. advertising. He admires your sneaker robot commercial and has asked that you be contacted to develop the advertising. Because he's afraid some segment of the population would panic if they knew this was official government policy, he directed us to start getting the message out in a way that doesn't involve Washington. We asked Meyer to get to you with the movie fabrication." He paused, then continued. "The President wants to see the advertising ideas. At the ranch. We had originally planned some of us close to the President would make the presentation. The unexpected, and usually one creeps in, is that the President wants both of you to present your own work to him. In person. At the ranch. Which is why we had to bring you into the loop. Much to Meyer's great relief. Meyer's character flaw as regards clandestine government missions is that the man hates to lie. Occasionally we encounter one of those. Pity really."

Meyer and Louis were both gauging reactions. Louis was searching for anything that would tell him how these two young men would do in the company of the President. Meyer wasn't worried about that. Although their values weren't formed on the playing fields of Eton, they were products of something equally effective. Stick ball in the street. Ringalevio in the neighborhood, school yard pick-up basketball. Meyer knew under their shell of irreverence was a layer of loyalty and dependability and when called up, courage, but was studying them for something else. Were they brothers betrayed? Or would they understand his dilemma? He decided they hadn't got there yet. Understandably. God. He was four days ahead of them and only now getting a perspective on the magnitude of what they'd been conscripted for.

A stillness filled Conference Room C as four brains were firing separate salvos. Marvin spoke first. "You coming Meyer?"

"Don't have any better offers for Saturday."

He looked to Louis Mortimer undecided whether to call him Louis or Mister Mortimer.

"As it turns out my Saturday is free."

Harry said, "Just so I understand this, we're going to meet the President at his ranch in Texas on Saturday and present our story boards, as if he were just another client. Except he's the President of the United States. And like any other client he'll ask for our recommendation and we tell him. A discussion on our rationale will take place, and if he disagrees we treat him like any old client and persuade him to accept our recommendation. That about it?"

They all looked at Mortimer. "One never knows for sure how something like this will go, but that is about it. Just be sure to tell the President exactly how you feel. He's the most powerful person in the world, and he'll recognize honest conviction. Lay it out straight. He's just another old client." Louis Mortimer was smiling. "Other details? We have a plane that will be standing by to leave Teterboro at 7:00AM. We've arranged a car to pick you up at 5:30. It's a three and a half hour flight. I can answer any other questions on the plane." He gave each of them a card. "If you have to reach me before tomorrow morning call this number. They'll get to me."

The very tall girl in tweed appeared with some documents. Louis Mortimer said, "I don't think that will be necessary. We all understand each other." She offered another big smile and left. Later Marvin thought that Louis Mortimer sounded like the Nazi officer saying, "Ve haf our methods." He did admit that was his own bias and Louis Mortimer really did seem okay.

As they were leaving Harry suggested to Meyer they meet for dinner around 7:00PM at a spot in the Village called Minetta's. Crossing Park Avenue on the way back to Black and White's offices, they found the traffic still barely moving. It seemed colder in the late afternoon shadows. Neither Marvin or Harry felt like talking.

When they were alone Meyer and Louis agreed Harry and Marvin would do just fine with the President. "They're both super high intelligence," said Louis. "They're up to the task."

"You have much contact with the President?" asked Meyer.

"Off and on. He's intuitive. At the 'agency' we concluded he can read minds. Has a great repertoire of crude jokes. If he likes you."

They got up. "Well Louis. Thanks for these front row seats." Meyer walked back to the Plaza Hotel, changed into jeans, spent an hour on the phone with his office, then got a cab to the Village.

"The arugula salad and rolled veal would be a good choice Meyer."

"Thanks Harry. I'll go for it."

"Same, here," said Marvin.

The waiter poured their wine. Meyer sampled and nodded. Harry swished and sipped. Marvin examined the dark purple vintage in his glass, offered a toasting gesture and drank down half making no pretense as to complexities of that particular year. "Little white lies among friends are okay Meyer. Especially when ordered by our beloved leader of the free world. You're forgiven."

Harry said, "We really do understand. As Louis Mortimer explained, your choices were limited."

"I hoped you would feel that way." They clinked glasses.

Marvin drank more of the wine, this time slowly. "If the President thinks there's enough of a possibility Extra Terrestrials exist, everything we thought we knew, about anything, changes. Are we supposed to take this seriously, or has he really gone batty?"

Meyer said, "We'll be able to decide for ourselves tomorrow. The people I've been in touch with have concerns, but it's the government. Professional liars. Not all, but enough. Some even lie to themselves. It's what gets the human race into quicksand. The truth tellers either succumb to the business gods or get out. A vote for war is a vote for profit. Keeps them in office. A few try and stay honest. But they're ganged up on. Labeled self-righteous. The club isolates them as kooks. Of course everyone is convinced their own policies are the only right ones. The compromises in Congress rarely are about conviction. They're negotiations. I'll trade you my vote on this for your vote on that. Covered up by deliberate confusion." Meyer swished his wine. "Still the political system of choice. Don't know anybody dying to immigrate to Russia. Or China. Our grandparents didn't dream of a new life in North Korea. It's not just our politicians can't help themselves. It's humanity."

The waiter arrived with their salads. Marvin said, "How 'bout delivering that speech to the President on Saturday. Get his mind off intergalactic rubberneckers." They started on the salads.

"You were right about the arugula," said Meyer.

After a few tastes Harry said, "Marvin. You've just inspired a thought that could change the world."

"Eat your salad," said Marvin.

"On Saturday we're having a couple of intimate hours with the President of the United States of America in the cozy atmosphere of his private sanctuary in Texas. What if..."

"I'm not sure I want to hear this."

"Listen. How many times have you thought, if I could just get the President face to face I'd pound some sense into him."

Still masticating salad Marvin said to Meyer, "Let's pretend he's not here."

"We shouldn't waste this one chance we'll ever have to achieve something that really matters. For America. For humanity. For our grandchildren."

"None of us have grandchildren," said Marvin.

Meyer said, "What'd you have in mind Harry? What would you say?"

Marvin said, "Don't humor him Meyer. He's experiencing one of his frequent lunatic episodes."

Harry stopped eating. "Haven't figured that part out yet. In the grand sweep of history some people have that one moment when they risk everything, regardless of the odds or personal consequences, to avert a calamitous incident. What if this was our moment and we did nothing?"

Marvin said, "I'm going to save the world by changing the

subject. Harry, tell Meyer about taking Shoshanna to the airport the other night."

"Small minds. No imagination. Okay. Shoshanna. She ordered up a limo. Very pleasant ride. Said she'd like to come back next summer when they auction off all the stuff her aunt left her, providing she can break away from medical school. Said something about seeing the West Coast. L.A. Mentioned she knew you had been married to a beautiful actress Meyer, and then tentatively, that you were divorced. From my limited ability to interpret the mind of a woman I'd say the groundwork's been laid. In a manner of speaking. Told her if she does make it back perhaps a handsome famous Hollywood producer might be persuaded to show her around. Got three warm hugs in the airport. She blew a kiss and I got back in the limo. If you can handle a confident gorgeous rich woman who knows how to shoot Uzi's, it appears the door is open and beckoning."

The waiter brought the rolled veal and poured more wine. Meyer said, "Auction not till next summer, eh? Own some Israel bonds, but never been."

The Ranch

On Saturday at 7:03AM a Saberliner 60 was third for takeoff at Teterboro airport across the Hudson River from Manhattan. Inside sat Louis Mortimer, Meyer Kaminsky, Harry Lang, Marvin Munchik and a fifth person who Louis introduced as Hector Eagleton, a muscular man about fifty wearing horn rim glasses, military cut blond hair and using a cane for a barely noticeable limp. "Hector is our in-house scholar on anomalous occurrences. When science is unwilling or unavailable we have Hector," said Louis.

"Sounds like an easy buck. How does somebody get into that line of work?" asked Marvin. Harry cringed, thinking don't ask these guys demeaning jack-ass questions.

Louis Mortimer said, "Having a Ph.D. in quantum mechanics, another Ph.D. in neuro-psychology and being a retired Special Forces major might get you an interview."

Meyer said, "Did you plan to submit an application Marvin?"

"Sorry. Is my face red?" Hector had a disarmingly warm smile. "For someone who's a legend in his line of work Louis does run off at the mouth." There's that bond, thought Harry, the fraternity of those who have been to war.

The pilot's voice came through the speaker system. "We're next for take-off. Should take three hours and twenty-eight minutes to travel the fifteen hundred nautical miles. Hope everyone's buckled up."

They were quickly in the air and as the New York skyline appeared in his window like a sharply defined cardboard cutout. Harry thought how nice it would be to afford travel by business jet all the time. Club seating made for comfortable conversation.

Louis said, "Never can predict what questions the President might have. Hector's knowledge of unexplained aerial phenomena, abductions, animal mutilations, could be an asset."

Meyer asked, "Abductions? Can you tell us anything?" Louis nodded affirmative to Hector.

"What Louis refers to as abductions have been happening for

centuries. The scientific crowd refuses to touch it. On the record anyway. Let's say you're a genius at a prestigious university involved in research, peer reviewed articles, respected in your field, attending conferences in Zurich, London, and you're presented with something like this. A thirty-four year old woman happily married with a couple of kids and a degree in English literature reports having been awakened at three in the morning by a presence in the bedroom. Her husband is next to her asleep. She can't see the figure but knows something is looming and tries to scream but she is paralyzed and voiceless. The mysterious being touches her head and fear diminishes. She feels herself floating up, travels through the wall of the house, rises up into the night sky watching her house and neighborhood and planet Earth disappear. Loses consciousness, doesn't know for how long, and comes to on an examining table in a brightly lit seamless room surrounded by non-human entities. One of them is inches away staring rivetingly and telepathically saying no harm will come. They examine her body probing with a thin metallic tube, taking longer with genitalia and reproductive organs. Any resistance results in eye staring and a sense of calm. Oddly, some of the beings feel familial, as if blood relations. Alternately enraged, aggressive, and resigned, she fades out, comes back in her bedroom with a headache and sense of disorientation. Husband still snoring. The clock says 5:30. Anxiety and uncharacteristic nervousness hang on for days. Tells no one. A month later the experience reoccurs. A couple of months pass and then again. Although she feels helpless one of the beings transmits a wonderful feeling of warmth, which is reciprocal and torments her because it's like love. The being telepathically tells her Earth is being devastated by pollution and war and she has been selected for something vital to survival."

Hector Eagleton takes out a pack of unfiltered Camels and a Zippo lighter with parachutist wings emblem, taps the cigarette, lights up and continues. "This woman sees a psychiatrist who finds her to be normal by all measures. The doctor is circumspect and most probably ignorant of what tens of thousands of men, women, and children around the world have experienced. Sometimes in their cars. Walking in the woods. Their descriptions track pretty much the same and hardly any ever had the slightest interest in extra terrestrial events. UFO's are invariably reported in the vicinity during their episodes."

Meyer asked, "President know this?" and Hector looked to Louis saying, "Probably, but not a priority." Harry looked at the clouds they were flying over and remembered his conversation that first night he met Audrey in Cleveland when they agreed living past lives was as much reality as anything else. He heard Meyer say, "Where's the government on this?"

Hector answered "about where the scientists are."

"And you?"

"Most of these people, experiencers, aren't nut jobs. I've met with a few. Witnessed some get hypnotized and call up memories. Some scream out. Tremble. Talk about dying rain forests, poisonous drinking water, our planet on the way to becoming uninhabitable. They describe parched deserts where farmland once was and the tears come. Maybe Extra Terrestrials are among us. Maybe it has nothing to do with outer space. Are these people at the front end of a continuing human evolution? Entering an as yet unexplainable stage of consciousness transformation? Opening a curtain to dimensions that might be thousands of years into the future for the rest of us? To a fish the entire universe is the water he's in. Yank that fish out of the water and holy shit. Who knew this other world was there? Parallel universes? Perhaps an explanation is that whatever our species evolved into is coming back through time travel from fifty thousand years into the future? Other realms beyond known reality? A non-physical spiritual reality? Fact is hardly any of the abductees are psycho. Another fact? Whatever it is, and it's something, we can't touch it."

Hector Eagleton stopped talking and put out his cigarette. Louis Mortimer got a copy of *Foreign Affairs* from his briefcase. The others looked at Hector hoping he would say more. When they decided he was finished Meyer said, "A few years ago a

Czechoslovakian film producer came to us with a script based on a true story he'd heard from a woman who worked as a secretary for an editor at *Pravda*. Someone named Nikola Tesla invented some sort of deadly ray gun that he sold to our Department of Defense. Said this weapon could take down four hundred enemy aircraft at the same time. In the screenplay our government used it to shoot down UFO's, including Roswell. When the Aliens retaliated by abducting several of our pilots with the planes they were piloting we stopped the aggression with ray guns. Nikola Tesla was found dead in a hotel room in New York. Not a hint as to what happened to our pilots and aircraft. Disappeared out of the sky. No wreckage ever found. Nikola Tesla's murder was never solved. We liked the story but the Czechoslovakian film guy mysteriously reneged and took off." Louis stopped reading and looked at Hector, then went back to his magazine. Neither responded. Meyer dropped it.

Harry and Marvin were beginning to realize nothing in their resumés prepared them for this. Nausea started building. Mustn't allow fear to fuck me, thought Harry. I've been drafted. This is my Vietnam. I will not freeze. Those kids in the jungle stepping on trip wire would much rather be in a plush private plane to meet the President. I'm not going to lose any limbs or have to kill peasant farmers in black pajamas. The agreement is go to war, make it back, and forever you're in the warrior brotherhood. Suppose I could talk to the Army recruiter in Times Square. Wouldn't trade career for Audrey. Do it for admission to the warrior club? Need admittance to a club restricted to members whose singular act of private courage would be diminished by publicity and whose reward is simply knowing. So what then? Stay in the same game? Doctor Sigmund. Doctor Stefan. Meaning. Sure is elusive.

Just as the pilot promised, three hours and twenty-eight minutes after getting airborne the Saberliner 60 came to a stop in front of an isolated hanger with a black Lincoln waiting. Two men in dark suits and short hair were watchful as the steps came down and five passengers exited. Two of the party seemed to know the very alert welcoming detail. As they all got in the big vehicle one of the Secret Service men said to Louis Mortimer, "He seems to be his normal self. Some columnist he doesn't think much of came out for a one-on-one interview and when told he was here said, 'don't have to tell me that. I can smell him.'"

As they drove up to the big winding two-story house the President was standing at a nearby white clapboard fence wearing a cowboy hat and open neck checkered shirt watching some Hereford cows chewing grass. He waved and walked to the car, an avuncular figure happy to greet some good friends. "Hello Louis, appreciate you all coming," looking at everyone, and after introductions put his arm around Mortimer and casually walked toward the house quietly talking as the group followed.

Inside the President said, "Come this way," and they entered a large room decorated in cozy western posh with cowhide and Frederick Remington art and bronzes of horses and dogs. He cordially gestured to some sofas and easy chairs as a short Mexican in black trousers and a white shirt wheeled in a cart with guacamole dip, small roast beef sandwiches, chocolate chip cookies, Cokes and coffee. The President said, "Thank you Vincente," and then applied a lifetime in politics to quickly sizing up the men, Harry first, then Meyer and lastly Marvin. Meyer saw shrewdness, playfulness, and an insecurity that could switch to pettiness, even cruelty.

"I've always admired the ability of advertising to affect the public perception. Takes an insightful mind to do that. First time I saw your T.V. ad for those children's sneakers I laughed out loud and thought whoever came up with that is pretty damn clever. Sure to sell a busload of those kid's shoes. Politics isn't too different than selling shoes. My Democratic brand is going to last longer than your Republican brand. Make your feet feel better. Congress is all about making America's feet feel better. You agree with that Louis?"

Before Mortimer could answer a phone buzzed and the President said, "Have him come in." Then to Louis, "Your boss just arrived," and the Director of Central Intelligence, tie-less in khakis and a blazer was shown in. "Have a seat Greg. These are the boys from the advertising agency, Harry and Marvin, and Meyer Kaminsky, you've heard of him. Big name in Hollywood."

Louis Mortimer said, "You just saved me from a trick question Greg."

"Greg is a card carrying member of the Georgetown liberal elite. That's why he shows up late for meetings with his President. Harvard men are like that. Or was it Yale Greg?"

Harry was thinking it was Saturday morning and instead of taking shirts to the Chinese laundry he was with the President and the Director of the C.I.A. about to show some story boards depicting Aliens from other planets appearing on Earth. Give his mother's mah- jong friends at the condo complex in West Palm Beach something to talk about between games. Then the President was saying his name. "Harry, can you tell us about that robot? How you came up with that particular idea? Don't mean to put you on the spot. Just like to understand those Madison Avenue brains. I didn't go to one of those New England Ivy League places, like Greg and Louis. Always felt that whatever job I had was too big for me. Not like these Wiffenpoofs."

"I know exactly what you mean Sir. Applied to Columbia but was accepted by Ithaca College." Louis and Greg had a closer look at Harry. Hector Eagleton's impassive face didn't reveal an inner smile. The President said, "Harry, you and I just might become good buddies."

"That would give my mother in Florida bragging rights 'till the snowbirds go back north."

The President said, "If I was running again might help us carry the state."

Meyer was staging camera angles and wondering if it were a movie what the next scene might be. Everybody showed respect with a controlled laugh and then Greg said, "I was wondering that myself. Exactly what is the story behind that robot commercial?"

"Marvin and I came up with that one together. The way it works is two guys, graphics and words, get the facts about the product, the customer, the competition, and then just bat ideas around. Mothers hope they don't have to spend money on new sneakers before the kids outgrow them. We had to demonstrate Kiddie Keds last longer. One of us said let's walk the shoes across America. That was the idea. But we couldn't get a kid to do it. Took about a week before we said let's have a kid size robot do the walk. We did consumer research and the moms loved it." Harry paused. Marvin decided that whether Harry stopped for dramatic effect or not, it was theatrically perfect.

It didn't elude Greg and Louis that the President was listening hard, looking shrewd, and Harry was his teacher. He only had a few weeks left in the Oval Office and wasn't going to allow himself to just coast home. His approval ratings had been in the high seventies and even eighties that first year in office but were now low thirties. He was vain, powerful, and insecure. He'd arrived in Washington thirty-five years before on the staff of a Texas Congressman whose ranch was larger than some European duchies, was calculating in his ability to pick influential mentors, realized early in his rise that quiet quid pro quo deals, ingratiation with the powerful, and talent at reconciliation were the rules of the game in Washington. He never hesitated breaking the rules to get where he wanted to go. And here he was taking Advertising 101 as the final curtain of his run was coming down. Greg and Louis exchanged a blink of eye contact affirming they both realized this President was still a formidable ruthless player, as three hundred Americans were dying every week in Vietnam. Hector caught the look and saw they were an outnumbered patrol waiting to be overwhelmed. He heard the President saying, "I'm going out to the pasture to take a piss and then let's see what you brought me Harry. Anybody care to piss in the grass with me feel free."

They all followed the Commander in Chief out to the white board fence where cows were still placidly chewing grass and in an asymmetrical oval relieved themselves. When everybody had zipped back up the President was still watering the pasture. He looked happy as the cows in his triumph.

The communal bladder relief diminished undertones of hierarchy, even with the President, and back inside Marvin and Harry got out the storyboards.

As Marvin handed over the first storyboard he saw a "what the hell" expression on Harry that was much like the look on Steve McQueen's face in the *Great Escape* when after the breathtaking motorcycle chase, he crashed and was recaptured by the Nazis. Hey fellas nothing personal. I just had to do this.

Harry began. "We have three different TV ideas, each we feel achieves the objective of subtly preparing the audience, America, for the possibility that Alien life from other worlds might someday land on our planet, but they are not to be feared. We should greet them as friends. Our mandate is that the government shall in no way be identified with this advertising." Addressing the President in Texas vernacular Harry said, "Sir, this was one sumbitch of an assignment."

This time Hector Eagleton let his smile hang out. The other two representatives from Central Intelligence hadn't formed any opinion of Harry, but the pleased look on the President's face was doing it for them.

"Now Harry, what would your momma in Palm Beach think of her sonny boy using language like that?"

"She wouldn't understand sir."

"Well I sure in hell understand. Go on."

"This first one takes place in the General Assembly of the United Nations...."

Meyer was still thinking film and saw that his lead actor in this dramatic scene was anything but intimidated in front of one of the more reviled Presidents. Harry pointed to each frame on the board as he described the action but his words were so vivid as to make the graphics superfluous.

The President was like a child being read a bedtime story. "That's slick as snot Harry. Let's have a look at the next one."

"A flying saucer lands, the Aliens exit and are met by the whole cheering town, high school marching band, mayor giving a speech, welcome wagon, embraces...."

In most client presentations Harry and Marvin explained the campaign together as a team, but this time Marvin saw the extent of his participation as simply handing over the boards and retaining details for later analysis—as recorders of historic meetings with major world figures do—contemplating a future book.

"Just like greeting kin folk on Christmas day son."

"This last one is done in animation, like the great Disney movies. Same endearing attitude America has for Snow White, magical...."

For thirty minutes Harry was Olivier, Chaplin, Paar, the Bard, and the President wanted curtain calls. Like Marvin, everybody in that Texas version of a stockbroker Tudor cattleman's sanctuary knew they would be exposed to Presidential barnyard ridicule should they attempt to showcase their own soaring I.Q's. The President got two of the small roast beef sandwiches and a Coke, chewing, walking and talking, in his slow confident big man in the county cadence. "Which of these fine TV commercials would you recommend?" The only one expected to respond was Harry, and for that the others offered their own personal prayers of immense gratitude. The President strolled, a patient man. From somewhere out in the pasture that had by now absorbed the various shades of urine a young steer bellowed, sounding like a rusty tuba.

He stood at a window looking out on his grazing land. From behind, framed against the distant grasslands, a lonely silhouette.

Harry organized the storyboards and leaned them against a small wooden stool carved by a local hill country craftsman to look like an old tractor seat. He addressed the President's back, "We have three distinct choices. From what we know about the American consumer any one of these commercials will get them thinking that if space beings ever land on Earth, they should not be feared or greeted with aggression. We have three routes with different scenery, all arriving at the same place. So which is our recommendation? Which in our judgment will be most effective? Mister President, none will. Because, Mister President, there's an even more powerful, more honest approach we haven't yet brought up for your consideration." Meyer's imaginary lens was on the anchored form of the President's back, shot in black and white, contrasting with the only movement in the scene being the breezy green luminescence of the grass through the window. He heard Harry's voice as if off screen.

"The folks who live in your hometown, any hometown, watch two, three, four hours of TV a day. Every week they see more than a thousand commercials; sometimes it's much more than a thousand. Few of those commercials will stop people from going to the bathroom or the refrigerator. But a speech from their President will. Nothing on TV gets a bigger audience than the President addressing the citizens. If you feel this issue is so threatening that history will condone a deception, then it's worth some straight talk. America is exhausted and furious. America is in no mood for subtlety. 1968 has been mean. Hitting them with the possibility of Aliens won't be a distraction from the caskets or rioting. Americans are straight shooters. All they want is a square deal. The truth. They want their President without the masks. They need you to show your soul. No politics. No nuance. This will be your last speech as President. Sir. A politician delivering a speech without giving a damn about the politics. Or party payback. Or contributors' agendas. It's beyond Americans' reach to even imagine the view of the world from the Oval Office. Facing the consequences of a bad decision. Wearing the final branding iron of history's assessment. They want a signal that their President is in touch with what is of true value in this life. The country needs you to not be a politician. Let them witness their President step outside of his own ego and embrace the universe. Their universe. Aliens and all the rest."

The President was anchored in stillness, like a bronze statue viewed from behind, a portrait of a lame duck, revealing nothing. The Director of Central Intelligence was the next senior ranking federal employee in the group and usually prepared with an opinion, but besides having no need to state one, he didn't know what it might be if asked. Louis Mortimer studied the rear view of the man who still ruled the world, from the cowboy boots to the cuffless tan twill trousers, the carved leather belt and red checkered shirt, stopping at the back of the head and outline of a very recent haircut. Louis felt pathos that comes from a Shakespeare play characterizing human darkness and ending tragically. Hector Eagleton was looking at Harry thinking this kid has just told the President what none of his advisors has the cajones for. It's either a Court Martial or a Medal of Honor. Meyer was road blocked as to how the movie should end. Marvin knew what it must be like to undergo electric shock treatment as his admiration for Harry's words caused a jolt of personal diminishment. Perhaps the time had come to be less critical of people, less exploitive of women, maybe find a shrink like everybody else and click down the wise-ass act.

There was just one person in the group who could legitimately respond, and he seemed to be telepathically linked to the cattle in the distant pasture.

Vincente appeared into the silence to replenish the snacks but saw that was unnecessary and with dignified Hispanic respect tiptoed out of the room. Slowly the frozen figure of the President began a melt into movement. Without turning from the cows his voice appeared to come from the same middle distance.

"Major Eagleton, I need to know more about the crashed UFO's, the ones we shot down, the Alien bodies. I understand there are few in government more informed than you. Even though some of this is at the higher levels of secrecy and my friends Harry," the President sounded laconic, "and Meyer and Marvin, are not cleared, they're much too smart to gamble vanishing into oblivion." If the President meant to sound funny he didn't. Marvin committed himself to honoring women as equal humanity.

Hector Eagleton got up to walk around the room as he talked. "At Area 51 we have several retrieved craft, some damaged and some in near perfect condition. We also have several bodies of E.B.E.'s, most are dead, but some were alive and one still is."

The President now faced the group. "E.B.E.'s?"

"Sorry. Extraterrestrial Biological Entities. Once we began to communicate, they picked up English rapidly; the information has been, understatedly Sir, useful. Their life span is three to four hundred years. They've been coming to Earth for fifty thousand years and controlling our evolutionary process. They say they have no plan to harm us, but they are advanced both technically and biologically, so far ahead of us that if they ever did have hostile intentions we'd most probably be close to helpless. Our best scientific minds are working on duplicating their technology. We've had some success, especially in learning to fly their craft. The ones we've interrogated over a period of years are...they're very nice. None of them are high-level actors, more of the mechanic level, Technical Sergeants, Warrant Officers. One of our own officers was deeply moved and saddened when one of the E.B.E.'s died. You might say he mourned the loss of a friend."

The President held up his hand and Hector stopped. "Thank you Major. You needn't continue," and sat down in the biggest cowhide covered easy chair. "Harry, I'm going to take your advice and give that speech. We won't be needing to produce any TV commercial. And the sumbitch that gave his President that advice is going to write that speech."

"You mean this sumbitch?" said Harry pointing at his chest.

The President got the phone next to the big cowhide easy chair. "I'd like the pick-up brought round please. We've got a sumbitch here from New York who'd like a private tour of the ranch." As the President rose to leave everybody else rose. Leaving the room with Harry following and not looking back he said, "Hope you boys can stay for a little Texas barbeque before flying out."

The group continued standing after Harry and the President disappeared, waiting for permission from someone to sit. Hector was first to punch out of the spell. "Well I'll be a sumbitch." Louis Mortimer found his pipe and tobacco then said to the Director of Central Intelligence, "Have you ever been anointed with a pick-up truck ride on these rutted ranch roads?" Greg thought over the question.

"The first time I came to the ranch after his inauguration and he asked me to stay on as Director I did have the pleasure, but half a dozen members of the press also came along. Except for the Secret Service this one is private."

Mortimer said, "I'd give a bag of silver to be a bug on the windshield."

Meyer saw they were together encased in a warm sort of circumstantial friendship. "Would probably take an academy award script writer to get down whatever it is they're talking about."

Marvin was about to put one of the miniature steak sandwiches in his mouth when Hector said, "You might want to think about saving your appetite for the President's barbeque Marvin." He didn't bite. "Just razing Marvin. Might have one myself."

A big mud streaked Ford pick-up truck was waiting in front of the house. "I tell the boys not to wash it when I'm at the ranch 'cause nobody 'round these parts drives clean pick-ups." They both climbed up and as the President put it in gear Harry saw two Secret Service vehicles appear and follow a few car lengths back.

"We'll be living here full time after January 20th and it can't come soon enough. The White House has been a fine home but it's the people's house. This place is mine. I suppose you could say for a country boy from Texas I did okay in life, but I'm going to enjoy running this ranch and doing some teaching and writing. Won't have to listen to crowds of young people on TV saying fuck you Mister President. Or be referred to as Uncle Corn Pone behind my back by some in the previous administration. As you said back there at the house Harry, nobody knows what it's like to sit in that Oval Office after the advisors and experts have gone home, making decisions in the night all by yourself. I did order a halt to the bombing, but it hasn't made the negotiations one bit more successful."

A jackrabbit zigged and zagged in front of the truck almost getting flattened but the President held steady. "Used to have fun shooting those bunnies with a Stevens .22 when I was a kid. Don't imagine you did much rabbit hunting growing up in Brooklyn."

"Only rabbits in Brooklyn are in the pet shops around Easter. Some of them are dyed pink. Most don't last long."

"Harry, I've tried to use the great power bestowed on the President by the American people to accomplish good for humanity, but apparently haven't achieved much, and whatever good has come out of my years in power has been crossed out by the damn war. January 20th will be one of the happiest days of my life, but I'll be leaving this office as a despised President. None of your friends back in New York will be grieving to see me go. I can't disagree with anything you said back at the house. When you write this speech I want you to convince those people in New York you work with and go to ball games with that there are reasons not to hate this President. I know they'll never love me like they love Kennedy or Roosevelt. Tell them there are other things in this world more important than contempt for this President. Nobody I know of in government can predict what our future will be, especially with those Aliens observing us on land and sea and in the air. Major Eagleton did say we've been on their agenda for fifty thousand years. They could announce themselves anytime. Tomorrow. Ten years. One hundred years. If it is in the next five or ten years and the world learns I'd been forewarned and didn't act, why that's just another reason to criticize this President. Reaffirm their hatred. You understand where I'm coming from on this? I've got a White House full of political speechwriters Harry, but I believe the man that came up with that kid's sneaker advertising will figure out how to get the American people to hate this President just a little less."

They came to a stop at a wide No Sag farm gate and the President got out. Harry jumped down to help and together they swung the gate open. The Ford pickup idled and they looked around at hilly grazing land and the three hundred sixty degree horizon. Except for an erector set style windmill by a large pond about a half-mile in the distance, nothing man made interrupted the Texas bigness. The President clasped his arms behind and allowed the wind to test him, showing the faintest smile to the hills that were not the people's but his alone. Harry saw a man trying to let the torment out. When they got back in the truck and slowly bumped cross-country without even cart tracks to follow, the President said, "I know you're not going to let me down on this son." In the side view mirror Harry observed both Secret Service vehicles come through the gate, watched as one of the men got out to close it, and couldn't decide who was in deeper shit. Harry Lang or the President of the United States.

As seatbelts clicked the Saberliner 60 swung onto the empty runway and without slowing first accelerated to takeoff speed. "We've got good tailwinds and should be at Washington National 10:43. Teterboro arrival 11:33. And please convey your pilot's appreciation to the President for the barbeque care packages. Mighty thoughtful of him."

"That would be a nice touch to put in your speech Har," said Marvin.

Meyer said, "You look a little nauseous Harry. Eat too much barbeque?"

Hector Eagleton added, "Saw you gag on that jalapeno Harry. Could be why you look so pale."

Louis Mortimer was lighting his pipe. "You've been drafted Harry, into the inner workings of high level government intrigue," pointing his pipe at Meyer, "just like this experienced hand. Of course you're in a more tenuous spot because with Meyer there's no paper trail. Your paper trail will be broadcast on every major TV and radio station in the world." With a twinkle and nod of mock sympathy his gesture meant I've seen worse. Continuing the sport Greg said, "The vast resources of Central Intelligence are available as you see fit." When the vultures abandoned the carcass on the side of the road with no flesh left on the bone Louis Mortimer switched to helpful and said, "We will do whatever we can to help Harry."

At 1:00AM Harry unlocked the door to his apartment remembering it was only nineteen hours ago that he'd left for the President's ranch. It was dark then as it was now. Inside the dimness was protective. He sat on the sofa with lights off. Shadowy illumination from the street blended with distant voices of Saturday night bar goers and he wrapped himself around the familiar, but envisioned standing on the windy Texas hill country with the President. I will soon escape into sleep, he thought, but Sunday morning there will be no escape. I'll rise slowly and recall that I, Harry Lang, the Don Quixote of American pop culture, entered history books yet to be written by offering advice to our President, which he found worthy, and then calculated that he who has advice for the President should bear responsibility for its execution. So now I must compose the last speech to be orated by the king of the world. First I will sleep. And with the sun will walk these quiet Sunday streets, sit alone in a café with a double espresso, no one realizing this is the author of the President's last speech. And then. And then. And then what in fucking hell to say?

Manhattan

Monday morning the door to Harry's office at Black and White Advertising was closed except when he came and went. Sandra knew he was not to be disturbed because he was writing a speech for the fucking President and she referred to him as a wise ass. The only one allowed in was Marvin. Rumor throughout the agency was they were working on a confidential new business presentation. Since they were advertising heroes it wasn't questioned. By chance the Chairman was in Lyford Cay for the week and no one else would attempt any serious snooping.

Harry was in a shell of isolation facing the empty sheet in his typewriter, fingers frozen on the keys lacking any brain signal to activation. Scenes replayed from two days before of the President in his aloneness positioned at the window, urinating in the pasture with those invited to join in a team bladder purge, delighting in the pleasure of simply driving his pick-up, so comfortable in his immense power, whether shown to the few in the room or the hundreds of millions under his care. To write this speech true to the man meant insight into the man. Curiously Harry was confident of that. The President's vulnerabilities were a primitive drumbeat from somewhere far away through humidity and surrounding rain forest, a rhythm heard only by Harry. He knew when the second sentence came he'd have his kick-start. The first sentence he had. My fellow Americans.

Sandra buzzed. A call from Meyer Kaminsky. "Just checking up on you Harry. If you'd like to bounce anything around call anytime day or night."

"Appreciate that Meyer. You may hear from me." Sandra buzzed again. Call from a Mister Mortimer's assistant.

"Louis asked me to check in and say he'd be available for input or as a sounding board should you be so inclined."

"Please tell Louis thanks and he just might hear from me."

Sandra buzzed again. "Guy named Hector Eagleton. Not sure I'd want to work for anyone who knows somebody named Hector Eagleton."

"I'm in New York tomorrow Harry. Can stop by if you like and chat. Might provide some additional insight."

"Sure Hector. I'm around all day. Stop by any time." At lunchtime Marvin walked in.

"Finished yet?"

"Just putting the final touches on it. Have a look." Marvin looked at the typewriter.

"My fellow Americans. That's a brilliant speech Harry. Let's go to lunch."

They passed a shoeshine shop on the way to the restaurant and Harry said, "Let's go in. Smell of shoe polish calms me. I'll buy you a shine." There were five large old-fashioned public library type chairs on a platform, all occupied by men wearing suits and in need of a shine, and three black men applying polish and brushing and buffing and jiving. An Italian and an Asian shoemaker were behind the counter, one at a whirring machine, the other at a workbench. A sign said "Heels in 5 minutes." Another said "Deposit required on all shoes left." Next to it one stated "We repair soles." A large calendar tacked to the wall with a winking smiling blond in her underwear partially covered another sign declaring, "Not responsible for shoes left over 30 days." *The Daily News*, *The New York Post* and abused copies of *Playboy* were scattered around. One of the shoe shiners was a whirling dervish of buffing action on a customer reading the sports page. With professional grace the black man snapped his chamois cloth and tapped the customer's shoe. "Next gentleman."

Harry motioned for Marvin to go first. He stepped up and opened a *Playboy*. Marvin's shoe shiner was older with smooth, high temples, distinguished steel wool-like blue-gray hair clipped short, and an expression that tolerated the two high energy younger ones who chatted and laughed and shucked as they shined. A loud radio was on the news station. One of the younger ones finished his customer and motioned for Harry to step up while jangling his pocket full of tips. His head was neatly shaven while the other had an Afro. All wore maroon aprons.

"How's it going?" asked Harry.

"Good man. Real good. Goin' good."

A Schaeffer Beer jingle celebrated, "the one beer to have when you're having more than one" and Harry could practically read the marketing plan targeting heavy beer drinkers. Then the news resumed announcing a body count of 437 Viet Cong and 197 Americans dead last week. The Afro'd kid mumbled "This shit gotta stop. No good. Ain't no good at all. Shit gotta stop," talking to the shoe he was working on.

"What you mumblin 'bout?" asked his cohort.

"Motherfuckin war man."

"Sheeet. That all? Ain't nothing you can do about it. No how bro. No how."

"Still a motherfucker. 'Cept for that Asian poontang. Everybody want some Asian pussy."

The older shoe shiner said, "You boys hush up. Customers not interested in your mouth."

Harry said to the old man, "Any idea why we are over there?"

"Yeah Pop. Why we fightin there?" challenged the one with the Afro.

The old one looked up at Harry to determine whether he truly was interested in an opinion, decided the question was sincere, and carefully applied polish to the sides of Harry's shoe.

"Who decides on these wars? Politicians with gray hair." He pointed to his head. "Or losing their hair like me. They look at the women and they want them. But the body can't do it no more. Not like they used to. No more. Then they see all the young men getting satisfaction, satisfying the girls, doing what they can't. So they get jealous and come up with reasons to start a war and send all the young ones that are doing what they can't to go fight. They'z just getting even. Always been like that. Always will. That's why we're over there in Vietnam."

Harry looked to Marvin. "Can't get more Freudian than that. Better than domino theories."

The one with the shaved head snapped his polishing rag. "Sheeet man. Can't get it up so the brothers got to die. Man, where you get those ideas anyway?"

Harry said, "You're making sense man," controlling the urge to talk jive. "Any way to chill out those guys in Washington?"

"Watermelon wine. Canadian whiskey. Or get their minds off their private parts that don't work. Don't know what that might be."

The Afro shoe shiner nudged his co-worker laughing. "Green men from Mars invading Earth get those dudes thinking sheeet...we all in this together."

Stepping down Harry handed the older one a twenty dollar bill saying, "This is in the national interest. Split it up man," and out on the street said, "Think I just got the theme for the speech. Will eat later. I'm going back to the office."

Marvin said, "I understand," and stood for a moment in the middle of the crowded lunchtime sidewalk on Third Avenue.

Sandra looked up. "Quick lunch Harry?"

"No calls Sandy" and shut the door.

The first paragraphs of the President's speech appeared on the page as fast as Harry could type.

My fellow Americans. This is my last speech as your President. These final weeks as the man you've elected to lead the country have been a period of hard, difficult decisions, and a time for hard and equally difficult reflection. You are aware of most of those decisions; history will be my ultimate jury. You are not aware however, of what I've been reflecting upon, and that's what these comments to the country will be about.

When you see a man or woman in the street, or on line at the grocery store or the filling station, you might be thinking, well there's a pleasant looking old man, or cross-appearing plump middle aged lady, or teenager who could use a lesson in manners, but in truth you know little about them. The pleasant looking man might have been in the battle for Iwo Jima and wept as he saw his buddies die in the sand and is carrying those images with him wherever he goes. The short tempered grandmother could have just buried her *husband and for the first time ever will be living alone in the house in which they raised their children. The inconsiderate teen-ager may be getting failing grades because his parents have decided to divorce and he's overheard too many threats and arguments about family finances and upheaval.*

We in the human race are quick with our judgments, but really know so very little about those we are with every day, those whom we take so for granted. No matter who they are, most of them want to be good people, good Americans, and most are fighting their own inner battles in their own way. I stand before you as your President with a confession. I am no different.

Regardless of the decisions any elected leader in any democratic nation makes, there will be loud objections. George Washington endured them. Abraham Lincoln suffered them. It's what you sign on for. During periods of crises the protesters' shouting gets louder, and sometimes their cries are justified. One thing I do know to be true is that every leader in every free society feels he's acting for the good of the people that chose him to lead.

In my quiet moments alone in the Oval Office I've asked is there anything in this world that might cause the nations on our globe to come together in united purpose? The best I can come up with is a fantasy that may or may not be witnessed in this lifetime, and that is visitations from Extra Terrestrials to this Earth. I've been up late in the White House puzzling over our own aggressive tendencies, coming to realize there are so many things we, that is, the nations of the world, the greatest minds we have, know so little about that we may as well just form an international welcome wagon and live in peace. Of course that's just the tired dreaming of an old man soon to become your ex-President and perhaps it's a subject best left to the philosophers, or the clergy, or Hollywood.

My fellow Americans, I have in my hands a pair of moccasins presented to me by the Tribal Council of the Jicarilla Apache Indian Reservation in New Mexico. During times of the most painful decisions of my term in office my wish was that each of you could walk in them.

Let us now enter a time of healing. Thank you. And God bless

America.

Harry looked at his watch. He'd written the speech in twelve minutes. It can take days to write a thirty second TV commercial. He re-read it once, saw it needed only slight editing, and decided to take a walk. The temperature was just a few degrees above freezing and the sun reflected harshly off store windows and car windshields in irritating flashes. He crossed Third Avenue going east, and then Second Avenue. The United Nations building was anchored like a massive square-rigged sail at the East River on land benevolently donated for world harmony by the Rockefeller family. He walked onto the plaza with school children on class trips, tourists looking up, and easy to spot Third World U.N. workers. He stopped in the middle of the plaza and turned to look back at the gray and glass jigsaw of midtown architecture, then continued toward the river and leaned against the railing. Flecks of sun on the river like migrating salmon sparkled in the current, and warehouses in Queens appeared as clear as a movie viewed through 3D glasses.

If the President doesn't find it to be what he expected, it will be between him and the speech thought Harry. I've done what I was drafted for. I am not a patriotic volunteer. But the words came easily and they are the right words. What would Doctor Rheinhardt say? "It sometimes happens." Even if the President thinks I've written a pile of shit, a pile of cow shit from his own pasture, I feel good. Not overwhelmed. Not intimidated. I've felt more pressure going into meetings with brand managers and marketing directors at disposable diaper companies. Because he called me son? No. Because he's going to like the speech.

Harry heard his stomach complain. Now that the speech was behind them a little food wouldn't hurt. He'd stop at a Gristiede's for a sandwich to go. Salami on Jewish rye with mustard and a side of coleslaw. That should do it.

He was in the office by 8:30 the next morning, even before Sandy arrived, and was enjoying the fresh percolated coffee aroma from a Schrafft's cardboard cup, pulling a very large soft prune Danish apart when Marvin entered feigning a stroke at seeing Harry in so early.

"Would you like a second opinion?" Harry handed over the typed speech. Marvin tore off a piece of Harry's Danish and stood by the desk reading. He then sat on the sofa and read it again with concentration that eliminated all sound and motion. Harry bit into a chunk of Danish and the coffee melted it into warm sweet sponginess.

Marvin finished and as his eyes went over it a third time said, "I hear him speaking the words. The cadence. I think you've called his bluff. Will he do it though?"

Sandra came into the office still wearing her coat and looking ruddy from the cold.

"Rode up the elevator with a big square jawed guy, had a blond crew cut and a cane. I was thinking this is what a Hector Eagleton should look like when he told the receptionist he was Hector Eagleton and looking for Harry Lang. Should I bring him in?"

"Thanks Sandy. I'll get him. He's a war hero and a scholar. Be nice."

Harry and Marvin went out to the reception area together. "Welcome to Mad Ave. Hector," and the handshakes were more than reflexive formality.

"You did say just stop by any time, so I thought I'd do it first thing. Giving a talk at Columbia at noon."

"On UFO's?" asked Marvin.

"We'll be skirting the subject. Science still in the closet. There is some good 'eyes only' conversation taking place though."

Sandra smelled of fresh lipstick and with a sparkly smile said, "May I get you some coffee Mister Eagleton?"

"Thank you. That would be very nice."

Marvin said, "One for me too Sandy?"

As they sat down Harry said, "Do you think the President's going bats? It's funny to say about the President, but I found myself feeling sorry for the man."

"He's tired. And gotten older quicker than most Presidents do in office. He's firm in his principles and his determination in civil rights and health care has improved the lives of tens of millions. But he'll never get the credit he deserves, and craves, because of Vietnam. And he knows it. This speech he's conscripted you to write is more about a proud and defeated man hurting for vindication than about Aliens. You've been tossed a fragmentation grenade with the pin pulled Harry."

"Sounds as if you two had this discussion before Harry wrote the speech," said Marvin.

"It's already written?"

"Show him the speech Har." Harry got the two type written pages from his desk and handed them to Hector who took his glasses off and bent over close to the paper. Like Marvin he read the speech twice, and then started talking as he went over it a third time.

"So now I understand why you fellows make the big bucks. It's all here. The President's instincts haven't disappointed. He knew you were the man Harry. Nobody else did. That's what brought him to the presidency." Hector Eagleton put his glasses back on and looked like a military commander forced to make a decision that will cause men to die. "How do you feel towards a President who's perpetually tormented by his own angry demons?"

"They're all his," said Marvin. "But I'm like Harry. At the ranch I could feel his struggles, felt sort of sorry for him myself. Wondered what he was like as a kid. What kind of reputation he had in grade school. When he was asking you all those questions about Aliens I would have thought he'd know more. He is the President, and Christ, Aliens?"

Hector said, "He sometimes does act dumb just to see if he'll pick up anything new. Point is, a lot of this is above top secret and some of the most powerful people in government don't agree on how to deal with any of it. He could have been sincere. Nobody really has the total picture."

There were still some boxes of Kiddie Keds on Harry's window sill and picking up a pair he said to Hector, "If you have any kids, or it would be grandkids wouldn't it, take a pair of these shoes that are responsible for demoting me to become the President's speech writer."

"No kids. No grandkids. Two ex wives. But I'm deeply moved by this grand gesture and I'd love a pair as a memento. Might get them bronzed."

Camp David

On Saturday afternoon a black government Lincoln went through the various security checkpoints at a facility in rural Maryland with one passenger in back surprised at how extensive the complex was. At an elevation of eighteen hundred feet in the Catoctin Mountains northwest of Washington, the wooded hundred forty-three acre compound was encircled by barbed wire topped fencing and protected by the United States Marine Corps. It was originally called High Catoctin but Franklin Roosevelt referred to it as Shangri la and Dwight Eisenhower changed the name to Camp David in 1953, for his young grandson. There were a heated swimming pool, a sauna, two-lane bowling alley, a trout stream, skeet shooting range, tennis courts, and a movie theatre. It was the perfect Presidential retreat, a short helicopter ride from Washington. One hundred feet below was a sanctuary for use should the need arise during times of war.

Harry had been told he'd be met at Union Station for his meeting with the President and when he got off the train was immediately approached by two men in dark suits very much resembling the types that'd met them at the airport in Texas. They knew who he was as soon as he stepped onto the platform and affably said, "Mister Lang? There's been a slight change in plans and we're going to Camp David instead of the White House. Hope you had a pleasant ride down from New York." Walking through the station chatting Harry felt they were observant of things he wasn't trained to look for, a confident American casualness projected through a translucent membrane signifying the bond between those who become brothers through combat arms.

The car stopped in front of a log lodge and a Marine sergeant about Harry's age said, "Welcome Sir, the President is in the sauna and will be with you shortly."

He was escorted to a rustic wood paneled locker room area that had brown leather easy chairs and brass lamps and looked like a place where very rich men would wear towels and smoke expensive cigars. Harry sat in one of the leather chairs and started to read a copy of Saturday's *Washington Post* when the President appeared from the sauna wearing nothing but an oversize towel. "Take off your tie and jacket Harry, and I hope you're feeling better. I understand you had a bad reaction to our Texas barbeque on the plane back from the ranch."

Harry heard himself giving it right back. "It wasn't the barbeque Mister President. It was the speech."

"Well your President would have felt real bad if it was the barbeque." He sat in one of the chairs parallel to Harry's, who noticed the President's roll of hairy stomach and warts and brown splotches that appear with age. The soon to be former most powerful leader on Earth crossed his legs, pinheads of perspiration all over his body from the dry heat of the sauna.

"I'm ready to look at the speech you've written for me." Harry reached over to his jacket and got a letter size envelope from the inside pocket and handed over two type written sheets. The President's fingers were still damp and the pages got stained with his thumb and forefinger imprints. His eyeglasses were fogged but he cleared them with the ends of the towel, held the speech low between his knees and leaned down to read.

Harry saw he moved his lips slowly and only went through it once but continued to stare at the page as if it was the corpse of a beloved pet that had died unexpectedly in his arms. He felt peaceful sitting there next to the mostly nude still warm and moist Commander-in-Chief. The hum from the sauna was a Zen chant and appeared to soothe the President. Then in a voice as if from deep sleep he said, "I've been thinking about death Harry. You ever do that? Wonder what happens If anything does continue, if we'd be aware it was us...have our memories...feel regrets...anxiety...nothing...observe the world as it goes on without us...if we become spirits...hang around in big houses, bumping and creaking in the middle of the night scaring the shit out of people?"

"Sure I've thought about what happens after you get dead. Whether it's just deadsville. Over and out. Or something else.

Get reincarnated. If we're reincarnations we sure as hell don't know who we got reincarnated from. At least I don't. So what does it matter? Nobody really knows anything, Mister President."

"You've written me the speech I needed to see Harry. Few would have had the gift of such a powerful perception, and the skill to pick these words. Now how do you explain that? That is, something told me you were the one to do this?"

Harry said, "I know a psychiatrist living in Jerusalem who would probably answer, 'It sometimes happens.' So it sometimes just happens Mister President."

The President put the pages on the floor and said, "So much of life does just happen. Regardless of how rich or intelligent or powerful or wise or lucky you happen to be. And there's not a god damn thing anyone can do about it." The President smiled, grinned, and then a soft private laugh. He pointed his naked toes at the speech on the floor and turned to Harry.

"If I was hypnotized these are the words that would come out. The only way. I will not deliver your speech. I will give instructions though to have it published after I'm six feet in the ground. Your President is a coward Harry. Do you understand?"

"I wouldn't agree you're a coward sir. But I understand."

"When I'm out of office and living at the ranch I'd like to invite you and your momma from Palm Beach to come down to Texas and have some barbeque with us. Would she do that for me?"

"Got any kosher cows on the ranch?"

The President got up and his damp towel fell to the floor covering the speech. He stood there bare ass and extended his hand. "You've done a great service for the country Harry. It took a special kind of courage. Thank you son."

On the trip back to New York Harry hoped nobody would sit next to him so he went to the last seat in the last car and was isolated from anyone interested in conversation. The train lurched and slowly accelerated to smoothness. The empty rows and only a few scattered passengers gave him thinking space.

Although he needed to be solitary there was sadness, the sadness that grows from an absence of somebody to love, somebody to try and figure it all out with. Find Sigmund's meaning. Is there a truth in any of it? Any of what? Suicide on Masada? Letting go of Audrey? Biological forms from different planets so ahead of us that to them we are as insects are to us? Swat. That's good for a chuckle. The unfulfillingness, the temporariness, of stardom. Endless squeezing of creative sperm for increased sales. Profits. Congratulations for the team. It's why we're here. Why we're here? And now hearing straight from the big enchilada he's a coward. *Congratulations son. You're a hero. I'm a coward. Your speech is an appropriate expression of my guilt. Guilty by reason of aggression. Thing is, can't get myself to admit it 'till I'm dead.*

Harry dozed through Baltimore and woke in Wilmington pitying the President for a future without knowing happiness.

He partially dozed to Philadelphia and then jerked awake in a fright with what might be camouflaged for him on tracks yet to travel.

Idling in mental neutral through Trenton and Newark, he shifted to active consciousness as the train slowed to a stop in Penn Station. There were empty cabs lined up on Seventh Avenue but he decided to walk. It's Saturday night, he thought. Couples on dates pressed into each other against the cold. I do need somebody to press into. To try and figure it all out with.

"So what's to figure?" he heard his mother's voice say, or was it Audrey, or was it Rivka, or was it Marvin doing an imitation of his own mother? Harry smiled the same way he pictured Doctor Rheinhardt smile. The same smile the President just had. So what's to figure?

www.ingramcontent.com/pod-product-compliance
Lightning Source LLC
Chambersburg PA
CBHW071128260626
47162CB00003B/710
* 9 7 8 0 6 1 5 7 4 5 6 5 7 *